Only in Your Dreams

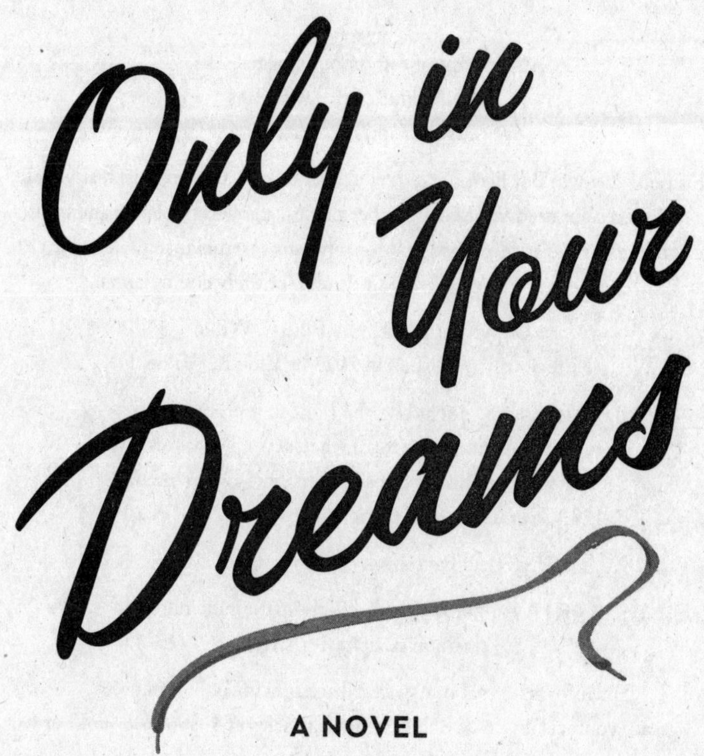

A NOVEL

ELLIE K. WILDE

ATRIA PAPERBACK
New York Amsterdam/Antwerp London Toronto Sydney New Delhi

An Imprint of Simon & Schuster, LLC
1230 Avenue of the Americas
New York, NY 10020

This book is a work of fiction. Any references to historical events, real people, or real places are used fictitiously. Other names, characters, places, and events are products of the author's imagination, and any resemblance to actual events or places or persons, living or dead, is entirely coincidental.

Copyright © 2023 by Ellie K. Wilde
Previously published in 2023 by Ellie K. Wilde

All rights reserved, including the right to reproduce this book or portions thereof in any form whatsoever. For information, address Atria Books Subsidiary Rights Department, 1230 Avenue of the Americas, New York, NY 10020.

This Atria Paperback edition January 2025

ATRIA PAPERBACK and colophon are trademarks of Simon & Schuster, LLC

For information about special discounts for bulk purchases, please contact Simon & Schuster Special Sales at 1-866-506-1949 or business@simonandschuster.com.

The Simon & Schuster Speakers Bureau can bring authors to your live event. For more information or to book an event, contact the Simon & Schuster Speakers Bureau at 1-866-248-3049 or visit our website at www.simonspeakers.com.

Interior design by Lexy East

Manufactured in the United States of America

1 3 5 7 9 10 8 6 4 2

Library of Congress Cataloging-in-Publication Data has been applied for.

ISBN 978-1-6680-9316-0
ISBN 978-1-6680-9317-7 (ebook)

For all of us who waited years for our one.

Only in Your Dreams

Prologue

Ten Years Ago

Melody

"I have something for you."

I snap my bedroom door shut. Then pause to listen for sounds of my parents coming to inquire why their daughter felt the need to sneak into the house after coming home early from a fully sanctioned final hurrah with her classmates the night before she leaves for college.

As it happens, that reason stands just feet away from me in the form of a tall, eighteen-year-old boy.

I give it a second before flicking on the overhead light. Even without it, I know I'll find his chin dipped to get a proper look at me, sending dark hair spilling onto his forehead. I know that eyes the color of molten caramel will be on me, conveying their amusement.

"Whatever happened to the *no boys in the bedroom* rule?"

I was right: his face is screwed up, a touch confused but amused as hell, as he wonders why I brought him up here.

I don't blame him.

In the four years that we've known each other, Zac and I have rarely found ourselves alone. Unless you count those few minutes in the boys' locker room at school before a game, but that ritual went away months ago with the end of the football season.

I've been third-wheeling with Zac and my twin brother Parker since the first time he trailed into our parents' house after practice, all quiet and lanky. Polite. New in town. At fourteen, Zac was already offering to help Mom set the table for dinner. When Dad went to drop him off at home later that night, Mom praised Parker for bringing home such a nice boy, who'd clearly been raised right by his parents.

Days later, we found out he was being raised right by his grandmother. Weeks later, we found out he wasn't so quiet once he got used to new people. Months later, he was the perfect middle ground between the Woods twins—the right balance between my relentless sarcasm and Parker's sunny smiles.

"It's still a rule. But you're you," I tell him. He follows me into my room and plops down on the end of the bed with me. An imposing figure, just like I always imagined he'd be if I ever got him in bed.

Not that I ever could.

"Elaborate on that for me, will you?"

"You know." I shrug. "You grew up with us. You're . . . basically a brother."

Zac's eyes sweep my bedroom, a space he's only ever glimpsed from the hallway. "Trust me, Melody. I'm not a brother."

"*Parker's* brother," I amend quickly. "You grew up here, with him. What I mean is, you hardly count as a guest. This is totally fine."

Zac arches an eyebrow, reaching behind him for the mini foam football sitting on my bed. "So why did you sneak me in through the back door?"

"I felt like taking the scenic route in."

His mouth twitches. "And why are we whispering?"

"So that the guy I keep hidden in my closet doesn't hear you and get jealous."

Zac laughs, a warm, deep sound that's been rewarding my snark for the past four years. He'd been one of the rare people in high school who hadn't immediately confused my dry humor with snobbery.

"It'll be weird not having you around, Clover," he says with a sigh. "You think you'd ever move back here? After school, maybe?"

I eye Zac in my peripheral vision, refusing to look at him on the off chance the rush of warmth coursing through me has me flushing. He's called me *Clover* more than a thousand times in those precious few minutes we've spent alone, but the way he says it tonight feels . . . different.

Quiet, intimate.

Like he can see into my brain and knows exactly how badly I need to hear that he'll think about me while I'm away. At least for a little while.

"Maybe. But Oakwood Bay is all I know. I've always liked the idea of moving to the city." When Zac only nods, I release a long breath. "Who knows, maybe I'll be in both places one day. A city apartment, and a big stone house on the bay here."

He looks around curiously. "A big stone house?"

I nod at my desk, where sits the large vision board we'd been tasked with putting together as a senior year project. "With a wraparound porch. A yellow front door, maybe a cute porch swing, and a patch of daisies. Or . . . you know. Something less cheesy." I rise, tucking my hands into the back pockets of my jeans. "Anyway, I wanted to give you a going away present."

Zac runs a hand over the stubble at his jaw that grew in way sooner than Parker's, much to my brother's dismay. "You're the only one going away for school. Shouldn't this be the other way around?"

"It should be." Pointedly, I study the pockets of his jeans. "But you seem to have forgotten my gift at home."

He rubs his lips together, trying not to laugh. "No, I didn't. It's in the car."

I squint at him. "So, first he forgets to get me a going-away present. And then he *lies* about forgetting to get me a going-away present."

He quirks a smile. Not a big one. Not the one that casts a glow on whoever he bestows it on. But it's just enough to trigger the very best part of it. His eyes go all squinty, as though he refuses to be anything but singularly focused on the joy of the moment. Laugh lines carve deep around his eyes, deeper than any eighteen-year-old I know, announcing to the world what kind of person he is.

He's Zac Porter, the golden boy of Oakwood Bay. Quarterback of the high school football team, on the cusp of taking the field for the University of Oakwood Bay, in just a few days' time. My brother's charming best friend, with a bevy of girls always trailing him. So confident and optimistic that everyone can't help but crave his company, just for a little taste of his warmth. Even me, the infamously grouchy Woods twin, standing in the periphery of his life. Close but never close enough.

Without warning, Zac tosses the mini football. It soars over my head and I scramble back to catch it before it hits the ground.

"Nice catch." He gets to his feet, shrinks the distance between us. Standing this close together, I need to tip my head back to look at him. "Why'd you sneak me into your room, Clover?"

"To give you a present," I say breathlessly.

"And what kind of present is it?" Zac smirks, and I'm blushing again. "What kind of present requires you to sneak me into your bedroom, huh?"

There's no way he doesn't hear the rapid thump of my heart. I'm shocked my parents aren't already barreling up the stairs, every heartbeat sounding the alarm.

Boy in bedroom. Boy in bedroom. Let's go up and make this awkward as hell.

Zac nudges my chin, scrapes his teeth over his lower lip. "What are you gonna do to me, Clover?"

Is he . . . Is he making a move on me?

His gaze sweeps my face, and he fingers my chin. I think he's holding his breath, but I might be projecting.

Because we don't flirt, and he's never touched me like this. I'm not sure what's possessed him now, but it really feels like he might be . . .

He's just trying to get a rise out of you, same as he and Parker always do. Don't embarrass yourself falling for it.

"Ha-ha, you wish," I say, moving for my desk. "Only in your dreams, Zac Porter."

I force a laugh as I sort through the mess on my desk, trying to find what I'm looking for. Buying my cheeks enough time to dial down the heat, and so determined to move us past this moment that it takes a second to realize that Zac isn't laughing with me. To recognize the silence as heavy.

He huffs out a breath. "Well, fuck."

I turn to find Zac rubbing his face with rough hands. Every stroke reveals a couple of inches of flushed skin on his forehead, his cheeks.

Shit.

"I'm only kidding," I blurt. "God, that was so embarrassing. I know you'd never actually wish—"

"I'd better get back to the party," he says, finally surfacing from behind his hands. When he does, there's not a trace left of that smirk. He eyes a spot on the wall above my head, cheeks still flaming. "I left Grams to fend for herself with the rest of the guys on the team."

"Summer's there," I say of my best friend. "They were wiping the floor with Parker at poker when we left—"

"I'll be quiet sneaking out. Don't worry." Zac flashes me a quick smile, turning for the door. "I'll see you around, Mel."

"Wait."

I dash for the door, push it shut just as he starts to pull it open.

I'm panting. Maybe from rushing to catch him. Maybe because

he's standing so close, soft brown eyes staring at his feet, or because my heart is shoving the air from my lungs with every one of its rapid beats.

I can't seem to pull together any other words, so I raise a hand between us.

Zac's gaze lifts as I twirl a stemmed four leaf clover between my thumb and forefinger. The way I always do, at least ten times a year. Our pregame ritual since we were fourteen, and I'd caught Zac nervously pacing the quiet halls of our high school before his first game, dressed in his gear from head to toe. A quarterback unable to coax himself out onto the field with the rest of his team.

"Can't let you leave without it."

He holds out his hand, accepting the clover. Staring down at it like I've just poured fairy dust into his palm. He swallows. "I don't know how I'll make it through a game without one of these."

"You'll pull through. This happens to be a very special four-leaf clover. I spent all day doing all kinds of crazy magic over it."

"You're saying it'll never wilt?"

"It'll wilt, and you definitely want it to," I tell him. "Because it so happens that the person who's carrying it when it wilts will inherit its magic. They'll throw a million touchdowns every game. Ace all their exams. Never get a hangover."

With a soft laugh, Zac folds his fingers over the clover. Tucks it into his pocket. He's still not quite looking me in the eye. His shoulders are still deflated, and a prickle builds at the back of my neck.

Like I'm missing something.

Like it's staring me in the face, but I can't make it out.

Zac slides a hand into the pocket of his jacket and produces a new pack of shoelaces. They're red, the same ones he wears on his cleats.

"What are you doing?" I ask when he rips open the package.

"Giving you your present."

"You bought me a pair of shoelaces?"

"No, I didn't," he says. "You were right. I forgot to get you a going-away present and I'm feeling like a pretty big jackass over it. Hold out your arm for me."

When I do, he loops a red lace around my wrist. Once, twice, three times. Double knots the bracelet in place.

"Now do me," he says, holding out his arm and the other lace. With lightly shaking fingers, I loop and double knot it around his wrist.

"There," he says with a breath. "I didn't get to do crazy magic on it or anything. But maybe whenever you feel down or . . . or if you ever miss home? Maybe you look at it and know that someone here is thinking about you. Missing you."

I think I might be suffocating.

Intense, all-consuming weight builds in the pit of my stomach, drifting upward, as I stare into his eyes. They peer down at me, fixed on mine like he feels them, too: the flurry of unsaid words now surrounding us. Words that mean nothing in isolation, but that, if I could just figure out in which order to string them together, could maybe change everything.

Because this feeling hardly makes any sense to me. Other than the weekly ten minutes we spend alone when I deliver his good luck charm from September to February, I'm number three in his friendship with Parker. The spare.

Except, right now, I feel like the one.

How many times have I wished he'd look at me like that?

We're standing so close our socked toes are touching. And I'm filled with the most overwhelming urge to run my fingers through his hair. Feel the stubble along his jaw. Touch the lean muscle he's built up from years of quarterbacking to a full-ride college scholarship.

"Kiss me."

The words leave my mouth before my brain processes them. I

wait for the kick of humiliation. For the regret, the urge to say something to erase the words. When none of that comes, all I do is stare.

Zac has gone completely still. I can't get a good read on his expression, but I can tell he's holding his breath.

"That's not funny." He says it so quietly I can barely hear the words over the sound of my own heart.

"I'm not being funny. I want to kiss you."

Zac swallows hard. Once. Twice. "You're not fucking with me?" I shake my head, feeling my throat dry out. "You really want to kiss me?"

I nod, suddenly overwhelmingly nervous.

And then his chest swells, and he takes such a long and thorough breath it's like he's surfacing from the deep sea.

"Stay here."

I rear back. "What?"

"I have to . . . I have to go do something." Zac opens my bedroom door, eyes still fixed on me. "Stay here and wait up for me, okay? I'll be right back."

"But—Zac, I just—"

I reach for him, but he shakes his head with enough intensity that I hit the brakes. He slips out of my bedroom, inching the door shut between us, eyeing me through the shrinking crack.

"I'll be back, Clover, I promise. Wait up for me."

Chapter 1

Melody

"What a jackass."

I focus on the pale-blue cashmere sweater I'm folding, tucking it into the dresser drawer with so much care you'd think it was my most prized possession.

It's not. What I'm really doing is ignoring the man sitting at the foot of my new bed. His eyes are burning into my back, waiting me out, but he should know me better by now. I don't cave when it comes to Parker Woods, and he's also stubborn when it comes to me.

Just not as stubborn as I am.

"Melody, I am begging you to say words to convince me you know exactly what kind of jackass this guy is. He *dumped* you."

"I know he dumped me. You don't think I know he dumped me? I'm back in town, moving in with you, aren't I?"

"Specifically, he dumped you so he could fuck his way through a boys' trip to South America. You do know that's what he's doing, right?"

I wheel around to face him, immediately regretting the way I plant my hands on my hips like a stern mom. But I've committed to it, so I throw in some narrowed eyes for good measure. "You don't have to rub it in. Okay, maybe he dumped me. Maybe I just spent the past month wallowing in our old apartment by myself. But it really was a great relationship while it lasted, and I don't see why I can't remember it fondly—"

With a groan, Parker falls dramatically onto the mattress. He's freshly home from work, still dressed in a pair of athletic shorts and a T-shirt adorned with the UOB Huskies logo on the sleeve.

"Correction: He's a *manipulative* jackass. He's out there sleeping around, and he's got you here *remembering him fondly*. I don't know what you ever saw in him, Mel. Is it the rich guy thing? Did he at least buy you nice things for tolerating him all these years?"

I move to the bed where one of my suitcases sits open, still full to the brim, and stare down at Parker who's now glaring at the ceiling.

There are boy-girl twin combinations who look totally alike.

That can't be said for me and Parker. We have the same blue eyes, the same scowl when we're pissed off, and the same talent for conveying our disdain with just a half-second glance.

But we're opposites in every other way. He's brown-haired where I'm blond, and he got blessed with several extra inches in the legs. He's spent his whole life here in Oakwood Bay, graduated from UOB and took a job as a physical therapist in its athletic rehab center.

Meanwhile, I moved to the city for college ten years ago and never made it back home outside of the holidays.

Except now, courtesy of the demise of my six-year relationship.

"Is this what it's going to be like, moving in here with you?" I ask him. "Look, it's bad enough I had to move out of the apartment I shared with Connor—"

"*And* hightail it out of the city you've lived in for a decade—"

"That part had nothing to do with him. I couldn't afford to live there alone on a part-time salary."

"Because *precious Connor* couldn't stomach the idea of the independence you'd gain having a full-time job. And then he goes and throws you to the curb. How are you still sitting here defending him? Where's the rage, Mels? Where's the hate? Why aren't you telling me about the bonfire you made of his belongings on your way out of that absurd apartment you shared?"

"There's nothing to hate. He always treated me well. Looked after me. He got me my job—"

"Which you despise," Parker interjects. "I've never once heard you gush about the prospect of making rich white men richer for a living."

I ignore him, but he's not wrong. Maybe I'd graduated college armed with a math degree and no clue what to do with it, but crunching numbers at the same investment bank where Connor worked definitely hadn't been on my bingo card. Until it was.

But at least I'd found a job, as aimless as I'd felt back then. At least I'd been earning something, paltry as it had been. At least they'd hired me as a remote worker, letting me move back to my hometown after it became glaringly obvious I could only afford to live—quite illegally and perilously—in a street-side federal mailbox post-breakup.

It might have been the gracious thing to do to let me have the apartment we shared, but it was Connor's apartment, really. He bought—well, his parents bought—a stunning condo in a high rise in the heart of downtown, high enough to peek over the surrounding skyscrapers for a glimpse of the river and the deep orange sun as it crossed the daytime sky. That apartment was pure glamour. Everything a small coastal town girl pictured when she imagined a life in the city.

And Connor ratcheted up the glamorous lifestyle when he sweetly refused to split the mortgage with me and my part-time salary, insisting he was thrilled to afford it for the both of us and that it made little sense that we'd both run ourselves ragged working demanding jobs. That I should go out and enjoy my life. Which, other than the three days a week I spent in the home office he lovingly put together for me, consisted of lengthy, directionless walks along the river, various fitness classes, and lunch with the other barely employed girlfriends within our circle.

Parker plucks a high-necked blouse adorned with pearls from my hands, holding it up by the shoulders with a grimace. "Let me guess: He bought this for you?"

Also true. I'll never deny that I lived a very spoiled life with my very doting boyfriend. Ex-boyfriend.

I snatch back the shirt and go to hang it in the closet. "I already know my life is in shambles, Park. I've had to crawl back home to live with my *baby brother* at twenty-eight."

"*Hey*—first off, I'm only a minute younger than you. Are you always—"

"Yes, I will always hang that minute over your head. You know it's my favorite thing to do."

"Second, I may live above a bar—"

"Oakley's is the *only* bar in town."

"—but I'm living a very adult life, in this very adult apartment. You know, I think it'll be really good for you, being back. Have you told Summer you're here?"

She'd be happy to see me, I know she would. Growing up, my friend Summer was a refuge in a world where I was constantly surrounded by boys, between Parker and his football teammates. Maybe I'd detached myself from Oakwood over the past decade, but she'd always made it a point to come around when I was back for the holidays. Still, though . . .

"No, I haven't told her," I sigh, fiddling with a shirt sleeve in my closet. "As much as I love you for letting me move in while I get back on my feet, you have to admit it's all a little embarrassing. Getting dumped out of nowhere. Crawling back home, not being able to afford my own place."

"Trust me, the only person who should be embarrassed is that idiot ex of yours."

"Actually, Connor is incredibly smart. He's the youngest person at our company overseeing a Fortune 500 CEO's portfolio."

"Oh, for fuck's sake, Mel," Parker groans. "*I know.* It's all he talked about the last time I had the misfortune of enduring his company, the pompous prick."

When would that have been? Parker made the three-hour drive to meet me in the city all the time, when I first moved out there—a good thing considering I started avoiding Oakwood Bay like the plague, and I love the hell out of my brother. His visits dwindled, though, the further I got into my relationship with Connor. Parker wasn't a fan of the so-called pompous prick. But Connor also wasn't a fan of Parker's many opinions, and the way he'd supposedly espouse them as fact.

I never felt like I could have them both equally in my life, and seeing as I lived with Connor, it was my relationship with Parker that suffered.

Not for the first time since the breakup, the image of Connor in my favorite shirt of his—the fitted polo that brings out the blue of his eyes—comes to me. He sits me down and takes my hand, then shares with me that he isn't happy anymore. Tells me how much I mean to him, how he'll always be grateful for me and the years we spent together, even when we go our separate ways. And then we do—we go our separate ways.

I finger the hangers in my closet, waiting for the tears to hit. They did, quite badly, the night of our breakup. Then the confusion settled in and hasn't left me since.

I didn't feel the monotony he said he felt. Had no idea what he meant when he said our futures no longer lined up. He left me so perplexed by the end of our talk that I spent the rest of the week trying to sort his words into an order that made sense. He'd stayed over at a friend's place that first night to give me space, and by the time I woke up the next morning, he'd left for his month-and-a-half-long

South American sabbatical. I'd never had a chance to ask where I went wrong.

Maybe that's why I'm feeling this way. Maybe the confusion is why I haven't shed a single tear since the initial shock of the breakup.

It might explain this inexplicable lightness, this strange relief deep down in my bones.

What else could it be?

Parker blows out a breath. His eyes are soft, sympathetic as I sink onto the bed beside him. I don't know why. Perhaps we've developed some kind of twin telepathy sometime in the past twenty-eight years, because I haven't made a peep about this *I don't miss my boyfriend of six years* thing. It's entirely heartless. Better kept to myself.

"You know what? What you need is a good distraction," Parker says suddenly. "A change of scenery to get your head right. I have to skip the annual Labor Day camping trip this year. There's a friend coming into town last minute, and I can't miss seeing her."

I make a face. "The French exchange student you met at UOB? Or the Australian?"

"She's from Sweden." Parker wiggles his eyebrows. "She's loud. Enjoys a little voyeurism—"

"Gross, Parker. I get that hearing questionable sounds is probably part of the deal now we're living together, but I thought you'd at least give me a grace period."

"You do get a grace period, sis," Parker says with a shit-eating grin that instantly has me dreading his next set of words. "You won't be here this weekend to hear it."

"And where exactly will I be?"

"You'll be taking my spot on the camping trip."

I return a deadpan stare, letting the thought sink in. Waiting for some part of it to appeal to me. But it doesn't. Spending my first weekend back home camping with Summer and . . .

And Zac Porter.

Absolutely fucking not.

"I'm not certain that's the best idea," I say, folding a pair of crisp, inky blue jeans.

"It's a brilliant idea. You'll have a great time. Get your mind off Connor. You can hitch a ride out with Summer, and you'd get to meet our friend Brooks—"

"I will not be attending."

Parker laces his fingers behind his head. "Then I should warn you: I'm loud in bed. And she's not a quiet little mouse, either."

"You're disgusting."

"Yup," he says, popping the *P* sound. "And I won't tame my impulses in my own apartment, big sis. So unless you wanna go out and buy yourself a pair of industrial-grade earplugs, you're in for a very long, long weekend."

"Parker," I groan, giving up on unpacking and tossing that pair of jeans back into my mess of a suitcase. "This is a horrible, *horrible* idea. I haven't even got a tent!"

"You won't need one," Parker says. "I'll make sure everything's set up for you by the time you arrive at the campsite."

I gesture at my suitcase. "Look at all this. I don't have any camp-appropriate attire—"

He waves away my words. "You have until tomorrow morning to figure that out."

"But—"

Parker grins. "You know, Ava and I have this thing for bondage. Rope, restraints . . ."

I rear back. "You do that kind of thing? God, what am I asking—stop talking about this. Right now."

He shrugs. "It's great, if you've got the right partner—"

"Oh my God, *okay*," I say loudly, tone begging for the end of this disturbing conversation. "I'll go camping. But be prepared to take the brunt of my bitching when I'm back, and you'd better stock up on After Bite because mosquitos *devour* me."

Parker pouts. "Poor *wittle* Melody and her mosquito bites."

I smack him on the knee. "You know they turn into these insane red welts—"

"It'll all be worth it, Melo. You'll see," he says, grinning at the ceiling and proud as hell of himself. "This'll be the best thing that's ever happened to you."

Chapter 2

Melody

"I feel like a proud dad walking his kid to her first day of kindergarten."

"Shut up," I grumble under my breath. "I can't wait to pay you back for this."

Turns out, Parker wins in the stubborn department. No amount of moaning and groaning last night got this camping idea out of his head, and as we emerge onto the street from Parker's apartment, we find Summer's car already waiting at the curb.

It's really a funny town, Oakwood. Its personality is a cross between devoted college football town and docile catch-all for the surrounding coastal fishing towns. Aside from UOB, which brings in students from up and down the coast, our schools are mostly populated by kids from bordering towns who live too close to the outskirts to qualify for their own school system. Our single inn is constantly booked out by tourists who waited too long into the fishing season to get a spot anywhere else. And over the summer and holidays, the town's population plummets to barely anything once UOB breaks and students head home.

Though it's named after the bay, it's not even really set on the water. You have to drive to the very perimeter of town to get anywhere near the ocean.

The main strip itself is all colorful doors, cobblestone sidewalks, and vintage streetlights, and is mostly occupied by a sweet corner diner and a handful of bait and tackle shops. Parker lives right over Oakley's Pub and immediately next door to Callie's Shop, the single women's boutique in town.

This town is far from awful, to be fair. I never resented the place until ten years ago.

The dread that's been festering in the pit of my stomach since Parker foisted this trip on me is alive and well as we near Summer's car. With a final scowl at Parker, I hike the backpack up my shoulder and slap on the bright smile: the one Connor always said made me feel *warmer*. More inviting.

Growing up, especially next to sunny Parker, I'd been told to perk up more times than I can remember. Connor used to work overtime trying to get me to smile. Trying to tickle me into laughter in that cutesy way of his.

Smile, Melly. It won't kill you.

Cheer up, Melly. People are starving in other parts of the world. What do you have to be so serious about?

As if my cheerful mood would cause the heavens to open up and deliver food and water to the people who need it. It's not like I'm perpetually upset. I just don't see why I have to walk around with a beauty queen smile if I don't particularly feel like giving one.

It seems to work now, though. Summer returns my grin, appraising me and Parker from the driver's seat.

"I can't believe my eyes. Oakwood Bay, blessed with both Woods twins after all these years. Better batten down the hatches."

I haven't seen her in nearly nine months, not since Christmas, but Summer doesn't look any different.

The dark hair that hits just above her shoulders in a collection of messy waves.

The tiny silver hoop piercing her nose and the perma-tan from her hours spent surfing.

The breadth of her smile as she leaves her car to pull me into a bone-crushing hug before drawing back to get a look at me.

"You going to church or something?"

"Oh, come on." I look down at myself. "Do people wear leggings to church these days?"

"Couldn't tell you. But I bet you'd see plenty of these sweaters in the pews." She pinches my sleeve, feeling the fabric. "What is this, cashmere? You're wearing this camping?"

I smooth a hand down my front. Summer's wearing a pair of leggings and scrunched-up socks with a baggy sweatshirt that makes her look like she just walked off the set of an ancient Jane Fonda workout video. Mostly, though, she looks a hell of a lot comfier than me and my fitted cashmere top.

I can admit my sweater collection is lacking. But I moved back home for the sole purpose of saving money for my own place in the city. I don't exactly have extra cash to spend on camp attire.

So, the so-called church outfit it is.

Summer nudges Parker by way of hello before hopping back into her car. My brother takes me by the shoulders and wheels me to the passenger door, like I am indeed a reluctant kindergartener.

"So, it's true, then? You're really back?" Summer asks as I slide into the seat beside her, letting Parker shut the door behind me.

"For now," I say with a breath. "Just until I find a job that lets me afford to move back to the city alone."

"What happened to the guy you were with?"

"He dumped her to fuck his way through a boys' trip to South America," Parker says promptly, dropping my backpack into the back seat. He taps the roof of the car, looking pleased as punch with himself despite the death glare I'm sending his way. "Have a good time, kids."

Summer watches him saunter down the sidewalk back to the nondescript blue door leading up to his apartment. "He broke up with you? When did that happen?"

I drop the coffee I brought for Summer into a cup holder, shaking up the green juice in my own travel bottle for no other reason than to buy myself time. I don't care what Parker says. This is utterly humiliating. I'd been so proud of my life, proud that I managed to make it in another city on my own when everyone I knew stuck around Oakwood.

But I didn't make it, did I?

I'm back here, with barely a penny to my name. With nothing but a few suitcases full of clothes that I didn't even buy myself, because I'd been constantly spoiled by the man who's now left me with hardly anything.

"He broke up with me a month ago, right before his trip," I tell Summer as she fires up the engine and pulls away from the curb. "I've been staying at our place—*his* place—while looking for my own. And then it became clear I couldn't afford to live alone, so . . . here I am."

"You didn't have any friends you could crash with?"

Apparently not. There'd been nothing more sobering than getting those couple of texts the week of my breakup. My request for a round of drinks with the women in our circle was met with apologetic yet firm denials, considering how *awkward it would be* to meet up with me now that Connor and I were no longer together.

I still haven't stopped shaking up my juice. The sound of sloshing liquid fills the car, hopefully sufficiently drowning out the tremble in my voice as the sting of those texts hits me all over again. "After some reflection, it turned out all my friends in the city are actually his friends. That would have been a little awkward."

"I'm sorry, Mels," Summer says with a sympathetic wince. "I remember that gray area after my last breakup, trying to divvy up the friend group between me and my ex. It took a while to figure out, but everyone landed where it made sense in the end. I even inherited a couple I thought for sure would side with him, and he got my college roommate in the swap. I'm sure they'll surprise you."

Shake, shake, shake.

"No," I mutter, fixating on the pickup truck overtaking us in the next lane. "I mean that every single one of them started out as his friend, and it's staying that way. I lost touch with my college friends a while ago."

Summer tips her head, hair swinging to one side as she follows the up and down trajectory of my bottle before settling her gaze back on the road. "Really? What happened?"

"Some of them moved back across the country after graduation. Connor wasn't a fan of the rest of them. There were a couple of nights where I went overboard with the cocktails during happy hour."

I'll never forget the sheer disappointment in Connor's face the night I came home teetering in my four-inch heels after a glorious night out with my girlfriends. The mortification I felt when he pointed out I was slurring my words. It culminated in a painful, lengthy lecture the next morning about making sure we surrounded ourselves with trustworthy, responsible friends who wouldn't let me embarrass myself that way. When I pointed out he was suggesting I drift away from my only friends within a three-hour radius, he folded me into his own circle with the women who'd all go on to side with him in the breakup.

"Did you not have any friends from work, then?" Summer asks.

I shake my head. "The job he got me was completely remote."

I can feel Summer's eyes on me, but when I chance a glance, I find her focused on the road with a small pull to her eyebrows.

"It's so weird hearing you say all this, Mels. I've listened to Parker rant about him for years, but whenever you mentioned Connor, it was all glowing reviews. But everything was on his terms, huh?"

Shake, shake, shake.

Was it?

I eye the road ahead of us, thinking back. Connor always had a vested interest in my life. Made sure I had a good job, was eating well. He spoiled me with my entire wardrobe. Sure, maybe his hobbies became my hobbies. Maybe his friends became my friends.

But isn't that normal? He was my boyfriend, after all. It's completely normal to get wrapped up in a relationship, especially over six years.

So why don't you miss him, you heartless wench?

We did everything together. Came up with a bucket list of the most outlandishly extravagant restaurants in the city, and checked them off one by one over the years. Traveled everywhere I ever dreamed of going, and then some. The way he smiled over at me that day hiking in Ecuador, with waterfall spray slowly drenching us, nearly tipped me off the edge of that platform.

It's not that I'm doing okay. I haven't had a decent night's sleep in weeks, tossing around, obsessing over this breakup and where it is I went wrong. How did I get someone like Connor, who doted on me so profusely, to walk away without a thought?

I loved him, and I lost him, and I have no idea how. I thought I'd been doing everything right to make him happy.

"What's this about a trip to South America?" Summer draws me out of my spiral, flicking on the windshield wipers as rain starts to drizzle onto the car.

"Parker's exaggerating—it had nothing to do with wanting to be single on a boys' trip. He told me he wasn't happy anymore."

She doesn't seem convinced. "Are his friends single?"

"One of them is. And . . . and the other just got dumped by his fiancée," I admit, overheating under my sweater.

Summer doesn't say anything. Only stares out at the road ahead of us, the thick tree line to our right, the pines sparsely dotting the land off the bay to our left. The sky above dark, threatening a downpour, reflecting every confused thought swirling in my head right now.

Shake, shake, shake.

I clear my throat, forcing a smile. "Well, if that's really why he did it, I suppose the silver lining is that he didn't cheat, right?" I focus on the road, feeling Summer's eyes on me again. "And there's no sense dwelling on it. We aren't together anymore, and . . . I'm moving on with my life. Staying positive."

Shake, shake, shake.

"Mels, I'm begging you—" Summer's hand darts out from the wheel, forcing my arm still. The green juice stops sloshing at once. "What is this stuff?"

I flip open the lid and take a swig. "My breakfast. Celery juice with a shot of turmeric—Connor's recipe. I make it fresh every morning. That juicer is the one thing of Connor's I snuck away in the breakup."

"How sentimental." Summer chuckles. "And there I was, stealing my ex's comfiest sweater as a memento. I ended up tossing it into a dumpster a week later, anyway, once I remembered what an ass he was."

It didn't occur to me once, in my days of packing, to steal something that smelled of Connor.

There's seriously something wrong with you.

I cast back, trying to remember when Summer's last relationship ended. Two years ago? Three? God, I'd really isolated myself from my life here, hadn't I? It's the problem with coming from a small town. There's no way to keep in touch with the people you love while successfully avoiding those you don't want to see.

"How's playing the field?"

"Playing the field is exhausting," she admits. "I've been stuck in an endless string of bad dates. I haven't been on a second date in months."

I rub my face. "Is that what I'm in for?"

Her mouth pulls down sympathetically. "First things first: I think you need a rebound. A fling. Quick and dirty. Get your mind off Connor and get your mojo back. It was the perfect thing to get me back into the mindset of dating, after years of monogamy."

Into the mindset of dating. After six years of feeling like I was the center of Connor's world, it's a mindset I never thought I'd have to revisit. I thought we were heading for an engagement, not an out-of-the-blue breakup.

We zip down the freeway, taking the familiar road to the campsite Parker and I grew up going to with our parents, the same one we'd introduced to our friends in school. The first couple of years it was the four of us, plus Zac and Summer, going a few times a year.

Eventually, Mom and Dad weaned themselves off the trips. We thought they'd been the coolest parents, trusting us and our friends to hang out in the woods alone without cell service for a weekend.

After a while, we realized they were just as excited to have the time for themselves. They never really grew out of their sense of adventure, even after the birth of their twins—as exhibited by the way they promptly sold everything to live out of a silver Airstream RV and travel the country the second Parker and I graduated college.

I used to love these camping trips. Back then, they were a glorious excuse to spend an uninterrupted forty-eight hours in Zac's company. Now?

I'm so nervous, I already have to pee. Twenty-three minutes into the two-hour drive.

I sigh, taking a sip of juice. "So, who's the new guy Parker says goes on these trips with you now?"

"Who, Brooks?" Summer looks around. "Wow, I forgot you wouldn't have met him. Brooks has been around for years now. He played at UOB with the guys, then went to the NFL for a few years. He's great."

"How's it been, being the only girl around all these guys?"

Her laugh tells me everything I need to know. "I swear, I caught myself manspreading on a date one night. And did you know there's such a thing as televised video game competitions? Because I do, and I'm so happy to have you back." She flicks on her blinker and speeds into the next lane. "Other than that, it's like having three protective brothers bodyguard you through life. Parker cheers you up, Brooks sits with you for touchy-feely chats until the sun rises, and then there's Zac . . ."

My stomach plummets at hearing his name thrown around so casually. Like it's nothing.

Then again, it *is* nothing for Summer. I never told her—never told anyone—what happened that night in my bedroom.

Wait up for me, he'd told me ten years ago.

I had. I'd waited up all night. Chastised myself every time I felt tears start to well after the first hour. I'd waited until the damn sun came up, and then some more in the morning, until my dad loaded up his car with my luggage and drove me out to my new school.

I'd waited because it was Zac.

Maybe we hadn't been as close as he and Parker had been. But I was the girl who brought him four-leaf clovers for good luck. That meant something to me. And from the way he'd look at me when I twirled that green stem between my fingers, I'd thought it meant something to him too.

I'd fallen for him over those ten-minute rituals. They were our thing. This little secret between us, one of the few things in life I didn't share with my twin.

I knew there was no way he felt the same, seeing as he rarely spoke to me outside of Parker's company. But I thought he'd at least come to care for me in other ways.

As Parker's twin sister. His deliverer of good luck charms. Whatever.

I never thought he'd turn out to be as heartless as he'd been that night. He'd tied a piece of red rope around my wrist, sent my stupid teenaged imagination into overdrive. Told me to wait up for him. Left me hanging. And never came back.

Never sought me out or tried to explain. Ignored the single text I ever sent him, asking if he was okay. Nothing for ten years.

"Have you seen much of Zac since you moved?" Summer asks, eyes on the road.

"I haven't seen him since that end of the summer party. Right before I left."

"Then you're in for a real treat. He's . . ." She casts around looking for the right word. "Different."

"What do you mean?"

"I like to call him the Ogre of Oakwood, which *greatly* pleases him," she says with a bite of sarcasm. "He bought himself this massive plot of land on the outskirts of town a few years ago, built this great big house. Spent the past few years terrorizing the good residents of Oakwood with a crappy mood."

I frown. She says all this matter-of-factly, but there's no way it's true. Zac Porter, in a crappy mood?

It's . . .

I think back to that deep, warm laugh, and the easy way he'd smile. The laugh lines around his eyes.

It's not just impossible. It's unfathomable.

Anyway, I don't care. It took me ages, but I stopped caring about Zachary Porter a long time ago. I'm not about to resuscitate those feelings just because he's turned into a miserable person. It's none of my concern.

I just need to survive the weekend. Survive the next few months living with Parker. And go back to never seeing or thinking about Zac Porter again.

Chapter 3

Zac

It's a good thing we've known each other for years.

That we grew up like brothers since the first time he brought me over to the Woodses. He heard me at practice talking about growing up an only child to diplomats, who shipped me off to live with Grams once they caught on that all that moving around probably wasn't doing me much good.

For a friendless fourteen-year-old entering high school in a new town, Parker was a godsend.

Maybe we're not as close as we used to be back then. Maybe my patience with *Prince Parker* has waned over the years.

But if he were just about anyone else, I'd kick his ass for sticking me with setup duty for the fifth year running of this camping trip.

It's typical Parker.

We always hang out at his place because it's convenient. At the bar downstairs, because it's *right there*. He takes his sweet time getting to a campsite so that his tent is all set up by the time he arrives, and I'm the one to do it because our sharing a tent is *tradition*.

And I'll say all this to his face, too, if he ever decides to show up.

Tossing his sleeping bag over the blown-up air mattress he'll be using, I'm very aware that my bad mood is misplaced. What I'm really on edge about is those painful forty-five minutes I spent in my boss's office this morning, where he let me know, in no uncertain terms, that my newly minted title as head coach of the UOB Huskies football team was acquired through a wild stroke of luck.

The front office hadn't managed to attract a new coach to fill the vacancy left when they fired my predecessor at the end of yet another horrific season. It's not altogether surprising that they didn't manage to recruit someone else. Who'd want to coach a team that hasn't won a single game in two years? We can barely recruit decent players anymore.

So, according to my boss, the only viable option was promoting me from my job as the team's offensive coach.

But it wasn't a reward for good behavior. Had nothing to do with the fact that I quarterbacked this team to a championship while I was a student. Nothing to do with the fact that I never considered coaching anywhere else once I graduated.

It wasn't even a favor.

It was a matter of necessity, and he assured me he felt no sense of loyalty toward me. I had a handful of games to turn this team around, or I was out. And considering our pathetic showing in the first two games of the season, his hopes aren't high.

I'm a few weeks off from unemployment.

I should be at home, plotting my next move. Figuring out how to squeak out a win while not a single person on the field seems to be able to catch a pass from the exceptional quarterback we've somehow managed to keep around after two failed years. I'm only here because Brooks convinced me I was due for a distraction from work.

I listen to Brooks fumble around outside trying to erect his tent in the brutal wind. Right on cue, the wind picks up, flapping my own tent so loudly it almost drowns out Brooks's loud, "Shit!" When I stick my head out of the partially unzipped opening, I see his tent has tipped over on its side, the two front pegs flapping uselessly after being ripped from the ground.

He's a big guy, with the kind of build and long limbs that served him well during his stint in the NFL. But right now, he's struggling to get a hold of this piece of canvas bouncing with the wind.

"You need any help, man?" I call to him.

He leaps for the edge of the tent and wrenches it to the ground, shoving a spike back into the dirt. "Got it."

If I were an ass—which I rarely like to be, despite the shitty mood I'm usually in—I'd give him my smuggest *I told you so*. I sent a text just this morning asking if we should rethink camping in this kind of weather. Besides the wind, the sky's been threatening a torrential downpour for the past week.

No one else seemed especially concerned about it, though.

I leave Brooks to it, making myself comfortable on the air mattress Parker has suddenly decided he needs, after years of going without. I pull out my phone out of habit, except there's no cell service to speak of here, so I toss it down on the sleeping bag I'll be using next to Parker's mattress.

My fingers find the red, worn-out shoelace around my wrist. Twist it around compulsively. It's nearly impossible to do given how tight the thing's become. I've been retying it within an inch of its flimsy life every time it's fallen off over the past ten years.

Really, I should cut it off.

Burn it in a purging ritual or something.

Hope it finally cleanses me of these incessant thoughts. Stops her from popping up in my head every other second.

I blow out a breath, shove the bracelet as far up under my sleeve as it'll go. Stare at the roof of this tent until I finally hear the sound of tires crunching on the ground at the outskirt of our campground. Two car doors slam shut.

Prince Parker blesses us with his presence at last.

"Too bad nobody warned us about the weather, huh?" I hear Summer say loudly, clearly meaning for me to hear it.

"Ah, don't be a wimp," Brooks replies breezily. "It's no worse than the time we . . . Who's this?"

Silence ensues and I sit up slowly, shoving the hair off my face.

Senses tingling.

Hair rising on the back of my neck.

"Oh," Summer says after what feels like an eternity. "I keep forgetting you two haven't met." There are goose bumps crawling up my arms, under the sleeves of my flannel.

"Hey, I'm Brooks."

And then I realize what's missing in this exchange. Not a single peep from Parker.

More silence. A throat clears. And then: "I'm sorry. I assumed Parker gave everyone the heads-up I was coming. I'm Melody, Parker's sister."

Mother. Fucking. *Fuck.*

Like it's got some kind of tether to the woman standing just feet outside the tent I'm now absolutely hiding in, the bracelet on my arm starts burning my skin. Like it needs me to know that Melody Woods is here. Like I don't remember the sound of her voice.

It's funny how life works. I've lived an entire decade without her. Went to school, ridden the highs and lows of college football both as a player and coach. I've made friends she doesn't know, dated women who weren't her. Yet, here I am, heart still pumping in anticipation of the girl who stole my heart the first time I ever saw her.

I have been desperately, pathetically, feel-nothing-unless-she's-in-the-room in love with Melody Woods for fourteen years.

She's the *what if* I've never been able to let go of. The regret that lives in the back of my mind. The fantasy of something that could've been so good, but never got to take off.

"I hope it's okay I came," Mel says. "I just moved back home for a bit, and Parker seemed to think it was a good idea. Though I did protest . . ."

She sounds different. Bright. Chirpy. I can *hear* her smile.

It's so contrary to the girl I remember. The one who only gave out smiles when you earned them. Who scowled so good she could skewer you with a glance.

Ever the gracious host, I hear Brooks stride across the campsite and picture him getting Mel into one of his suffocating hugs.

"Of course it's okay," he tells her. "The more the merrier. Is Parker not coming?"

"He has a . . . He needed me out of his apartment for the weekend. But he said I could take over his spot in one of the tents. Which one's his?"

No.

No.

What the *fuck* is he playing at—

"It's the one right over there. Go make yourself comfortable," Brooks tells her, oblivious to the utter fucking meltdown happening in the tent *right over there.*

Then it's nothing but the sounds of wind and footsteps muffled on dirt, heading for me. I scramble off Parker's bed—*Melody's* bed, because my oldest friend fucking hates me—and move toward the tent opening, heart beating uncomfortably fast. I fiddle with the zipper, get it all the way open just as the footsteps come to a stop outside.

And that's how I find myself crawling around on hands and knees at Melody Woods's feet. Sounds about right.

I let my gaze rake up her body. The spotless white sneakers that look brand new. The dark leggings confirming that my memory of her perfect legs has been serving me well all these years. The fitted sweater, hugging the curve of her waist.

The way she looks down at me, blue eyes wide, lips popped open.

Long blond hair curtaining her face as she takes me in, kneeling before her.

Mel's mouth shapes over a word that never makes it out.

We're still staring at each other, and I can't tell whether her heart is about to give out, too, or if it's just me feeling all this. The pounding in my chest. The light layer of sweat building at the back of my neck, even though it sure as hell isn't warm out, even for early September. I'm also brutally aware of the two other people taking in this wordless exchange.

"Melody."

The sound of my voice seems to snap her out of this loaded staring contest. She takes a step back, away from me. And then another.

"I'm about to become an only child," she mutters, but I don't think she's speaking to me. "I am going to *kill him*—"

"You and me both."

I don't know why I'm still kneeling on the ground. But it's where I continue to stay, staring, as Mel throws me a look—scathing and maybe a bit afraid—and digs her phone out of her back pocket.

None of those phony smiles for me, I guess. "There's no cell service for miles, remember?"

Her eyes widen. "Are you seriously talking to me like it's nothing right now?"

I know what she's getting at. What she's already accusing me of. Despite the cheery tone earlier, she's still Melody Woods. The Melody Woods I know doesn't let anyone off the hook when they've fucked up as big as I did.

And damn if I'm not aching to see her in all her no-nonsense glory. I missed it. "How would you like me to talk to you?"

She takes another step away. "I don't. I want you to get off your knees and help me reason with the others."

"Reason how—"

She faces our audience of two. Brooks towers next to his tent, hands stuffed into the pocket at the front of his sweater, hood up against the wind, eyeing me curiously. Summer has her arms crossed tightly over her chest. She's staring like she can barely believe Mel's there, as though they haven't just spent a two-hour car ride together.

"Are the tent assignments final?" Mel asks.

I finally rise. She doesn't turn, and there are a good couple feet between us, but she feels me behind her and her shoulders immediately stiffen. It stings. But I move a few steps away, giving her space.

Brooks's gaze drifts in my direction in the wake of Mel's question, clearly sensing the tension, though he doesn't have any context to go off of. He raises his eyebrows.

You want a way out of this? he's silently asking me. Do I?

It's clear she wants nothing to do with this sleeping arrangement. With me, altogether. But if she's really moved home, we're going to have to air things out.

I'm going to have to explain myself. Without the audience. With my eyes on Brooks, I shake my head.

"Ours is final," he announces. "Isn't that right, Sum?"

"We can—"

"Nope." He throws an arm around her shoulders. Gives her an obnoxiously cheerful smile. "I've got my heart set on you, hun. You know Zac's a terrible spooner."

Summer immediately shrugs off his arm, giving him a funny look. Thankfully, she doesn't argue.

"Well, that's settled, then," I say, clapping my hands together. Quietly, I add, "Looks like you're stuck with me, Clover."

"Don't call me that."

She mutters it under her breath, only for me to hear. Doesn't even look at me. But she doesn't need to. The hushed disdain in her voice conveys exactly how much she means it. That the nickname no one's ever used but me isn't going to fly anymore.

I deserve that, after what I did to her. The way I left her that night. The way I never reached out, didn't go to her until I finally cracked five years later. Five years ago. Only to find her holding hands with him. The lucky fucker who was smart enough to see what he had in front of him. Who didn't screw it up.

I don't deserve to use that nickname.

Mel's shoulders rise all the way with the force of her inhale. "Okay." She nods, head turning to survey the campsite before her. "Okay, I guess this is happening."

Hitching her backpack up over her shoulder, she swerves past me and disappears into our tent. The rest of us stare at each other in dumb silence. If it wasn't for the quiet rustling behind me, I'd put money on a mutual hallucination.

I beeline for Summer, and I'm so focused on her face that I don't notice the firepit until I'm stumbling into it, almost losing my footing. Brooks snickers, but I don't have it in me to care.

"What the hell, Summer?" I say tightly, peeking over my shoulder to check that Mel's safely tucked into our tent. This won't be a fully private conversation, but the wind is loud enough to give us some coverage. "How do you just spring this on me? On—on all of us."

Brooks looks at me curiously. "You know her?"

"Yeah, she was . . . She's Parker's twin. We were all in the same grade."

"I didn't think you'd mind if she came," Summer says, scanning me. "You're always asking for news about her."

She's exaggerating. I only ask once in a while.

Every couple days, when not knowing how she's doing starts to feel unbearable.

"You look like you're verging on some kind of aneurysm," Summer tells me now. "Anything you need to share?"

What do I need to tell them?

Last time I saw her, she made a move on me and I fumbled it. I haven't spoken to her since I left her that night.

I still haven't figured out how to stop thinking about her.

"I'm sharing a tent with her," I say to Summer. "I haven't seen her in ten years. Don't I get a little sympathy?"

"Sympathy for what?" Summer rolls her eyes. "She's having a rough go of it right now. She just got out of a relationship."

Hold up.

I narrow my eyes. "What does that mean, *she just got out of a relationship*?"

Summer gives me an odd look. "It means she was recently broken up with," she enunciates, like I'm some kind of moron.

I don't blame her. My brain does seem to be short-circuiting. Because . . . he *dumped* her? He actually dumped *Melody Woods*?

Is he insane?

"She's trying to get back on her feet after a bad relationship, dealing with some controlling stuff she doesn't seem to have wrapped her head around yet," Summer goes on. "You want to talk about sympathy, then you go and give that some thought."

Despite my best efforts, the image of Melody walking out of a skyscraper pops into my head. It had been dark out. Wet, the tail end of winter, slush around my feet. I'd been in the city that night and sat in the cold for hours, trying to build up the nerve to go in there, knock on her door. To figure out whether she still thought about me the way I thought about her. Only to see her come out holding hands with some buttoned-up guy in a peacoat and tightly wound scarf, who monologued his way down the sidewalk with her trailing just a little behind him, a flaccid smile taped on her face. Seeing her with someone else cut me good, but the whole scene felt off in a way I couldn't quite place then.

"Controlling how?"

The tent behind us flaps open and we turn to watch Melody crawl out, unfurl herself as she stands. Her hair catches in the wind, fluttering behind her and looking so whimsically beautiful I feel some of the tension in my shoulders start to ebb. She gives a big, restless sigh, eyes taking in the campsite.

God, I fucking missed her. The rare sound of her laugh, the shape of her eyes.

I missed her scowl. The one she gives when you've royally annoyed her. The one that looks like she's on the verge of your murder, unless you know to look for that little twitch in the corner of her mouth, telling you she's only trying to get a rise out of you. To see if you can keep up.

And then, with another deep breath, she staples a smile on her face. It doesn't reach her eyes.

"I think this calls for a drink," she announces, planting her hands on her hips. "Any chance I can snag a beer off someone?"

I stare at her dumbly. I'm so stunned by the sound of her voice that Brooks is already halfway to the cooler before I recover.

"Thank you," she tells him, cracking open the can he offers. "I completely blanked on bringing anything for myself. This is what happens when you're basically sober for six years."

"You're sober?" Summer asks, watching with alarm as Mel tips the can to her lips and takes a long sip, then winces as she swallows.

"No, I'm not. It was part of Connor's whole *healthy living* thing. My ex-boyfriend," she clarifies for Brooks's benefit. "Rule number two: no drinking your calories."

What the fuck?

"Pardon me?" Summer says sharply. We exchange a look. She looks just as disturbed as I feel.

Mel clears her throat, deepens her voice, makes it go a little lofty. "'It's a waste of calories, Melly. You don't need it.'" She gives a weak smile. "That's not exactly what he sounds like, but you get the picture."

Brooks gives Mel an up and down. "I'm not a nutrition expert or anything, but you don't look like you need to be counting your calories. What was rule number one?"

She shrugs so nonchalantly I know instantly I'm going to hate whatever she'll say next. Not just because it's already clear this ex *was* a controlling motherfucker. But because she doesn't even seem fazed by it. Like he's robbed her of all fight. Everything that made her *her*.

"Rule number one: stick to the meal plan. It was our thing. Working out, staying healthy."

"And did *he* follow a meal plan?" Brooks asks, tone suggesting he already senses the answer.

Mel rubs her lips together, seemingly stumped by his question. "I gained a few pounds a few years back," she says slowly, picking through her words. "I got hooked on these salted caramel cupcakes from a bakery across the street. He said . . . he was concerned about my health."

So he put her on a bullshit meal plan under the guise of mutual *healthy living*, and conveniently never stuck to one himself.

That motherfucking *fucker*.

I'm properly seething, rage boiling the contents of my stomach, making me sick. But mostly, making me want to commit a crime.

My fingers twitch toward my pocket like they expect to find keys there. Like I was the one who drove here today, and I can climb into my car and race to the city just to deck that sleazy piece of—

"Mels, you're tiny," Summer says delicately.

Melody swallows so hard I can see her throat move from where I stand across the campsite. Her eyes dart around the space between us, like she's seeing things that aren't there.

Putting puzzle pieces together.

Mel takes another tentative sip of her beer. "I think I need to stop talking about this now."

Like me, Summer seems to have grown roots from her toes. Shocked into silence and into place by the horrifying direction this conversation has turned. I widen my eyes at Brooks, and it's a mark of the depth of our decade-long friendship that he seems to know exactly what I'm asking of him.

He lays a hand on Melody's shoulder and squeezes. "Then let's stop talking about it. What do you feel like doing? Pounding our entire supply of alcohol in one sitting? Going for a swim? The wind's pretty bad, but we should be okay if we stick close to shore."

Mel closes her eyes a moment, inhaling deep through her nose, centering herself. "You know what I want? Food. I want to fall face-first into every single calorie I never got to have."

"You've come to the right place," I tell her without thinking. "The way Brooks packs for these trips, you'll make up for it within the hour."

Melody's gaze skims the tree line behind me, as though she didn't hear a word over the wailing wind. But her hand tightens around her beer can.

"I can confirm that's true," Brooks says, kneeling to throw open his cooler. "Should we try to start a fire?"

Chapter 4

Melody

"One fully loaded cheeseburger, with extra pickles on the side."

I stare at the paper plate Brooks deposits on my lap. For a cheeseburger thrown together in the middle of a campsite over an open flame, it looks amazing. Orange cheddar oozing down the sides, the whole thing piled high with layers of bacon and pickles and caramelized onions he had pre-prepared.

Summer was right. This guy is awesome.

"This looks fantastic." I beam at Brooks. "Thank you."

Truly, this burger is the stuff dreams are made of, especially in the wake of my sickening revelation.

Connor had always been a doting boyfriend, since the very first date. He'd showered me with love, affection, and gifts. Told me all the time how beautiful I was. How much he cared. How he wanted me to do well, how we'd spend the rest of our lives together.

He'd always been keen on his own wellness. He took great care of his body, ate well, worked out. At the time, I'd been convinced setting me up with a meal plan and workout regimen meant he cared. That he wanted this to be *our* thing.

I spent years thinking nothing of his obsession with my diet. And then I saw the three dumbfounded faces staring back at me earlier.

Well, two dumbfounded faces.

The third looked like it was one wrong word away from going scorched earth on anyone who got too close.

But I'm not thinking about Zac.

I'm not looking at Zac.

Not seeing how round and full his shoulders are, even under layers of clothes. You know those people who peak in high school? Zac isn't one of them.

He's tall and solid. Deep brown hair so perfectly tousled in all this wind. The familiar straight jaw, brown eyes like soft caramel. The laugh lines around his eyes, deep and worn in like smiling is his favorite thing to do. It always had been.

If Zac Porter wasn't Zac Porter, I'd let him destroy my life and ruin my credit rating.

But I'm not feeling anything at all about the man kneeling by the fire a few feet away from me, dressing his own cheeseburger.

Instead, I fix my eyes on the plate in my lap, trying to figure out how much of a massive, inconsiderate bitch I'd be if I told Brooks that I'm brutally lactose intolerant.

So lactose intolerant, I'm afraid of even *smelling* this cheese.

But he's gone out of his way to put together this dinner for me. And he was so sweet earlier, when he cooked a totally overzealous lunch once I made my demand for calories.

And here I am, ungrateful, thinking about throwing this gesture back in his face.

The length of my breath is half galvanizing, half stalling tactic. But before I can reach for my burger, fully intending to suck it up and quietly suffer the consequences deep in the woods with nothing but the moon and crickets as witnesses, the plate vanishes from my lap.

A new one appears, near identical. The tall burger, the stack of extra pickles. No cheese oozing off the sides.

By the time I register what's happened, Zac is already planted in the canvas chair next to mine, taking a massive, nonchalant bite from the cheese-filled burger he just plucked off my lap. As though it were perfectly normal that he'd remember my severe dairy intolerance after all this time.

I should be grateful, but I can't help the twinge of bitterness. We haven't spoken a word to each other all afternoon. Not since those tense few seconds by the tent, when it became clear I'd be spending the weekend sleeping at his side.

Maybe Connor was the last man to break my heart. But Zac? He taught me the meaning of heartbreak.

And now he's here. So self-assured, and staggeringly attractive. Making me cheese-less burgers as though nothing happened between us. As though the memory of that night only exists in the deepest, darkest part of my brain where I've made it live for a decade.

No longer feeling the least bit hungry, I force myself to dial back into the conversation around the campfire.

"So, he's already sitting at our table by the time I make it to the restaurant," Summer is saying. "And—"

"He didn't pick you up for your date?" Brooks interrupts, pulling a face. He's sitting with his hood drawn up against the wind, covering his dark cropped hair, the soft light from our fire bouncing off his face.

"I've been on so many bad dates lately, I prefer to have my own getaway car at the ready. So I sit, and he gives me the whole up-and-down, and tells me I look amazing, even better than I do in my dating app photos."

"So far, so good," Brooks says, biting into his burger.

"So far, so good," Summer agrees. "But then he says—and I quote—'thank God I beat off before coming here.'"

Brooks chokes on his burger.

"*What?*" I say, gaping at her. "What do you even say to that?"

"Well, he spared me from answering by adding, 'don't worry, I was thinking about you.'" The sip of water Brooks has just taken blows out of his mouth, spraying into the fire.

Summer passes him a napkin. "At that point, I just got up and left."

"This is why I don't date," Brooks groans. "It's the wild, wild west out there."

I sink into my seat. If Brooks is right and Summer's stories are a real glimpse of what's out there, I might join him in the land of no dating.

For the thousandth time since that last conversation with Connor, I'm hit with all-consuming dread. I never thought I'd be back here. Starting out again after six years. Left with barely anything, because I relied on Connor for so much. He made sure of it, didn't he?

"I'm sure it's different for guys," Summer tells Brooks soothingly.

"Is it? Because Naomi—"

"Naomi was a status-starved jerk, and you're better off without her."

Beside me, Zac heaves a deep sigh. I find him staring grimly into the fire. Summer was right about his crappy mood. He hasn't cracked a smile all day. It's . . . unsettling.

Not that I care.

"Who's Naomi?" I ask, picking up a pickle from my plate.

"His college sweetheart," Summer supplies. "She broke up with him after . . ." she trails off, eyeing Brooks, who's sat back in his chair to glare at the dark sky.

"It's a funny story," he says wryly. "I got drafted to the NFL. Played in California a few years, got served up a nasty concussion last year, never played again. I guess Naomi decided she'd grown accustomed to the glamour of dating a professional athlete. She left me for a former teammate."

I freeze in the act of biting into another pickle. "God, Brooks. I'm really sorry. About the concussion and Naomi."

Brooks takes a swig from his bottle of water. "Thanks. At this point, I miss the game more than her, you know? I think it's a sign it would've ended either way. If it was the real deal, I'm not sure I'd have ever stopped missing her. But I did."

I nod slowly, painfully aware of Zac at my other side. "What do you do now?"

"I'm a wide receiver coach." He tips his head in Zac's direction. "You're sitting next to my boss."

Out of the corner of my eye, I see Zac is still staring into the fire. He's not as tense in the shoulders as he'd been a moment ago, though, and I wonder whether his frustration came out at the mention of Naomi, and how she treated Brooks.

Summer launches into another terrible first date story, and I occupy myself with my last pickle.

If it was the real deal, I'm not sure I'd have ever stopped missing her.

By Brooks's logic—

"You want these ones, too?"

His voice is soft, barely audible over the wind. I turn my chin just enough to find Zac holding out his plate, indicating the extra pickles.

"Stop doing that," I mutter, dragging my gaze back to my plate. "Just stop."

I can feel his eyes on me. We've got a whole campfire to spread around. Yet he still chose the chair next to mine, and now he inches it closer.

"Stop doing what?"

My gaze flicks around the fire as Brooks and Summer burst into laughter, missing this hushed side conversation. "Stop with the pickles and the burger."

"Clover, you shouldn't have eaten all that cheese. You'd be doubled over in a second—"

"I asked you to stop calling me that."

I feel a flood of guilt the second my mouth shuts.

In my peripheral vision, Zac leans forward, pushing his elbows onto his knees. My entire body stiffens. Hair rises at the back of my neck. Muscles start to vibrate, anticipating the onslaught.

For him to tell me not to be a bitch.

That it's not fair that I'd speak to him like that, think the worst of him when he's been so attentive to my needs.

But Zac only releases a long, low breath. "You're right. It slipped out."

I turn, watching the shadows from the campfire dance over his face. He's looking at me like I have a right to be upset with him. Like he's going to let me hold his feet to the fire over the way he hurt me.

Right now, though, he can't seem to take his eyes off me. With the curved brows and the tic in his jaw, he looks like he's working hard to keep a string of words bottled up.

"I want to explain—"

"I need some water." I stand abruptly and set my untouched burger on my seat.

I go for the cooler just as Brooks moves to help. We crash into each other and the momentum jostles his water out of his hand so that it lands on his sneakers, spilling over the hem of his sweats.

My stomach drops and my heart leaps into my throat. "Oh my God, I'm so sorry," I say in a rush.

You're such a fucking klutz, Melly.

I drop to my knees, catching the bottle, but by now the damage is done. It's empty, its entire contents now covering the bottom of Brooks's pants, soaking his socks and shoes.

Panic rises. The muscles in my shoulders stiffen painfully as I stare at my mess. "I am so sorry . . ."

"Hey, it's okay—"

"I'm so sorry, I'm sorry—"

I pull my shirt sleeve over my hand and dab frantically at his shoes, heart pounding, trying to soak up the water.

"Mels—"

"I'm—I'm . . ."

I can't breathe. My eyes prickle with tears.

Such a fucking klutz.

My breath catches in my throat, but my lungs can't seem to stop trying to expel air, and it all builds up in my chest, excruciating and painful, doubling my panic. I pat Brooks's ankles, blood rushing in my ears.

I'm—why can't I breathe—

"Melody."

It takes me a moment to realize Zac is crouching beside me, looking alarmed. An entire eternity seems to pass, and it's just us staring at each other, noses close together. And then I let out a labored gasp, or maybe it's a sob, and Zac reaches for me, raking back my hair with his fingers and cupping the nape of my neck.

"Breathe, Clover."

It's long but inaudible over the rushing wind. And as soon as that air hits my lungs, my heart steadies out. I suck in a breath, and then another, and my muscles unclench.

What the hell was that?

Zac's eyes mirror my question, but with a knee-buckling layer of concern wrapped around it. I stumble to my feet. Brooks stares in shock. Across the fire, Summer is standing, watching apprehensively.

Color floods my face, my neck, probably my entire body. I back away from the fire. "Sorry, that was . . . such a strange reaction. I think we need more firewood. Right?"

I hurry to the path leading into the woods, scrambling over raised roots and stones to get as far from that campsite as I can without losing sight of the fire to help guide my way back in the dark. I come to a stop by an enormous tree, clutching it to help keep me upright.

What the fuck have I been doing?

Better yet, what the fuck has Connor been doing to me?

I just had a meltdown after accidentally spilling water on a guy who didn't care.

You're such a fucking klutz, Melly.

Connor used to say it with a laugh. All breezy, like we were both in on a joke. But I wasn't, was I?

Because what came after the laugh were the pointed remarks. The looks of disdain. The walking on eggshells if I'd done something he was particularly offended by. No amount of apologies would soothe him until he decided he was done being upset with me.

How . . . how the fuck am I only seeing this for the first time now?

None of this—the control, the walking on eggshells—had occurred to me in the month since the breakup. And how pathetic am I that it took four people gently pointing it out within the span of a couple days to realize how I'd been living?

I turn my back to the tree and slide down its trunk until my ass hits the ground. It helps shield me from the roaring wind, which seems to have picked up in the past few minutes.

I am so stupid.

This is why I haven't missed him, isn't it?

"Melody." Zac's voice is clear over the wind and my heart sinks.

I'm sitting here panicking over the last six years of my life. I don't need him to add another four years to the pile, up for examination.

Zac easily finds me in the dark and crouches in front of me.

"I can't handle any more right now," I tell him. "Whatever you've come here to say, please just don't."

"I want to make sure you're okay."

"Do I look okay? Did any of that back there look okay? I just lost it over spilling a bit of water on your friend's shoes."

He's silent for a beat. Then says, "Was he ever physical with you? Connor?"

I rear back, the back of my head hitting the tree I'm sitting against. "Never. That wasn't how he'd get."

"How would he get?"

"Just . . . I'm not sure," I say slowly, shoving the hair off my face. "I guess I felt guilty a lot."

"You were going to eat that cheese, weren't you? Instead of saying something?"

"He made me feel ungrateful a lot, too."

What the fuck have I been doing? What the fuck, what the *fuck*—

Zac releases a quiet breath. "Fuck, Mel. I'm so sorry."

I curl my hands into fists, refusing to let myself cry in front of him. I've humiliated myself enough today—shown my weakness to a man who's already proven he'd shove a spear into my heart given the chance. And now he's here, acting like he cares.

It dries my tears right up. Simmers my blood in a way I haven't felt in years.

I stare at the dark outline of him. "Do you want to know how you make me feel?"

The words feel foreign to me. In the pit of my stomach, I expect him to say no. To brush me off.

Zac stills. "Yes. I want to know how I make you feel."

Triumph flares in my chest. "You remind me what a silly, stupid girl I am. You make me feel bitter and resentful that you left it the way you did. You confuse me and I don't trust you. I don't know what you want from me."

He nods slowly, as though not a single one of my words surprised him. "Right now, I want to make sure you're okay."

"I'm fine."

"Then I'd like to explain why I left—"

"You've had ten years to explain," I say, getting to my feet. He follows me up. "I don't have it in me to sort through the dumpster fire of my last relationship while revisiting . . . whatever the hell happened that night. So, unless the reason you never came back involves some horrible tragedy that had you occupied for a decade, I don't want to hear it right now." I squint at the dark outline of his face. "Is that what it was? Did something happen to you that night?"

But Zac shakes his head. "No. There was no good excuse."

My heart splits in half all over again. That's it. Confirmation that he was just a bad guy. Nothing like I made him out to be in my head when we were younger.

I seem to be an expert at it. Building up men who don't deserve it. "Then I'm going to bed. Get out of my way."

~~~

The inside of our tent is loud.

Deafening. I can tell something's wrong even before my eyes spring open.

It's pitch black, and then it's not. A light appears at my side, and I blink myself to full consciousness to find Summer kneeling at the foot of my blow-up mattress with her phone lighting up the space between us. When I tip back my head to stare at the roof I realize it's being pummeled by rain, so hard the canvas sags threateningly above me.

"Mel, get up. Now." Summer grips my arm, tugging to encourage me into a sitting position.

"W-what?"

I can't have been asleep for more than a couple of hours. A flash of lightning illuminates the rest of the tent, revealing a purple sleeping bag on the ground. Summer and Zac must have traded spots after I fell asleep.

Summer tugs at my arm. "Something's wrong, Mel—this storm—I think we might have to go. This doesn't feel right—"

"*What?*"
~~~

"Mel, get *up*—"

Oh my God. She's serious. This isn't a dream.

I scramble off the mattress, feeling around for my things just as the top half of Zac's body appears inside the tent. He's soaked to the bone.

"We need to get out of here," he shouts urgently over the pounding rain. "We need to go. The property owner just came to say the roads are flooding over—trees are catching fire from the lightning. We have to leave. Grab whatever you need and get into a car. Now."

Chapter 5

Zac

As if to punctuate the urgency of the situation, another flash of lightning splits a tree not ten feet away from the tent. Melody pats around her mattress looking for something, and I indicate to Summer that she should go outside.

"Get to your car. Brooks is already out there. We're right behind you."

She slips past me, and the second Mel's hand closes around her phone, I grab a fistful of her sweater, haul her out of the tent and on her feet.

The campsite around us is a dark wall of heavy rain, making my flashlight all but useless, with only the bright taillights from the two cars telling us where to go.

Melody stares around, disoriented, instantly drenched. She turns her wide eyes on me. "Oh my God—"

"Let's get the fuck out of here."

We race for the cars. I take Melody's arm as she slips on the muddy ground, crowd her until she makes it to Brooks's car, rip open the door, urge her in. Summer's car is already running, and frankly I don't have a fucking clue how we're supposed to be driving out of here considering I can barely make anything out a few feet ahead of me.

"Get in, Mel—hurry."

But she pauses in the doorway and attempts to duck back under my outstretched arm. "I forgot something—"

"Leave it—we can come back for everything else. Let's get out of here—"

"I can't. It'll only take a second," she shouts over the rain. She slips past, dodging me as I try to catch her. "Go without me. I'll jump in Summer's car. Just tell her to wait for me."

"Melody!" I shout after her as she disappears into the rain.

Fuck fuck *fuck*. This woman is hell-bent on destroying me today.

"Are you getting in?" Brooks throws over his shoulder.

"Apparently not—just get out of here. We'll get home with Summer. Go."

He doesn't have to be told twice. His SUV lurches down the mud-covered path to the main road as I run almost blindly back to camp in time to see Melody disappear into her tent. I dive in after her.

"What do you think you're doing?" I shout as she shoves something into the pocket of her shorts. "What the hell's important enough—"

"I told you to go without me," she shoots back, trying to move around me. "I don't need a sitter—"

"Get your ass into a car, please—"

She brushes past me without another word, back out into the pouring rain. I have to double my steps to keep sight of her through all this fog, have to grab her hand and wheel her in the right direction, past the campfire we almost trip over, toward the trees. Searching for Summer's taillights until I manage to make out a pair of tire tracks through the mud at the edge of the woods.

We follow them a few feet.

And then another few. Brooks's car is gone. He left like I told him to, but— "Where . . ."

I move us deeper into the woods, refusing to let Melody out of my sight. Especially now, with the panic rising up my throat, threatening to block my airway completely. With my heart beating in my ears even louder than the rain as I find a second pair of tire tracks, leading away from the campsite, too.

No. "Zac."

The panic in Mel's voice tells me she's putting the pieces together, too, and coming to the same conclusion: both cars are gone.

Both of them.

They're just fucking *gone.*

I'm properly panicking now. Because this can't fucking be happening. We can't be stranded here. *She* can't be stranded here in the middle of this kind of storm, without proper shelter, without anything to keep her warm—

Melody pauses when I forge forward, forcing me still because I refuse to let go of her, terrified that she'll disappear on me, too.

"Zac," she shouts over the downpour. "Why did Brooks go? We were getting into his car."

"I—I told him to go," I say, and I can barely hear myself over a clap of thunder. "I told him we'd ride with Summer."

She stares uncomprehendingly. "Why didn't she wait?" Fuck. *Fuck.*

I shake my head. "I thought . . . She must have noticed him pulling away and assumed we got in with him."

"You didn't tell her to wait?"

She pulls out of my grip and pushes past me as though refusing to believe our reality. Determined to confirm this for herself, to make sure that we really are stranded here in the middle of the woods, in a brutal storm, with no cell service to speak of.

She only makes it another couple of steps before wheeling around again, this time with fury permeating her panic.

"I told you I'd be right back," she shouts. "I told you to tell Summer to wait. I told you to go without me—"

"And look how that would have turned out!" I feel sick at the thought. "You'd be here by yourself, while I'm out there thinking you made it home with Summer."

I force a breath into my lungs. Wrench my fingers out of the tight fists they've balled into at my sides, willing myself to beat back the panic. To get it together for her.

But when I look at her, standing close enough to see her through all this fucking rain, I already know it's a lost cause. Her crinkled eyebrows. Gaping mouth.

The way her eyes are asking me: *What the hell do we do now?*

Chapter 6

Zac

"Melody, I'm going to need you to show signs of life. Say something."

Mel sits frozen on Parker's air mattress, terror etched over her face. She's so pale that her lips are turning a little blue, and I gather her sleeping bag and throw it around her, rubbing over her arms in an effort to help her regain some warmth.

"Hey. You're going to be fine, okay? It's gonna be fine."

But Mel doesn't say anything. Just keeps staring at the other end of the tent in silent shock. Her hands are clasped so tightly together they look several shades paler than the rest of her. When she doesn't move, I reach for her chin, gently tipping it so that she looks at me with wide, blank eyes.

I cast around for something with enough shock value to snap her out of it.

"I . . . You know how I coach my old college football team now? Well, we haven't won a game in years. I mean, we hadn't won a game before they made me head coach, to be fair. But it's not looking good. I'm on the verge of being fired, and we're only a couple of weeks into the season."

She only stares at me, so I try to come up with something better.

"Do you know how long it's been since my last date? Yeah, me neither. I've never been . . . I mean, I've dated casually but . . ."

Christ, why the fuck am I telling her this?

My gaze falls to her clenched hands, sitting in her lap.

"If you didn't run back here to grab fuck-knows-what out of this tent, we wouldn't be stuck—"

"You're blaming *me* for this? You didn't tell them to wait for us!"

There she is.

She's glaring, and I don't know whether it's the sleeping bag doing the trick, or if my words have pissed her off that much, but she even has a tinge of pink staining her cheeks.

I sort through the stuff I salvaged from Brooks's tent. The clothes we all left, the cooler full of food. "Maybe I didn't tell them to wait, but they wouldn't have had to wait if you did what you were told and got into the car. Here, change into this. It's dry." I hold out a sweater of Brooks's but Mel stiffens, staring at it like it's drenched in pig's blood. "What?"

She takes in a long breath without meeting my eye. "No. No, thank you." She wraps the sleeping bag around herself.

"What's happening here?"

"Connor . . . Well, if you insist on knowing, Connor used to dress me."

"Excuse me?"

She lets a breath rattle through her teeth. "He liked to buy me clothes. Really nice, really expensive clothes. As a gift. I can't remember the last thing I picked out for myself."

"Why?"

Her gaze drifts to the roof of the tent, still being hit with heavy rain. Thank God I had the sense to pack the waterproof one.

"He was always really sweet about it. Liked to spoil me with stuff." She shrugs, and the nonchalance of it looks like it takes some serious effort. "But now that I'm . . . you know. Seeing it for what it is? I find I'm starting to overthink it all."

And I'm starting to feel real fucking murderous over this guy. He was telling her how to dress?

I gather the entire pile of clothes I pulled from Brooks's tent and lay it at her feet. Drop my own bag beside it.

"Then take your pick," I tell her, sorting through my bag and brandishing a pair of clean boxer briefs. "Wear these on your head if you feel like it. Just get out of those clothes before you catch pneumonia."

Her lips twitch. Just a tiny movement, like she was contemplating a smile that didn't quite make it out. But it was there, and suddenly this entire shit show of a day feels worth the trouble. Melody reaches for the original sweater I offered and then tugs free a pair of Summer's leggings from the pile.

I grab my own change of clothes and shuffle to the other end of the tent to change—back turned, trying to block out the sound of her undressing over the rain. Eyes firmly averted.

I must have had the restraint of a god back in high school.

I don't know whether it's the years apart or the regret. It could even be the heightened emotion of our current circumstances, amplifying everything to a near breaking point. Because I'm nowhere near as confident in my ability to keep my hands, my words, and my mouth to myself anymore. Which is the very last thing I should be doing, seeing as I've watched this woman struggle through the worst kind of epiphany today. Her breakup is so fresh, her pain even more so.

"They have to come back for us, right?" Mel says suddenly.

I can't resist a glance over my shoulder. Her head disappears into a tank top, the fabric falling down her bare back.

Jesus Christ. I whip around again.

I pull on a fresh pair of sweats, and wait until I hear her settle back onto the air mattress before turning again.

"I told Brooks we were riding with Summer," I say grimly. "And Summer wouldn't have left unless she thought we were already gone with Brooks."

Mel's whole body deflates. "Parker's not expecting us home until three days from now. There's no cell service. We're trapped here—that's what you're saying, right?"

I shuffle over to Brooks's cooler and swing open the lid. "We have all the food and water we planned to eat this weekend. We'll be okay for three days. Longer, by the looks of what Brooks decided to pack."

"Maybe they'll message each other in the morning," she says hopefully. "Maybe they'll figure it out."

"Maybe," I agree, though part of me doubts it. I could see one driver asking the other if they made it out all right, and if the answer's yes on both ends . . .

I rummage inside the cooler. It'll be impossible to get another fire going with how wet everything is out there, even if the rain stops. So all these eggs and meats are useless. But there's enough bread, dry cereal, and granola bars to keep us afloat. Plus . . .

Jesus, Brooks.

This guy and his sweet tooth. He packed a full assortment of homemade cookies, muffins, and Danishes, enough to have fed the three other campsites surrounding us if they were still occupied. He always makes sure to bake dairy-free stuff for Parker's sake, so Mel should be all right. I extract a massive bag of candy from the cooler, grimacing. The least he could have done was pack something better than gummy worms.

"I swear, I'm a good person," Mel says quietly.

"What?" I say absently.

"Please don't interrupt me. I'm trying to remind the universe that I am very much a good person. A good person who only recently realized she was being gaslit through a six-year relationship. I've earned some good karma, I'd say."

"You're better off without that jackass."

She gives me a withering look. "And now I have to bear snide commentary on my relationship from the very last person who deserves to have an opinion on my personal life, my dating life, my life in *general*—"

I slam the cooler shut. "*The very last*? You mean you're ranking me worse than that piece of shit ex-boyfriend?"

"It's my ranking system. So yes, right now, when I'm stuck in the middle of a torrential downpour with nothing but a flimsy tent for coverage, I'm ranking you worse."

Little brat.

She scowls at me like she fucking hates me. But at least she's talking to me now. I move to sit next to her on the air mattress.

"What do you think you're doing?" she asks sharply, throwing out an arm to block my path.

"It's this concept called sitting."

"Not here you're not," she says. She jerks her head at the space behind me. "The only way we're surviving this is if we set clear boundaries. You have your side of the tent. I have mine."

"You want me to sit on the ground while you hunker down on this air mattress that I blew up for you?"

"You blew it up for Parker, technically. Now," she indicates the other end of the tent, "off you go."

I blink. Melody waits until I've settled on my side, then reaches for the pile of stuff I grabbed from the other tent and bundles herself under the two extra sleeping bags.

"There. Nice and toasty warm." She gives me a delicate *fuck you* smile.

I sigh dramatically. "You know what? I'm starving. Absolutely famished."

I flip open the cooler beside me and pull out one of Brooks's chocolate chip cookies, almost downing it in one bite. She looks so immediately sour I have to work real fucking hard to suppress a laugh.

"What? You don't . . . oh. You don't happen to be hungry, do you? I'd pass you a cookie if I were allowed on that side of the tent.

He bakes them dairy-free for Parker, too. But I don't make the rules around here."

"At least you've got something right," she mutters, lying back on the mattress. She stares at the roof of the tent, watching it sag under the weight of the rain. "I can't believe this is actually happening. I told Parker coming here was a bad idea."

"Bad idea why?"

"You know why, Zac. In the long list of things I'd like to do with my time, hanging out with you doesn't even crack the top one hundred."

I slip into Summer's sleeping bag. The fabric is damp and I notice water starting to seep through the corner seam of the tent. Surreptitiously, I kick my foot out to soak up the moisture with the end of the sleeping bag before Mel notices and it sets her off again.

At least she'll be safe up on her air mattress. And if she wants to put me in my place after the way I fucked up with her, then I'm going to sit here and take it like a good boy. Tail firmly between my legs.

I deserve it, and you won't hear me say otherwise. It's not my choice whether she lets it go or not.

But man, this fucking sucks.

"Can we talk about it yet?" I say quietly.

Mel takes a long breath.

"No, we can't talk about it. I don't have the stomach to hear it without having the space to lick my wounds without you around."

"Fair," I say. "But for the record, Mel? I haven't stopped being sorry. I'd do anything to get us back to what we were that night."

Melody sets her gaze on me again, and for a while, that's all we do. Stare at each other in the light coming from the lantern in the middle of the tent.

She looks grim and skeptical, and I lie here both withering under the weight of her distrust and wondering how it is she's even more beautiful than she was back then. How I had the stomach to walk away from her that night. Whether she'll ever forgive me, and if I'll ever manage to forgive myself.

"We weren't anything that night."

Each of her words deliver a sharp blow right to my chest.

We lie in silence so that all that's left is the sound of rain and earth shuddering thunder. Finally, I drag the cooler across the tent, setting it right in the middle between my sleeping bag and her mattress.

After a beat, and without another look at me, she helps herself to Brooks's box of cookies.

Chapter 7

Melody

I guess this is actually happening.

I am actually stranded in the woods with the man who broke my heart the last time I saw him.

I must be a terrible person.

Maybe I've been unwittingly messing up over the years. Maybe every time I've aimed for a trash bin, my coffee cups have bounced off the rim and onto the street. Maybe I'm secretly a litterer and this is my comeuppance, come to get me at last.

I wake up to the bright morning light diffused by the thick PVC tent material, our salvation against yesterday's onslaught of rain. The bright dot I can see through the top tells me the sun is out, and I stare at it resentfully, as though it came out to personally mock me and my circumstances. It's eerily quiet after last night's storm. The wind has stopped, and all that cuts the silence is the chirping of birds overhead, and lake water hitting the shore in the distance.

I don't know whether I really believed I could go through the rest of my existence avoiding Zac. Presumably there would have been something, at some point, that would have thrown us together. Maybe Parker gets married one day, and I'd have to force my gaze away from the other side of the aisle, where he'd be flanking my twin. But until that day, I was happy to hide behind the hurt of the last time we saw each other.

I was happy pretending he didn't exist.

I peek over the sleeping bag up high around my head. Zac is still sound asleep, breathing softly, face buried in his pillow so that his cheek smushes underneath him, brown hair flopping across the pillowcase. His brow is crinkled like he's thinking very hard, and the sleeping bag he's using is pulled up to his nose.

I shuffle off my bed, get the tent half-open before throwing a glance over my shoulder.

The other side of the tent—Zac's side—has a visible layer of moisture pooling over the ground, seeping in through a small tear in the corner of the PVC. The bottom of his sleeping bag is wet, several shades darker than the part covering his body.

Shit. He slept in a puddle of water.

Very careful not to wake him, I lay one of the sleeping bags I'd been using on top of him. I may resent having to spend the next couple of days at his side, but nothing feels good about seeing him cold and wet like this. Hopefully, the sleeping bag still has enough of my body heat to help.

Outside, our campsite is a wreck.

I stand ankle-deep in thick, wet mud. Massive tree branches litter the ground. The shore is closer to camp than I remember it being yesterday, helped along by the rain, and Brooks's tent has completely collapsed overnight. Gingerly, I pick my way across the mud, back down the path where the cars had been parked yesterday, like I expect a vehicle to appear at my side via light beam. But I don't have that kind of luck.

Deciding I might as well follow this path up to the road, I walk the flooded tire tracks through the trees. Every so often, I get hit by a stream of rainwater trickling off high branches as the wind picks up. But otherwise, the forest is still.

It's the kind of calm you'd only see at the climax of a horror movie. When the beaten and bloodied heroine limps through the dark woods, frantically trying to escape her would-be killer.

I'm so focused on my feet and trying not to slip through this mud that when something shifts in my peripheral vision, it catches me off guard.

I shriek loudly as a bush to my right bursts open with the force of the world's smallest chipmunk darting out toward me.

Melody Woods versus chipmunk.

It's bound to forever go down as the most humiliating moment of my life. I already know it. Because I end up in a frantic standoff with that chipmunk as it tries to dodge around me.

And before I can understand what's happening, it decides that the best way to go is *through*, and darts between my legs so quickly I trip over my own feet, trying to move out of its path.

With a hard grunt, I land in a muddy heap. And it is indeed the most humiliating moment of my life, because I fall on my ankle completely wrong. The searing pain shooting up my leg is immediate.

"*Shit*," I breathe through a clenched jaw, sawing my teeth against the pain. Slowly, I move on all fours and try to get to my feet— "*Ow*. Nope. *Nope*."

I flop back onto my ass, wincing as I try to peel Summer's leggings up my calf to get a look at the damage. Everything's covered in mud, but even so, I can see my ankle is starting to swell.

Why? Why is the universe hell-bent on torturing me?

Tears of frustration prickle my eyes. It's not enough to get dumped, to realize I've been living with wool over my eyes for the past six years with Connor. It's not enough to have to move in with Parker, to be stranded here with Zac.

I have to be down a limb, too.

"Melody?"

My stomach sinks. Zac's voice floats through the woods from the campsite.

What are the odds I can scale this hundred-year-old tree to hunker down sloth-style until someone comes to rescue us?

"Melody? *Mel?*" Zac calls again, louder than before. I can hear the panic in his voice. "*Melody!*"

"I'm over here," I call back. Completely unhelpful, considering *here* could be anywhere in these woods, but already his footsteps squelch through the mud in my direction. I wipe the tears from my cheeks with the only part of my sweater not covered in mud.

"Mel, if this is some kind of twisted game of hide-and-seek . . ."

Zac emerges onto the path. He looks barely awake, hair sticking out at all angles, pillow creases covering his cheek. Totally disheveled in his sweatpants and the long-sleeved shirt bunched around his hips, leaving a strip of skin between it and his sweats as though he dove straight into a search and rescue mission without minding himself first.

Not that he needed to. The shirt leaves absolutely nothing to the imagination, and damn him for it. How does he look in even better shape now than when he played football?

It's offensive.

I feel personally victimized.

He doesn't see me right away. Zac sweeps the area at eye-level, before finally finding me in this puddle of mud. His mouth is ajar as though he's not really sure what he's seeing. And then his gaze glides along my legs, zeroing in on the ankle I'm clutching.

"Are you hurt?"

It's like someone's lit a firecracker in his pants. Zac powers forward, so focused on me he nearly wipes out in all this mud at least twice before reaching me.

"What the fuck happened?" he growls, dropping to his knees by my feet. He slides off my flip-flop so gently my foot doesn't even jostle.

"Well, I had this idea that I would make a bad situation worse by twisting my ankle." Zac shoots me a searing look, utterly unamused as he carefully brushes the skin along my ankle. I bug out my eyes. "Sheesh. Tough crowd."

"How bad is it? Can you move it at all?" He steadies my calf as I make an attempt to rotate my ankle. I clamp my mouth against a whimper, and with a wince he grips my toes to stop any further movement. "Easy. Let's get you back to camp. I'll find something to wrap it up with before the swelling gets any worse."

He moves to my side, arms outstretched, and I dodge his hands so abruptly my ankle twinges. "Ow, *fuck*!" I cry through clenched teeth. "What do you think you're doing?"

"I'm picking you up."

"No, thanks. You don't get to waltz in here acting the hero." I plant my hands into the mud and attempt to heave myself up, gritting my teeth as my ankle protests the movement. It hurts so badly that tears sting my eyes again.

"That's enough." Zac gives me a hard look, daring me to defy him, before tugging me into his chest and winding his arms around me.

"I'm heavy," I warn.

Zac rolls his eyes. "According to who? I could fit you in my pocket, Mel."

I don't answer him. Connor would say so in passing all the time. When he noticed my feet hurt after a night out in heels. *I'd carry you to the car, but you're a little heavy, Melly.*

The tic in his jaw tells me Zac's question was rhetorical. He lifts me in a smooth movement so that I'm cradled in his arms. For a split second, I almost forget myself. Almost sink into him, lay my head on his shoulder. Let myself admire the faint laugh lines at the corner of his eye. I used to love those laugh lines. They're visible even when he's not smiling.

It's a smile I have yet to see this weekend.

I turn my gaze to the canopy of leaves above us as he moves down the path, and cross my arms over my chest to resist the urge to wrap them around his neck. It probably looks like he's carting around a grumpy, sleep-deprived toddler.

"If I ever meet this ex of yours, there's a good chance he's face down on the pavement two minutes in."

My stomach squeezes at the promise in his voice. "How very primitive of you. Since when do you fight?"

Unlike so many of the football players we'd gone to school with, Zac had never been prone to aggression, not even on the field. He was always as gentle as they came, and I loved him for it.

Zac marches us across the soaked campsite toward our tent. "Since never. But I grew up surrounded by guys who'd pummel each other over a ball. I picked up a few tricks."

"Could your delicate quarterback hands handle giving out a good pummeling?"

"I'd be willing to find out."

Inside our tent, Zac deposits me onto my mattress before rummaging inside the cooler.

"For the patient." He waits until I wipe the mud off my fingers and hands me one of Brooks's chocolate chip cookies. Then he sorts through his bag to pull out a white T-shirt. "Don't you dare try to move, Melody. I'll be back in a second."

Zac returns by the time I've finished my cookie, the T-shirt in his hand now completely soaked. He crouches at the foot of the mattress. "All right, Mel. Here's the deal: you're covered in mud."

I look down at myself, at the thick layer coating my leggings. "What an astute observation, Zachary. Gold star for you."

"Anyone ever tell you you're an absolute brat?"

I smile innocently. "No one whose opinion matters."

"Case in point. Do you plan on spending the rest of the day covered in mud?"

"No?"

"Then I'm going to help you change."

I cough out a laugh. "*In your dreams—*"

"Believe it or not," he says wryly. "When I dream about you naked, you're not usually so hobbled, and you're a lot more enthusiastic about it."

I choke on my laugh. When he . . .

When he dreams about me naked? What the hell?

There's a faint flush in Zac's cheeks and a touch of caution in his eyes, as though the words slipped out despite better judgment. He clears his throat when all I do is stare. "I'm going to help you out of these clothes. Okay?"

I eye my busted ankle, now visibly swollen to twice its size. There's no way I can shimmy out of these second-skin leggings on my own without excruciating pain.

"Fine," I say tightly. "But for the record, I'm doing it with prejudice. And I forbid you to add this to your spank bank. Which supposedly involves made-up images of me naked? Get a grip, Porter."

Zac chuckles sheepishly. "Put your arms up for me."

After a split second's hesitation in which his waiting hands hover by my hips, I lift my arms. He jimmies Brooks's baggy sweater out from under my ass and peels it off. I only get one single moment of gratitude for the tank top I'm wearing underneath before noticing the pulse at Zac's jaw, the way he seems to force his eyes off me.

That would be because I'm wearing a fitted white tank top. No bra. Enthusiastic nipples. Great. I fist the sleeping bag underneath me. I'm unable to tear my own eyes away from him, the profile of his face as he focuses on the tent wall, the long breath he inhales. The way his brows twitch when he notices I haven't made a move to cover myself.

What's the point? It's about to get worse. Zac clears his throat. "Ready?"

I nod.

"Keep your ankle steady."

He curls his fingers into the waistband of my leggings and I plant my hands behind me, lifting my hips off the mattress just enough to let him tug them down my ass. Determined to keep his eyes off my body—or else to make this situation as horrific as possible—Zac keeps his gaze on my face. Creamy brown eyes pierce mine as he peels my pants down my legs.

"The eye contact is making this worse," I say, and my voice has dipped lower and a hell of a lot huskier than I ever intended.

His teeth scrape over his lower lip. "Where would you like me to look?"

Fuck looking. I want you to dive in and eat me out so good they hear me in the next town.

Wait, no. Scratch that.

"I don't care. Just don't look at me like that."

I squirm against the mattress and Zac's gaze drops to take in the movement. Mine drops too, but it's to confirm that I'm not wearing my period underwear. Fortunately, Connor kept my lingerie drawer stocked with the nicest stuff, and I'm grateful for the lavender lace now covering me up.

Zac pulls one pant leg over my good foot, and I grit my teeth against the pain as he peels them off completely. If the wind picked up right now, rattling the leaves above us, I'd have missed the near-silent groan coming out of Zac. But the world outside seems to hold still, breath held, dying to see how this moment unfolds.

He takes in my bare legs. With a swallow, I try to unclench my thighs.

"You always had fucking incredible legs, Mel."

His words settle low in my stomach. I don't know what's happened over these ten years apart. Maybe the distance changed his perception of me as a kid sister, or maybe he hasn't got his dick wet in a long time, but something's different.

The brazen confessions, the loaded eye contact. Maybe it's not completely intentional now, if the renewed color in Zac's face is any indication, but we'd never flirted back then. It had always been as platonic as it could get until I opened my big mouth and asked him to kiss me. "There's a pair of shorts in my bag," I whisper.

He nods. And nods, and nods, like he's talking himself through something in his head. "Okay," he says at last, rolling back his shoulders. He reaches for my backpack. "You don't have any pants? You'll be freezing."

"The ones I wore yesterday are still soaked." I flush as he sorts past clean pairs of panties. "It's fine. I'm not going anywhere in this state. I'll stay huddled under these sleeping bags."

"If that's the case, let me do you one better." He switches bags, digging through his own and pulling out a pair of sweats. "You'll have to tie them up within an inch of their life, but they should be comfier."

Instead of helping me pulling them on, Zac takes the T-shirt he'd gone out to soak in the lake and carefully cleans the mud caking my feet and ankles, moving to wipe my hands off, too. There's a tiny furrow in his brow, and he curls his lips into his mouth and bites down in a look so familiar the nostalgia nearly overwhelms me.

I'd seen that look thousands of times growing up, whenever he was singularly focused on a job. Poring over a playbook before a big game. Helping my dad shovel snow off our driveway in the winter.

He glances up to find me watching him. "How're you feeling?"

"Thoroughly embarrassed."

He pulls his sweats up my legs, warm fingertips skimming my skin along the way, up my calves, my thighs, while his eyes follow their trajectory almost ravenously. By the time he's cinching the drawstrings, I'm sweating.

When he's done, Zac shuffles toward the tent opening. "I'll be right back."

"Where are you going now?"

"I need a minute."

"For w—"

"I need a minute, Mel." Zac turns over his shoulder with a look so dark and frustrated that my breath catches in my throat.

Holy fuck.

His back is turned to me so I can't peek at the only thing he could mean, with a look like that and a voice that gruff. My pulse seems to have settled between my legs.

I expect him to walk off into the woods, but he only stands outside the tent opening. When the leaves still outside, I can hear the deep breaths he's taking. I follow his lead, trying to settle the dull ache in my body.

I can't help it, though. When Zac crawls back inside, looking a lot less tense, I let my eyes wander down the front of his sweats—

"Eyes up here, Melody."

Shit. My gaze zips to meet his. "There was nothing there. Don't worry, I'm sure you manage to keep your ladies satisfied in other ways."

He snorts. "Such a brat." He hands me a fresh sweater out of his bag and watches me slip it on. "What happened out there, anyway? With your ankle?"

I clear my throat. "Well, I was out on a perfectly innocent walk. And then a wolf decided to dart from behind a bush—"

His lips twitch, threatening a smile. "It's the middle of the day."

"So?"

"So, wolves don't tend to roam around in broad daylight. Was it a bird?"

"Of course it wasn't a bird. I'm not a wimp."

"Squirrel?"

"I told you it was a wolf. I escaped within an inch of my life."

He hums. "So, you're a brat *and* a liar, huh?"

I bat my lashes. "Aren't you thrilled to be stuck here with such a lethal combination?"

He smirks, brushing loose hair off my forehead. "I don't hate it."

I bite my lip, warming under the playful look he's giving me. Too late, I go to swat away his hand, but he's already long gone. "It was a chipmunk. It flew out of a bush and—"

Zac coughs. "A *chipmunk*?"

"It—it was quite a *large* chipmunk—it launched itself at me—"

Zac erupts. A loud laugh, so warm and familiar, eyes crinkled into barely open slits. And damn him, I can't stop my own gurgle of laughter before it makes it out into the open.

"I can't stop picturing it," he manages. "You getting buckled by a fucking *chipmunk*—" He snorts, succumbing to another peel of laughter.

I pinch his side, trying and failing to wipe the grin off my face when he yelps. "Stop laughing, you ass. I've been crippled—"

"By a *chipmunk*—"

"You don't know what it was like, okay? It was looking at me all beady-eyed—" Zac sucks in a steadying breath, wiping at his eyes. "With its little tiny teeth—"

He rubs his face. "Fuck, that's the best thing I've heard in a long time. Thank you for that."

With a shake of his head, Zac digs another T-shirt from his bag and pulls at the hem until he rips it in half, then rips it again. He takes the long strip of fabric and wraps it around my foot and ankle, the way I'd watch Parker do when he tended to minor injuries after a football game.

"It's not the best job, but it'll do." Zac knots the brace in place. He puts a pillow under my foot to elevate it and then pulls a slightly melted icepack out of the cooler and props it on my ankle. "Bless

Brooks and his six-hundred-dollar cooler, huh? Everything in there is still cold."

"Most of all, bless his chocolate chip cookies."

Zac passes me one, tops it with that smile of his. "Bless his chocolate chip cookies."

Chapter 8

Zac

"You're sure it's not in there?"

I sort through Melody's backpack for the hundredth time in less than two minutes. Ignore, once again, the urge to sneak that pair of black mesh panties into my pocket when she isn't looking, because that would be wrong. Really wrong.

But it's so damn tempting.

I unzip the front pocket of her bag, looking there, too. "There's no lip balm in here, Mel."

She holds out her hand until I pass her the bag. "There has to be. I specifically remember putting it in here. I couldn't find my overnight-bag lip balm, so I packed my purse lip balm. Which meant that I had to put my nightstand lip balm into my purse, and my car lip balm on my nightstand . . ."

I collect the deck of cards we've been using to entertain ourselves all day and stuff it back into the carton, unable to hold back an affectionate smile as I watch her get increasingly irritable with every pocket that doesn't turn up a lip balm.

Fuck, she's adorable. I'm addicted to her scowl. Always have been. "And why do you have so many lip balms, exactly?"

"Because I enjoy having silky-smooth lips." She squints at me. "You're telling me you don't use lip balm? Like, ever?"

"Never."

"And your lips don't get all dry and cracked?"

"Why?" I wag my eyebrows at her, tossing the box of cards off the mattress. "You wanna take 'em for a test drive? Feel for yourself?"

The scowl melts off her face. The second I catch the tinge of pink on her cheeks, I know I fucked up.

"Shit. Mel, that was—" I shake my head. "I'm sorry. That was tasteless."

We've been tiptoeing around each other all day. This sort of dance where for one shimmering moment, she forgets she resents me and we slip into this easy, comfortable thing where we just *gel*. Bounce off each other so well, it's like no time has passed since the last time we saw each other. I'm having to remind myself to dial it down, to curb the overpowering instinct to act on the attraction. She's doing her best not to show it, but I know the post-relationship clarity is hitting her hard, and I want to respect that.

And then she blinks and awareness returns, and before I know it, we're lapsing into uncomfortable silence where she looks anywhere but at me, shutting me out all over again.

Whenever I imagined seeing Mel again, I definitely pictured a lot more groveling. So many apologies that she'd tell me to shut up already. I pictured confessing that I've been crazy about her since the second I saw her hop down the stairs of her childhood home in that fuzzy purple bucket hat and a yellow dress that seemed to be made out of some kind of terry cloth material.

I still don't particularly understand that dress to this day. Are you meant to wear it after you get out of the shower, or . . . All right, not the point. Mel reclines into a stretch so deep I can hear her back crack. It's proof that she's been forced to sit around doing nothing all day with her ankle propped up. The sun has completely set by now, and the two lanterns lighting up the inside of our tent cast creepy shadows against the walls.

I move my fingers over her swollen ankle for something to do. I can't see much in this light, but I can make out the purple bruising that's developed around her makeshift brace. It seems to have stopped swelling any bigger, at least.

"How's the pain?"

"Bearable, as long as I stay perfectly still." She sighs over the sounds of the lake crashing on shore. "I think I'm going to try to go to bed. Every sleep means getting closer to our rescue, right?"

Don't remind me.

I need the time with her. If we don't leave here on better terms, with some kind of reassurance that she won't avoid me when we're back in town, I don't know what I'll do.

I unfold my legs from underneath me. "I did get a pretty terrible sleep last night."

Mel shimmies off the mattress, gingerly crawling outside the tent, careful not to jostle her swollen ankle. "Yeah, about that—"

"Where do you think you're going?"

"I need some private time in the woods." She circumvents me and I hurry to steady her as she balances on one foot outside. "Where do you think *you're* going?" She holds up a lantern to cast its light over my face. Her eyes have turned to slits so narrow it's impressive she can see at all.

"I'm coming with you. It's one thing to hop into the woods in broad daylight. You're not doing it in the dark. Think of all the chipmunks you'll trip over."

She throws me a look of pure venom—the kind I remember fondly from back then—and it's so good that I have to force down an exhilarated laugh.

"You're really asking if you can come with me to the bathroom?"

"Who says I'm asking?" I lift her up before she can argue some more, marching us across the campsite.

"The blows just keep on coming, don't they?" she grumbles. "It's not enough to get dumped and be so broke I had to flee the city for lodging. Now I need an escort to relieve myself."

I let it out. The question I've been dying to ask since yesterday. "Were you ever happy with him?"

As much as it pains me to think about Mel with another guy, I desperately need her answer to be yes. Knowing she's been unhappy for six years—thinking about how both our lives could have been different if I hadn't been an idiot that night—might cause the excessive amount of chocolate chip cookies and M&Ms I've eaten today to come right back up.

"You know what? I was, for a while." Mel thinks a moment. "But now . . . I can't stop overthinking it all. These things that never phased me in the moment, and now I can't believe I was stupid enough to fall for them."

"What do you mean?"

She fixes her gaze on a nearby tree. "He was always very caring. Very invested in me and what I did, how I was doing. Loved to look after me, spoil me. Looking back, I realize everything always had some kind of ulterior motive. Strings attached."

"Like what?"

"The apartment," she says, considering. "He bought it, moved me in rent free. Said there was no need for me to work full time because he could afford to look after us both, that I should go out and enjoy life instead of being stuck behind a desk. And he was incredibly gracious about it all until we'd argue or . . . I'd point out something I wasn't happy with, and he'd list off everything he'd ever done for me. All these ways that I was suddenly indebted to him."

I stare grimly. "So you let it go? Whatever you were fighting about?"

"Every time. I never had the room to be upset over anything." She shakes her head, releasing a frustrated breath. "He'd always find a way to turn whatever I was upset about on me. I'm ungrateful. I don't see the good in him. I'm moody. *You* know—you grew up with me. You know I'm not a sunny person, but . . ."

"You aren't moody, Mel. You're discerning. You're playful in a different way, and that's beside the point. You're allowed to be angry. You're allowed not to shit rainbows and butterflies at all times, and you're sure as hell allowed to put someone who hurt you in their place—me included—without being called moody."

"Bitchy, then?"

"He called you names?" I ask sharply.

She shakes her head. "It was never *bitch*. And he'd never call *me* bitchy—it was always something I did or said that was bitchy, so it never occurred to me. In hindsight, he was just covering his own ass, right? It was his way of calling me names without doing it outright. He'd give me a kiss right after, and that was always a good sign he was tired of arguing, so . . . that was it."

God fucking damn it, I will *dismember* that guy if I ever meet him.

Crickets chirp as I pick out a bush with decent enough coverage for her. "Why'd you put up with it? I never knew you to let someone walk all over you. Hell, I can barely get you to look at me without murder in your eyes."

"That's because I don't care if you like me." She smirks, but I can't return the humor.

"But *him*? The way you talk about it sounds like you turned into . . ." I struggle to find the words, wanting to ask but not wanting to judge.

"A doormat? Bending so he'd keep loving me?" she finishes for me. The lantern illuminates the shame in her face. "All day, I've been trying to figure out how the hell that happened, in between kicking your ass in rounds of poker."

"And?"

She releases a breath. "All that stuff? The arguing, the guilt-tripping. The backhanded doting. It was never that way at the start. Everything was amazing that first year with Connor—even now, I can't pinpoint a single thing wrong with the way we were then, other than it all being a lie, I guess. I loved him and I trusted him with everything. I never saw the manipulation for what it was because he'd never given me a reason to doubt him. He surrounded me with people who sang his praises, always made him out to be this amazing guy I was lucky to have. It wasn't hard to believe I was the problem in the relationship. Needless to say, I'm humiliated."

I hold her tighter, as though to shield her from her palpable self-disgust. "He's the one who should be humiliated. He's the one who did a bad thing—not you."

"I let it happen."

I shake my head, feeling so poorly equipped for this conversation. Except this is the woman I've loved all my life and I can't stand to see her beat herself up over something that I *know* wasn't her fault. Mel has always been tough, the no-nonsense one of the group. The fact that she fell victim to this piece of shit says more about his ability to manipulate so convincingly than it does about her. That I'm sure of.

"I'm not sure it works that way," I tell her. "Can you stop something from happening when you don't realize it's happening in the first place?"

Mel blows a loose strand of hair off her face. "I don't know. But it's never going to happen to me again, I can tell you that much."

I set her on her feet, holding her elbow as she steadies out, and then turn to give her privacy. I'm painfully aware of the questionable sounds coming from behind that tree nearby, but I'm going to believe it's just the chipmunk that got us into this mess to begin with.

"Zac? You could have told me the ground was flooding last night. You slept in a puddle."

I turn to find her staring at me thoughtfully, balancing against a tree. "Oh. It wasn't so bad. Refreshing, really. Have you never slept in an inch of water before?"

I'm full of it. It was wet and cold, and fucking terrible, and the only reason I managed to get any sleep is because my brain forced itself to power down at around six o'clock. But I'd sleep in a flooded tent another year if it puts me back in her good graces.

"You just said you had terrible sleep."

"Only because you kept waking me up. You were moaning, *oh God, Zac, please* in your sleep."

She rolls her eyes. "Trust me, I was having a night terror."

"Yeah?"

"You're my sleep paralysis demon. I was begging you to spare my life."

I snort. She's trying not to smile, but I can tell she's pleased she got a half-laugh out of me. "Turn around, please. I really need to go."

I take a few steps away, staring at what I can see of the branches on nearby trees swaying in the breeze.

Melody clears her throat. "So, I was thinking it would be okay if you wanted to sleep on the mattress tonight. As a thank you for helping me today."

"I don't want you sleeping on the ground, Mel."

"I wasn't offering that. I'd also be on the mattress. With you."

I force my gaze straight ahead, despite the urge to turn and get a read on her face.

A decade ago, I decided—got told, explicitly—that anything with Melody beyond platonic was strictly off the table.

But the truth is, I don't want platonic. I didn't that night in her bedroom. I didn't the day I caved and went to find her hand-in-hand with Connor. I don't today.

Fuck platonic. I *want* her. And I won't keep that to myself this time. Not if she ever shows signs of interest. Extends an olive branch.

"Totally platonic mattress-sharing, of course. Everyone keeps their hands to themselves," she adds.

Fuck.

"Still with me, Porter?"

"Yeah, I'm still with you. Look, I . . ." The rest of that sentence dies in my throat. The hair at the back of my neck stands up.

I'm now preoccupied staring at a dark shape only feet away from me, just out of reach of the light from our lantern. This shape that's about a thousand times bigger than a chipmunk.

"Okay, point taken, Zac. I was just trying to be nice," Mel grumbles, oblivious behind me.

Get her out of here. Now.

Without telling her what's happening because the second she sees this, she'll lose it and—I force a breath into my lungs just as the four-legged shape in front of me takes a step closer.

"Mel?" I say, forcing calm into my voice. "Do me a favor."

"What?" she says absently, and I hear the sounds of her pulling my sweats back on.

"Can you make out the path back to camp from here?"

"Yeah, why?"

"Well," I force out, and I swear this is karma for laughing at her chipmunk story. It has to be, because I'm fairly certain I'm now in a standoff with a fucking wolf. "It's my turn to go, and I can't do it with you around. Can you make it back to camp on your own? I'll be right behind you."

"Actually, I think I've become accustomed to being carried around."

My hands start to shake and I ball them into fists. "Get back to the tent, please."

"What—"

"*Melody*," I say through clenched teeth. The dark shape takes another step toward us. "This is the one and only time I'm going to need you to do what I say, no questions asked."

She doesn't listen. She hops closer. And closer. And then she's steadying herself with a hand on my shoulder and following my gaze to—

It happens fast. Mel starts to scream, the dark shape starts moving, and I throw this woman over my shoulder so fast I almost wind myself. I dart down the path, countering Mel's panicked stream of *oh my God's* with *it's okay's* and I swear I've never moved this quick. Not even when I had men twice my width barreling toward me in solid padding, looking to destroy me over a football.

But my footwork is NFL-caliber tonight. We emerge onto our campsite and I dive into the tent, tossing Mel onto her mattress so hard she almost bounces off it as I zip up the opening.

This is, without a doubt, the stupidest hiding spot.

Any wild animal worth its mettle would smell us from a mile away, but I don't know what else to fucking do and so I kill the second lantern and clamp a hand over Mel's mouth when she still won't stop her panicked stream of words.

"Zac—"

Her voice is muffled against my hand, and I double my grip. "Shh. I need you to stay quiet, okay?" She whimpers this terrified sound that shatters my heart into a couple million pieces on the tent floor. I crawl onto the mattress behind her and gather her into my chest. "It's gonna be okay, Clover. I just need you to stay quiet, all right? It's gonna be fine. Nothing will happen to you."

I strain my ears, trying to hear movement outside the tent. I can't hear anything, but my body is still so tense I'm sitting rod straight, even as I wrap an arm around Mel's waist, tucking her into me, willing her body to relax. And then I feel it. Little wet drops hitting the fingers I'm holding over her mouth.

"Shh," I whisper. I recline until my head hits her pillow and cradle her into my side as she gives muffled sobs into my hand. "You're okay. I don't think it followed us. You're okay. I'm gonna move my hand, but you need to stay quiet, all right?"

After a moment, she nods, and I give her another second to collect herself before releasing her. I can't see her at all, can't see anything in this pitch-black tent, but I feel around for her tears and try to catch as many of them as I can manage.

Mel shivers against me and as quietly as I can, I pat around for a sleeping bag. "Don't leave me—"

"I'm not going anywhere." I throw the sleeping bag over us both and a fist closes around my heart when she burrows into my side, clutching the front of my shirt into a fist as though she's scared I'll slip away. I feel more tears drench my shirt and I let her cry it out for a while, just holding her to me like she's my only tether to sanity as I wait for an incoming threat.

Outside, a twig snaps somewhere to our left.

"Say something," Mel begs me. "This is unbearable. Tell me a story. Tell me something."

I release the breath I've been holding. "I . . . Clover, I'm kind of drawing a blank right now."

She lifts her chin, and I'm hoping it's too dark for her to tell just how panicked I am. There's a fucking animal out there, stalking us. And who knows what might've happened if I'd let her go out there alone.

The thought sends my heart into overdrive.

Melody releases my shirt and smooths her hand over my chest instead. "Tell me about work," she says at last. "You said yesterday your team is struggling. Tell me about it."

So she did hear my rambling as I was trying to snap her out of her state of shock once we got stranded. Which also means she heard me say that I couldn't remember the last date I went on—

Something rustles outside our tent. I think I hear the sound of a lawn chair toppling over, and the last breath I took might have been around the same time as my last date.

"Zac, talk to me," she whispers, so low I can barely hear her though she's plastered against me.

I force some air into my lungs. "I . . . I'm not sure I'm cut out to be a coach."

"I can't imagine that's true. You used to mentor your older teammates in school."

I close my eyes. "I inherited this team in a rebuild phase. Started out as an assistant coach after I graduated there and it went from bad to worse over the years. They fired the guy I coached under after last season, tagged me in as the interim replacement, and then just never hired anyone else before the season started."

"That's good for you, though, isn't it?"

"They weren't shy about telling me they're taking a gamble with me. Made it clear that I only had a handful of games to prove I could do it and keep the job."

The hand she has splayed on my chest moves a few inches to the left, over my pounding heart. "So basically, win games or get fired."

"And I've already lost two. I have an NFL-level quarterback without a receiver who can keep up with him."

"Tag me in, Coach." Somehow she musters a chuckle. "I haven't caught a football in years, but I'm sure it's like riding a bike."

Despite the terror, I feel my muscles start to loosen. "It's not a bad idea, you know. You were always pretty good, Clover."

"It's what happens when you grow up with a bunch of dumb jocks."

"Wasn't I your math tutor?"

"I was *your* math tutor—you and Parker always begged me for help. It's what I do now. Math. Data analysis for an investment bank."

"This is the job Connor got you?"

"The one and only. We don't work directly together, and thankfully, I work from home. But he comes back from his trip in a couple weeks, and . . . I hope we can avoid each other. Until I find a new job."

My ears are still straining, alert for sounds outside our tent. But I can feel my heart rate go down as she keeps talking.

Melody blows out a soft breath. "Remember those couple months in senior year when Parker busted up his elbow?"

"I remember."

"And how you were a total freak back then, always wanting to train outside of practice? You and Parker made me sub in for him so you'd have someone to practice with."

There's no way I'd ever forget the sight of her dressed in my too-big football gear, my jersey. She wanted to look the part while she practiced catching my throws, as Parker and Summer looked on.

"Yeah. I remember."

"Well, by the time you were done with me, I'm pretty sure I could have given Parker a run for his money for his spot on the team. You know, if we didn't live in such a persistently patriarchal society."

She wrenches a chuckle out of me. "You definitely could have. The patriarchy sucks so hard."

"Seriously, Zac. If you could get scrawny little me to hang with a quarterback like you, I know you can do it again."

We're back there. In that hallway at school.

I'm new in town. Friendless all my life after being endlessly plucked from country to country, following my dad's job. I've finally got a group of kids I'm meshing with. I'm a second from the starting whistle of my first game, and I'm terrified to fuck up. To be the new kid letting down my first ever friends—the entire school—just weeks into the school year. I'm pacing the hallway, and then I turn around.

Mel pulls a four-leaf clover from her pocket and tells me I've got this game in the bag. She just has a gut feeling about it, she says, and those big blue eyes look at me like she believes every word. Getting that vote of confidence from Melody Woods, the infamous skeptic, is enough to make me feel like I can conquer anything.

Every week for four seasons, she finds me before a game, home or away, to give me my good luck charm. Even when I lose, it feels okay. Because there's a blue-eyed girl out there somewhere who believes I can do it. If not that game, then the next one.

It wasn't the clovers that did it for me. It was her. She *was* my four-leaf clover.

I can't exactly see her right now, but it feels like Mel believes in me now, too, and it's an instant mood shift.

This night, with a wild animal circling our tent. My next game, and the one after that. "Thanks, Clover. Can't tell you how much that means."

She pushes her face into my shoulder. "You're really not supposed to call me that."

"I know," I whisper. "Can I anyway?"

She doesn't say anything—just nods into my shoulder—but my chest swells. "Do you think it's gone?" Mel whispers after a while.

It's not gone. It's out there somewhere. "Yeah, I think it's gone. We're fine. Try to get some sleep, okay?"

Mel releases a long breath. She's still pressed so hard against me there's not a sliver of space between us. "Can we stay like this?"

"We can stay like this. Go to sleep, Clover. I won't let anything happen to you, I swear."

Still, she tenses at every little sound outside this tent. Every chirping cricket. Every time the breeze makes the tent walls shudder. It's not until a couple of long, painful hours later that I hear her breathing start to slow. That I feel her melt into me, lose the tension in her body.

Mine stays put, though. I stare into this dark tent, straining my ears, clutching her to me until the sun comes up.

Chapter 9

Melody

Seeing as he spent the better part of the night fidgeting, I expect to find Zac passed out cold beside me in the morning. He can't have slept more than an hour or two, but when I wrench open my eyes, he's already gone.

Even with a wild animal on the prowl—God, the way its eyes shone in the dark makes me shudder out of my skin—there had been something so comforting in being plastered together on this air mattress.

Maybe it's that, despite his best efforts, he let that controlled façade of his crack open last night. He was terrified by what he saw in the woods, and after spending a decade resenting him, the whole experience was incredibly humanizing.

Last night, he wasn't the guy who broke my heart. He was the boy who made my heart squeeze every time he'd look at me.

I gather a fresh shirt from Summer's pile of clothes and the pair of leggings Zac washed off for me after the chipmunk incident. The campsite is quiet when I surface from our tent. I limp toward the lake, managing to put a little weight on my injured ankle today.

Zac probably went out for a walk along the road like I tried to do yesterday, hoping for a car to pass by. I may as well take the opportunity to wash up in the lake while he's—

Oh.

Oh my—

God. Truly. I'm watching an underwater god surface from Atlantis.

Zac isn't walking along the road. He's out in the waist-deep water, his back to me, wet streaks running down the slopes of his bare skin and . . .

I've seen him shirtless. That comes with the territory of living my teenaged summers with him at this very campsite. But it was never like this.

He was never like this. He'd been mouthwatering then, a teenage fantasy come to life. Now, though?

That's a man effortlessly pushing strands of soaked hair off his face, like he's in some kind of pornographic shampoo commercial. Every inch of him glistens, muscles bunching as he bends to splash more water on his face, and his hips lift out of the water, all tight and dimpled lower back.

He's naked. Not a stitch of clothing on, and I'm on the edge of my fucking seat, willing the water to part like the Red Sea.

I'm relieved. *Relieved* to know that I can feel that kind of want, and this hot, near painful lust, so soon after my breakup. I can get Connor out of my head and my system. It's possible.

Still, though. I shouldn't be . . . A tingling sensation shoots down the length of my legs. Zac raises an arm to ruffle his hair and is there anything hotter than a man's broad shoulders, muscles rolling as he moves?

I really shouldn't be staring— Zac glances over his shoulder. Shit.

"Mel?"

I swivel, start limping back to our campsite like my life depends on it. Like there's even the slightest chance he hasn't noticed me shamelessly gawking him.

Problem is, my ankle is still messed up, the freaking traitor. I barely make it a few feet by the time Zac splashes out of the water behind me.

"Melody, wait."

Please don't still be naked. Please don't still be naked—okay, maybe a little bit naked—

I turn, plastering a practiced, nonchalant smile on my face. I don't tend to smile at this guy, but I'm hoping it's at least weird enough to help deflect from this disastrous situation.

Zac is tugging a long-sleeved shirt down his body, clutching a towel around his waist. And damn him, it does nothing to dull the pulse between my thighs. The shirt is sticking to every wet dip and rise of his torso. His dark lashes are clumping together, water dripping from his hair, and even *that's* enough to amplify the ridiculous fluttering in my stomach. He is just . . .

He's really something else.

Zac nods at the towel I have slung over my arm. "You going in?"

"You and I had the same idea, it seems," I say, coughing when my voice comes out paper thin. "But on second thought, I don't think my ankle is up for it. So, if you'll excuse me, I'll head back to my trusty air mattress—"

"I can help you wash up. If you want."

"I don't think . . ." My lips part at images of Zac's wet body next to mine in the water, the gentle way his fingers would sweep my skin like they did while looking after my ankle.

Zac drags his teeth over his lower lip, looks down the length of my body. Shoulders rise and fall in one deep breath, and we might both be there. In that imaginary water, where my nails would dig into my palms, willing me to behave until we both finally snap and—

"*No*," I say firmly, holding up a hand between us to drive the point home. My fingers are shaking and I hope he doesn't notice. "You . . . you stay over there. Way over there. Far, far away. Over there."

Smooth as ice, Mel.

Zac doesn't have any trouble catching the drift of my alarm, and I wrench my eyes away the second I see his mouth shape into a playful smirk.

"Don't look at me like that while you're . . . dressed like that."

"I'm practically fully clothed. Yet you seem to be blushing, Clover." Oh, not the nickname, too. What's this guy playing at?

I limp away. "Don't come back to camp until you're fully dry and—and clothed. With *pants* on. There'll be no funny business at this campsite. Mark my words." He doesn't say a thing. No, he does me one worse.

Zac lets out this soft, husky laugh. And I pick up speed before I do something really stupid.

~

I keep myself preoccupied all day.

Take down Brooks's storm-crumpled tent. Limp around gathering firewood only to realize that Zac was right when he said everything is still far too wet and mud-covered to manage a fire. I drag a canvas chair down to the lake so that I can stare out at the water rather than at the man I've been avoiding.

If there's one good thing about Zac, it's that he takes a hint. He gives me a wide berth as the sun moves through the sky. Whenever I chance a glance over my shoulder from the shore, I find him still in his own chair, poring over a massive binder in his lap. Muttering to himself, scribbling things down on a yellow legal pad of paper. He sounded stressed, talking about work last night. But he really looks it now as he obsesses over whatever's in that binder.

Thing is, stressed Zac is my weakness.

It always has been—it was how our four-leaf clover ritual got started in the first place. Zac walks around with all the confidence in the world. But those moments when that swagger slips . . . There's something so painful, even now, seeing him like this. His face isn't meant to look anxious. His smile is just too damn good to go without.

That's what has me rising from my chair now. My ankle's slowly improved throughout the day, but my steps are still unsteady as I head for the tent I dismantled earlier. I don't look, but I can feel Zac's eyes follow me as I cross the campsite.

"I'm bored," I announce. I hear the sound of Zac's binder falling shut. "I found this inflatable canoe in Brooks's tent. I think I'll take it out."

"Are you inviting me to take a canoe ride with you?" Zac arches a dark eyebrow from where he sits.

You need a rebound. Quick and dirty— Shut up, Summer.

"I suppose I could allow it," I say briskly. "If you inflated it and did most of the rowing, of course."

He rises from his chair and shrinks the gap between us. "Are you trying to punish me for catching you staring earlier?"

How does he make his eyes twinkle like that? The nerve of him.

"I was staring in horror. It was like spotting the Loch Ness Monster emerging from the depths."

A laugh bursts out of him, emphasizing those laugh lines around his eyes. "I don't think so. You haven't looked me in the eye all day."

Zac tips his head, all six feet and God knows how many inches of him looming over me. Making me feel the kind of small he can easily toss around, manhandle in the most knee-buckling way.

Quick and dirty— Shut up, *Summer.*

I bend down, fully intending to scoop up the deflated canoe, but the damn thing is a lot heavier than I thought. I stumble forward on my unsteady foot and end up crashing straight into Zac's chest. His hard, toned chest, so fucking warm and drool-inducing—

"If you wanted to feel me up, all you had to do was ask."

Cocky prick.

Mustering all my reserves of dignity—which at this point could barely fill a thimble—I wrench myself upright and wave at the deflated canoe at my feet. "I'll leave that to you while I get changed, shall I?"

Twenty minutes later, we're coasting along the shore of the deserted lake. Behind Zac, the sky is streaked pink and orange as the sun sets, casting a warm glow over his skin, and he's such a perfect specimen of a man that I'd easily believe I was staring at a painting if I weren't living this moment for myself.

"Thanks for suggesting this." Zac settles the oars inside the raft. "Swear I was going to lose my mind staring at that playbook another second."

I gaze at the flowering lily pads dotting the water to our left, the family of ducks streaming past us in the water. From the corner of my eye, I see Zac studying the setting sun.

"Personally, I'm starting to think this was a terrible miscalculation."

"Why's that?"

"It's a bit . . ." I gesture around us. "It's a date out of a Nicholas Sparks novel, isn't it? Any minute swans will swim by, curving their necks into a heart-shaped omen."

I make the mistake of letting my gaze drift toward Zac, who's already looking back and gives a shameless smile at being caught. I zero in on the lily pads again, cheeks flushing.

"Would that be so terrible?" he asks.

I shrug. "I wouldn't mind seeing swans, I guess. But I didn't think they came out here."

Zac snorts. He's rubbing his face with both hands. It might be a trick of the light, but his cheeks look a little flushed. Was he . . . did he mean about the date, and not the swans?

And does that mean—

God, this has to stop. I feel eighteen again, trying to decipher the words and actions of a guy who only wound up disappointing me. I'm past this. Past him.

"Did you ever miss—" Zac starts, surfacing from behind his palms.

"What time do you think—" I say at the same time.

He chuckles. I blush some more because, evidently, I stumbled into a time machine at some point in the past twelve hours and re-emerged as a lovestruck teen.

I need to put this man at a safe distance before I make a fool of myself with him all over again.

"What were you going to say?" he asks after another awkward beat.

I fiddle with the knot from my swimsuit at the back of my neck, tucking the strings into the oversized T-shirt I borrowed from Brooks. "I was asking what time you think we'll get rescued tomorrow. I'm hoping by early afternoon, but that might be wishful thinking if Parker is still . . . entertaining."

"Still dying to get away from me, huh?"

Yes.

"I think a return to civilization is what's best for everyone. What were you going to ask?"

The corner of his mouth tilts in a wry smile. "I was wondering if you ever missed home while you were away."

"Oh," I say quietly. "I guess I missed some parts of it. Parker, mostly. He visited me in the city at first, but . . . he wasn't a fan of Connor, and Connor wasn't a fan of Oakwood. It's been hard, not seeing him as much."

"So, Connor's the reason you stayed away all this time?"

I'm overheating under Brooks's T-shirt. "He found it a little boring here." I don't even need to look at him to know he knows I'm lying.

Connor's dislike of Oakwood and its slow pace was a convenient excuse to limit my visits to Thanksgiving and Christmas, but my main gripe with Oakwood Bay is that it's nearly impossible to avoid anyone, especially when they run in your circle of friends.

My main gripe sits in front of me now, in this blown-up canoe, fingering something underneath the sleeve of his shirt without looking away from me.

Yeah, this sunset canoe ride was definitely a mistake. "Maybe we should turn back. Before it gets too dark."

"I thought we were turning a corner," Zac says abruptly. "After almost getting mauled by a wild animal last night."

What he really means is the way I let him cradle me against his body as I cried terrified tears. The way I coaxed him into conversation, long enough to feel the panicked pace of his heart slow under my palm.

I reach for the oars at the bottom of the boat. "I don't hate you, if that's what you're concerned about."

"Yet you want nothing to do with me."

"Look, we ended our friendship—or whatever it was—on bad terms." I stare at the shoreline. "We've both managed life just fine without each other, and just because I'm home doesn't mean we have to . . . I don't know. Revive things? I don't plan on being back in town for long, anyway."

Zac frowns. "What do you mean, you're not in town for long?"

I slot my hands between my thighs. "I'm moving back as soon as I can afford to on my own."

His gaze drifts at a point over my head. "So, how long? Until you leave?"

"Why does it matter?"

"How long, Clover?"

I finger the end of my ponytail, pick at my shorts. Shove the box I put him in all the way at the back of my mental closet, where it belongs. "Hopefully only a month or two."

"A couple months," Zac mutters absently, still staring off at the sky like he's working something out in his head. "Okay. I can work with that."

I shoot him a funny look. "I hope you don't think I was inviting you to come with me."

"No," he says with a breath, like he's steeling himself for something. "Not yet, anyway."

Okay, the man has clearly lost it.

"Now we're definitely turning back. You're looking a little crazed."

He takes an oar and feeds it over the edge of the canoe. "I'm not crazed. I want you to forgive me. I want us to be good again. I'll get you to trust me if it's the last thing I do. You'll see."

All the confidence in the world, this one.

Still deep in thought, Zac holds out his hand, presumably so that I can pass him the other oar. And then we realize his mistake. Namely, letting go of the oar that's now slipping the final inches off the side of the canoe.

I dart forward to catch it just as Zac does the same. And this really must be a sappy romance novel come to life, because we end up missing the paddle completely and grabbing each other's hands instead.

The paddle splashes into the water, but I'm now badly fixated on the way Zac's hand is holding mine. His skin is warm and soft and his hand is so big and—

"Oops," I say, and the laugh that follows is fake and shrill as hell.

I jerk away and it happens fast. The hand I have braced on the soft edge of the canoe slips, my bad ankle buckles. My squeal pierces the peaceful lake, and a bird bursts out of a tree on shore just as I splash into the water.

The lake is cold, cooled down by this weekend's storm, and I surface with a massive shiver to find Zac busting a lung in laughter.

Ass.

I send a wave of water splashing over the edge of the canoe, but it misses him by inches. "I'm so glad I could be your personal sideshow this weekend," I grumble at him.

I shove the hair off my face and reach for the floating oar, launching it into the canoe. The jerk still hasn't stopped laughing, wiping tears from the corners of his eyes, and I hold out a hand toward him.

"Here, help me up."

Zac shakes his head at my outstretched hand. "Fuck no. You have vengeance etched in every inch of that pretty face, Clover. And I know exactly how cold that water is."

Wimp.

With a sickly sweet smile, I swim up to the canoe, assessing it. Its length, its weight. The probability I can manage to . . .

"Actually, I think the water's warmed up. Why don't you give it another go?"

"Melody," Zac warns, as I get a handle on the boat. "Don't you fucking—"

I guess all those hours in the gym with Connor really paid off. One hard shove and the canoe tips over easily, sending Zac into the water with me.

Chapter 10

Melody

I jerk awake.

It's bright out. Birds chirping. Lake water crashing on the shore.

There were no midnight animal encounters, but the simple knowledge that there was something out there stalking us just a day ago was enough to keep me up most of the night again. For the third night in a row, I don't think Zac slept at all. I felt him shifting around at least until the sun rose.

But it's finally Monday. Parker expects me home this morning and the second he realizes I haven't made it, he'll message the others. They'll figure out they left us here, and this will all be over.

I can digest the horror that was my last relationship without the utter mindfuck of having Zac Porter sleeping next to me.

Unlike yesterday, Zac is still in bed, dead asleep, with an arm and leg thrown around me as though to shield me from an incoming threat. I'm pressed against him so tightly I can feel every bit of his solid body. Every little—

Oh my God.

Every not-so-little bit of him.

I lift my chin, making sure he's still out cold as I try to shimmy out of his grasp. When I don't manage to slip away, I flip onto my back, which isn't much better because it means that his arm and leg are now pressing down on my front, his cock into my thigh.

Zac hums in his sleep and somehow manages to tighten his hold. I wiggle an inch away. He tightens his arm, reels me back in.

"Quit moving," he mumbles groggily, eyes still closed. "I just fell asleep."

I attempt to twist out from under him anyway. "You're using me as a body pillow."

"No different from what you did with me last night. Return the favor. I'm comfy."

"I need to go to the bathroom."

He holds me closer. "No, you don't."

I let out a sharp sigh. "Zac, I regret to inform you that you've got morning wood digging into me right now."

Zac's eyes snap open. He dips his chin, giving me a sleepy stare. It takes a whole extra second for my words to properly sink in and then—

"Oh." He flips onto his back, settling comfortably into the air mattress.

"*Oh*? What kind of a reaction is that?" I shuffle to the other end of our makeshift bed. Against my express wishes, my gaze falls down his body.

Holy mother of—that thing is . . .

Zac calmly rubs the sleep out of his eyes. "What's the end of that sentence?"

"The end of *what* sentence?" My voice is so high-pitched, dogs in the next state over can surely hear me.

"You just said *holy mother of, that thing is . . .*"

My cheeks have become the surface of the sun. "I did not. I did not say that."

"You did. Clover—"

"Don't call me that! It's supposed to be sweet and wholesome. Don't call me that with your—"

He turns to look at me. Lifts an eyebrow. "With my hard cock sticking out between us?"

"*Don't* say cock."

He's chuckling now. The absolute *audacity* to give me that kind of a chuckle with his hard cock sticking out between us.

Zac lies there completely unperturbed. Dark hair a disheveled mess on the pillow we've been sharing, shirt bunched up around his waist and exposing several inches of perfect, tanned abs before he tugs it back in place. He looks so at ease with the entire thing. Not a shred of embarrassment over the way his cock tents the front of his sweats—the fucking *size* of that tent—

An unacceptable pulsing starts between my legs, so bad I press my thighs together. Zac catches the movement.

"Don't," I say. "Don't say it. You didn't see anything."

"Forget the squirming. You're looking at me like you're ready to hop on. Why do you think that is?"

"You—" I struggle for the right words. "You're hitting on me. You realize that, right?"

"I've been hitting on you all weekend. Thanks for finally noticing."

"I—you—why are you hitting on me?" I sputter. "Zac, *why are you still hard*?" I reach for the sleeping bag we've been using and throw it over his waist.

"I'm hitting on you because I'm attracted to you," he articulates carefully, as though trying to make me understand. "And I'm still hard because it appears my body has finally decided to give up all pretense when it comes to you."

"What does that mean?"

"It means you get anywhere near me, I get hard." With a sigh, he props himself up on an elbow. "I'll admit you weren't supposed to see it, but I didn't manage to leave the bed before you woke up this time."

I flush. Is that what he was doing in the lake before I showed up yesterday? Taking care of a hard-on?

I try to unclench my thighs, but the beating is so damn uncomfortable my legs snap shut again. "It's not about you," I quickly explain when he watches me do it. "I haven't had sex since Connor."

Zac's eyes turn to slits. "I'm gonna need you to refrain from mentioning that piece of shit any time we're in bed together. Talk about a boner killer."

Out of sheer, morbid curiosity, I lift the sleeping bag off his lap. Nope. Still there.

I throw the cover back in place, taking a long, bracing breath. "You can't possibly think you have a chance with me, can you?"

"Are you telling me I don't? *Ever?*"

It seems to be an honest question. Zac looks at me like it is, anyway, and it stumps the hell out of me. This whole weekend has. The flirting, the hitting on me.

You get anywhere near me, I get hard.

Where is all this coming from? It's never been like this between us. Never, and it's really messing with my head.

"I'm going to wash up in the lake. Alone." I reach for my backpack before I do or say anything stupid. Like offer to take care of this particular hard-on.

Zac zeroes in on my ankle. He starts to reach for it, but I jerk away, unconvinced I can stand to have him touch me without properly combusting.

He holds up his hands in surrender. "How is it? The bruise looks pretty bad."

"Sore," I say truthfully. "I'll be fine. Just stay in here a few minutes while I clean up, okay? I'll be back in a bit."

~

Someone should come for us any minute now. Any hour.

I tug up my leggings and continue down the path leading to the road, hoping to catch the early signs of tires crunching.

Three days post-storm and it's still wet out. The mud under my feet is soft, and the leaves above me leak rainwater whenever the wind blows hard. Not that it's blowing much today. The sun's out in full force, and the early-September cold snap brought by the storm has evened out to a warm end-of-summer temperature.

I'm going to miss spending fall in the city this year. The walks along the river. The professional sports seasons starting up. Not that Connor had ever wanted to go to those with me.

The more I think about our relationship, the more I feel like what I was really cheated out of was the experience I'd wanted from living in a bigger city. His hobbies became mine, his friends became mine, and it was just as much my fault as it was his. Maybe he'd been carefully manipulating me under the guise of love, but I'd let myself get swept up in Connor. Trusted him, relied on him for so much.

I still can't believe how wrong I'd been about him. How blind I'd been to all the red flags. I've never trusted my own judgment less.

Which is why I'm staying the hell away from Zac until someone shows up for us. I'm not prepared to revisit any kind of relationship with him beyond platonic. I was wrong about him once, and considering my losing track record with men, I'm not risking it again.

He can consider himself friend-zoned for all eternity.

"Melody?"

Zac's voice echoes through the woods from the campsite, and the sound of it sends a rush of warmth below my waist. He went into the lake for a makeshift bath after I did, and I made my way out here to avoid any chance of seeing more than I should. Again.

God knows what would have happened after this morning.

I shiver at the thought of him yanking me to him, all strong and wet and—

I push deeper into the woods, off the path and away from the sound of his voice calling my name. This breakup has me all turned around. That's all it is.

I haven't been with anyone since Connor, that's all it is.

Summer is right. I need a palate cleanser. A rebound. I need someone to drown out the last memory of me and Connor together. I need my skin to stop crawling at the thought that he was the last man to touch me. To relieve some of this tension built up over the course of this nightmare weekend with Zac.

I have no idea how I'll find someone in a town as small as Oakwood, where everyone knows everyone's business, but . . .

"Mel? What are you doing over there?"

Zac finds me at last and picks a path toward me. I don't notice the panicked look on his face until he's within a few feet.

"You scared the fuck out of me." He grips my shoulders. "Don't ever wander off alone again, do you hear me? Who knows what's out here—"

"What, like you expect an axe murderer to pop out of a bush and chop me up?"

He lets a breath hiss through his teeth, pressing his palm into his eyes. "Better a fucking axe murderer than whatever the hell was out here stalking us that night."

He looks so on edge it makes my chest twinge. Stressed Zac. It's always been my Bat Signal.

"How is an animal worse than an actual *axe murderer*?" I say, scoffing just enough to distract him. "Ever seen *Friday the 13th*?"

He drops his arms to regard me with a raised eyebrow. *That's better.*

"We watched it together, you absolute brat. You peed your pants at the one scene—"

My jaw drops. "I did not *pee my pants*."

"Oh, that's right. You 'spilled your drink.'" He makes air quotes with his fingers, pairing them with a slow, derisive nod and looking all the way amused now. "Conveniently over your crotch, but who's to say what really happened."

I flush. This has backfired hideously. "I *begged* you and Parker not to put that stupid movie on. We were only fourteen—"

"Hold up," Zac says and raises his palms, grin spreading over his face. "Please confirm for the record that you just tacitly admitted that you *did* pee your pants while we were watching *Friday the 13th.*"

"You're such an ass," I mutter.

He snorts. "I can't believe this. The mystery of Melody Woods's soaked crotch, revealed at last. We need to commemorate this moment. Quick, find me something sharp enough to carve into this tree. *Here marks the spot where Mel Woods finally confessed*—"

"Do me a favor and leave all matters related to my crotch out of your head and mouth."

"Trust me, that's easier said than done."

I brush past him, aiming for the campsite. "I know I happen to be the only other warm body for miles, but for the record, the whole desperate-to-get-laid thing really isn't working for you."

"I don't care about getting laid." Zac easily falls into step with my pace. "I want you to tell me you won't avoid me once we get back to town."

I pivot to face him. "Why do you care? I haven't heard from you in years!"

"Exactly. I made that mistake once. I'm not letting you go on bad terms again. Not after having you back. The weekend's been a bit awkward, but we needed it—"

"Having me back? *A bit awkward*?" I splutter, trying to grasp onto the right words. "This weekend has been a living disaster. We got stranded in the woods. I messed up my ankle. You—we—if you had just stayed in the car—"

"And left you out there to get stranded by yourself?" he says incredulously. "How the fuck would I have been able to live with myself if something happened to you?"

"Stop acting like you suddenly care how I'm doing." I take a step backward, away from him, and my back hits a tree. "Frankly, it's a miracle you haven't driven me half insane by now."

"And now you know how it feels. To be driven out-of-my-mind insane every time you're around." Zac shoves up the sleeves of his shirt and shrinks the gap between us, feeding me his body heat. "Swear to me you won't avoid me the second we get home."

The absolute audacity of his request stuns me into silence. He's the one who lied and said he'd come back for me. Who never reached out after.

Zac lifts a hand to sweep the hair off my face. He's standing so close my eyesight is full of him. His skin, his body, the soft brown of his eyes.

The flash of red at his wrist as he lowers his arm.

"What's that?"

He winds his arm behind his back, hiding it from view, but I grasp it and tug. My heart is suddenly pounding in my ears, because it kind of looked like—

"Show it to me."

Zac's muscles lose all resistance against my grip, and he lets me draw his arm out from behind his back, staring at a point on the tree above my head.

It's a red shoelace—the same one I'd tied to his wrist ten years ago. I'd taken mine off the moment I came to terms with the fact that he wasn't coming back for me like he said he would. His lace seems barely more than a scrap of string anymore. It's short and tight to his wrist, like it's broken off and been retied over and over.

I feel Zac's eyes on me, but I can't seem to face him. I'm fixated on the red string. "Why are you still wearing that?"

He takes back his arm, tugging his shirtsleeve over the shoelace. "Why did you ask me to kiss you that night?"

Finally, I look at him. We're in a standoff. Unblinking. I can't seem to take in a breath, and I'm not sure he can, either.

"I told you we're not rehashing that."

"You want me to keep to myself why I walked away, then fine," Zac bites back. "But I was there, too. You asked me to kiss you, and I get a say in whether we talk about that part."

I clench my jaw. "I don't owe you anything."

"Why, Mel?" The set of his shoulders, the way he doesn't look away, tells me he isn't letting this go.

"It was a . . . I was feeling sentimental."

Zac's gaze skates over my face. He shakes his head. "You're lying. Try again."

I clench my hands into fists, forcing them to stop quivering. "I thought I might miss you—"

"Try again, Clover."

It's the nickname that gets me. The way it melts me. The way he just wielded it like a weapon, trying to get what he wants out of me.

Fine. If he wants the truth, wants me to make him feel guilty about it, then fine. I square my shoulders. "Because I had feelings for you, that's why."

I don't know what he thought I'd say, but it's immediately clear that this certainly wasn't it. Zac lets out a harsh breath, body almost sagging at my words.

"You had feelings for me?"

"I was in love with you."

His lips part, and for a beat he only stares at me, stricken. "And now?"

My heart throbs at the thread of vulnerability in the words. And I realize he doesn't look guilty at all. He looks like a wounded animal.

Oh God.

Was I right about him? About the way he looked at me that night?

"It was a long time ago," I say delicately. "I just got out of a six-year relationship. Maybe Connor wasn't who I thought he was, but I really loved him. I moved on, Zac."

I think I catch a tremble in his jaw, but he clenches it so tight I can't be sure. "Lucky you, getting over it."

"What's that supposed to mean? You expected me to pine over you for a decade after the way you left things? I reached out to you the next day, asking if you were all right. I gave you the opening to explain. I don't understand how you can expect any more from me after you left me hanging."

"I don't expect a thing out of anyone," he says simply.

It's gone. Any trace of the playfulness, the old Zac I managed to needle out of him this weekend. Taking a step away, he looks every bit the bitter man Summer made him out to be on our car ride over.

"What happened to you?" I ask him.

He doesn't even look at me. "What are you talking about?"

"You're different. You used to be . . . happy. You used to smile, laugh all the time. It was your thing. I used to love that about you."

"That was a long time ago."

"Seriously, what's with you? Summer calls you the Ogre of Oakwood, so I know it's not about being stuck here with me—"

"Let it go, Melody."

"How is it fair that we spent the past couple of days talking about my mess of a life, and when I ask you about yours—"

"Fine," he shoots, meeting my eyes at last. "You want to know what happened to that smile you love so much—"

"Loved." I don't know what makes me say it other than the need for him to know he hasn't held something over me all this time. "I don't love anything about you anymore."

He throws out his arms as though to say *exactly.*

"Welcome to the club," he says quietly. "Self-loathing is a hell of a thing, Clover."

I don't understand any of this. The red shoelace, the self-loathing. The look like I blew his soul right out of his body the second I told him I'd gotten over him.

The story is black-and-white: I put myself out there ten years ago. He walked away. If he's as crushed about it as the red string suggests, he wouldn't have left. Or he'd at least have reached out. Responded when I did.

This is utter bullshit.

My palms find his chest. And I mean to push him away. I mean to walk off, to get my stuff packed and ready for rescue.

I really do.

But my fingers seem to have a life of their own. They seem to forget who he is, how badly he hurt me. They curl, twisting the cotton of his shirt into my fists. Zac's gaze leaves mine, settles on the way I'm gripping him, keeping him close.

It's ten years ago, in my bedroom. We're standing at the door. He's about to leave, and I utter two reckless words.

Except, we're not. We're alone in this forest, backed up against a tree, with mud at our ankles. I've just realized the kind of monster my ex was, and learning that has shattered my heart into so many more jagged shards than Zac ever did.

Just this once, a tiny voice in my head says, searching for any flimsy excuse. *Just to know what he feels like.*

Just to get Connor out of your head. So he isn't the last person you've had. Let yourself indulge in the fantasy of Zac Porter. Just once.

Zac takes hold of my wrists where I'm still gripping his shirt. "Melody, I'm sorry I was harsh—"

"Kiss me."

He freezes. "What?"

My heart is thumping in my throat. I think I might be on the precipice of a huge mistake. I'm a terrible judge of character, after all.

Only, I'm not sure I care right now.

"I want a do-over," I tell him. "Kiss me."

Chapter 11

Melody

I think I've shocked the life out of him.

Zac stares down at me with pinched brows, lips parted like he's rewinding and hitting play on my words. Rewinding again, just to make sure he heard me right.

And then he raises a hand, cups my cheek. Lifts my chin. Eyes sweep my face, giving me the chance to change my mind. And—

He's kissing me. Zac Porter is kissing me. His hand is sliding across my cheek. His fingers are digging into my hair and bringing me closer to press me into his skin and we're touching everywhere.

I was the one to ask for it, but I didn't expect him to give it to me. Why would I, when he didn't the last time? For a second, it's all I can do to grip his shirt, try to stay upright, try to wrap my mind around this. Zac presses his mouth to mine harder, like he's trying to will me into the kiss I demanded. A proper kiss, one where the world goes black and nothing else matters.

But I'm so deeply in shock I can't move, not even when he pulls back to suck at my bottom lip, gently now like he's decided on a different tack, to ease me into it instead.

I can't move, I can't think, because Zac is kissing me—

And then my lips part for him, my tongue reaches for his, and he freezes. Pulls back a fraction, and my eyes flutter open to see the perfect brown of his eyes staring in utter disbelief, like he really didn't expect me to kiss him back. My chest heaves against his. One breath, two breaths, and then—

Our mouths crash together. He's pressing me back into this tree in a way that makes my legs weak, makes it hard to stand. But he gets an arm around my waist, steadying me. Tilts his head to kiss me deep, licks my tongue with his, moans into my mouth like a man starved for this very thing. And this time, I meet him pace for pace. I suck his lips between mine and breathe him in, that smell of pine and wood and lake he must smell on me, too.

I moan and he breaks away, panting hard. "Jesus fucking Christ, do that again."

"Do what?" I grip his chin, trying to get his mouth on me again. A second in, and I'm addicted.

"That sound. Moan again or I might die."

He looks like he means it. Like he's toeing the edge of a cliff, risking it all for the sound of my moan. Like he needed this just as bad as I did.

"You want that sound again, Zac?" I rest my head on the tree behind me, fascinated by the effect I seem to have on him. "Earn it."

"Fuck."

He's back on me. Dips to grab the backs of my thighs and lifts me up; I wrap my legs around him. His hands start roaming, touching me hard through my clothes, feeling the curve of my waist, cupping a handful of my ass, fingers coming up to touch my lips as he kisses me, like he's dying to feel the kiss through every sensation.

"Tell me now," he says, coming up for air just for a second. And then breaking away again when he realizes he never finished the sentence. "I know a lot of ways to earn that moan, Clover. But if this is all you want from me, tell me now."

He's touching me everywhere but where I need him most, the painful, desperate throb between my legs becoming unbearable.

Forget good sense. Forget heartbreak. Forget everything.

His swelling cock presses into my body and I push into it without thinking. The move seems to startle him. Zac staggers to the side. His foot must catch on something, or maybe it slips in the inches of thick mud on the ground, and then we're falling.

He manages to throw an arm behind my head to soften the impact as we hit the muddy forest floor and he flattens on top of me, air whooshing out of my lungs.

When he pushes the hair off my forehead, I can feel the streaks of mud his fingers leave behind. Not that it matters. I'm covered in it. It's in my hair, soaking my back. It's wet and slick, and holy fuck, does it make me more rabid.

Zac grinds his hips into me almost compulsively, then seems to think better of it. "Melody, are you okay?"

"Shut up." I wrap my legs around him and rock up into his body. "And do that again."

I grab a fistful of his hair and pull him to me. The kiss is messy. It's pent up. It's licking and biting and when Zac grinds his hips into mine, hitting me at an unbelievable angle, it's moaning and groaning, too. I'm drowning in wave after wave of utter bliss as his cock hits my clit, even with layers of clothes in between.

My body wants this, whatever this is. That red string around his wrist ripped open an old wound.

Just this once.

Zac swallows my whimpers with a kiss and he's rolling his hips against me at a steady rhythm, cupping my breast with a mud-covered hand.

"*Fuck.* It's so good," I gasp against his mouth. Oh God, I think I might—

Heat surges down my legs with every brush of his body. Zac

breaks the kiss, staying close but looking down at us, at our bodies moving together. The way the front of my tank top pulls farther down the swell of my breasts every time he grinds into me. My fingers curl at his hips, digging into his skin.

"You're going to come, aren't you?" Zac dips to kiss up my throat, my mouth, any part of me not covered in mud. "I can see it in your face. You're so fucking close I can feel your fingers shaking."

Cocky prick.

I sink my nails into his sides, tighten my thighs around his hips, and flip us around. Zac lands on his back with a grunt. His jaw slackens the moment his eyes adjust to take in the way I've straddled him, with hair wavy from the wet ground cascading above him.

"Sit still and let me get myself off," I tell him, smoothing muddy palms over his chest.

God, he really is beautiful. Even dipped in mud the way he is now, hair disheveled from my fingers. His body is all sharp angles and hard, so, *so* hard, every part of him—

His clear irritation at my taking over only lasts the length of time it takes me to adjust my hips and find his cock again. At that point, his eyes nearly roll to the back of his head.

At this point, mine do, too. My shoulders drop in relief, head falls back, and maybe it does feel like a bit of a waste, using up our *just this once* on a fully clothed dry hump, a glorified mud-wrestling match. But I grind into him over and over, and everything is just wet and slippery enough, the friction so perfect I couldn't stop even if I wanted to. I couldn't. I really couldn't—

Zac tangles his fingers in my hair and brings me down to his mouth as I ride his cock, wishing he was in me deep instead. The whole thing feels so intense, so messy and rabid. There's no patience, no savoring. Just want.

I rock into him and everything inside me goes taut, tight, and searing hot, almost to the point of pain. My hips pick up their pace, and the last thing I see before my eyes close is the raw fascination in Zac's face before—

My back hits the ground again, and my eyes wrench open as the start of my orgasm fades. Zac's smirk is all I see now as he hovers over me on hands and knees. And then I catch his hand moving between us.

"What—"

"Let's get something clear, Clover." Zac brushes his lips with mine. "If someone here is getting you off, it'll be me."

God, there's nothing—*nothing*—like the sharp perfection of strong fingers moving over your pussy. Nothing, even with my leggings between us. Instantly my back arches off the ground, hips return the pressure of his fingers as he draws circles over my clit. My moan is desperate, hungry.

"I can't decide which of your moans I like best," he mutters against my neck. "How many more versions are you holding on to, Clover?"

He kisses down my neck as his hand crawls upward, fists the waistband of my leggings and tugs, shoving the seam against my clit. My eyelids flutter, and I let out a breathy moan that has the corner of his mouth ticking up.

"That was a good one."

I'm at his mercy, taking what he gives me, letting him coax these desperate sounds out of me with his fingers. The way his eyes devour me. The cocky-as-hell smirk that grows with every fresh note out of my mouth. He rubs my clit between two fingers and it's so good that the sound I make is more garbled than anything.

"I like that moan, too. You're so fucking needy, aren't you?" His smirk grows a fraction. "You wearing panties, Melody?"

He doesn't wait for an answer, or maybe he realizes I don't have any words left at my disposal. He feels me through my pants, fingering the thin band of my panties at my hip before shifting to slip his hand underneath my leggings.

He finds my pussy again, over my silky panties, and the friction is so decadent that I give a sharp cry into the woods around us. I'm overheating, entire body throbbing.

"All this mud is killing me," Zac says, kissing me hard, sliding his fingers over my clit. "I want my fingers inside you. I want to touch you, feel your pussy clench around me like you need me."

I do, though. I do need him, or my body does at least, because I know that if he stopped now, if he took his hand away, stopped rubbing me, I might wither away to nothing.

"Zac," I moan, and it's all I can get out.

"You need me inside you, don't you? Fingers are nice, but it's my cock you want, isn't it? Tell me."

I whimper. Every single soft word out of his mouth brings me closer to the edge, and I need him to keep talking. "I want it," I admit breathlessly. "I wish you were fucking me."

Triumph flares in his eyes, and I don't even care. "You wanna know what I want?" I nod frantically and he nips my lip. "I want to peel off these clothes." His fingers rub me agonizingly slow now. "I want you bare for me, nothing between us. I want to touch and taste every bit of your body. I want to spend hours between your legs, licking this perfect pussy until I hear each of your moans a thousand times, memorize them all."

I can feel how slick I am down there. My neck arches when his fingers pick up their pace.

Zac rakes his fingers through my hair, fists a handful and wrenches another moan out of me. "I want my mouth on you, want you to come on my tongue until you think you have nothing left to give me. That's when I'll fuck you. Prove you wrong, make you scream for me. Hard and fast and as messy as this. I want to see my cum drip all over you, out of you . . ."

"*Fuck*, Zac." My entire body goes weak, and I've never wanted anything more than this picture he's painting.

"You get it, now, Mel? I want you to remember all that the next time you think I'm full of shit."

He builds pressure over my clit and—I'm either coming or dying, I don't know—

"Remember that the next time you make the mistake of looking at me like you don't believe a word out of my mouth when I tell you I want you. That my body fucking *needs* you—"

His fingers pick up their pace and I'm on fire.

"I want . . . fuck, Melody. I want everything with you."

My breath catches. At the words, the sheer longing overcoming the heat in his eyes. With a blink, Zac seems to come to and realize how this has shifted. Swallowing, he bends to run wet kisses down my neck. And his fingers lose all mercy.

It comes quick, and God, it's so much better than clumsily using his cock the way I'd been doing. Everything rushes through me at once, the heat, the raging need to see it to the end. I grip his sides, his shoulders, scrape down Zac's back. Take fistfuls of his hair and I really have lost my mind today because I crush his mouth with mine, desperate to feel him in every way I can.

I break away with a whimper. "I'm—Zac, I'm gonna come."

"Do it," Zac says, pressing our foreheads together. "Let them fucking hear you in the next town."

"Oh my G—*Zac*—"

The rest of the forest falls silent. His eyes go wide and hungry, watching me squirm and shudder beneath him. I grip his wrist as he continues to rub me, like I'm afraid he'll quit on me right when it counts. My cries bounce off the trees around us, and thank God the neighboring campsites are deserted. Because there's no denying that these are the sounds you make when you get hit with the kind of orgasm that causes the world around you to crumble.

He kisses the tip of my nose as I gasp desperately for air. "You are so fucking hot."

Color rushes back to my vision and Zac's there above me, staring like he's having an out-of-body experience. I don't know if he means to be, but he's still rubbing me, drawing out sharp bursts of heat with every soft touch.

I'm not sure how my limbs are functioning. Somehow, I manage to pull his hand off me, make enough room to put mine between us instead, to reach for him through his sweats.

"You don't need to do that."

"There's no way I'm leaving the scales tipped like this."

The sound he makes when I close my hand around the shape of his cock will haunt me for the rest of my life. It's pure relief, pure greed, and immediately I want to hear it again. I feel my way along the waistband of his sweats, reveling in the shudder of his stomach under my touch. And then I pull him out.

The second I get a bare hand on him, his grip in my hair turns just short of painful—a knee-jerk response to the way I'm stroking him that fills me with intoxicating power. This man, for all his smirks and self-assuredness, melting at my touch. This is what I want. This is what I need.

Zac's eyelids go heavy as I start to stroke his cock.

"*Fuck*," he breathes in one long, drawn-out syllable. "Slow it down for me." He nods frantically when I do. "Yeah, like that. Keep doing that."

Zac is even louder than I was. He groans freely, breathes out my name, face screwed up in pleasure and *God*, there's something so hot about a man who's vocal in bed. It makes me work harder, chasing more of his noises. Little rewards as I play with his cock.

"Fuck, Melody, that feels so good."

His arms start shaking on either side of me. His breathing becomes ragged, moans drawn out, and I resent them now, knowing in the back of my mind that this is it. It's just this once, and I'll never get to hear those sounds again. So I soak it in. Stroke his cock just the way he asked. All the while, he doesn't take his eyes off me, like he's afraid to blink.

Like if he does, I might disappear.

The whole thing is almost as exhilarating as it was to feel his fingers move over me. I almost regret the slackening in his jaw, the way he whispers *oh fuck, oh fuck, oh fuck* like he wants it but wants to hold back, make it last longer, and he's running out of time to decide.

Zac arches his neck, groans so deep and lets go, spilling all over my stomach. Hanging his head, panting, he takes in the sight of me as he tries to regain himself. When I release him, he shifts and lands on the ground beside me, staring up at the green canopy of leaves above us.

God.

I expected to feel shame. Humiliation. I've spent years resenting this man, only to fall to pieces for him anyway. Maybe I expected to feel some guilt, too, at the fact that it's the first time in years I've been touched by a man who isn't Connor. I don't feel any of that, though.

I'm relieved.

Connor's not the last person who touched me. I'm still desirable. Sex can still be fun without him. He might have spent the past six years messing with me, breaking me and rearranging me at his will without my noticing, but he didn't ruin me. I can be fine without him.

Thank God.

Summer was right. This is exactly what I needed.

Beside me, Zac releases a long breath. "You have no idea how long I've needed to do that."

His voice is the kind of light I haven't heard over the course of the weekend. He's staring up at the trees without a speck of leftover tension. He looks content. Maybe from the orgasm. Maybe he's feeling the same kind of relief I am.

Did someone break his heart, too, since I last saw him?

I lift onto my elbows to get a better look at us. We're a wet, muddy mess. "I think this probably calls for another lake bath."

He cracks a smile so familiar my entire body throbs with recognition. "Together this time? I owe you a clean-up, after all that. Maybe another round."

"Nice try," I scoff, sitting up. "File this away under *never happening again.*"

His smile fades. "What do you mean?"

I frown. Why does he suddenly look so . . . confused?

I'm about to ask. But I cut off my own words, because I swear, I just heard— Our eyes clash, mine as wide as his.

Over the sounds of leaves shaking in the breeze, lake water flowing, and wildlife scurrying, I hear the distinct, miraculous sound of tires cutting through gravel from somewhere nearby.

I look around us. "Do you hear—"

"Melody, what does this mean?"

I scramble to my feet. "Did you just hear—"

"*Melody*," Zac says urgently. He stands, then nudges my chin until I focus on him again. He's staring at me almost frantically. "What does this mean?"

My brows furrow. A car engine roars somewhere to my right. "What are you talking about?"

"This," he says, and looks between us before fixing his eyes on me again. "The kissing. Everything after. What does it mean?"

My mouth forms around a word as I hear the car come closer. Zac shoves the hair off his face, smearing more mud in the process.

"I . . . It was nothing," I stutter.

"*Nothing*?"

Now I'm confused. "Weren't we . . . We've had this tension going all weekend. We were just giving in for a minute. Isn't that all it was?"

Zac deflates.

Almost immediately he shakes his head, as though waking himself up. "No. That's not at all what I thought it was. I wasn't *giving in for a minute*, whatever the hell that even means."

"Then—"

The sounds of tires come closer.

"You asked me for a do-over. That's what I thought we were doing," he says hurriedly. I turn, trying to find the source of our rescue, but he cups my cheek and forces my gaze back on him. "Melody, I'm trying to tell you something."

At last, I properly take in the pleading look on his face, the tension in his shoulders. The determination in his eyes. He looks like he's on the verge of a confession that's weighed heavy on him, and he's finally ready to let it out.

A honk breaks the delicate silence. Then another.

And we turn to see Parker's Jeep tearing down the path toward us, coming to a halt just feet ahead.

We're covered in mud and other questionable fluids. Our clothes are askew. We're a mess.

Parker hops out of the driver's seat and slams the car door shut behind him. Looks back and forth between us.

"What the hell happened here?"

Chapter 12

Zac

Six days.

That's how long it's been since I've exchanged a single word with her. Since we got rescued from that campsite, since I got dropped off at a house sorely missing her presence. Her snark. The reluctant smiles she'd give me whenever we hit our stride with the back and forth.

Six days is an improvement on a ten-year gap, but still. I'm feeling a little vulnerable here, on account of the whole discovering-my-red-shoelace thing.

The whole being-on-the-verge-of-confessing-my-undying-love thing.

I whip my phone out of my back pocket for the hundredth time in the last five minutes, and what's got to be the millionth time since we parted ways. Only to once again remember we don't have each other's numbers. After we cleaned off and packed in silence, the car ride back with Parker had been too awkward to get a chance to ask her for it.

"You need another coffee?"

Brooks sidles up to me, his eyes on the group of large men

running drills up and down the UOB football field. The place got a major facelift the summer I graduated and transitioned from quarterback to assistant coach. It's a lot better than the patchy grass we used to play—and win—on.

I think the school was riding a high off the end of a championship year when it decided to invest in the stadium, only to then embark on a miserable losing streak. Spending that kind of money on a losing team definitely explains the frustration from the higher-ups.

I mold my baseball cap so that it properly shields my eyes from the sun, shoving the binder with our next game's playbook under my arm.

"Why would I need more coffee?" I ask, watching yet another fumbled catch on the field.

"Because you've been averaging five a day since you got back from the camping trip."

I throw Brooks a look. "Is that what we're calling getting stranded in a storm with nothing but cookies and gummy worms for sustenance?"

"There was bread." Brooks shrugs. "And the cookie boxes were empty when you handed back the cooler. Not a single M&M left over. I don't know what you're complaining about."

My reply drifts to nothing as we catch sight of a lanky player breaking off from the drill and jogging in our direction. Brooks takes a few steps away from me, which isn't altogether necessary, but he knows how careful I am about being overtly friendly with him in front of the team or management. I encouraged him to go for the job, and put in a good word for him.

But I'm a young coach, who basically fell into this job and hasn't earned his keep. I don't need anyone thinking I'm running my coaching team like some kind of fraternity on top of that.

"Hey, Coach." Noah strips off his helmet, gripping it at his side by the cage. He rubs along his hairline at the red helmet creases over his forehead. The kid towers over me and my six-feet-three-inches, with the kind of build that makes you question how he manages to retain perfect control over his limbs. But I've never, not in my two decades of playing and then coaching football, seen a guy so perfectly suited to throwing that ball. He's light-years better than I ever was as quarterback.

I still cringe every time I see an opposing player twice his width charge toward him. But part of Noah's magic is that he's damn near impossible to sack, tackle, or grab.

The kid should have been a dancer or something.

"You're point-two seconds over your drill time, Irving," I tell him, motioning with my binder. "Did you have a big breakfast?"

"Bit creepy of you, tracking me that closely, Coach." He gives an unperturbed laugh.

This is a kid who knows how good he is. He's barely got a sheen of sweat going while I can see some of his helmet-less teammates wiping their brows on the field. And maybe he's over his time now, but the second he hits the field on game day, he'll be breaking his own records.

Not that it does us any good.

"Hey, so I was thinking." He moves closer and shoots a look over his shoulder at the rest of the team. They're loud and preoccupied, but he drops his voice anyway. "Maybe we give Matthews a shot at throwing next Friday. He's looking pretty good out there, and he and Doke trained together over the summer. They've got a good thing going."

I look over his shoulder at his backup quarterback throwing a ball around with one of our main roster receivers.

"That should be you over there. And that should have been you training with Doke over the summer. You're his quarterback."

"We did get a bit of training in," Noah says with a shrug. "But they both live in the same state, across the country, and I live here. They've become a pretty decent tandem."

"I'm not looking for *decent*. I can't believe you're even coming to me, suggesting I bench you for our home opener." I study him, the tired circles under his eyes. "How're things at home?"

Noah shifts his weight. "This has nothing to do with home. We went an entire season last year without winning a game. And I can hand off the ball all you want, but you know I'm just a regular guy, with regular skills unless I'm throwing. And if I have no one to throw to . . ."

"Don't be a fucking martyr, Irving. It doesn't impress me."

"I'm not trying to impress anyone. I'm trying to win us some games."

I jab a finger in his direction. "See, that's the wrong answer. You should be trying to impress scouts *while* winning us games. I know you've got some kind of good-guy complex, kid, and that's great. But I'll never be able to live with myself if I was coaching the NFL's next greatest quarterback and didn't make sure your ass was on the field every minute it was supposed to be there. No one's saying Matthews and Doke can't play a decent football game. But they're not who scouts come here to see."

"What good is having scouts coming to see me when I'm not even throwing? I'm not getting drafted anywhere this way," he says, rubbing at the cropped sandy hair on top of his head.

"I'll find you someone to throw to."

"With all due respect, Coach, that's what the guy before you kept saying. I'm in my junior year, and still nothing."

"I'll find you someone," I say again. "And if you don't get drafted in the first round this year, I'm quitting my fucking job."

"Who's being a martyr now?"

"I'm not a martyr, Noah." I drop my voice. "I'm a coach who sees an insane amount of talent in the player in front of me. A player who, setting aside the game for a second, deserves to have his fucking dreams come true after all the shit he's been through." Noah's gaze falls to the grass under our feet. "You're sure everything's okay at home?"

He shrugs helplessly, and the clear defeat in his shoulders makes me wish that the ground would open up underneath me and swallow me whole. It kills me, hearing him talk about his home life. The screaming matches between his parents. The holes punched through walls, the way he's the one looking after his dad when the fucker drinks himself into oblivion.

Noah's here on a full-ride scholarship, could have played anywhere, yet still lives at home for the sake of his parents.

I will never be able to understand living in that kind of environment. Maybe my home life wasn't picture-perfect, with my parents always somewhere halfway around the world. That's the life you end up with when you've got a diplomat for a father. But I had Grams to put down roots with.

Noah's situation? It makes me infinitely grateful to live in the house I do. It's just out of town, on the water and away from prying eyes, with enough bedrooms to have housed both Noah and Grams, if she were still around.

Noah turns his chin over his shoulder, eyeing the field. I'm getting this kid out of that home if it's the last thing I do.

"Get back out there," I say abruptly, snapping back into coach-mode. "You sure as hell won't be winning us any games by slacking in practice."

With a lackluster parting salute, Noah dons his helmet and gets back on the field at a jog. "Is he still trying to get out of playing?" Brooks mutters, retaking his spot next to me.

"He's brought this to you before?"

He nods. "I told him to get over himself."

"Just told him about the same. He isn't wrong about any of it, though." I rip off my hat and shove my fingers through my hair. "How far into the season do you think I'll make it before they give me the axe?"

Brooks winces. "We'll figure it out, all right? It won't come to that."

Problem is, the longer I go without finding someone who can hang with Noah, the closer I find myself to an early retirement. Who the hell would hire the guy who couldn't win a game with an NFL-caliber quarterback? My predecessor started the season without a new job.

I'm royally fucked.

I pull out my phone for a distraction. Also, because I've once again forgotten Melody doesn't have my number. "Hey, have you heard from Mel at all?"

Brooks shoves his hands into the pockets of his jeans. "Why would I hear anything from Mel? I met her for half a day."

"But nothing through Summer? Parker?"

Brooks eyes me, amused. "You know, it all came together the second she showed up."

"What did?"

"Why you've been stubbornly single since we met freshman year."

I force my eyes toward the field. "Was I that obvious?"

Brooks shrugs. "Nah, you were fine overall. But to my well-trained eye, you were definitely a little shifty. What happened while you were stuck together?"

"Nothing."

"My well-trained eye says that's bullshit. You can't convince me that you were stuck alone with the love of your life and it led to nothing."

"She isn't the love of my life."

Liar, liar.

"The girl you've been obsessed with since you were a kid, then."

"I'm not obsessed with her."

Liar.

"The girl you fucked while you were stranded together in the woods," he ventures. When I don't agree, he narrows his eyes. "The girl you fondled?" I roll my eyes. "Kissed?"

"Give it a rest," I groan. "I said nothing happened."

I refuse to give him an inch on this. She and I never got the chance to talk about how we'd address what went down between us before Parker showed up. The kissing, the touching. I refuse to make that call without her blessing. Grams didn't raise me to run my mouth like that. Locker room talk was never my thing.

I'm not sure he entirely buys it, but Brooks pulls his phone from his pocket. "I'm gonna do you a favor, even though I'm fairly sure you're lying to me." He types at his phone, and a few seconds later mine vibrates in my back pocket. "There. Summer just added her to the group chat."

"You guys work fast," I mutter, pulling out my phone. "How does this help me?"

"You know her number now."

I stare down at the nondescript phone number now at the top of our group chat. "Who says I'm a shitty friend, huh?" Brooks nudges me.

I tap Melody's number and add it to my contacts, thumbs hovering over the screen after I open up a new message thread. "I never said you were a shitty friend."

"But I've felt like a shitty friend," he says, voice dipping solemnly the same way it has every time he's launched into an apology since Monday. "And once again, I am sincerely sorry I didn't realize you were both missing. I swear I would have driven right back if I did . . ."

I tune out the thousandth apology speech. I can tell him it's fine, can pat him on the back as many times as I want, but Brooks's guilty conscience knows no bounds. He just needs to get through it and he'll be fine until the next time it occurs to him how bad he feels.

I stare down at the pulsing cursor on the screen as I figure out what I want to say to Mel.

Did you really mean it when you said kissing me meant nothing?

Because if my head wasn't already brutally screwed up over you before, I'm a downright mess now.

Instead, I type *hey* and hit send before I lose my nerve.

I spend the next thirty seconds staring, horrified, at the three letters contained in that blue message bubble, instantly wanting to claw them back. Hey.

Hey?

She had a fist around my cock the last time I saw her, and all I can come up with is *hey*? And then I realize I actually punctuated the *hey* with a period. A damn *period*.

Fucking. Kill me.

My heart leaps into my throat when I see three small dots flicker at the bottom of the text thread.

ZAC: Hey.

CLOVER: Hey with a period, Porter? What are you, a serial killer?

I let out a laugh, and Brooks shoots me a weird look. He tries to look over my shoulder, but I shove him away. "Get back to work."

"Not obsessed with her, my ass," he mutters under his breath, before striding closer to the field and saying something to one of the players.

ZAC: It's a fair assumption, given the text. How did you know it was me?

CLOVER: It was either you or Brooks in that group chat, and he didn't strike me as a hey with a period kind of guy. Aren't you at work?

ZAC: I am.

ZAC: How are you?

ZAC: I've wanted to see you.

I've never been so damn embarrassed by my own text game.

I stare down at my screen, as those three gray dots flicker for an entire fucking eternity before her next message finally comes.

Oh, fuck yeah.

Chapter 13

Melody

The pen cap digs into my head, delivering acute relief to my screaming scalp from the sharp sensation of hair follicles pulled taut in the same direction for far too long, in variations of the same chaotic bun I've had on top of my head for the past week.

The relief is fleeting. The real solution to my follicular problem involves a shampoo and blow-dry I haven't been able to muster since the shower I took upon my rescue from camp. It's a good thing Parker is the only person I've seen all week. I'm an overtired, greasy-haired mess, and even though there's no fooling anyone that I'm a woman in crisis, he knows better by now than to question me when I resort to one-word answers.

What happened at camp before I showed up? Nothing. What are you doing hiding in your room all day? Thinking. What do you want for dinner tonight? Pasta.

Again? Yes.

I toss the pen down on the desk in the corner of my room. It bounces off my keyboard and the computer screen comes to life, immediately exposing my shame. Half the screen is covered by a spreadsheet I've been toiling over for work, market trends for a Fortune 500 client who seeks to increase his infant son's trust fund from a cool however many millions to however many more millions.

But it's the webpage on the other half of the screen that really takes the cake.

What is Love Bombing? Seven Signs to Look For.

Apparently, Connor's type of love has a name.

I turn back to my closet, glaring at my collection of clothes as though each piece has a sin to answer for. It's right there, at the top of that list of seven signs: *unexpected, needless gifts and tokens of affection.*

Pretty, shiny, designer things Connor showered me with as proof of his love, only to use them against me later.

Simple yet oh-so-fucking-effective, wasn't it?

I've been existing in a stolen, oversized sweatsuit of Parker's since the camping trip, unable to stomach the thought of wearing anything Connor purchased for me.

"And to think," I say, flicking the sleeve of a silky white blouse. Connor's favorite, and the current object of my disdain. "I thought we were all friends."

The blouse slips off its hanger in response. It lands on the closet floor.

"Well, screw you too, then."

I've truly gone insane from this six-day insomnia.

I pause, reaching for the offending blouse. The back of the closet I'm using is lined with bent-out-of-shape cardboard boxes all marked *Parker's Stuff*, collected from my brother's childhood bedroom before our parents sold the house a few years ago. But there, at the very top of a corner stack, is a single box with my name scrawled on the side in black marker. I hadn't noticed it when I moved in.

I heave out the box, causing more silky-bloused casualties in the process, and the clear tape barely offers resistance when I rip the top flaps apart.

It's a pile of old clothes and other random knickknacks from my childhood bedroom. A variety of miniature footballs, both foam and badly deflated leather—a staple for a homegrown resident of a football town like Oakwood. A length of rope my old sitter insisted I use to practice my bowline knot before she allowed me behind the wheel of her sailboat at the age of twelve. Sinking to the floor, I dig out a folded piece of cardboard from the very bottom of the box, smoothing it out in my lap.

Ten years from now, my life looks like . . .

My stomach sinks. It's my senior year vision board, depicting the life eighteen-year-old me declared would be hers. It's not particularly ambitious—not that it needed to be, at eighteen—but the images are splashed with warm yellows, happy blues and greens that scream of optimism for this open-ended future.

Ten years ago, I didn't have much of a plan beyond knowing I was headed to the city to study mathematics. That didn't scare me. Parker and I grew up with adventurous, fly-by-the-seat-of-their-pants parents, so it didn't feel odd to any of us that I'd look to a change of scenery for inspiration. I was excited to explore a new city, meet new people outside of the forever–safety net that was my twin brother. My free-spirited parents encouraged it.

But between the images of a city skyline, a stock photo of a young, happy family, and some goofy-looking dachshunds contained in this vision board, eighteen-year-old me would be in for a brutal awakening if she saw me now.

I left Oakwood Bay optimistic about the future. I returned to my hometown aimless, emotionally damaged, to be judged by this decrepit piece of cardboard and internet search results that tell me just how foolish I've been for the past six years.

I eye the corner of the old vision board, where a missing photo must have torn off in my parents' move. I can't remember what used to be there, but I bet I never made that happen, either.

I rub at my temples. If only I could manage a decent night's sleep. Maybe then I'd be able to cobble together some sort of life plan . . .

My phone chimes from its spot in the middle of my unmade bed. I set aside the vision board, blocking my old dreams from view.

SUMMER: Adding the better-looking Woods twin to the group chat . . . You're welcome, everyone.

PARKER: What the hell, Summer??

I snort, and it's as close to a laugh as I've gotten in my week of wallowing and psychoanalysis. If there's one thing about moving back home, it's feeling like I've got people like Parker and Summer in my corner again. She's been messaging me nonstop since our return from camp, asking how I'm doing at least four times a day.

I finally got it out of her that the first time she checked on me was to satisfy her own concern. And every time thereafter had been to satisfy Zac's.

I almost asked her to give me his number for the sake of telling him to take a breath. But that would require finding a way to cut through the awkwardness we left between us after that tumble in the mud, and I can't even muster the will to shower these days.

I blow an errant strand of hair off my face just as my phone dings again. A text from one of the anonymous numbers at the top of the group chat.

"Who . . ." I click open the message.

Hey.

The snorting thing happens again. This time, it's followed by an odd gurgling from deep in my chest, bubbling up my throat, and the sound of my own laugh hitting the dead silence of my bedroom is a shock to my system.

I stand, shrugging out of Parker's too-big sweater as we exchange messages. Whatever awkwardness there was after our hookup last week, the man seems to have recovered just fine. More texts come through, three in a row, and I stare at the final one for a long minute.

ZAC: I've wanted to see you.

I tug my hair free of its bun prison and massage my aching scalp.

I have no clue what possesses me in the seconds that follow. One moment I'm clutching my phone, eyeing my bath towel. Contemplating that much-needed shower. The next . . .

MELODY: Give me half an hour. I'll meet you at the stadium.

~

"What are you doing?"

Zac ushers me into the plush swivel chair behind his desk in his office at the UOB stadium. He crouches at my feet but pauses in the act of reaching for my sneaker.

"Can I check your ankle?"

"It barely hurts anymore," I tell him. But the earnestness in his face—the fact that he *asked*, when being told had been the norm during my six years with Connor—has me toeing off my sneaker anyway.

Zac peels off my sock and studies the bruising underneath it. "Rotate your ankle for me."

I do so, wiggling my toes for good measure. Then he runs his fingers over my skin, checking every bump and angle with all the concentration in the world, lips curled into his mouth like he does when he's really being careful with something. His touch is delicate and, to my horror, goose bumps erupt over my bare legs and crawl up my body.

I mean, can you blame me? The day I last saw him, we rolled around in the mud together. All wet and slippery, feeling so good.

Sex with Connor had never been an issue—it was the one thing I could consistently get right with him. But it had never—*ever*—felt the way things did with Zac. We'd gone six years without falling into the kind of effortless rhythm Zac and I fell into that day. Reading each other without even trying. My body never ached for Connor the way it does for Zac.

Zac follows the trail of goose bumps up my legs, disappearing under the ancient, too-tight sundress I plucked from the cardboard box of my teenaged belongings.

"It's really cold in here," I mumble.

He tips his head. "They don't run the AC in here on Sundays. This is an extra practice."

Right on cue, beads of sweat erupt at the back of my neck. I rub my lips together and his eyes zero in on them. His jaw slackens a little.

God, this has to stop. I don't know what brought me here to see him, but this wasn't it.

I turn, scanning the room. Zac's office doesn't have any windows, but it's decently sized, with wall-to-wall shelving loaded with binders lining the far wall. Behind me hangs a framed white-and-maroon UOB Huskies jersey with the name Porter over the number ten. It's the same number he wore in high school.

Apparently satisfied with his examination, Zac carefully slips my sock back on, followed by my sneaker.

"What's the prognosis, Coach?"

"Almost good as new." He sits on the edge of his desk, scanning the rest of me. "How have you been?"

How have I been? I've been flip-flopping between angry tears and snapping at inanimate objects in my closet all week. But at least I finally washed my hair.

"I'm great, actually. Parker's been working overtime to apologize for sending me on such an ill-fated trip, so that's been fun. He's been cooking every night. Set up a desk in my room for my work." I shrug. "In fact, I came here to ask you to please stop harassing Summer with texts asking how I'm doing. You're really starting to freak her out, and as you can see, I am perfectly fine."

Zac crosses his arms, nonverbally rejecting my claim that everything is a-okay, but he doesn't push it. "Do they know about . . . everything right before we got rescued?"

I raise my brows. "What happened right before we got rescued?"

His mouth tugs into a smirk. "Do they know you let me play with your pussy, that you practically begged me to fuck you—"

God.

I roll my shoulders back, feeling a little hot around the nonexistent collar of my dress. "Oh, *that*. I haven't told anyone. And I think it's a good idea to keep it that way."

It hasn't been easy, though. It had been a quiet ride home with Parker, but the second he dropped Zac off, he kicked off an inquisition so thorough I had to pretend to go have a nap as soon as we got home. And the second I resurfaced from my room for dinner, it started all over again.

It was strange. We grew up with Zac, in the prime of my teenaged sexual awakening. But he'd never once asked if anything outside of the platonic happened between us.

Not that it could have, given Parker was always around.

I reach for my purse, fish out some lip balm, and pop off the cap. Zac's gone suspiciously quiet, and I find him staring at my lips. The tip of his tongue grazes the corner of his mouth, and he looks utterly mesmerized. He doesn't even seem to be breathing.

Just like hearing—*feeling*—his response to my mouth and my hands last week, there's something incredibly intoxicating now in rattling someone so otherwise composed. The way he looks at me makes me feel viscerally wanted. Like I'm one swipe of lip balm away from seeing him snap.

I cap the tube and hold it out to him. "You want some?"

"Hm?" His brows twitch. He snaps out of his daze, taking the tube of lip balm and turning it over in his hands. "This stuff is gold, you know. Your lips are so fucking soft, Clover."

"And yours could definitely use some." It's bullshit. He's a fantastic kisser. Zac examines the tube, and I pause on the dark circles under his eyes. He looks just as tired as I feel. "Are you having trouble sleeping?"

He fiddles with my lip balm. "I don't know what it is. Residual panic after the animal thing, I think. I'll drift off and a second later jerk awake, thinking I'm back in that tent. I look around for you, freak out until I remember you aren't supposed to be in my bed."

How did he just manage to make insomnia sound almost . . . sweet?

"I haven't slept either." He finds the dark circles under my eyes, identical to his. "I've tried everything. Working out to help tire me out. Herbal tea. I'm driving Parker crazy, pacing my room at night."

"Because of the animal thing? Or everything with Connor?"

"Both," I sigh, swinging his swivel chair from side to side. "I wake up at the slightest sound, start obsessing over the Connor thing, and never fall back asleep. I can't get my mind to shut up."

"What's it saying?"

"Aren't you sick of listening to me talk about him?"

He caps and uncaps my lip balm without losing eye contact. "I fucking hate the guy, but it's what's going on in your life, which I want to be part of. You tell me about processing your breakup, I bore you with stories about my impending unemployment. It comes with the territory of getting to know each other again."

I nod, smoothing my palms on my thighs. I suppose there's no real reason we can't become friendly while I'm still in town. It'll certainly make things a lot less awkward for everyone.

"In that case, I've been trying to put together the *why me* of it all. Why was I the one Connor chose? After some deep self-reflection, the conclusion I've come to is that I'm a gullible, desperate idiot."

"I doubt that, but go on."

I hesitate. I've spent the past week trying to dissect my own brain. Trying to figure out why I let myself get sucked into the mess that was Connor. My conclusion hits a little close to home for Zac and me.

But that's the point, isn't it? I was biting my tongue in favor of a man's feelings. I refuse to do that anymore. I force my gaze off my shoes, up to Zac's face.

"It was kind of the perfect storm, really. No one ever showed interest in me in high school. The guys we'd all hang around with were always weird with me, which wasn't great for my teenaged self-esteem. And then . . . that thing happened with us. And I'm not blaming you for anything, but by the time I got over you I'd spent a long time feeling undesirable."

My cheeks warm under the humiliation of that confession. It sounds so pitiful said out loud, but it's the truth. I was single until I met Connor at twenty-two, and after a while, it was hard not to think there was something seriously wrong with me. The guys in high school would get shifty whenever I'd innocently chat them up before making some excuse to run off somewhere else. Couple that with the years it took me to let go of Zac, and my confidence was shot.

Zac has the grace to drop his gaze. When I hold out my palm, he hands me my tube of lip balm.

"Anyway, Connor was into me right away, and everything that followed was . . . fast. He wanted to be exclusive after only a few dates, we spent every night together. He was my first everything, and it felt really good to be wanted like that. That's where I went wrong, wasn't it? I was such an easy target for his brand of manipulation, because I so badly wanted to believe I could be special to someone."

Zac looks a little ill now, and I have no idea why I felt compelled to spew all that to him when I have a perfectly understanding brother who'd have listened to me. I have Summer, who would no doubt launch into a speech about how much better off I am without Connor.

"You want to know the worst part?" I continue anyway.

Zac fingers the red string on his wrist. "What?"

I grind my teeth, refusing to cry another tear over my own stupidity. I've done enough of that this week. "He told me he loved me two weeks in. *Two weeks*, Zac. And I actually believed him. How stupid am I? You don't fall for someone that fast. It's impossible, and I ate it up. All the signs were there, weren't they?"

"You're not stupid." Zac rises from the edge of his desk, running his fingers through his hair. "It's possible. I don't know about this guy, but it's possible, okay? Between the right people, falling in love can happen quicker than a blink. And that kind of love can last an entire lifetime, waiting for the right moment to show itself."

"I don't believe that. Not anymore."

"Trust me, I would know—"

"It's not possible, Zac. It's total bullshit."

He clamps his jaw against a counterargument. This is the part I might hate Connor most for. I'm a skeptic by nature, always have been. Still, I held out hope that this blink-and-you-fall, never-goes-away kind of love existed. I wanted it from Zac so badly back then, and again when I met Connor.

That optimism got me eyeballs-deep in emotional manipulation for six years of my life.

"I'm so fucking mad at myself, Zac. I should have known better. I should have left him. I was stupid enough to think the way he cared for me was genuine. I failed myself so fucking badly, I have no idea how to start trusting my own judgment." My nose prickles painfully as I beat back tears. "So, tell me again how I'm not gullible and desperate."

But Zac shakes his head and crouches to bring us almost to eye level. After a moment's hesitation, he reaches for my hands. "You are neither. You don't own what he did to you, okay? None of that was your fault." I open my mouth to argue, but he shakes his head. "Let me get this out. I can't ever apologize enough for the part I played in it. I've been sorry since I left that night, and fuck, I think I'll stay sorry until they put me in a grave one day. And to think you spent even a second of your life thinking you weren't desired . . . I wouldn't blame you for not believing me when I say this, but I desired you then. And if last weekend wasn't indication enough, I desire you now."

Well, shit. Here come the waterworks.

I'm aching for it to be true, from him of all people, but he's right. I don't believe him. I'm forbidding myself to believe him. My guard is up so high I can barely see around it, and that's how it should be.

Before I can do anything more than clear my throat, catch my own tears, Zac scoops me up in his arms and falls back into his chair, cradling me in his lap. The space outside his office is deserted, silent save for the occasional muffled whistle we can hear from the field. Zac lets me cry uninterrupted tears into his shoulder, doing nothing but holding me to him for so long I lose track of time.

"You should be out on the field," I say after a while, and my voice comes out scratchy, thick with tears though they've started to dry up. "This isn't what I came for, I swear. I can't believe I dumped this on you while you're working."

"I don't give a shit about work right now."

Zac smooths the hair off my face, tucks me closer, and sinks us down into the plush chair. The effect is instantaneous. My limbs soften. Brain stops whirring. I can barely feel my own body, but his is warm, lulling me into the kind of peace I haven't felt in a week.

The same way it did the night we were stalked by a wild animal, every beat of his heart against my body seems to send a message to mine in its own Morse code.

Safe here, safe here, safe here.

"Clover?" My eyes have started to close and I wrench them open to see Zac watching me drowsily. "You're falling asleep."

"You look sleepy, too," I mumble, nuzzling his shoulder. I can't seem to make myself care about boundaries right now. I am so fucking tired.

"What if . . ."

I wrench my eyes open again. "Mm?"

Zac sinks deeper into his chair, taking me with him. He rests his head back, closes his eyes. "Do you think we can only fall asleep together?"

I frown, giving up on having my eyes open. I mean to tell him that's ridiculous, that the sleep deprivation is getting to him. That it can't be true.

But the words never make it out.

Chapter 14

Zac

ZAC: 5121 Hillside Road.

ZAC: In case you feel like sleeping tonight.

I slam shut the playbook on my lap, staring out at the dark grounds and the moonlit waves rolling through the bay at the foot of the property.

Seems my brain is just as muddled at one in the morning as it is in broad daylight, which isn't a great sign considering my job is hanging by a thread. Today's abysmal practice was attended by my boss, Harry Nunez, whose patience and good humor apparently departed the school in the same cardboard box as my predecessor's belongings.

This time, he decided to remind me how close I was to unemployment right there on the sideline, turning me into a sideshow in front of my entire team—my entire coaching staff. He knew what he was doing. Putting everyone on that field on high alert that if they didn't get their shit together, they'd be leaving their so-called beloved coach hanging high and dry.

I need to get some fucking sleep. I haven't managed a second of it since that euphoric nap in my office yesterday, with Melody in my lap.

I took a gamble and sent her my address hours ago. Still nothing.

I'm about to head inside when I hear the distant sounds of a car out on the road. Living on the outskirts of town, it's rare to hear a sound past seven o'clock, let alone this late into the night. And then the car seems to turn onto my driveway, and holy shit. The second I hear light footsteps climb up the front porch, I dive inside.

There's a knock at the door and I wrench it open so fast Melody's fist is still hanging in the air.

Fuck, yeah.

She sours the second she sees me, like she hoped I wasn't home, and it takes everything I have not to break into a smile at the sight of her scowl. She's sweet when she's grumpy. And she's especially grumpy when sleep-deprived.

"Hello to you too, sunshine." I inject just the right amount of enthusiasm into my voice to elicit an impatient eye roll. Fucking adorable. "I'm glad you caved. I'm dying for some sleep."

"I still think it's a ridiculous theory. That nap was a total coincidence." She peers around me into the house. "Can I come in?"

I pry the backpack out of her hand and lead her to the kitchen at the back of the house. Mel takes in the soft gray cabinets, the butcher-block countertops. Turns and scans the living room from the doorway off the kitchen. I follow her gaze, suddenly self-conscious as I examine my own furniture. The blank, white walls around us.

"What did your grams think about this place? I can't believe she let you move her into a house without floral wallpaper everywhere," she says after a moment.

"I wallpapered her bedroom while she was still around. It's still up." My stomach squeezes uncomfortably, the way it always does whenever I think too hard about Grams. Four years gone and I still hear her voice in my head, outraged at the house's blank walls. "I wasn't sure if you knew she was gone."

Mel's eyes go pink around the rims. "My mom mentioned it. I

thought about coming home, but . . . I wasn't sure it was the right thing to do."

"I get it."

I was barely hanging on when Grams died—she'd been my parent, my person since I was fourteen. Having to see Melody on top of that might have driven me right over the edge.

"You know, the longer I'm here, the more I regret letting what happened between us keep me away," she says. "All that turmoil over something as silly as high school puppy love."

Jesus Christ, is that what we're calling it?

Maybe that's what it had been for her. But I don't think puppy love sticks for fourteen years. "What are you saying?"

"I'm saying that I really appreciated you listening to me vent yesterday. I thought it made sense to go our separate ways after camp, but there's really no reason we can't be friends."

Oh, fuck no. I didn't spend the last fourteen years of my life pining over this woman, only to get friend-zoned the second she's back in my life.

I wanted to tell her so badly yesterday. Explain to her how seismic my love for her has been since the moment I met her. In hindsight, I'm relieved she stopped me. Her ex showered her with his feelings right at the start of their relationship. And given that he turned out to be a love-bombing, gaslighting piece of shit, I realized a love confession a week into a ten-year reunion probably isn't the right move here.

I wouldn't trust it, either.

But her return to my life has an expiration date on it, if she's serious about moving back to the city. I can't waste a second of it playing coy. I need to show her that her experience with Connor had been a one-off. That she's been desired to a maddening degree since the moment I saw her. That she's as deserving of true love and a relationship built on care and respect as anyone else.

And, hopefully, she'll grow to want that with me.

"Point of clarification—"

She raises her eyebrows. "Unfortunately, I'm not accepting addendums at this time."

"*Point of clarification*," I say again. Her eyes narrow, but I catch a definite twitch to the corner of her mouth. "Whether you want to admit it or not, things between us have shifted in a no-turning-back direction." I push the hair off her shoulder, and there it is—the evidence that I'm right. That not-so-subtle catch in her breath when my fingertips drag along her skin. "So, unless you're telling me you go around dry humping all your friends, let me be very clear: You and me? We aren't friends. Not even close."

She breaks into a grin specifically designed to annoy me. "Not with that attitude, we're not."

That bratty smile dies right off her face the second I pick her up and drop her ass onto the counter, stepping between her open thighs. She's wearing a pair of leggings like she had on at camp, ones that hug her toned calves and bite-worthy thighs. If I didn't have a point to make, I'd be trying to figure out how to convince her to let me reach into them again, just to see if her pussy's as wet as it had been the last time I touched her.

The way her chest heaves tells me maybe she wouldn't let me stop at a touch. She's staring at the way I'm gripping the counter next to her thighs, desperately working to keep my hands off her.

Focus, you horny jackass.

"You want to sweep our baggage under the rug, Mel? You do that. But I'm not sweeping anything away. I did something to you that I intend to make up for. And I don't want to be your friend while I do it."

"Oh? And what is it you want?"

"You."

She frowns, stumped. "What do you mean, *me*? Like a friends-with-benefits thing?"

"There you go, using the word *friends* again. Believe me, I want the benefits. But I want the other stuff, too. I want you visiting me at work, me looking after you when you face off against chipmunks." I let out a breath. "Go out with me."

"What?"

"Let me take you out. Anywhere you want."

Her eyes turn to slits. "What is this? Some weird way of trying to make up for the fact that I had a thing for you before? Or is it what I said about not feeling desirable? Because I'm not interested in a pity date."

"It's not a pity date. And it's not about what happened ten years ago."

"Then what is it about?"

"It's about . . ." I search her face, like I'll be able to succinctly articulate the reasons I love this woman when I've failed at it for years. It's a long fucking list, but I shoot for the thing least likely to alarm her. "It's your scowl."

"My scowl?"

"Yeah. It's charming. And I like the way you keep me in line with that bratty mouth of yours. Plus, you smell nice."

"I . . . smell nice," she deadpans.

"Like vanilla and cinnamon." I play with a strand from her ponytail. "You smell so sweet for someone so bratty. I like it."

I think I've lost her. Mel's gaze travels to the far wall, trying to add up my words. "I'm not going out with you, Zac," she says slowly.

It stings, but I nod. "Because you're fresh out of a relationship."

"That. And also, because . . . Look, I swear I'm not trying to be a bitch when I say this, but—"

"Just so you're aware, it's not required that you preface your feelings by calling yourself names. It's not your job to keep my ego intact, least of all, by minimizing the way you feel."

She rolls her lip between her teeth. "Then I'll preface it with this:

I swear I'm not trying to hurt your feelings when I say this, but I meant what I said at camp. I moved on. I'm not going out with you."

It doesn't hurt any less hearing that the second time. "Yet. You're not going out with me *yet*." I want to *devour* that scowl. "Look, that night in your room? I hurt you by leaving. I broke your trust by not coming back. It wasn't what you deserved, nor were the years of silence after, and I'm going to make it up to you."

"That's so unnecessary." Melody's skeptical gaze drifts to the kitchen doorway, like she's considering making a run for it. At least she hasn't told me to go fuck myself. "We need some sleep. We can pick this up when we're both thinking clearly."

I've never had a clearer thought in my life.

But it's also clear I'm not winning this battle tonight, so instead I say, "Then let's get you to bed."

~

I'll be honest, here.

This isn't how I ever pictured having Melody Woods sleep over for the first time. She's in the adjoining bathroom now, and it feels like I should be lighting candles around the entire perimeter of my room, sprinkling rose petals everywhere.

A little mood lighting. A little mood music, maybe. But no, that would definitely freak her the fuck out.

I put fresh sheets on the bed yesterday, thank God, but I hustle to the basket of unfolded laundry, shove it into the closet. Then double back with an armful of clothes I discarded after my shower and throw those in the closet, too.

There. Good enou—

I rush to the bed, fluff the pillows for good measure. Okay, this is fine. Absolutely fine.

Problem number two: How do you dress for bed when you're on

a mission to break a brutal cycle of insomnia with the woman you're in love with, who recently let you worship her body?

Do I leave on my sweats and T-shirt? Go for a simple boxer-brief thing?

The bathroom door squeals open. I wheel around to find Mel dressed in a full, oversized sweatsuit I think I recognize as Parker's. Like she's determined to cover every bit of skin in cotton armor.

Well, that answers that question.

"You're sending very clear signals," I tell her. "Socks too, huh?"

"What's wrong with wearing socks to bed?"

My feet are moving, and I'm aching to touch her just as badly as if she came out wearing nothing. Despite the evident *we're not fucking tonight* outfit, her lips rub together as she watches me come closer, stop just short of her. Fuck, it takes everything in me not to pull her close, pick her up, bury my face in her hair. Drop to my knees and beg her to let me have a taste of her. Just a tiny one, a small lick.

I bet she's the sweetest thing.

"Which side of the bed do you want?" I ask instead.

Mel bites her lip. "We were spooning the last time we slept."

Oh, Jesus. Is it too late to rub one out before we do this? "Middle of the bed it is."

There are a few seconds of awkward shuffling as we settle in bed and she wrestles with her oversized sweatshirt when it twists around her. A moment later, Mel sits up with a huff.

"Why are you a furnace?" She glares at me in accusation.

"Yeah, I'm the problem here. It can't possibly be the snowsuit you're wearing to bed."

"I was trying to keep things PG-13."

She rips the sweatshirt off then smacks me in the shoulder when I bark out a laugh at the sight of the long-sleeve shirt she's wearing underneath. She strips off her socks and throws them over the edge of the bed.

Then, with an aggrieved sigh, she drops onto her back and shimmies around under the covers. She pulls her sweatpants out from underneath and throws those overboard, too. I peek under the sheets. She's wearing a pair of polka-dotted, silky-looking shorts.

"I was expecting long underwear."

"I couldn't find any!" she says keenly. "I tried to steal a pair from Parker, but then he caught me poking around his room and I had to pretend to offer to do his laundry, which of course he agreed to. I spent the night washing my brother's underwear!"

"Okay, this is all a little insulting. Did you expect me to jump you or something?" She gives me a scathing look and shuffles closer, back under my arm. "*Oh.* Oh, I get it now. I was thinking you were wearing an armor. It was a straitjacket, wasn't it? You're the one who can't control yourself."

"Shut up," she grumbles.

"Don't worry, I trust you with my virtue." I kill the light and then shift her so that she backs into my front. "Though if you feel your hands start to wander in the night, just go with it. See where it takes you."

I gather up her hair, gently untucking the strands caught underneath her and twisting it all up on the pillow so that I don't accidentally roll over it in the night.

It's so dark this far out of town that I don't have curtains on the windows. The moonlight filters into the room, lighting up her wary eyes as she peers over her shoulder.

"You're insufferably nice sometimes, you know that?"

"You're welcome. Now, admit you were psychologically cueing yourself not to get handsy with me."

"You just ruined it." She arches her back, ass nestling into my crotch as she nuzzles the pillow we're sharing.

Uh . . .

I'm sorry, but . . .

"Really, Zac?" she hisses, jerking away from my cock, which is very much getting the wrong idea.

"I—fuck. You were grinding your ass into me—"

"It was an accident—*Zac*!"

"Okay, *that* was absolutely an accident," I say quickly, ripping my hand from where it landed on her breast as I tried to pull her closer.

She huffs, rolling onto her back.

"*Fucking hell*, Melody—"

"No—I didn't mean—"

"You just cupped my dick."

"I didn't mean to. I swear."

"Hands where I can see 'em, Woods." I fish them out from under the covers and tug them over her head. I end up hovered over her in the process, and if my dick was confused before, he's downright accusing us of shenanigans now.

Mel stares back with parted lips. My eyes trail down the curve of her neck, taking in the rapid rise and fall of her chest.

Bless that moonlight. Bless that moonlight and the way her nipples are visibly hard under her shirt.

"I can't stop thinking about it," she confesses. She doesn't need to say what. That tussle in the woods is on both our minds. "And you were totally wrong."

"What about?"

"This sleep thing. Here I am in your bed, and I don't feel the least bit tired."

"Just so you know"—I don't mean for it to happen, but my voice has definitely dropped to a sex octave—"I'm definitely open to . . . fucking hell, I'll do whatever you want, Mel."

My words hang in the air, almost like a dare.

She wets her lips, leaving them all shiny, and that's my only point of focus now. "I wouldn't want anyone to know. Brooks, Summer. My brother. And I wouldn't be your plaything."

"I'll be *your* plaything. I'd wear the title like a badge of honor and eat you out on command."

For a while, it's only the sound of our breaths, short and tight, bordering on desperate. My cock is painfully hard and digging into her thigh. Grams really must have raised me right because somehow, I manage to resist the urge to grind into her. And then Mel spreads her fingers so that mine thread between hers.

Oh, fuck yeah.

I roll, taking her with me so that she lands on top of me. It took giving her the control that day in the woods to get her comfortable, to make her let go. And maybe it's not the way I usually like to play it in bed, but I'll give this woman whatever she needs to trust me again.

She tips her head, long hair swinging sinfully over her shoulder. A smirk plays at her lips. "What exactly do you expect me to do up here, Zac?"

"Take. Do everything to me or don't give me anything at all. It's enough to hear you moan again. To hear you call my name as you come."

"That doesn't seem very fair." Her voice is dripping with sex. Wrapping me more tightly around her finger like I haven't already spent the past fourteen years twisted around it. She toys with the hem of my T-shirt. "Take this off."

Fuck. I can't. I won't risk letting her see me like that. Not yet, anyway. Not until she lets me properly explain why I left her that night.

"Shirt stays on tonight."

Mel gives me a funny look, but her hands run through my hair and I'm breathing so fucking hard. Her own shirt is so fitted her nipples are straining underneath. I reach for her, grazing her nipples with my thumbs. Then change my mind and let my hands crawl underneath the fabric, watching her breath hitch as they make their way higher and higher, until I can touch her nipples, pinch them skin-to-skin. Fuck, I hope I get to put my mouth on them this time.

Mel's head falls forward as I play with her tits. She gives me an appreciative little hum, shifts around, sits her pussy right over my cock. Those shorts are so flimsy she feels unbelievably warm even through my sweats. It doesn't get any better than this: Mel's eyes on mine, hair cascading everywhere, tits pressing into my palms.

I'm greedy as fuck tonight. I leave a hand under her shirt, but the other finds her thigh, sweeps up and back to take a handful of her insane ass as she rolls her hips.

Holy shit, I think I'm about to fuck Melody Woods. I have no idea how I got this lucky.

"You're so fucking big. So hard," she murmurs, dipping to kiss my neck, sliding up and down my cock. "I don't know how to fit you inside me, but I can't wait to try."

Fuuuck.

"I'll fit you so good, Mel. You and me, we were made for each other. You'll see."

Her hair is creating a gorgeous, vanilla-scented curtain around us. Melody sways her hips, drags her pussy along me and wrenches a desperate moan from my throat.

"Touch me," she murmurs into my neck.

My hand leaves her ass and she gasps when I find her soaking through her panties. I run a line over her pussy with my knuckles, once, twice, then slip underneath the fabric.

My impatient girl hitches her hips and my fingers are inside her. She's whimpering in my ear, squirming into my hand and I'll never get enough of this. She's setting her own pace, fucking my fingers and kissing my neck and it is so. Fucking. Hot.

"You like this?" I ask when her fingers twist in my hair.

"Yes," she admits. But she reaches down, pulls my hand away. "And no. It's not how I want to come tonight."

And then she brings my hand up, lays my glistening fingers against my mouth and I think I'm asleep. I'm dreaming this.

That's it, right?

Any minute I'll wake up and I'll be alone. Those fingers won't be there for my tongue the way they are now, won't taste this fucking perfect as I lick her off them.

And Mel won't be straddling me, bending, and she sure as shit won't actually be darting out her tongue to help me lick clean my fingers with a sinful glimmer in her eye. Fucking fuck.

Our tongues graze together from opposite sides of my fingers and I hope I never wake up. When we finish, I take a fistful of her hair, tug enough to hear her moan.

"I don't know why I ever thought you'd go shy on me the day we finally fucked." I twist her head to one side to kiss her neck. "You're a dirty fucking girl, aren't you?"

With a mind-numbingly sexy laugh, she dips to kiss my jaw. I cup her cheek and pull her up, needing her mouth. Her kisses are truly something else, and I've been dreaming of having my lips on hers since the second our last kiss ended. But the moment I lift my chin, she jerks away.

"No kissing," she tells me, backing off when I try to pull her closer. What?

I squint at her through the dark. "We've kissed already."

"We shouldn't have. We're just fucking, okay? Kissing makes it personal."

"No kissing?" I ask, just to make sure. She shakes her head. It fucking hurts, but her denial injects me with a much-needed dose of good sense. "Then we're not doing this."

I lift and drop her next to me, sitting up and adjusting the front of my sweats. I'm fucking aching. Struggling. About to burst into flames. My cock is painfully hard and demanding the very thing I was on the verge of getting.

But I'm an idiot, getting swept up in a longtime fantasy and almost failing to see things for what they are. Me and her? It's as personal as it gets. Sneaking around our friends is one thing, but having her only to see her move on with someone else someday? It would crush me.

When you've been desperately in love with someone for fourteen years, a fling isn't good enough. I want to be her last, and I need her to be mine.

She's still panting but looking disoriented. "You don't want to sleep together? You said all those things the last time we . . ."

"Trust me when I say it has nothing to do with want. But I need a few things to fall into place first."

And because I can't just leave it like that—with there being any doubt that I'm dying to have her—I bury my face into the crook of her neck and lay kisses along her soft skin. From this close, I can feel the accelerated pace of her heart. I hope she can feel mine.

"You're so fucking sexy, Clover. This is the second hardest thing I've ever had to do in my life."

She inches away and I can practically see her defenses reassemble, brick by brick, when she crawls off the bed and starts sorting through her backpack.

"You don't believe me," I tell her. "You don't believe I want you."

"It doesn't matter."

"It does to me, and that's why we can't do this. I want you to trust me. I want to earn you."

"It's fine, Zac. It was a bad idea, anyway." She frowns at her bag. "You have to be kidding me."

"What is it?"

"I specifically remember putting my nightstand lip balm in here." She screws up her face. "Or maybe it was my desk lip balm? I can't keep track of them all."

She seems to be in a constant game of hide-and-seek with these lip balms. I don't understand it. Giving up, Mel tosses her bag to the ground and crawls back into bed. I'm relieved that she doesn't make an effort to create an abnormal amount of space between us.

I gather up that gorgeous hair again, move it safely out of the way, and hold her to me. "Are you angry?"

"Of course not." Her cheek smooths over my chest. "I'm confused as hell, but you're allowed to say no to sex. Let's just sleep, okay?"

The moment she settles, the edges of sleep come for me. If this theory works, if I can really have a reason to keep her here every night, I might be able to pull this off.

Win her over. Make her fall for me again.

"Zac? What was the hardest?" I blink to find her looking up at me, eyes already heavy with sleep. "If that was the second hardest thing you've ever had to do, what was the hardest?"

I pull her closer, kissing the top of her head. My cynical Melody, all sharp on the outside but soft as velvet on the inside. A hopeful at heart, and I'm so damn grateful for it. I won't let her down this time.

"Leaving you that night, Mel. That was the hardest thing I've ever done. I still don't know how I managed it."

Her moonlit eyes linger on me for one long second. And then she tucks her chin and succumbs to sleep.

Chapter 15

Melody

The morning sun blinds me the moment I open my eyes, and I immediately snap them shut.

Despite how strange this bed feels with its flat pillows and flannel sheets—flannel sheets in the summer, God help this man—I feel the kind of well-rested I haven't been in over a week. In over a month, actually. Since the night Connor sat me down to inform me we were breaking up.

For the first time since then, I feel energized. I feel like something *good* has happened to me. I got my life back, or control over it, at least. Sure, it's a whole mess right now. My job doesn't pay enough, and I'm living with my brother. I made a pretty good fool of myself last night, making moves on a man I don't even trust to begin with.

But it's my mess. Mine. I no longer have some manipulative asshole telling me what to do and disguising it as love.

Fuck Connor. Fuck letting myself get swept into a man's mind games. I can get my life back on track.

I throw off the covers and groggily stumble into the bathroom to freshen up. Trip out of the bedroom, following the smell of coffee to the kitchen. The entire place is as bright as Zac's bedroom, completely curtainless.

I poke around the kitchen until I find where Zac keeps his mugs. I wonder if . . .

I heave myself up on the counter to peer deep into the shelves, looking for hints of shiny yellow among the monotone mugs, and sit back on my heels in disappointment when I don't find it.

"It's drying by the sink."

Zac leans in the doorway of the sliding doors leading to the back porch. He's already dressed in a pair of dark jeans and a fitted polo with the UOB Huskies logo embroidered on the sleeve. The shirt surely wasn't intended to look like that. I mean, there's no way a college purposely designed a shirt that makes their head coach look like he belongs on stage with Chippendales, rather than shouting at uncooperative players from the sideline.

"What is?" I have no idea what we're talking about anymore.

Eyes on mine, Zac motions to the sink with the hand not holding a cup of coffee. With the fingers that found their way inside me just a few hours ago. I've never gone to sleep feeling so hard up and confused by the abrupt shift in my life. Last night was shaping up to be the hottest of my entire existence, until his rejection.

It stung, but I refuse to let it get to me the way it did ten years ago. I force my mind off it every time the humiliation seeps in. Try to tell myself something about it being his loss.

"Your mug," Zac says. "I just gave it a wash. It's been out of commission a long time." Mug. Right.

I hop off the counter, shaking out my hair so that it lies in front of my shoulders, obstructing my enthusiastic nipples from view. I pluck the mug off the drying mat, admiring the yellow polka-dots covering its surface. Parker and I had our own mugs at Grams's old house. I haven't thought about this thing in years, but it's intensely satisfying that someone felt it worth saving.

I fill the mug nearly to the brim with coffee and use the hem of my shirt to wipe the counter after my sloppy pour.

"What are the odds you have—"

"Top shelf in the fridge."

With a suspicious look over my shoulder, I wrench open the fridge. "Why do you have lactose-free cinnamon creamer?"

"Because I woke up early and went into town for lactose-free cinnamon creamer. I also made breakfast." He drops his mug on the counter and reaches into the oven, resurfacing with a plate stacked with blueberry waffles.

By the smell of it, my favorite blueberry waffles. The ones Grams would make every time Parker and I would stay overnight.

I stare at the plate, dumbfounded. I can't tell which part gets me more. That he remembers these tiny, nothing details from school, or that he actually bothered to wake up early enough to do all this in the first place.

Most importantly . . . *why* did he do all this? What the hell does he get out of it?

"I took a gamble that you still liked all this." Zac looks a little uncertain now. "I also got you plain creamer in case you prefer that now. And eggs, bacon, and all that if you want me to make something different."

I eye him over my mug, taking a deep sip of coffee. Still clutching his plate, Zac opens a cabinet by the fridge and pulls out a few boxes of cereal. "I got this, too. Wasn't sure if you'd like the healthier kind or the stuff packed with sugar, so there's a bit of everything."

I hum. Reach for the waffle at the top of his stack. "Anyone ever tell you that you're annoyingly thoughtful?"

His eyes crinkle up in a smile.

I take a bite of my waffle. Delicious. "Why are you waking up early, anyway? Did you not get to sleep?"

"I slept. I'd ask how you did, but I got a good earful of your snoring when I woke up and that's probably answer enough."

"I don't snore."

"You do snore, and it's adorable."

I follow Zac out onto the porch, pausing when I catch sight of the rolling green lawn that drops off into a sandy beach.

What the hell?

It's not enough that this house is absurdly large. The freaking place sits on the water.

I guess I shouldn't be surprised. I've been around football long enough to have a sense of what college football coaches can bring in. But seeing all this attached to Zac is a shock to the system. In some ways, all I see when I look at him is the kid I used to know. But it's a man now who sets the plate of waffles down on a large glass table, next to a heavy binder with *UOB Huskies Football* emblazoned on the front.

"What's with this house?"

Zac looks up from his binder. "You don't like it?"

I stare at the massive porch that wraps around the corner of the stone house. A few feet away from the table where Zac sits is the sweetest-looking porch swing, hanging from the roof overhang, facing the bay. Down by the water, near the tree-lined edge of the property, a wooden bench sits in the middle of a patch of flowers. Daisies?

I've never set foot here before. But it feels strangely familiar.

When I look back, Zac is still intent on me. As though he'd consider tearing it all down, starting from scratch, if I hated it.

"It's beautiful," I say at last. "Was it always here?"

He shakes his head without taking his eyes off me. "It was just land when I bought it. You like it?"

"I love it." I rub my lips together, trying to decipher the prickle of awareness at the back of my neck. I move to sit in the chair next to Zac's. "It's just that . . . I don't know. It feels so familiar somehow. How long have you lived here?"

Zac pulls his binder closer and throws it open to a page he'd been holding with a pad of yellow legal paper. It might be the sun that's beating down on us, but I think his cheeks are a little flushed.

"Four years."

I wouldn't have been surprised if he said he only moved in last week, aside from the missing cardboard boxes. The interior is just furniture. Nothing on the walls, not even a speck of color, like he moved in and forgot to make the place his own.

"What time do you have to head to work?" I ask when he doesn't say anything more.

"Not for a couple hours. But I thought I'd get a head start on figuring out how the hell I'm going to win a game this season."

I lean in to get a look at the binder. It's a playbook, same as he was studying back at the campsite. "What do you have so far?"

"You mean, how do I plan to miraculously coach the team to its first win in two seasons?" He picks a blueberry out of a waffle. "Right now, the plan involves making Brooks shave his facial hair and enroll as a student, and praying no one notices there's a guy pushing thirty on the field."

A burst of laughter escapes me, and Zac gives me a look of such pure affection, I feel it down to my toes.

"Speaking of Brooks." I fiddle with the handle of my coffee mug. "I need to ask you a favor."

"Anything."

I set down my coffee, bracing myself for an argument. But this version of me, the one who's taking charge of her life? She's going to set clear boundaries and stick to them.

"If we have to do this, if we have to be together to get any kind of sleep, then I don't want anyone knowing about it. Least of all Parker."

"What does that mean?"

"It means we pretend we don't see each other outside the friend group. No one finds out about us, okay?"

Zac stares. "You can't be serious—I thought you wanted to hide hooking up. Not everything else."

"I'm perfectly serious. I don't want to deal with the questions. Besides, I'm not sure Parker would take too kindly to the idea that I'm hooking up with his best friend."

"We're *not* hooking up."

"As if he'd really believe that. And not that I need his permission, but I don't want to start something with him over nothing." I study the glass tabletop. "Maybe he'd take it well—"

"Trust me, he wouldn't." Zac's binder falls shut with a snap. "Luckily, I don't give a shit what Parker thinks."

I rear away at the sudden edge in his voice, trying to remember if Parker mentioned a falling out. But I'd been very careful about avoiding the topic of Zac over the years, and there's a real chance I'd have descended into a fugue state at the simple mention of his name.

"Did something happen between you two?"

"Me and Parker are fine." Zac drains the rest of his coffee and drops the mug on the table.

I stare him down, knowing he's full of crap.

Zac glances my way. "I said we're fine, Mel. Let it go."

He seems to want to play this just as stubborn as I am. I'd be highly impressed with his perseverance if it wasn't getting in the way of the intel I'm after. There's no way I can bring this up with Parker without raising suspicion about why I'm suddenly asking about Zac.

When it's clear he's not willing to let me win this round, I sink back in my chair. "Then what do I have to do to get you to hide this sleeping arrangement?"

He doesn't miss a beat. "Let me kiss you again."

"Not happening."

"Then you'd better hope you're as sneaky as you think you are. I'm not hiding you, or our sleepovers."

"Then I'd better get out of here," I say innocently, jumping to my feet. "I need to sneak back into Parker's before he notices."

"Sit your ass back down, Melody." Zac catches the hem of my shirt and tugs me into my chair. "We both know you couldn't pay Parker to wake up this early. You have a couple hours, at least."

Stifling a laugh, I help myself to another blueberry waffle. "Maybe I want to get a head start on work. This feels like the kind of day made for changing my life."

"Oh yeah?"

"Yeah. I mean, look at all this." I gesture around us. "There's waffles. Not a cloud in the sky. I just had the best sleep I've had in ages. If today's not the day, when is?"

Zac hikes a knee up on his chair so that he can turn to face me fully. "Can't argue with that. How are you changing your life?"

"I haven't quite thought that far ahead yet. I've been wrapped up in Connor for so long, I barely know what I want anymore."

"You said before you wanted to move back to the city."

I nod, staring out at the shoreline at the end of his property. "I want to move back on my terms without help from a shitty boyfriend with a rich mommy. I want . . . I want everything I thought I had with my ex before it blew up in my face."

"Which is what?"

"I want my own place. A job that doesn't give me the Sunday scaries every single night of the week. I want to be in love. To start a family with a good person who doesn't get off on messing with my head. I just need to figure out how to get it all without completely losing myself in the process again."

"So make yourself a playbook."

I tear my gaze away from the bay. "What do you mean?"

Zac nods at his binder. "At work, we've got a playbook for every team we play against. Maybe we're playing football every time, but the opposing players change constantly. The field changes with every away game. We adapt our plan accordingly. Maybe life is like a game of football—"

"Okay, Forrest Gump—"

He jabs my thigh. "Let me finish. I'm saying you spent the past six years with that idiot Connor, playing your life a certain way. Maybe your goals are the same, but your circumstances have changed. You want to move to the city, have a family. You can still have all that. You just need a new playbook. A new way to get there."

Zac plucks up a pen sticking out of his binder. In big block letters, he writes *Clover's Playbook* across the top of his legal pad and slides it toward me, dropping the pen on top.

I eye the page. "You realize you're encouraging me to come up with a plan to meet a guy, right?"

"Nah, I'm just waiting for you to realize you can check that off your list at any time. You've got one sitting right here." I make a show of looking around, but he cuts off the beginnings of my comeback with a pointed, unamused look. "That would be me, you brat."

With a laugh, I pick up the pen, posing it under the words *Clover's Playbook*. "Well, play number one seems pretty cut and dry. If I want to move back to the city, I need a job that lets me afford it."

I write *1. Find a job that pays better* on the legal pad.

"Do you like what you do?"

"Absolutely hate it," I say, staring down at the page. "I was scrambling pretty hard to find a job after graduation. And in came Connor."

"Then add *a job that doesn't give me the Sunday scaries* to the list."

"May as well dream big." I suppress a smile, holding out the pen. "Maybe you should be writing this."

"Nuh-uh," he says with a shake of his head. "That's part of the deal, Clover. You've spent six years following someone else's playbook. This one's yours, all the way through."

My entire body tingles, starting in my chest, spreading slowly outward until I feel it in the tips of my toes.

Annoyingly, irritatingly, breathtakingly thoughtful.

I tear the page out and slide his notepad in front of him. "What's this for?"

"It's your playbook. You've got a job to keep. A few games to win as a start, but a championship sounds pretty good, too, doesn't it? You look miserable every single time you mention work. How are you going to get happy?"

He digs a second pen out of his binder, and after a quiet moment, bends to start writing. The red shoelace peeks out from under his sleeve, and not for the first time since finding it, I wonder why the hell he's still wearing it. A token of guilt maybe, given the pained way he talks about that night?

I turn back to my page and write:

1. Find a job that pays better (and doesn't give me the Sunday scaries)
2. Purge my life of everything that isn't mine
3. Cut all ties to my ex
4. Do something I've been dying to do, but never have
5. Never hold back how I feel (dirty thoughts excluded)

It's not exactly a master plan for success.

But maybe, just maybe, it's enough to get me in a happy place again.

Done with his own list, Zac leans over my page. He takes his time reading, as though committing it to memory, then bursts into laughter. I watch him ride it out, taking in the laugh lines around his eyes, the way his top and bottom lashes nearly tangle together with the force of his crinkled eyes.

"I might have to contest that last one."

He does a double take when he finds me staring. His smile grows an impossible inch, so wide and genuine. My insides scramble. My heart falls into my stomach, brain lodges itself in my chest.

I swallow, drop my gaze. Nod at his page, which he's folded in half. "Do I get to read yours?"

"Maybe one day." Zac buries the sheet of paper in the heart of his binder. "I like yours though. Think you'll start today?"

I peruse my list. "I'll start easy. Maybe purge my closet or something. The thought of wearing anything Connor bought me makes my skin crawl. I'll have to save up a few paychecks to afford to replace it all, but my parents left some old things of mine with Parker. It should be enough to tide me over." I pause, staring thoughtfully at the water. "Maybe I'll get a second job. Help speed up the process."

"You'd work two jobs?"

I shrug. "If that's what I need to do. And I might have an idea where to start."

Chapter 16

Melody

"Now, this might confuse you a touch. The serving trays go all the way over here. See? Over here."

I rub my lips together, trying to keep as straight a face as I can as Wynn Sheffield mimes transporting a round tray from a spot by the industrial latte machine on the counter where they used to be kept, to the tall stack of trays by the pass window.

"See? They go over here now."

I suck in my cheeks. "Aye, aye, Captain."

New tray location or not, the nostalgia slaps me in the face as Wynn passes me a worn black apron, equipped with a tiny spiral-bound notebook and pen. Paired with the black skirt and peach polo T-shirt with *Sheffield's Diner* across the back, it's exactly the same uniform he had me wearing when I served here over my high school summers.

Back then, I'd be at the colorful diner for family breakfast, even on my days off. Wynn himself would often sit with us, entertaining us with the latest town gossip, of which he was an avid follower.

"Now, do I need to train you on the coffee machine again, or do you think you have the hang of it?"

That's assuming I'd had the hang of it the last time I worked here. I eye the massive stainless-steel machine. This thing used to be my absolute nemesis. I could never figure out the damn milk frother, but I was safe as long as I stayed on drip coffee duty.

"On second thought, let me give you a refresher." Wynn watches me like he remembers exactly how many times I managed to detonate frothy milk bombs at this very counter.

"Probably for the best." I even pull out my notebook to take notes as he demonstrates.

See? I am the picture of dedication.

So determined to get my life on track that I now officially work two jobs, splitting my Mondays to Saturdays between Sheffield's and my regular gig.

"I'll give you as many breakfast and dinner shifts as I can," Wynn says over the whistle of the damned frother. "But seeing as you're only part time and temporary around here, you'll probably get stuck with the lunchtime crowd more than anything. I gotta make sure to keep my regular team happy. But I'm afraid it may mean lousier tips for you."

I stick my pen into my ponytail in a move that very much makes me feel sixteen again. "I'll take whatever you give me, Wynn. Honestly, I can't tell you how much I appreciate you helping me out."

"Never mind that. It's nice to see your face in town again." Wynn hands me the canister of freshly frothed milk. "Now, see this? There's still a tad bit of milk at the bottom, which you'd pour into the cup before you scoop in some of the froth. Think you can manage a couple of practice rounds?"

There's precisely no way I can manage anything when it comes to this machine. "And if I screw it up?"

Wynn pats my shoulder, moving for the line up at the register. "Then you try again. And if that doesn't work, I'm just a froth-dripping-from-your-hair holler away."

Ah. He really does remember.

"Okay, you merciless contraption," I mutter at the coffee machine, pouring fresh milk into the stainless-steel canister Wynn handed me. "You and I are getting along this time, if it's the last thing I do."

I poise the canister under the frother. Hit the button—

My eyeballs are greeted by the retina-singeing flash of a camera just as a stream of cold milk backfires on me. I slap off the machine.

Parker grins at me from the other side of the counter, turning his phone toward Summer, who gives a delighted laugh at an apparent photo of me with milk streaming down my face.

"Really, guys?"

"Melody Woods, server extraordinaire," Summer says, appraising me as I wipe off my cheek with my apron.

"Terrifying adults and kids alike with her many scowls." Parker taps at his phone. "I'm sending this picture to Mom. She didn't believe me when I told her you picked up some shifts here."

I smooth out my skirt, then pick up a bar rag to dab milk splatters off the counter. The Sheffield's lunch crowd is already dwindling, leaving most of the peach-colored bench seats empty.

"I don't blame her. If there's anything to make you feel like you've gone backward, it's having to default to the job you left at eighteen."

Parker pockets his phone. "You haven't gone backward, Mel."

"I'm back here, aren't I?" I make a show of looking around. "I also spent six years ignoring the red flags of my relationship. Spent the past few days purging my closet because *Boyfriend Dearest* paid for all my stuff, to the point where I'm now working two jobs just to afford my own place and a new wardrobe. Wearing my brother's oversized sweaters and too-small dresses our parents kept from my high school wardrobe in the meantime."

I suck in a breath, trying to center myself. I wish there was a roadmap for this stuff, color-coded with precise goal posts to get me through the next few months.

I'll get over being manipulated through a six-year relationship by then. Will forgive myself for falling for my ex's bullshit by then. Will trust myself not to make the same mistakes by then.

"You've got this, Mels," Summer says kindly. "You should really be proud of yourself, you know. You could easily be hiding out at home feeling sorry for yourself, but here you are putting in the work."

Oh, I've done plenty of greasy-haired wallowing. But I'll keep that secret shame where it belongs: between me and the four walls of Parker's guest bedroom.

And Zac. Zac and the way he let me cry very wallow-y tears into his shoulder in the middle of his workday.

Summer's right, anyway. Maybe I'm mourning the loss of my free time now that I only have one day off a week, but I am pretty proud of myself. Zac's playbook idea lit the kind of fire under my ass I haven't felt in a long time. Maybe ever.

"Between this and the Great Closet Purge of Oakwood Bay, you're really kicking ass," Parker agrees with Summer. "Before you know it, you'll be dating again."

Yeah, that would be a resounding *hell fucking no*. I won't be jumping into anything until I have my life entirely in order. Lessons have been learned over the course of this breakup, thanks very much.

Given the look on Parker's face, I seem to do a poor job of hiding my revulsion. "Come on, let me set you up with someone," he insists. "I'll use our special twin powers and find you the love of your life, you'll see."

Over by the register, Wynn calls out for a tray of waters and coffees that I dutifully start pouring.

"I don't know, Park. If the love of my life lives here, wouldn't I have met him by now? This town doesn't exactly have influxes of newcomers our age. I know everyone there is to know, and none of them ever showed interest when I lived here."

Parker waves away my words as I pass Wynn his tray of drinks.

"That was because of the Hands-Off Melody Woods Rule. Things are different now."

Summer frowns at my brother. "The what rule?"

"The Hands-Off Melody Woods Rule," he says again, picking at a piece of lint on his shirt. "To preface this, I'm not at all proud of it. But I did spread it around with the athletes at school that they weren't allowed to go near you."

Summer and I exchange a look. "Why the hell would you do that?"

"Because I was also an athlete. I had a firsthand look at the way they'd talk about girls in the locker room. At the things they'd get up to at parties, the way they'd fuck with their heads. I didn't want that for you."

You have got to be kidding me. It's all dancing through my mind. A whole freaking slew of high school boys who'd never look me in the eye, even when I'd say hello.

"You do realize Summer and I exclusively hung around athletes because of you and Zac, right?"

Parker blinks. "What's your point?"

"My point, you absolute jerk, is that I was single until I made it to college. No wonder no one came near me. I always thought there was something wrong with me!"

Parker's face falls, and he rubs the top of his head thoughtfully, rumpling his hair in the process. "Shit. I thought maybe you didn't want to date."

I try to whip him with my bar rag, but with a whole counter between us, it's not even close. "I went to prom alone! I almost skipped it—I cried for days leading up to it!"

"Is this awkward for anyone else?" Summer mutters, looking around as though we have a full audience.

"You ended up having fun at prom!" Parker says defensively. "Zac didn't have a date, either. You looked like you were having a good time!"

He's not wrong, to be fair. The lead-up sucked hard. I'd been the only one out of our friends not to get asked. But then Zac's date fell through at the last minute and the entire night ended up being an incredibly fun friend-date along with Parker, Summer, and their dates.

But I'm not letting Parker off the hook that easily.

"I was—*I was a virgin until Connor*!" I hiss as Wynn passes Parker on his way behind the counter. He drags his feet and surveys our scene with interest befitting a gossip at heart.

"Yup, definitely awkward," Summer says under her breath.

"So? You could be a virgin today and there wouldn't be anything wrong with it."

I try again with the bar rag. "That's not the point, Parker. None of that was my choice. You turned me into a pariah with all the guys I ever interacted with."

"I said I'm not proud of it!" he says, hands held out in surrender and cheeks crimson red. "Fuck, Mels, I'm sorry. Let me make it up to you. I'll set you up with someone—"

"Oh, I think you've done more than enough—"

"I might be able to help. I came by Parker's place to find you, Mels," Summer pipes in. She motions to her hair, the honey strands she showed off when she popped by Parker's just yesterday. They hang above her shoulders in signature beachy waves, from all the time she spends surfing in the ocean. "As you can see, I'm all about shaking things up these days. Any bit helps when you're in a dating rut like mine, and based on the scene in your bedroom, it looks like we're on the same page."

I turn my glare away from Parker, who's suddenly become engrossed with the glass pastry display and the assortment of donuts behind it. "I assume you're referring to the clothing explosion littering my bedroom floor?"

"Are you replacing all of it?"

"Once I can properly afford to. I'm trying to sell it all, but I'll be saving everything for a deposit on an eventual apartment. The second job is supposed to help."

Summer claps her hands together. "Well, it never hurts to check out what's out there, and I'm currently in the market for a shopping buddy. I have my eye on this guy I met at work the other day. He's quite a bit younger, but he seems really promising."

Like most residents of Oakwood, Summer works at the college, in the same athletic rehab center as Parker.

"Aw, I'm honored, Sum," Parker says, tucking her under his arm. "But you know I have a strict policy against messing around within the friend group."

Shit.

I freeze in the act of adjusting my ponytail, and my hair tumbles out of my grip, spilling over my face.

Zac was right. There's really no chance of Parker taking it well that we've been having sleepovers. It's why, for the past couple of days, I've made sure to sneak out of the apartment after Parker goes to bed. I down Zac's waffle breakfast at warp speed to sneak back into the apartment before my brother gets up. It's a shame, actually. I could get used to the mornings on Zac's porch, drinking coffee while staring at the water, listening to him talk game strategy. But at least I can avoid Parker's barrage of questions.

I shove the hair off my face. "Anyway," I say loudly. "I'm assuming I'm the shopping buddy in question, Sum?"

"Well, that's just rude," Parker says. "What if she came here to ask me?"

"Yeah . . ." Summer says slowly. "I'm not inclined to take advice from the guy who owns a collection of Hawaiian shirts."

"I wear them ironically."

"No, you don't," we counter in unison.

"Fine," he says, crossing his arms. "Fine, I see how it is. Melody comes home and suddenly I'm the unfavorable Woods twin."

Summer gives him a sweet smile. "That would assume you were at some point favorable."

"Get out of here, the both of you. I refuse to take this kind of abuse at Sheffield's, of all places," Parker says, jabbing a thumb over his shoulder.

I grimace at Parker. "My shift ends at four."

"Perfect, I'll wait for you." Summer plucks a menu card from a stand by the register. "I'll just have a late lunch."

"Fine, then I'll go," Parker grumbles. "But if you happen to come across an interesting Hawaiian shirt while you're out shopping, I will accept it as penance."

Chapter 17

Melody

By shopping, Summer meant visiting one of the few storefronts along the colorful main strip of Oakwood Bay that doesn't cater to the surrounding fishing towns. The front door of Callie's Shop chimes to announce our arrival, and I trail inside after Summer.

"Summer Prescott, don't tell me this self-imposed shopping ban of yours is called off already," a loud voice calls from somewhere around the register.

The years have aged Callie beautifully. She looks over from the counter with silvery gray hair, ends tickling her shoulders. Her face is sun-kissed from summer, and I wonder if she and her wife still own that sailboat they used to take me and Parker on as kids whenever they babysat for my parents.

Summer grins, completely unashamed. As athletic as she is, with her job and her love of surfing, no one can rival Summer's heel collection. "Aren't you of all people supposed to celebrate my addiction, Cal? How have the books been since I stopped coming by?"

I follow Summer past the front display table, laden with marked-down summer clothes surrounded by racks of wooly fall sweaters and trousers.

"Books have been fine, smart-ass," Callie replies dryly. "This ban of yours only lasted five days . . . Well, well, well. If it isn't Melody Woods, come back from the dead. A little birdy told me you were in town."

Callie's gaze has zeroed in on me over Summer's shoulder. I step out from behind her, tucking my hands into the pockets of Parker's too big sweater. "The dead? That's a little dramatic, no?"

Callie regards me sternly from over her dark-rimmed glasses. "Is it, now? Might've been dead for all I knew, after all these years. I never saw one of you without the other, and suddenly it was just this one." She nods at Summer, who's strayed to a clothing rack at the back of the shop. "Would've taken it personally if I hadn't compared notes with Wynn over at the diner. But he claimed he hadn't seen you, either."

"You really think I'd have the guts to show my face on this street without coming to see you?"

Callie snorts and breaks into a wide smile, rounding the counter with her arms thrown out. I meet her halfway and she swallows me up in a warm hug, patting my back so heartily my chin bounces off her shoulder.

"How're your parents, huh? Haven't seen them since they high-tailed it out of here. Are they still enjoying their travels?"

"Loving it. They're somewhere in the south right now," I tell her when she lets me pull away. "I actually moved back for a couple of months. I'm living with Parker next door."

"So I was told. Here's hoping that curbs the train of pretty tourists he has coming in and out of there. Well, I won't hold up your shopping." She eyes my sweatsuit. "Looks like you need it, love. You couldn't pay me to hide a figure like that under all those layers."

"Actually, we're here for Summer. She has a date on Friday."

"We're here for you, too," Summer calls with a stack of clothes already piled high in her arms. "We're both shaking things up, Callie. She just got dumped by a real piece of work."

Callie nods. "That explains it, then. Pick out whatever you want. It's on me today."

"Absolutely not—"

"Call it a welcome home gift from your old sitter."

I'm about to protest some more, but the argument dies in my throat as I'm overcome by the desire to create more separation from Connor. Saving up enough for a new wardrobe will take me weeks, and the deposit on an apartment should be my priority anyway.

"Are you sure?" I ask Callie.

"Completely sure."

My sigh is pure relief. "Callie, thank you. You have no idea how much I need this."

"Of course, love. And make sure you check on that rack over by the door. There's a green dress somewhere in there I'd say I brought in just for you, if I'd known you were coming in more than a couple of days ago."

I drift toward the rack in question, immediately finding the fitted green dress she must mean. Connor would have *despised* a dress like this.

"How did you know I was coming a couple days ago, Cal?" I ask absently, pulling out a dress in my size.

"Never you mind," Callie says, just as her phone starts ringing. "Help yourselves to the dressing rooms when you're ready, ladies."

~

"Oh my God, Summer."

In the dressing room next door, I hear the vague sounds of Summer trying on her own loot. She probably can't hear me whisper over these high dressing room walls, and I don't really mean her to.

I forgot how much fun it is to shop for myself, how utterly flattering the lighting in dressing rooms can be, how you're suddenly imagining all the places you'd go wearing your new clothes. But Summer had thrown a pair of cut-off denim shorts into my pile of clothes, and . . .

They're ridiculous.

Cut so short, the insides of the front pockets peek out from under the rough edges of denim. I'm practically wearing denim panties. I study myself in the mirror, turning around to get a look at the back.

They do my legs justice, I'll give them that. I feel tall and leggy in a way I absolutely am not. And they really do something spectacular to my ass, if I let myself get a little conceited.

Connor would have hated them. It's a tick in favor of the shorts, really.

I dig my phone out from under the pile of clothes and snap a photo of my reflection. Then stare at it like I expect it to reveal a different view of myself closer to the version I'm more accustomed to. Modest and prim, the way Connor would dress me. But it doesn't.

I feel . . . sexy. Strangely confident.

On a total whim I'll hate myself for in a minute, I open up a text thread and send the photo before I can think better of it.

MELODY: Is this too cliché of a rebound outfit?

The shorts are barely down my thighs before my phone chimes. I open the text to see Zac has replied with a photo of Brooks, who looks mid-angry shout with his arms thrown out, face contorted.

Why the hell would he send me a picture of Brooks?

I zoom in, confused, only to notice that the front of his white T-shirt is splattered with brown droplets. Before I can make sense of it, Zac's name flashes across my screen.

"Whatever happened to a simple *you look great*?" I say, picking up the call. "I'd even have settled for a respectful *take that off, you're embarrassing yourself*."

"I just sent you the biggest compliment I could have paid you, Clover," Zac says, and in the background I hear the sound of a whistle going off. He must be running a practice. "I made the mistake of opening that picture with a sip of coffee in my mouth. Spat it out so hard Brooks won't even look at me."

I stifle a laugh, bending to remove the shorts. "I'm sorry. That was probably incredibly inappropriate to send you at work. At all, really."

"I'm going to pretend you didn't just apologize for giving me the best gift I've received in years. You are so fucking hot. I'm getting this picture blown-up and framed at the first opportunity." I can hear him moving, the sounds of activity on the field dimming as he goes. "How's shopping?"

I hold the phone between my ear and shoulder, freeing my hand to take the green dress off its hanger. "How'd you know I went shopping?"

"You just sent me a picture of yourself in a changing room."

"Right. Dumb question." I shimmy into the dress, letting the fabric stretch over me. "It's going great, actually. I found some really good stuff."

"I hope to God that means you're buying the shorts."

"They're in the *maybe* pile. Hold on a sec."

I put the phone down long enough to twist around and zip the dress. It's skin tight, cutting off at mid-thigh. I snap another picture of myself and fire it off, ignoring the near-instant hit of embarrassment that causes a rush of heat to my cheeks.

What the hell are you doing, you sad, desperate—

"Fucking hell," I hear Zac mumble. He's not speaking into the phone. It must have picked up his voice as he looks at the photo. "Fucking killing me."

Even from afar, I hear his words come out thick, loaded as hell, and I watch in the mirror as goose bumps erupt over my skin. I drag my fingers across the slippery fabric covering my stomach, feeling so heated it's like he's wedged in this tiny dressing room with me, fucking me with his eyes.

"What do you think?" I ask when he still hasn't said anything directly to me.

He clears his throat, and it sounds like he has the phone to his ear again. "You first. Do you like it?"

I stare at my reflection, running a hand up and down the fabric. The dress looks like it's been painted on.

"I do, I think." I lean against the wall of the dressing room. "Connor never would have gone for it. God, I feel like I'm fourteen again, sneaking racy outfits into my backpack behind my mom's back so that I could change on the bus ride to school."

"I remember that. A bunch of you girls did it." There's a smile in his voice. "You'd make me shield you on the bus so that no one could see what you were doing. Parker did the same for Summer."

I love that he remembers. That I'm not alone in greedily hoarding memories of him, and the way he made me feel back then—worthwhile, and tingly from head to toe whenever he'd look at me.

Not so different from how I feel now. "Did you ever peek over your shoulder?"

"Trust me, I really wanted to. You look insane in that dress, Melody. It was meant for you. But for the record, you could walk around in a tarp and I'd still ogle the hell out of you. As long as you're happy wearing it."

I catch my reflection in the mirror. I look ridiculous, and it has nothing to do with the dress. It's the pink cheeks, bright eyes. The silliest, out-of-control grin on my face. God, he's just as charming as he always was. I feel myself falling into the trap that is Zac Porter like it's ten years ago.

It's insane. I've lived since then. Experienced, learned lessons. Connor was a charmer, too, and look how that turned out.

More than once in the past few days, I've had to remind myself to pump the brakes, to keep myself from losing my head over sweet smiles and platitudes. The next time I fall for a man, it'll take a whole lot more than that.

I turn from the mirror. "Okay, I think you'd better start charging me for these therapy sessions."

"Does that mean you're getting the dress?"

"I'm getting the dress," I confirm, shimmying out of it.

I almost jump out of my skin at the sound of a knock at my dressing room door. "Mels?" Summer calls from its other side. "Who are you talking to in there?" Shit.

"No one," I call. "I'm talking to myself. I'll be out in a second."

"Ouch—did you just *no one* me?" Zac says in my ear.

"No—"

"You did," he says with a laugh. "You totally just *no one*'d me to Summer."

I purse my lips, trying not to laugh. "What was that? Zac, I think I'm losing you. You're cutting out—bad reception in this dressing room—"

Zac laughs, and having the warm sound of it pouring straight into my eardrum triples its effect. My chest fills up with something sweet and warm. A flurry of goose bumps bursts over my skin.

"See you tonight, Clover."

Chapter 18

Zac

"You have to admit it's clear you have a problem here. You've got an NFL-caliber quarterback and still can't manage to win a game."

What a dick.

It's bad enough having to sit through these press conferences outside of a game day. But with our home opener around the corner, these are now getting scheduled all over the place, forcing me to withstand pointed abuse from local sports reporters looking for blood.

I'm not expecting to be handed roses given this team's track record. But my job satisfaction has taken a definite hit.

"You got a question somewhere in there, Scottie?"

Harry Nunez has been at this a lot longer than I have. My boss leans his elbows on the table, fixing the reporter with an expression that clearly states, *why is it always fucking you, Scottie?*

Wouldn't mind an answer to that question myself.

"Yeah." The reporter spares me a glance before settling back on Harry. "The general consensus is that you've been too forgiving of your staff over the years, and it's now cost the team twenty-six losses in a row. You're already oh-and-two on the season. A grace period is to be expected with a new coach, but how long will that be this time around? How many more losses would it take before you consider another coaching shake-up?"

Yeah. It takes a real fucking prick to start calling for my ass to get fired when I'm only two games into the job. Can't a guy get some credit around here?

I lean toward my mic, molding the brim of my hat when a couple camera flashes go off. "I'm not expecting a lifelong grace period, Scottie. What I do expect is the chance to coach a few more games before the pitchforks come out."

Out of the corner of my eye, I see our PR coordinator's shoulders slump. Talking pitchforks was definitely not part of the training she put me through once I got promoted.

Harry takes over the mic. "Four games, to be exact." I go still in my seat. There's a simultaneous frown going around the room. "The question was at which point in the season do I consider a coaching shake-up. That would be four more games, to the midpoint of the season. I need to see a win sometime in the next four weeks."

Are you fucking kidding me?

Cameras flash. My stomach drops and lands on the floor by my feet. I do my best to smooth my face. Act like my boss hasn't just dropped a bomb on me in a room full of cameras and salty reporters.

We've apparently done enough to piss off the PR coordinator because she steps up to the table. "All right, looks like we're at time. Thanks for coming, everyone."

The second she calls it, I get to my feet. "I gotta get out to practice," I mutter before Harry can manage to corner me. I've had enough of his scathing assessment of the team, as though I don't spend every waking moment obsessing over it already.

Well, *almost* every waking moment.

A little over a week into our new sleeping arrangement, and the corner of my brain normally reserved for thinking about Melody Woods on loop has spread across an entire hemisphere. Now I see her every day. Go to sleep with her at night. Wake up to her in the morning.

Yeah, maybe she only shows up after midnight and leaves before she's even finished her cup of coffee, but it's more of her than I've had in a long time.

Apparently, my obsession has turned into full-on hallucinations. Out on the field, my eyes immediately catch a flash of pink on the sideline next to Brooks.

I was always wildly fascinated by Melody's wardrobe. You meet the girl, take in the snark, the way she makes you work hard just for a two-second glimpse of a half-smile, and you expect to see her dressed head to toe in muted colors. Then she shows up in a yellow terry cloth dress or a bright pink one like today, blond hair strewn around her shoulders.

In high school, anticipating which blinding color she'd show up wearing that day made it damn hard to dread going to class.

Brooks catches sight of me first, and then Mel twirls around in a way that makes the dress spin around her thighs. She doesn't smile. Just fixes me with that look where her eyes twinkle as she decides between a simple *hello* or a teasing quip.

"You're forty minutes late to your own practice, Coach," she says. Mystery solved. "I caught Brooks here trying to stage a coup. Steal this team right out from under you."

"You know what? He can fucking have it." I rip my hat off and toss it down on the bench beside us, then shove my fingers through my hair. "Let's see how he does knowing the entire town wants you unemployed. Probably even exiled."

Funny how fast they can turn on you. When I played here, I couldn't make it down the main strip without getting stopped for a friendly chat every few feet.

"Interviews went well, then?" Brooks says.

Melody turns those massive blue eyes on me. Fucking hell, she's pretty. Fourteen years in, it still hits me straight in the chest every time I see her.

"Media," I tell her by way of explanation, and she winces. I don't need to say more. She grew up in this world with us. Knows exactly how rabid the fans can be.

Brooks gets called over by a player, and Mel eyes the stands behind the bench. It's Thursday, which means open practice, and the seats are usually pretty well occupied by reporters and students.

I scan the area, looking for signs of Scottie or any of his fellow vultures, but it's just a couple groups of college kids dotting the stands. I recognize a few girlfriends of some of the players huddled together. There's also a kid I've never seen before sitting a few rows up from them, legs draped onto the seats in front of him like they're too long for the small space between rows. He adjusts his glasses as he looks down at the textbook in his lap, pausing to stare out at the field every so often.

"You're probably wondering why I've come to see you outside of sleeping hours," Mel says. She's wearing a pair of high-top sneakers a few shades darker than the pink of her dress.

She looks like a walking valentine, and I fucking love it.

"You're beautiful," I tell her, sidestepping her opening. As far as I'm concerned, she could come to me in the middle of a colonoscopy and I'd be thrilled to see her.

"Oh." She looks down at herself and swings her hips, admiring the way her own dress flutters around her. "Thanks. It's new, obviously. Considering the entirety of my old wardrobe was fit for a funeral. Connor had very particular taste."

I really hate that fucking guy.

"I wasn't talking about the outfit. Though, to be clear, this dress really does do you justice."

She wrinkles her nose at the compliment, but the flush in her cheeks betrays her. "Anyway, I actually came to—"

"Heads up, Coach!"

Our heads swivel toward the field. Noah is off in the distance, waving his arms frantically in our direction. I manage to cut to the left just in time to catch an errant ball before it bashes Melody on the head. She squeaks as I jostle her to make the catch, and I quickly reach around her, pressing her to me before she falls over.

A chorus of howls go off on the field, players tipping their heads back as though baying at the moon. The Huskies Howl. That cheer used to thrill me when I played here. You'd hear it whenever we scored or pulled off an impressive play. Not that it happens much these days.

I wave them all quiet. "You okay?"

She grips the front of my shirt, disoriented by the sudden shift in our positions. And maybe that's why she stays plastered to me a few seconds longer than necessary. Why she blinks up at me with her lips a little parted. But I've never been one to take my blessings for granted. She's going to have to pry herself away from me.

"I'm . . ." Her grip tightens, and it pulls her body into mine like there'd even been the room for it. "I could have caught that, you know."

I know. I've seen her reflexes in action. She used to throw around a ball with me and Parker back then, and I'd put money on her making that catch every day.

I abandon the ball to brush a strand of hair off her cheek. "It's all yours next time."

Her mouth pinches into a reluctant smile. I want to kiss this woman so bad. Every night I tell her *goodnight* without touching her, kissing her, and it feels like carving a chunk out of my own soul.

With a lingering tug of the front of my shirt, Melody steps away, putting a respectful couple feet of distance between us. I whip around, finding Noah.

"Keep your passes under control or your ass is on the bench," I bark at him.

The entire field collectively freezes. Even the quiet guy in the stands raises a curious gaze from his textbook.

That was probably a bit much.

Melody watches, amused, as Noah sheds his helmet to reveal a shit-eating grin as he approaches. "Wow, Zac. You really set him straight," she says.

"Everyone knows his bark is bigger than his bite," Noah tells her when he reaches us. "And experiencing said bark is totally worth it if it gets me some answers. I didn't realize you were seeing someone, Coach. Let me tell you, it's about fucking time—"

I cough loudly. Melody takes in the traitorous color in my face and presses her lips together in an amused semi-smile.

"Oh, we're not together," she tells Noah. "He begged me for a date, but I politely declined."

Little brat.

"She likes to play hard to get," I clarify innocently. "Only a matter of time, though."

She's the one blushing now. "He's just an old friend of my brother's. We all went to high school together."

"She sleeps over every night."

"The key word there is *sleep*."

"In my bed. Every night. She can't stay away."

"It's completely platonic."

"Only because I *politely declined* her advances. Did I mention there's spooning?"

Noah glances between us, now amused as hell. He puts a hand out toward Mel. "Melody Woods, right? I haven't seen you around town in years. You look amazing."

Excuse me?

The punk ass kid actually allows his eyes to drop the length of Mel's body. They hover several milliseconds too long on her thighs.

Oh, hell fucking no.

"Why do you look so familiar?" Mel asks, taking Noah's hand.

"If you went to school with Coach, then you were probably in the same grade as my sister Georgia. I'm Noah Irving."

Mel's eyes light up in recognition. "Wow, I remember you now. You're all grown up. Are you the big-shot quarterback Zac keeps talking about, then?"

Let's be realistic, here. Am I *actually* threatened by a twenty-year-old golden boy?

Yes. Yes, I am fucking threatened by a twenty-year-old golden boy.

I *was* that golden boy. I know the kind of shit you can get up to, if you're not too busy pining for your childhood friend's mildly grumpy twin sister.

"That'd be me," Noah tells her with a grin. "Nice to hear you have me on the brain during pillow talk, Coach."

"There's no pillow talk," Mel says promptly.

Noah's still got her hand in his and I separate them, swatting their arms impatiently.

"Wow," Noah says flatly, eyes widening. "This is very believable. I am one hundred and ten percent convinced that you're just old friends who have never had a single moment of pillow talk. Completely convinced."

"All right, that's enough. Shouldn't you be out there making yourself useful, Irving?"

Noah flashes Melody a conspiratorial grin, like he's telling her, *can you believe what a dick this guy is?*

"Sheesh." Mel returns Noah's look. "Lucky you with a coach like that. And they call me the grumpy one."

Noah bites down on his tongue, trying not to laugh at my very evident irritation. "We are pretty lucky, actually. And if there's a list of people who owe him one then I'm at the very top."

"What do you mean?" Mel asks curiously.

"Nothing. He means nothing," I cut in before Noah can get

going. We don't tend to advertise the ways in which I help him out, and all this talk about owing me for it annoys me to no end. "Get back out there, Irving."

I wave him off and he starts to back away from us. When Melody bends to tug up her sock Noah locks eyes with me, indicates Mel, and throws his head back as he fans himself.

"That's quite the dynamic you've got," Mel says, catching the tail end of Noah's nonsense. "Are all your players so . . . involved in your life?"

I stuff my hands into my pockets, resisting the urge to flip him off. "That's just with Noah. He's . . . a bit of a kid brother. I help him out sometimes with a place to stay when things get a little rough for him at home."

She turns her gaze over her shoulder. Noah has made it back across the field and is having a laugh with some of the other players. "I assume that's what he meant about owing you one? Why wouldn't you want him to talk about it?"

"He can talk about it all he wants; it's his life. But I don't deserve a medal just for helping out a good kid who badly needs someone in his corner. He doesn't owe me a thing."

That look. Mel's softening eyes, the way she rubs her lips together like I've stunned her out of a vocabulary. That's the reason I don't advertise my relationship with Noah. I'm not some kind of saint. The kid deserves to have someone look out for him.

Her eyes follow the trajectory of my hand as I reach up and run my fingers through my hair. I realize her attention is on the red shoelace around my wrist. She looks at me like she's trying real hard to figure me out, and I start to sweat like I expect her to formally deliver the results of her assessment, right here, right now. Gavel and all.

Worthy or not worthy.

Over her head, I see an assistant coach looking at us curiously. And that's when I realize how utterly risky this is.

Ken Matthews knows Parker. He's lived in Oakwood long enough to know exactly who Mel is. Most of the staff would, seeing as they're all long-timers.

Mel is dead set on her brother never catching wind of . . . whatever the hell it is that's going on with us. Me, though? I want to reach for her hand. Pull her into my chest. I want everyone here to witness it, to recognize us for what we are, even though Mel can't see it for herself yet.

See this? Me and her, we're an us.

Parker's consequences be damned.

Ken is still watching, and I'm a heartbeat away from tucking that loose strand of hair behind her ear just to see how this unfolds.

But Mel peers over her shoulder, finds him there, and takes a step away—the moment is gone. She unzips her bag, and I think it's supposed to look casual, but she fumbles it a couple of times.

"What are you looking for?"

She drops her wallet back into the main pocket of her bag. "Lip balm. But I think I moved this one to my car. I swear, I need to put GPS trackers into the caps or something."

"Check the front pocket?"

"I never put them in the front pocket," she says absently, unzipping it anyway. "Oh—yeah, there it is." She studies the uncapped tube with a frown before swiping some on. "Actually, I came here to ask if you were craving anything. I thought I would order us a late dinner after you finish up practice as a thank you for all the breakfasts."

I know what she's doing. Playing a game of tit-for-tat with me, making sure she doesn't leave herself indebted the way Connor made her feel.

It's the last thing I want, the last thing I'd do to her. But I'll play along if she needs me to. "Dinner sounds great. But you didn't have to come all the way here just for that."

"I was going to text you, but I wasn't sure you'd check your phone during practice." Her cheeks go a bit pink. Hang on a damn minute.

"I've answered your calls during practice," I point out, and I can't help the satisfied smirk taking over my face. "Melody Woods, you wanted to see me."

She rolls her eyes.

"And you're not even denying it. How many fingers?" I'm wiggling three fingers in her face.

"Don't be smug."

She shoves my fingers away and I'll be motherfucking damned, but she holds on to my hand far longer than she needs to, sliding her thumb along my palm as she releases me.

Something's happening here.

I don't know what. I don't even know if she means for it to be happening, but—

"Zac—come here a sec!"

I will ruin his life.

Brooks waves me over from where he and an assistant coach pore over a playbook, and I don't think I've ever felt this murderous in my twenty-eight years.

"I should go," Mel says, but I take her by the shoulders, holding her still.

"Don't you dare. I'll be right back."

In fairness to Brooks, they couldn't have worked through this new play without me. We huddle over the binder spitballing strategy. At some point, I become vaguely aware of some kind of commotion in the stands behind me. But I don't have a chance to inspect as Brooks turns to the field and starts calling out directions at the guys, and I watch them all hustle into their new positions to run the play.

It's not perfect. We're still horrifically underutilizing Noah. But these are desperate times and it might have to do.

I'm relieved to find Melody still standing where I left her, though she doesn't acknowledge me when I come over. Her gaze is fixed on the stands, at the kid reading his textbook. Then she bends, picks up the ball I'd caught earlier, and hands it to me. "Tell Noah to cross the field at the fifty-yard line and throw this into the stands."

"What?" I stare down at the ball.

She rips her eyes off the guy with the textbook. "Tell Noah to cross the field and throw this ball at that group of girls up there." She jerks her head to where the players' girlfriends are sitting.

"Why?"

"I just saw . . . That guy over there. In the glasses? I just saw him catch a stray pass and . . . trust me, Zac. You want to see this."

Without taking my eyes off her, I turn my chin out toward the field. "Irving, get your ass over here!"

When he's within proper earshot, I toss him the ball and nod at the far sideline. "Get out there and throw that at your buddies' girlfriends, won't you?"

He's immediately horrified. "Do you *want* me to get my ass beat—"

"Just do it."

With a parting bewildered look, he does what he's told. Lines up the throw, and it spirals perfectly toward the girls, who go on chatting obliviously.

That is, until Melody shouts, *"Heads up!"*

They turn toward the field and immediately start to scramble out of the way as the ball comes for them and—

Holy. Fucking. Fuck.

The kid in the glasses leaps up like a real-life motherfucking Clark Kent, bouncing from row to row so gracefully he might be in the middle of a ballet recital. He throws himself in front of the girls and catches the ball—no, he *snatches* it right out of the air like he was the pole and it was the magnet. He crashes to the ground, and after one terrifying moment where he doesn't seem to move a muscle, he gets up, shakes it off, and says something to the group of girls that has them instantly laughing.

Ahead of me, Brooks gives me the same *holy fuck* look I'm surely wearing. And then he turns, hops the fence, and beelines for the kid.

That might've been enough good to tide me over for a few days. Until the reality inevitably hits that we're likely about to put a guy on the field who's never practiced a day with this team.

But then I catch sight of the grin on Melody's face. Big and bright and cocky as hell. Radiating self-confidence, proud as fuck of herself.

She tips back her head and lets rip a damn good Huskies Howl. And that might be enough to tide me over into the next century.

Chapter 19

Melody

Spending the day scouring investment trends for my boring-as-hell job at my ex-boyfriend's investment bank: easy peasy.

Carrying a serving tray loaded with three full English breakfasts, a stack of pancakes bigger than my head, and an inordinate amount of breakfast beverages across an overcrowded diner on a Saturday morning?

A real fucking challenge.

"Here we go," I say, sidestepping a couple kids racing toy cars down the aisle between table sections, to finally deposit the tray onto a table of visibly hungover college kids. They look up at me like they can't remember what the hell they're doing at Sheffield's in the first place. "So, I believe you ordered the coffee, you the smoothie, and—"

If I didn't feel solid ground beneath my feet, I'd think I was invisible. The suffering occupants of table fifteen reach for my tray and help themselves to their designated breakfasts before I can finish my sentence. The guy at the far end of the table downs his glass of water in one long gulp before dousing his pancakes in syrup.

"I'll leave you to it, then."

It's one of the rare mornings Wynn managed to score me a breakfast shift, and four hours into it, I am already drained. Between my three weekly shifts at Sheffield's and three days dialing into the office, I barely have time to think anymore.

"It's worth it, it's worth it, it's worth it," I chant under my breath. The second I bank enough for a deposit on an apartment and land a new job that lets me afford that apartment, my aching feet will become a distant, worthwhile memory.

If only I could figure out what that job could be.

Parker and Summer knew off the bat they wanted to combine their love of sports with their frightening scientific abilities. They both ended up rehabbing athletes at UOB.

Zac, a people person since I met him, spends his days coaching college kids.

Connor's ambition was always money—maybe a product of growing up with a rich mom—and there he was, becoming an investment banker. Taking me along for the ride when poor little Melody graduated with her math degree—the only thing I ever loved studying in school—and had no idea how to apply it.

I'd hoped moving away to the city, leaving the confines of Oakwood Bay and everything I knew, would spark some inspiration. But I'm just as aimless now, with my spray bottle and bar rag, wiping down this diner table that probably consumed more syrup than whoever was sitting here last.

I move to check on the next table, a much more wholesome scene than the stale-vodka-scented one I just served.

"Hey, Ingrid. How're we doing over here?"

Ingrid Reeves, who may very well be the only person in this diner more exhausted than me, blows out a breath so impressively loud that I can hear it over the shrill *vroom vroom* sounds coming from the six-year-olds playing with their cars behind me. She and her eight-year-old son Killian were here over two plates of pancakes on my last morning shift. Her husband was our physical education teacher while I was in the seventh grade, before he joined the military.

"The food is perfect as always." Ingrid sighs. "You want to know what's not so perfect? Trying to run through my kid's homework when I'm working off half a brain cell this morning, and nearly flunked all my math classes as a kid, anyway. Sean usually handles homework duty when he isn't deployed."

I pull a face, peering at her son's workbook as he gnaws on the end of his pencil. "Whatcha working on today, bud?"

Killian answers by way of a wordless grumble.

"They're onto probabilities now, which makes perfect sense given the probability of my being able to make him care about this is precisely zero," Ingrid supplies, taking a sip of orange juice.

I slide into the booth next to Killian. "You mind if I have a look?"

He shoves the workbook in my direction. "Numbers are boring," he announces.

"Hmm, I'm not so sure I agree with that. You just need to get the hang of them, and then something really cool starts to happen."

"What does?"

"They start telling you a story." I peruse the page he's stuck on. "What would you rather be doing if you weren't studying math?"

"Watching football," he says morosely, bitter that I'm reminding him. "The Huskies have their home opener on Friday, but Mom says we can't go because Grandma Janet is visiting from Ireland and we can't afford three tickets."

Of course. This town really does live and die by football.

Across the table, Ingrid lifts her gaze to the ceiling as though begging the heavens for patience.

"Well, I can't do much about Grandma Janet visiting, but I can probably help you out with this." I answer Ingrid's inquisitive look with a shrug. "I'm only a part-time server. I work in data analysis on the side."

Or maybe I'm a server on the side. Honestly, I can barely make sense of how I split my week anymore.

"Okay, so forget about all those funny drawings in this book and humor me for a minute," I tell Killian. I pull straws out of the tabletop dispenser and lay them out as yard lines across the table, then pick up a brown sugar packet. "Let's say this is your quarterback—"

"Irving," Killian pipes up with a sage nod. "The best quarterback the Huskies have ever seen."

"Yes, Noah Irving. Excellent quarterback," I agree. "So, it's the Huskies home opener, right? And he's on the field, lining up a pass, but the other team is closing in on him fast." I pick up a handful of white sugar packets and scatter them around my makeshift football field, dot two brown sugar packets among them. "The white packets are the opposing players, and these two brown ones are the only Huskies open—"

"One of them can be Hudson Jones," he adds. "Freshman, wide receiver, joined the team just last week."

Zac and I have taken to calling him Baby Clark Kent, but Hudson Jones it is.

"Sure thing. So, it's just Hudson and this other guy open, and they're surrounded by five opposing players. What are the chances a Husky gets that ball?"

"Well," Killian drawls. "If Irving fakes to the left—"

I chuckle, contemplating my makeshift field and the way the sugar packets are scattered. "You're probably right. If he fakes to Hudson, this other guy might be able to take the handoff. But let's focus on the numbers, bud. We'll leave the rest to his coaches." I point to the table. "There are two Huskies and five from the other team."

"The ball will probably hit one from the other team."

"Right. And what are the chances the ball makes it to a Husky?"

Killian purses his lips, staring down at the mess of straws and sugar packets before him. "Only two out of seven?"

"Nailed it." I pick a berry off his plate and mime throwing it across the straw field until it lands on a white sugar packet.

Killian sinks down on the bench with an aggrieved sigh. "Dad's right. The Huskies *are* losers."

Shit. Probably should have reversed that example.

"Look," I say loudly, drawing his workbook closer. "It's the same thing with these weird-looking marbles in the book. See? Two plain marbles, five with the squiggles on the inside."

With a determined frown, Killian moves the berry so that it sits on a brown sugar packet. At least I didn't kill his spirit.

"Any chance you're open to working a third job?" Ingrid says, passing Killian his pencil. "I'll pay you whatever you want to keep turning math problems into football analogies. Extra if you put the Huskies on the winning side."

With a chuckle, I slide out of the bench and collect my serving tray as Killian flicks the white sugar packets off the makeshift field. "No need. I'm usually on the lunch shift on Mondays, Tuesdays, and Saturdays. If you ever need help, just stop by."

She groans her appreciation. "You're a saint."

I slip behind the counter and dump my serving tray under the pass window. Despite the sneakers, my feet feel like they've ballooned to twice their size. I shake them out, one after the other, as I survey the restaurant.

It's loud and happy this Saturday morning, and I might be a down-to-the-bone kind of exhausted after a couple weeks of working six-day marathons, but there's something else there, too, as my gaze sweeps over my section of tables. The kids racing their cars down the aisle, couples young and old laughing over cups of coffee and between mouthfuls of eggs. Killian watching with rapt attention as Ingrid patiently counts out packets of sugar as she references her son's workbook. Hell, even my table of hungover zombies seem to have regained a bit of life since I left them.

It might not be much—the coffees and the food and the impromptu tutoring—but it really feels like I've done something here this morning. I've been productive. I've made these people happy, at least for the length of their breakfast. It feels better than any of those aimless walks along the river on my days off back in the city.

It feels amazing.

"I can't tell you how wild it is seeing you back there again."

My stomach swoops. I hadn't noticed him coming up to the counter, but Zac now presses his elbows on the pale green surface and leans over it to blatantly rake his eyes along my body from the ground up.

Something pleasantly warm blossoms in the depths of my chest. It's not even the way he's looking at me, nor is it the fit of his T-shirt, though that certainly doesn't hurt. I find that, a few weeks into our sleeping arrangement, I've developed something of an addiction to him.

I've been stretching out our porch breakfasts with the lamest excuses, in the same way teenaged me would loiter around the house whenever he and Parker were around.

Oh, look. There's a family of ducks crossing the waterfront the exact moment I finally got up to leave. How quaint.

Despite my insistence that it's all about sleep, this thing is quickly going from reluctant sleeping arrangement to . . . something I can't quite articulate.

He's nice to be around.

Really nice, actually. I pinch the sides of my black uniform skirt and dip into a curtsy. "Probably not as much of a mindfuck as it is to be the one back here. Are you getting something or are you just here to stare at my legs?"

Zac nods to the to-go cup of coffee on the counter between us. "Came for the coffee, stayed for the legs."

I duck behind the pastry counter, mostly to hide the embarrassing smile attempting to claw its way onto my face. As great as the tips are on a breakfast shift, it meant leaving the comfort of Zac's bed criminally early—definitely no coffee on the porch this morning. He did get up in time to see me off with a pack of travel waffles, though.

It feels wrong to have missed him, when I swore I wouldn't entertain the idea of another man until I got my life in better order. But I did miss him, hard.

I surface from behind the counter to place a glazed donut on a plate in front of him. "Here, these are fresh out of the kitchen. I've already snuck myself three, but don't tell Wynn."

Zac mimes zipping up his mouth but goes straight for a bite.

"Mel, mind pouring me three coffees and a grapefruit juice?" Wynn calls from the register down at the other end of the counter.

"On it," I call back.

"How's the shift going?" Zac asks as I lay out some purple mugs.

"Let's just say there's nothing more humbling to a desk worker than serving a morning shift at Sheffield's." I pour out the coffees. "No disastrous latte experiments yet, though I might have turned your biggest fan against you by accident."

Zac peers over his shoulder when I nod at the nearby booth, where Ingrid and Killian lean over his math workbook.

"Killian? Impossible. The kid always sits right behind the visiting team bench just to heckle them. He's got a pair of lungs on him."

"You might miss him at Friday's game." I pause, bottled grapefruit juice in hand. "Actually, do you think you can get them three tickets to the home opener? Ingrid's mom is visiting this week."

Zac shrugs, going for another bite of donut. "Easy. Tell them it'll be at the gate."

He's left a fleck of frosting on his lip, and smiles when I reach across the counter to wipe it off and suck it off my finger. Wynn shoots us a curious look before collecting his drinks and running them to his table.

Shit. The last thing I need is Mr. Town Gossip on our trail.

Hastily, I grab a tray of empty glass dispensers and heave a large tub of syrup on the counter in a makeshift barrier between me and Zac.

"How's Baby Clark Kent doing at practice?" I ask, pumping syrup into a dispenser.

Zac picks up a bar rag and reaches to wipe up a streak of syrup dripping down the side of the dispenser. "He isn't bad. Well, no—he's good. Lots of natural talent. But it's pretty damn obvious to anyone watching that he's never played with this team. It's disjointed as hell right now, Mel. Doesn't help that I'm only being given four more games to prove my worth, or I'm out."

I pull a face, moving to a fresh dispenser. "They have to know it'll take some time to get the chemistry right, though? How can they expect you to slot in a new player and see magic right away?"

"Doesn't matter. The media doesn't care. The fans are impatient. Viewership is down, which means sponsorships are down. It's becoming harder to scout for the school because no one wants to play for perennial losers." He sighs, fiddling with the bar rag. "I'm the perfect scapegoat. I was never supposed to have this job in the first place—it was supposed to be interim until it wasn't. I'm young, inexperienced as a head coach. I inherited the other guy's insane salary, which I haven't even come close to earning. I'm expensive and, so far, all I've delivered are losses on the season. I'm royally fucked."

Every bit of his body carries signs of defeat. The deflated shoulders. The tilt of his head, the curve of his eyebrows. My chest pinches. It's so rare to see Zac without his signature swagger. The confidence that's so infectious he deals it out like candy to everyone around him, making them feel as capable and valuable as they are through his eyes.

It's how he makes me feel, anyway.

Also, screw his boss. It sounds like Zac was set up to fail from the start, and it makes me absurdly storm-the-stadium-with-a-pitchfork-and-torch angry on his behalf.

"You've always been a football whiz, Zac. I can't see this going any different."

"Good players don't always make good coaches. And head coach . . . it's a completely different skillset." He shoves his hands deep into his pockets, scanning the diner over his shoulder like he's expecting an angry mob to ambush him any moment. "I'm responsible for the success of an entire staff. I need to be able to take things in stride when they go wrong—"

"Like you did when we got stranded at the campsite?"

His brows pull together. "To motivate the team when the odds feel stacked against them—"

"Like you did when you had me write my playbook?" I raise my eyebrows when Zac feeds me a funny look. "By all means, keep pointing out the ways you think you fall short. I could do this all day."

The corner of his mouth lifts. "When'd you become such an optimist, Clover?"

"Since I've seen firsthand how much your team respects you. And I'm willing to bet they'll work just as hard for you and your job as you will for them and their career prospects. Keep the faith, Porter. That championship is in the bag, and I, for one, cannot wait to celebrate."

It's a proper smile he gives me now. "Championship, huh?"

"We're aiming high this year, you and me." I wipe my fingers on my apron and hold a fist out between us, pinky in the air. "If I have to find a new career that makes me happy, then you have to start believing you'll win that trophy. Deal?"

"Deal." We're both leaning so far over the counter separating us that he barely has to reach to twist his pinky around mine. His eyes go soft the second we connect. "Melody, I'm dying to kiss you."

He looks like he means it, too. My gaze settles on his mouth.

Why'd he have to be such a phenomenal kisser? I'm not itching to dial up the emotional dependence between us—no more than I already feel building despite my best defenses, anyway—but it's impossible to forget how weightless I felt kissing him back in the woods.

Our pinkies are still connected, sitting between us on the counter. Zac brushes his thumb over my knuckles, just once, and my entire body thrums pleasantly.

The diner door chimes open and a familiar Hawaiian shirt walks in.

"Shit." Our fingers disentangle, and I drop my gaze to the syrup dispenser in front of me.

Behind Zac, Parker strolls across the diner. I really should have known he'd be here this morning given the maddening lack of a coffee machine in his apartment.

"Maybe you should . . ." I nod over Zac's shoulder.

But Zac only takes an unperturbed sip of coffee at the sight of my brother, who stops to chat up a table of college girls on his way to the counter.

"I'm not running away from your brother, Mel."

I might, if he catches wind of whatever's going on between us. Parker's never been one to mind his own business. His interrogation would be long and painful. Full of questions I'd have no idea how to answer, considering my own feelings are a mess.

"Fine, just . . . act normal," I whisper. Zac's smirk turns pure filth. His gaze finds my legs again and damn him, I'm blushing. I swat his arm.

"What?" he says innocently. "You said act normal."

"Act *friendly*. Stop checking me out." I clear my throat when Parker sidles up to the counter. "College girls, really, Park? Don't tell me you go for them that young now."

Parker gives an overzealous gasp. "She's a student, Mels. On the tennis team. I've been rehabbing her shoulder. I am the picture of professionalism." He does a double take when he finds Zac nonchalantly sipping his coffee beside him. "Oh. I never see you in here."

I've been back a few weeks now, but aside from the painfully awkward car ride back to town when Parker rescued us from camp—which consisted of silence, followed by more silence—I haven't seen these two interact at all. More than once, I've tried to needle Zac into explaining his shift toward my brother. I haven't found an opening to grill Parker.

Zac shrugs and motions with his coffee cup. "Don't tend to enjoy my coffee with a side of angry football fans."

"Yet, here you are, having your coffee anyway. What's the occasion?"

"The legs."

I fumble the pump I'm using. Douse the front of my shirt in a stream of syrup. Parker frowns. "The what?"

Without even a glance, Zac pushes a bar rag in my direction. "The eggs. Ran out of them at home. Got hungry, and here I am."

"Right." Parker nods, but his gaze is more than a little suspicious.

Mine flicks back and forth between them, trying to make sense of this. They're polite, perfectly friendly. But they're acting like casual friends who catch up every couple of months rather than the pair I used to know. Back in the day, you couldn't get these two to shut up. They ribbed each other like brothers, did the same with me whenever I was around. Now, I'd love nothing more than to submerge myself in this tub of syrup just for the sake of escaping the awkward dead air.

I give a very obviously forced cough. "So, it should be a good game on Friday. Word around the diner is there's a new receiver on the team."

Parker lifts a brow. "Yeah? Any good?"

Zac's only response is a polite nod.

I cough again. "It's Hudson Jones. Freshman. Wide receiver. Joined the team last week." Both Zac and Parker feed me a funny look. "I spent some time with Killian this morning."

Parker peers over his shoulder, finding Killian and his mother. "A freshman? Did he come in on a scholarship?"

"Nope," Zac answers against his coffee cup. "Found him by accident. We're optimistic."

"Good. That's . . . great." They exchange quick smiles. When Zac meets my *what the hell is going on* look, he only shrugs.

Parker clears his throat. "Anyway, Mels, I came here to see you about something. There's a rumor about you going around town these days I was curious about."

"What?" My voice comes out closer to a squeak. "What are they saying?"

"Something about you popping up at the Huskies stadium now and again. Looking cozy with the coaching staff." He glances to his left, where Zac carefully ponders the colorful pattern on his to-go cup.

Oh, fuckitty fuck. I stare at the ground under my feet. Despite my begging, it refuses to open up and shoot me straight to the earth's burning core.

I knew it was stupid, going to visit Zac at work. Knew it would bite me in the ass, in more ways than one, that I couldn't seem to make myself call or text him, on account of not being able to see his face that way. His warm, handsome, completely unhelpful face as he studies the menu board, seeming bored to tears by this conversation.

"I didn't believe it at first," Parker continues, "and then I noticed something interesting. Any guess what that might be, Mels? No?" He tips his head when I shake mine. "You mind explaining why you've been sneaking out of the apartment after midnight every night? Sneaking back in the morning?"

This is swirling into the gutter. Parker leans his elbow on the counter, clearly settling in for an inquisition and looking so damn pleased with himself at having caught me. "Go on, Mels. Tell me who you're with every night."

Zac raises his brows at me in a way that very much feels like a challenge.

Tell him. I dare you.

God, this is really happening, isn't it? Never mind the awkward questions. Never mind Parker denouncing relationships within the friend group just a few days ago. If Zac was right and Parker doesn't take it well, we're about to have a blowout in the middle of a breakfast shift at Sheffield's.

"I . . . Look, Parker, I need you to be cool about this," I say, swallowing hard. "It's that . . . well, it sort of started out of nowhere, and really, nothing untoward has happened—well, *mostly* nothing. There was this one time where we, uh . . . you know. Certain things *did* happen, very adult, very consensual things . . . Nothing crazy, nothing like the bondage stuff you said you did, which . . . God, I wish I could forget about that. Anyway, there was an almost-time after that, too, where we were about to . . . You probably don't want to hear about this part of it, do you? What I mean to say is—"

"It's Brooks. She's seeing Brooks, all right?"

My mouth pops open. Parker's elbow nearly slips off the counter. Zac glares at the ceiling, clearly irritated by his own words.

"*Brooks*, Mels, really?" Parker squints at me like it'll somehow help him see into my brain, but it would serve us both better if he tried analyzing his best friend's.

What in the hell just happened?

Zac drags a hand down his face, and when he finally meets my eyes he looks completely resigned. "Just go with it," he mouths silently.

"It . . . appears so," I tell Parker, trying my best to look casual as I screw on the lid to the syrup dispenser I had long abandoned, while shouting silent questions at Zac. "Me . . . and Brooks. Having all kinds of sleepovers."

Instead of shedding any kind of light on my apparent relationship status, Zac collects his coffee cup and turns to Parker. "Brooks is a good guy. You know that; you've been friends with him for years. Take it easy on them."

He flashes me a look of apology and I watch with more than a little confusion as he walks away.

Parker fixates back on me. "So . . . what? Are you dating Brooks? Seeing each other? Is it serious? Why him?" Damn it.

He shoots the questions at me so rapidly I barely have a chance to digest one before the next comes out of his mouth. I knew he'd get like this.

I hop onto my toes, catching the nonexistent eye of a nonexistent customer across the diner. I grab the coffee carafe at my side. "Excuse me, I need to make a coffee run."

"Mel, seriously. What's going on—"

I hurry around the counter before he can get on another inquisitorial roll. "You're the one who encouraged me to get out there, Park! I'm only following your brotherly advice."

Chapter 20

Zac

"This is, by far, the dumbest plan I've ever heard."

I'm standing over my desk, staring at tonight's playbook like it's spontaneously grown new pages that I haven't been obsessing over all week. I can feel Brooks's eyes boring into me from where he sits on the other side of my desk, but I don't have it in me to return the eye contact.

Between tonight's home opener and the utter fucking agony of asking him to pretend-date the love of my life, I'm not in the mood to indulge his facial expressions.

"I never said it was a smart plan," I mutter. "I panicked, all right? She came within an inch of telling her brother we were fooling around the other week. It slipped out."

Mel's confusion had turned to smugness by the time I saw her after the diner. Because she'd been right. Letting on about our situation seemed a lot easier before I was faced with the reality of telling Parker. Things between me and him are delicate enough as it is. Haven't been the same in years. And if I'm going to have any kind of shot at a relationship with her, keeping the peace with her brother is important.

In the end, I managed to convince her it was for the best we all go along with the fake relationship. Parker might be on her case about Brooks, but it's nothing compared to the turmoil there'd be if he knew it was my bed she's in every night.

"Something did happen between you and Mel, then. I fucking *knew* it."

I give Brooks a long look. "Parker and I have . . . a sensitive history. I knew that conversation was headed down a bad path. I just need him off our backs while she and I figure out what the hell's going on with us."

"And the long and short of it is," Brooks says as he leans back in his chair, "you both had a thing for each other in school without knowing it, and now you're . . . sleeping together while not *sleeping* together? And you're in full-on grovel-mode, trying to win her back?"

"Something like that." He's utterly baffled, not that I blame him. It's an insane plan. "Will you fake-date her or not?"

"What are we talking about here? Going out? Meeting the parents?"

Planting my palms on the desk, I look out into the office space through the open door of my office. It's buzzing with the coaching staff and trainers making last-minute preparations for tonight's game. On the other side of the wall behind my desk, I hear the thumping bass of hip hop music—Noah's beats of choice—coming from the players' locker room.

"No," I say flatly. "Absolutely none of that. It's a show you'd put on in front of Summer and Parker, and nothing else. It'll be casual, so you can still go out and date other people. There'll be no touching, no staring. No cutesy nicknames. Don't smile at her. You know what? Don't even look at her."

"So, act like I hate her while pretending to date her. Got it."

"I'm not kidding, Attwood."

Brooks grimaces. "I really wish you were. You realize you're being possessive over nothing, right? I'm not *actually* interested in dating her."

My eyes narrow. "And why not? You think you're too good for her, or something?"

"*What*? Did you bang your head into a concrete wall before this conversation?"

"Because she's out of your league. And she's way out of mine."

"You're acting unhinged."

I feel unhinged. "Answer the question, Attwood."

"I can't believe it's even a question," Brooks mutters, scratching at the scruff along his jaw. "I'm not trying to date her because *you* are, okay?" He adjusts the zip of his shirt with a Huskies logo on the sleeve. When I don't say anything, he adds, "Zac, you're asking me to fake-date the woman you've loved since you were fourteen. Fake or not, this is so fucking messy. And I don't see a version of this that has you and your feelings coming out completely unscathed."

"I don't think I'm that fragile."

"I think you are," Brooks says, eyes firmly on me. "Maybe I didn't have the full picture until now, but don't think I haven't noticed how . . . *still* you've been, since I met you in college. You could have coached anywhere, lived anywhere, but you stayed here. Any time a girl you were seeing tried to get serious, you found a reason to break it off. Like you were in a constant holding pattern, waiting for something. And then Mel shows up, and you . . . it's as alive as I've ever seen you, man."

His assessment comes like a punch in the gut. It's not like I hadn't known how badly I failed to move on from her. It's that I didn't think anyone else noticed.

This is what makes Brooks a true gem of a friend.

He's gone through hell and back. Was on top of the world in his dream career, playing for the NFL team he grew up watching. And then one bad hit on a random Monday night put it all to an end. Still, through all that and his eventual break up with Naomi, he's always kept a good eye on me.

Thing is, though, I don't care how stuck I've been. She's what I want. I can't help that.

"It'll all be worth it if she comes out on the other side wanting to be with me," I tell him.

"And you told her how you feel?"

I slam shut the playbook on top of the desk. "She knows I'm interested, but not the extent of it."

"Why the hell not?"

"Because she's trying to figure out where she's at in life, and she deserves to do that without the pressure of knowing I've been losing my mind over her since we were kids. She should be able to tell me *no* without wrestling with the guilt of shutting down a lifelong . . . I don't even know what to call this anymore." I sit in my chair with my head in my hands. "Man, I really need you to do this for me. I know it's putting you in a weird spot with Parker—"

"Knock, knock."

My head snaps up, chest seizes. Then my entire body eases, like the very sight of her just eliminated everything that's wrong with the world. Melody stands in my doorway, flashing Brooks a small smile before fixing her full attention on me. She's wearing a pale purple dress and sneakers, and a denim jacket with a floral pattern embroidered throughout it. The look is so vintage-Melody I feel a tug in my chest.

"Is it safe to come in?" she says, hesitating by the door.

"Not really," Brooks mutters for my ears only.

"Yes," I tell her, rounding my desk to lean on its other side.

She crosses the room to sit in the chair next to Brooks's. "I assume by the awkward silence that Zac told you the plan?"

"Mels, I'd give anything to turn back the clock to half an hour ago, when I was blissfully unaware of this scheme. It's ridiculous and completely unnecessary."

She deflates. "So you won't do it?"

Brooks sinks into his chair. "Of course I'll do it." He turns to me. "But let me make it clear that I'm never again paying for my own drinks when we're out together. They're all on your tab, man."

"Deal," I say quickly. "That's more than fair."

"Well, all right then. I'll leave you guys to it." Brooks gets to his feet and grins down at Mel. "Enjoy the game, *girlfriend*."

At the door, he turns to give me as close to a firm look as he can muster. "And you. While you're with my girlfriend, there'll be no touching. No staring. No cutesy nicknames. And don't even smile at her. Do you hear me?"

With a laugh, he dodges the pen I launch across the room and shuts the door behind him. Melody gives me a funny look. "Why can't you smile at me?"

"Don't ask," I say, rubbing my face.

"Okay . . ." she drawls, taking me in. "You look nervous. Do you have a bit of time before you have to get out there?"

"I've got all the time in the world for you, Clover. Ask me to blow off the game and I'd do it."

"Stop that," Melody mumbles, covering her face with her hands. "Stop being so damn sweet, Porter. It's nauseating."

"You love it." I'm smiling stupid-big. It's so charming when she's bashful.

She surfaces from her hands with flushed cheeks. "I don't love it. I tolerate it."

I hum. Crook a finger to beckon her over. To my surprise, she gets up without protest and stands between my outstretched legs as I lean on the edge of my desk. I stroke her cheek with the back of my finger.

"You're blushing pretty hard over something you only tolerate."

Mel fiddles with the ends of her hair. It's different from the way she normally wears it. Kind of curly tonight, and she's wearing different eye makeup, too—a black line over her eyelashes that kind of flicks up at the ends, like a little wing.

"You changed your hair," I tell her, reaching for a few strands and watching them sink through my fingers like soft Caribbean sand. "It looks great."

"You don't think it's too much?"

"What do you mean?"

"Connor preferred me looking natural. And then I realized that his version of *natural* actually involved a full face of neutral makeup. Just no winged liner or bright lipstick, or whatever."

Fascinated, I take her chin, moving her face from side to side to have a better look at the black lines. Jesus, that's gotta take some skill. Those lines would be wonky little nubs if I had a hand in them.

She gazes at me anxiously. "Are they uneven? I'm a bit out of practice."

"They're perfect. You got them on the same angle and everything." I study her eyes. "You're beautiful, Clover."

With my fingers holding her chin, I can feel the give in her face at the words. Her eyes go soft and she rubs her lips together, drawing my attention there.

No kissing. No kissing, no kissing, no kissing— "Lip balm addiction kicking in?"

She grimaces. "I left it in the car."

I lift my ass off the edge of the desk and pat around my back pockets, pulling out a tube.

Melody stares, not making a move to take it. "Don't tell me I turned you into a lip balm devotee."

"It's yours. You must have dropped it the last time you were here."

Reluctantly, she takes the lip balm and uncaps it. "You know, the strangest thing keeps happening," she says, staring at the tube. "All these lip balms keep popping up right when I need them."

I tip my head. "Isn't that the point of you putting them everywhere? Your car—"

"My overnight bag, your nightstand . . . the wrong pocket in my purse? I even found one in your kitchen this morning." She gives an exaggerated squint. "You want to know what's even weirder? All these tubes are brand new. Never used."

Fuck.

What kind of idiot doesn't think to break in a lip balm that's supposed to be hers? I've been sprinkling them around, hoping she wouldn't think anything of it.

I don't know what my face looks like, but the very corners of her mouth tick up. She's caught me and she knows it.

"Why do you think that keeps happening, Zac?"

I take her hands, palm to palm, and thread our fingers. Give a little tug and pull her closer. Her eyes catch on the flash of red at my wrist, the old shoelace bracelet breaking free from under my sleeve.

"I guess I forgot to tell you about the gnome problem at the house," I say, drawing back her attention.

"The gnome problem?"

"Yeah. It's been happening since I bought the land. Up until now, they've been leaving bags of Flamin' Hot Cheetos everywhere. I guess they're onto lip balm now. I hear that stuff's addictive."

She digs her teeth into her lip, trying not to laugh. "You're telling me you have an infestation of benevolent gnomes, who leave around your favorite snack and my exact brand of lip balm?"

I shrug. "In hindsight, it explains the cost of the property."

"And what do these gnomes want in return for their kindness?"

"Oh, everyone knows the best way to hurt a gnome's feelings is to try to pay them back. Just enjoy the silky-smooth lips, Clover."

She gives a skeptical hum, squeezing my hands before extracting her fingers from mine. "Well, I don't know about that. But I did come here hoping to give you something to ease your nerves tonight."

"What's that?"

"First is a reminder that it's only one game, and you've got three more ahead of you to make this work. You can do this, Zac. Even if you don't tonight, it's not an indicator of how the next game will go. How the rest of the season will go. You'll bounce back because you're good at what you do. You love this game and your players, and knowing you, you won't rest until you make this happen for them. They're lucky to have a coach who cares as much as you do."

I nudge her thigh with mine. "How would you feel about delivering my pregame speech to the team, huh?"

"Not that you need me, but I'm happy to do my part to get that win. This next thing is just for you, though."

Mel reaches into the pocket of her jacket. My heart, my entire fucking *being,* melts when she pulls out a tiny four-leaf clover.

She twirls the stem between her thumb and forefinger, fluttering the four little leaves. Gives me a tiny smile, blue eyes twinkling up at me.

Ten years.

She hasn't done this for me in ten years, and the surge of emotion inside me almost cripples me. I'm aching. This persistent, delicate ache that originates deep in my chest and radiates through the rest of me, and I know that if I were to lift the sleeves of my shirt, I'd find myself covered in pinprick goose bumps.

I am so . . . God, I am so fucked.

I will never, ever, fall out of love with this woman. It'll never happen.

"Clover." My voice is so soft you can barely hear it over the music next door. "You went out to look for one?"

She softens at the shameless affection in my voice. "Of course I did. Same spot I used to find them for you."

That fucking ache. The most intoxicating kind of pain there is.

Melody drops the clover into my open palm. Leans in, touches a hand to my shoulder to steady herself before placing the sweetest kiss on my cheek.

"Good luck, Coach."

Chapter 21

Melody

"So, we've got a monthly happy hour get-together. And if ever you don't feel like braving these crowds, the team sets up a screen in a room off the coaches' offices where we can watch. But I have to warn you, it tends to get even crazier than out here, with all our kids running around."

Emily Davies—welcome wagon to the Huskies coaches' wives and girlfriends group that apparently exists and I am now a part of—gets it all out in one single, loud string of words I can barely keep up with.

Obviously, my inability to focus has absolutely nothing to do with the absurdly gorgeous man on the field below. Despite the clear nerves I witnessed in his office, Zac now looks so attractively competent and in control, giving out orders to his players down there. I pity the state of my panties, after almost two quarters of watching him coach this game.

I don't even know how Emily got wind of my dating Brooks, given we've barely been "official" for a couple of hours. My best guess is that Wynn was privy to Zac's declaration back at the diner and is just as much the unofficial town crier as he was when I last lived here.

"Oh! And how could I forget." Emily smooths down the front of her Huskies jersey, tossing her perfectly blown-out brown locks. "There's the annual WAGs flag football game on Tuesday. Really, it's just an excuse for the guys to use us as pawns to compete against each other, but it can be a lot of fun."

A play on the field is whistled dead and I rip my gaze off Zac, who's gesturing at one of the refs. "A WAGs flag football game? As in, it's the wives and girlfriends playing?"

Emily doesn't seem to hear me. Out on the field, Baby Clark Kent, the Huskies' new wide receiver, manages to fake the defender. The crowd gasps in anticipation as Noah lines up a pass, makes the throw—and gets flattened to the ground by an opposing player.

I jump to my feet. "What the hell was that?" I add to the chorus of angry roars. "He wasn't in possession!"

"Throw the fucking flag!" Emily shouts, jabbing her finger at the field.

I look down at her, impressed. She's got a few years on me, and the kind of perfectly tamed hair I was used to seeing in Connor's circles, but Emily wears her disdain almost as good as I do. I decide, then and there, that I like this woman.

The Huskies bench seems to be in agreement with us both. Down below, I catch sight of Zac striding across the sideline toward a ref. The brim of his hat sits low on his face, so I can't make out his expression. But his shoulders are tense, his gait clipped, and the way he wrenches up the mouthpiece of his headset as he speaks to the ref tells me he isn't one bit happy about what he's hearing.

"Ah, that's bullshit," Emily says as play resumes without penalty, but I'm too distracted watching Zac pace up and down the sideline to muster a reply.

I forgot what it's like to come to a Huskies game.

In a small town like Oakwood, their home games command the same kind of reverence as Christmas. Other than Oakley's—which keeps its doors open to the overflow crowd who aren't able to snag a ticket into the stadium—the main strip shuts down early. It's a good guarantee that every TV in town is tuned in to the game, and the Huskies stadium itself becomes the chaotic home of drunk college kids and rowdy locals.

I'm not sure whether it's because I haven't been to one of these games in forever or because it's the first home game of the season, but the crowd seems unusually unruly. Angry. We're sitting a couple rows up from a group of college guys down to their underwear, painted head to toe in the Huskies' maroon color. A decent contingent of fans from the opposing team sits across the field, countering the Huskies Howls with boos whenever something happens remotely in our favor.

There's a fumbled pass on the field. A voice behind us, which had been calling for a flag only a few minutes ago, turns completely hostile.

"This is what you get for throwing a jersey on a freshman and calling him a wide receiver. They hire a washed-up townie for a head coach and think it'll make it okay that this team can't win a game—"

Anger ricochets through me. "How is he washed up? He's the youngest coach in his division."

Emily pats my knee. "I do feel for him, too. We all do. Zac," she clarifies when I look confused. "Don't know how he can stand to live in this town when they all turn up their noses at him. And I hear he's lived here since he was a kid. You'd think they'd be kinder to him."

Yes, Emily. Exactly.

The hardest part about sitting here tonight hasn't been the score, which I can admit is atrocious. It's been hearing people from around town trash-talk Zac like he hasn't lived among them since he was a kid. Like his grams hadn't been everyone's favorite person.

Like he doesn't care about this team, like he doesn't work his ass off every day to get them in a better place, like—

"Oh, there's your brother coming back," Emily says, jumping up as Parker files into our row. "You'll make sure to come to the WAGs game, yes? This Tuesday at the stadium! I know the girls would love to meet the one who managed to pin down Brooks Attwood. We'd all be lying if we said he wasn't the team heartthrob."

Brooks, the heartthrob?

I find him on the sideline, standing with Zac. He's objectively good-looking, sure. The tattoos covering his arms do give him a certain edge and, yeah, he was an NFL star until his injury.

But are these women blind?

How do you even manage to pay attention to another man when Zac Porter is standing beside him? Have they *seen* him smile? How competent he looks, coaching down there?

Also, he smells pretty wonderful, and he's very warm when you cuddle in bed. He makes sure to move your hair out of the way so it doesn't snag in the middle of the night.

Also, his body is the kind of mouthwatering that stays imprinted on the backs of your eyelids, so that whenever you close your eyes, you can still see the way he looked bathing in that lake.

Also—

Parker plops down in the seat just vacated by Emily, with Summer at his other side. "Look at you, Mels. We leave you for five minutes and you're already making new friends."

"That was Emily Davies—she's dating one of the coaches. Apparently, there's this flag football game I get to go to?"

Maybe spending a night acting the part of loving girlfriend to Brooks doesn't feel appealing. But I used to *love* flag football in high school.

"The WAGs game," Parker says with a nod. "Heard about that. They do it every year. Guess it's part of the package now you're one of them."

Summer pokes her head around Parker. "How *are* things going with Brooks, Mels?"

"Hm? Oh, it's good. He's really nice," I say vaguely. Parker turns his attention to his knee, working to dry the condensation mark his beer has left.

"He is," Summer agrees. "You know, I've known him since Zac started bringing him around. But I'd never have pictured you two together."

"Really? Why's that?"

"I always thought you'd be with someone with a little more bite than Brooks. Who isn't afraid to challenge you when you try to get a rise out of him."

I smile, eyeing Zac where he's standing huddled with Brooks. "He does a pretty good job of it."

Summer follows my sightline. "He's pretty fine, too. I'm sure that doesn't hurt."

The game has really taken a bad turn. Still, Zac is down there looking so good, visibly trying to pep up his players. He's oozing confidence despite the score, and I feel absurdly proud watching him command his team's respect like this.

"You have no idea. Seriously, he's a twenty out of ten," I say absently, suddenly distracted by the way Zac's pants fit him.

The whistle goes off, calling the end of the first half. Almost instantly, Parker and Summer are accosted by a group of girls I vaguely figure out play on the Huskies volleyball team.

I catch a glimpse of Zac following his players as they disappear through the opening under the stands. He scans our row of seats, eyes settling on me. It's not long. He doesn't get much more out than a soundless *hey* before we lose sight of each other, but seeing him manage a smile despite the state of the game releases some of the anxious pressure in my stomach.

After a while, I feel a tap on my shoulder. "Hi, love. I thought I'd find you here!"

I turn to see Callie, the town's boutique owner, dropping into the vacant seat on my other side. She's holding a plastic cup of beer in each hand, and the wide smile on her face tells me they probably aren't her first drinks of the night.

"Cal, look at you double fisting. I'm impressed."

She laughs, lifting the cup in her right hand. "I swear this one's for Amber. Assuming she shows up while there's still beer in it."

"'Atta girl." We watch a couple of maroon-painted college kids pound down the rest of their drinks and file toward the concession area. "Has it always been this rowdy here? I swear this feels different from what I remember."

"You'd be right. The crowd's definitely gotten meaner. We haven't made the playoffs in five years, now? Six? You know how it gets here. People aren't taking too kindly to seeing one of the few forms of entertainment in this town lose season after season."

"But it's like they're out for blood." I shake my head. "Like they think—it's not like the team's oblivious about how bad things have been. They're trying."

Callie pats my knee. "Good on you standing by your man."

Wynn Sheffield is at his absolute finest, it seems. It's truly impressive how much of the town he's already managed to cover with news of me and Brooks.

"Yeah," I say slowly. "The thing with Brooks is pretty new. But I don't like the way people talk about him. Them. The coaching team."

"Brooks? Brooks Attwood?" Callie frowns. "I heard the Joneses saying something about that a few minutes ago—they heard it from Wynn earlier this week, but you know how he is with his gossip. Never know what to believe."

"Yes, well . . . It's new. Very casual."

Callie appraises me as she sips her drink. "To be young and beautiful again! You're back in town just a few weeks, and already you've got all these men running around after you."

I laugh awkwardly. "He's quite tall, but I'm pretty sure he still qualifies as just one guy, Cal."

"Well, I can't wait to see how he'll try to top your other boy." Callie does a double take over her shoulder, spotting her wife coming up the stairs. She seems to forget both her hands are occupied and sloshes beer onto her lap as she tries to wave to her. "I know I'm blatantly biased here, but any man who treats his lady to an all-expenses paid shopping spree at Callie's gets my vote."

What?

I watch Callie rise unsteadily to her feet, the amber liquid in her cups bobbing dangerously around the rims. "Callie, what are you talking about? You said that shopping spree was on you—you said it was a welcome home gift."

"Hm?"

"Callie, wait a second—"

I stare after her as she moves obliviously toward her wife, fingering an embroidered daisy on my denim jacket.

My new denim jacket.

My new denim jacket that . . .

I told Zac that I wanted to replace my old clothes once I saved up enough money. And in came Summer just a couple days later, there to take me shopping.

I poke my head around Parker. "Sum? That day we went shopping at Callie's, how'd you know I was purging my closet?"

It seems to take her a moment to figure out what I'm talking about. When she does, Summer shrugs. "Oh, Brooks mentioned you talked about needing a new wardrobe. He put me on the case."

"I never talked to Brooks about that," I say, but the sound of my voice is drowned out by roars as the Huskies return to the field. I spot Zac and Brooks talking as they make their way to the bench, heads close together. They're focused, neither of them looking around at us.

I think Zac . . . what, exactly?

Orchestrated a shopping date with Summer. Paid for every single thing I bought and passed it off as coming from Callie. Never let on so much as a hint that he had anything to do with it.

Suddenly, I'm itching to strip off this jacket. The new dress, the pair of shoes. My new underwear. I'm spiraling. It's the same feeling I get whenever I think back on my relationship with Connor, and all the reg flags I ignored.

I've never been starved for gestures of affection. Connor would always think of me in that way. Picking me up a latte on his mid-day coffee break, bringing home my favorite flowers every couple of weeks. It took stepping away from the relationship to realize those gestures had been held over my head whenever he wanted to talk me into something.

Look at all this stuff. Look at this home. You know I'd never do anything that wasn't for your own good, Melly. There's the proof.

Down on the sideline, Zac slips a hand into his left pocket, where he put the four-leaf clover earlier.

I think about the clothes, the lip balms, the complimenting my makeup earlier. And all I can think as I look at him is: *What the hell do you want from me?*

~~~

I pace up and down the deserted coaches' office space, waiting for the game to end. I excused myself from Summer and Parker with two minutes left to go, unable to stand sitting there another second watching Zac move around without feeling brutally nauseous.

I don't even know why I'm in here, or what I plan to say when he comes in. But I can't sit on this. If this conversation doesn't go the
~~~

way I need it to, if I catch even a whiff of a motive, this is over. I don't care if I have sleepless nights for the rest of my life. I'm not going back to his place.

Sharp whistles go off outside, calling the end of the game. Within seconds, the sounds of players making their way to the locker room fills the space. I lean against the closed door of Zac's office, unable to stomach sitting inside alone. Rip off the denim jacket and hang it on the doorknob.

"Hey, Mels. You okay?"

I lift my head to see Brooks and a few other coaches trailing him into the office space, all giving me curious looks. I find the pockets in my sundress and stuff my hands in them, then change my mind and cross my arms instead.

"I need to talk to . . ." I nod at Zac's office door, unable to say his name.

"He'll be a while. He's out doing post-game interviews." Whatever Brooks sees in my face causes a crinkle in his brow. "Anything I can help with?"

"No, thanks. I'll wait."

He zeroes in on the denim jacket I've hung on the doorknob. "Who do you talk this out with?"

"Talk what out?"

"This . . . secret relationship. I know about it; I can be an outlet for Zac. Who's doing that for you?"

I shrug, shooting a tight smile at a coach giving me and Brooks a curious look over his shoulder. "The whole point is keeping this from Parker, which means keeping it from Summer, given how close they are. I guess that means no one."

Brooks nods, like it's the answer he expected. "All right, girlfriend. Let's go to my office. Come on."

He leads me a couple of doors down to an office identical to Zac's, and ushers me into one of the chairs in front of his desk.

"I know it's not ideal, considering I'm Zac's friend. But it's not fair that only one of you gets to talk things out with a third party." He sinks into the chair next to mine. "I promise I'll stay as diplomatic and unbiased as possible."

I shift uncomfortably in my seat. "I was going to speak to Zac about it tonight . . ."

"Good. Whatever it is, you should. And if you'd feel better just sitting here in silence while we wait for him to wrap up the presser, that's fine by me. But you can talk to me, too. If you want to."

I consider him. He mentioned back when we were camping that he'd gone through a terrible breakup as well. That his last girlfriend left him for a former teammate when he left the NFL.

"Did you ever try to date again—after your breakup with Naomi?"

Brooks shakes his head. "I haven't wanted to. The breakup, what happened with my career . . . it left me in a pretty bad place. Even now, I don't think my mind's right for a relationship."

"Why not?"

Brooks tips his head thoughtfully. "I've got a lot to be grateful for. My parents, my sister, my friends. My dog," he adds with a laugh. "I played long enough that I'm not hurting for money. But if you ever asked me what I wanted out of life, it wouldn't be this. Zac's a great coach. He's smart, patient. He's got this natural way of making others see their own potential and motivating them to be better. He was meant to do this. I'm not, and I know it. It's been a year since the injury and I'm still not over it. I miss playing. I'm not at my most happy, and I'm not doing much to help myself. I'd be a terrible partner."

"It sounds like you need a playbook," I say without thinking.

"What do you mean?"

"Oh." I flush. "It's this idea Zac had. I wrote out the ways I was going to work on myself, so that I could take back control of my life after Connor. Like a playbook for my life."

Brooks's gaze drifts to the far wall, where he stares for a moment.

"Of course, that's something he'd come up with. It's not a bad idea, you know."

I watch Brooks run his fingers along his hair. "If I ask you about something, can you keep it between us? I swear, I'll speak to Zac about it, too. But for now?"

"All this stays between us, Mels. Besides," Brooks cocks his head, "I'm pretty sure that if I ever tried to spill your secrets, even to him, Zac would straight up wallop me. And I've never seen him turn a fist on anyone."

I nod, staring down at the jacket in my lap. "When you told Summer to take me shopping"—I watch understanding dawn on Brooks almost at once—"I assume Zac asked you to do that?"

He leans forward, pressing his elbows on his knees. "This is a hypothetical scenario, right? Because if that really did happen, he'd also have sworn me to secrecy."

I chuckle. "Yes. Totally hypothetically, would Zac be the type to ask his friend to orchestrate a shopping spree for . . ."

"A woman named . . . *Belody*?"

I manage a laugh. "The one and only."

"Hypothetically, I do think that's something he'd do."

"And why would he do that? *Hypothetically*."

"Hypothetically, I think he'd be the best person to answer that. But if I had to guess, I'd think he'd have heard something that made him feel as though Belody needed it. And he'd have wanted to do that for her." Brooks studies me. "Was he wrong?"

"No," I sigh. "I did need it. Really badly. But I just got out of a relationship where I was constantly showered with gifts, and that didn't exactly turn out well."

"What kind of stuff would he gift you?"

"Jewelry I never asked for. Clothes he said would suit me. He was very full-on with that kind of thing. Looking back, the red flags are blinding."

"Do you see them here? With Zac?"

"I don't. But I only saw Connor's red flags in hindsight. How do I know I'm not making the same mistake?"

Brooks rubs a hand over his jaw. "It's a good question. I've asked myself the same thing after my breakup. How can I tell that the next person I'm with wants me, and not the . . . I don't know. The appeal of being with a pro athlete. Former athlete, I guess."

"Have you come up with anything?" I ask hopefully.

Brooks smiles kindly. "Yes, actually. Getting burned the way I did, the way you did . . . finding out the person you were with wasn't who you thought they were? It was a shit deal, Mels. But it's a lesson I'm never letting go of. I know the signs now, know what to look for. And as much as I'd work to give that new person the benefit of the doubt, I won't ever ignore my gut again. By the sounds of this conversation, you're in the same place as I am."

I clutch the denim jacket into fists. "My gut tells me Zac had good intentions," I admit. "He listened to me, what I needed, and he gave it to me. Right?"

He grins. "I wasn't there for your conversation. I can only really validate that by being biased."

"Then please, be biased," I say desperately. "Honestly, I really need someone to tell me I'm not crazy for believing he's just that good of a guy. That he did it purely to make me happy."

"As far as I'm concerned, if he wanted to hold it over your head or use it against you later, it would require him to tell you he was the one behind it. The whole thing is typical Zac. He did the same for me when I was trying to figure out my next move. Put in a good word for me with the Huskies and never told me. It wasn't hard to figure out he was behind it, but he never so much as let me buy him a drink as a thank you. If we ever talk about it in the months since I got this job, it's because I bring it up."

I think back to earlier in Zac's office. How quickly he swept aside that he's been replenishing my lip balms every time I lose one. And this? Having Brooks initiate a day of shopping with Summer, asking Callie to take credit for paying for it all. Brooks is right. It's so Zac, it makes my heart ache.

I sigh deeply, losing the weight of the hour and a half since Callie's drunk slipup. I nudge Brooks's foot with mine. "You know, you're kind of the best fake boyfriend I could've asked for."

Brooks grins. "So far, so good, huh? Maybe it'll be my next career move: Brooks Attwood, Professional Fake Boyfriend."

"I think it's kind of brilliant. And I'm proud to be your first."

Chapter 22

Zac

A seventeen to forty loss.

It was ugly, but there were flashes of good in there, too. It's not quite right yet, but it's clear that with a little more time, the chemistry between Noah and Baby Clark Kent can turn into something special.

Special enough to get Noah playing in the NFL next season, and safely away from his destructive father. Special enough to get us some wins and let me keep my job.

But it's hard to hang on to that optimism after a long team debrief, where no amount of inspirational talk could lift the guys from their dejected funk. And yet another press conference where people blatantly opined on the matter of my employment.

I'm out of my truck the second I kill the engine, moving for the inside of my house like I'm being chased by one of Mel's imaginary axe murderers. But the truth is, I feel a lot like a depressed moth desperately searching for an open flame.

My flame happens to take the form of a stunning, sharp-tongued woman in a bright sundress, who brings me four-leaf clovers for good luck before a game.

This late, I expect to find Melody in bed. Instead, I follow the sweet smells coming from the kitchen to find her leaning into the fridge dressed down in a pair of drool-inducing leggings. The sight of her perfectly sculpted legs is more than enough to lift my mood. But then she straightens and I swear, if I didn't just dart out to steady myself on the kitchen island, she'd find me on the floor.

She's wearing an oversized, ancient jersey. White with the teal accent color from our high school. The number ten, and my last name plastered on the back.

I can't tell whether I'm about to come or laugh or cry. It's a fascinating combination of emotions.

She borrowed that jersey mostly to annoy Parker back then, who bitched for days that it was weird that she wouldn't wear his jersey to our games, considering they shared a last name. But I always let my lovesick brain fantasize about a scenario where she wore it because she miraculously reciprocated the way I felt about her. That maybe she was Parker's sister, but when she was in the stands watching our games, she was there for me, too.

And maybe she was, if her confession at the campsite was true.

Mel finally spots me behind her, then scans me head to toe like she's trying to find answers to unasked questions.

"I didn't know how you'd prefer to recuperate," she says slowly. "So, I have three options prepared for you."

Is it too much to hope that one of them involves her face down on my mattress while I fuck the lights out of her in that jersey? Talk about recuperation.

"What are the options?"

Mel lays her palms on the counter between us, and you know what? That fantasy now involves her bent over this counter instead.

"Well, I put beers in the fridge so they're nice and cold by now. We could get so drunk we forget all about the past few hours. There are also cookies in the oven, if you prefer a sugar coma. And behind door number three is a hug from yours truly." She outstretches her arms as if driving the point home.

I hum. "How long is this hug?"

"How about . . . thirty seconds. Full-bodied, and I'll throw in a bit of a back rub out of the goodness of my heart." She offers me a tiny smile to top off the offer. "So, what'll it be?"

"I'm taking the hug, Clover. Every time."

With her eyes on me, Mel rounds the counter. The whole thing feels so strangely monumental, considering I've already dry-humped the fuck out of her. But she's making small moves tonight. The clover, the jersey. The way she winds her arms around my waist, slowly bringing our bodies closer.

With a palm spread over the small of her back and the other tangled in her hair, I leave no space between our bodies but the threads from our clothes.

"I'm sorry you lost your game."

At some point, I realize that I've transferred some of my weight on her. But she carries it without faltering, and so all I do for a while is inhale that sweet vanilla scent of hers. Let it turn my mood around.

"Think it's been longer than thirty seconds," I say after a while.

"I'm not done yet," she mumbles.

I smile into the top of her head, moving her hair out of the way so I can get a good look at my name on her back. "Nice jersey, by the way. Mind telling a guy how he's supposed to interpret something like this?"

Her face is still buried in my chest, but her shoulders shudder in a silent laugh. "I'm showing my support. Make of it what you will."

"And the reason you kept my jersey all these years would be . . ."

Mel pulls back to get those wide blue eyes on me, chin propped on my chest. "Honestly? I tried to get rid of it more than once. I never could."

This woman is as slow a burn as they come. I don't blame her for it one bit—she has a hell of an ex, moved back to town just over a month ago with barely a sliver of confidence left to her and all the distrust in the world. But then she shows up, clover in hand or with my name on her back and a tray of cookies in the oven. Tiny gestures to anyone else. To me, though, knowing what she's been through? She may as well be moving mountains.

And I need to kiss her. It's not a want. It's a *need*, this sudden, desperate, life-or-death thing I have to do before my body starts to split at the seams. Turn to dust, fizzle into nothing.

Then Melody parts her lips, chin still propped on my chest. I'm not the smartest man on earth. But I'm not stupid enough to pass up a chance like this.

I rake back the hair framing her face and cup her cheek, and she lifts her head. She looks nervous, but then, so am I. I might've kissed her before, back at the campsite, but it didn't feel like this. She didn't look at me like this.

"Oh, damn. Should I not be here?"

Melody's head snaps in the direction of the hallway, while mine snaps toward the beeping oven.

You *must* be joking.

You must.

There's just no way the damn cookies would finish cooking at this precise, inopportune moment. And then I follow Mel's gaze to find Noah hovering awkwardly at the entrance to the kitchen. He's still dressed in his postgame tracksuit and doesn't look worse for wear. But there's added depth to the dejected look he wears now, and I know instantly that something's gone wrong at home. That his overnight bag will be sitting by the door.

"Sorry, Coach," he says, backing away as Mel disentangles herself from me. "I'm just gonna . . ."

"Noah," I say sharply as he turns the corner into the hall. "Get your ass back in here."

He trudges back in and Melody rushes to the beeping oven, pulling out a tray of what looks like chocolate chip cookies. Noah's gaze snags on her back, and I assume he's analyzing the jersey with my name on it.

Hopefully, he takes a moment to clue me in once he figures out what it means. "Bet you regret giving me that key now, huh, Coach?"

"My only regret is that you still don't get that you're supposed to call me Zac while you're staying in this house."

He ignores the comment. Noah wiggles his eyebrows and glances pointedly at Melody, who's facing away from us as she carefully pries her cookies off a baking sheet.

"Way to go," he mouths silently.

"Shut up," I mouth back.

If it were anyone else, it would be weird, if not completely inappropriate, to tell a student to shut up. But Noah's stayed here more times than I can count since he joined the team three years ago. And with only an eight-year age difference between us, within the walls of this house, he's more like the kid brother I never had.

Rounding the island, I fill a glass with water and slide it across the counter to him. "You good?" I mouth now.

Noah's still standing there, so clearly he doesn't have an issue with Mel knowing he's here to stay the night. But I'm not going to be the one to make him talk about his home life in front of someone new to him.

With a shrug, he says out loud, "Same old shit. He tried to make it to the game tonight, but he was so drunk I found him passed out in the cab of his truck, still in the driveway. He blew up on me when he realized he slept through the game. Like I was supposed to sit on my hands and refuse to throw until he got his ass to the stadium."

Melody turns back with a plate of cookies, and for her benefit he adds, "My dad's an alcoholic. Coach—Zac lets me hang around here when he kicks me out."

"I'm very sorry that's something you deal with," she says softly. "If you'd like some time to talk alone, I can head home. Give you some space."

Noah shakes his head at the suggestion. "Nah, it's all good. Last thing I want to do after leaving there is rehash it here. Can I have a cookie?" He reaches for one when she slides the plate over, gaze bouncing from me to Melody. "What I'm really interested in knowing is when the no sleepovers rule stopped being in effect."

"No sleepovers?" Melody asks.

He nods in my direction. "He's a lot stricter than I'm used to at home. No sleepovers with girls while I stay over. And if I get here early enough on a weeknight, I have to study for at least a couple hours."

My face is flaming hot. From the way her hair is framing hers, I have no idea what Melody's thinking.

The kid's doing a damn good job of painting me as the fucking fun police. But I know how easy it can be to get lost in the adoration from your teammates, peers, and the people around town when you're in his position with the Huskies.

I'm dead set on getting this kid drafted to the NFL this year, which means he likely won't come back for his senior year of college. Players at his level rarely do. But that doesn't mean I won't do whatever I can to make sure he keeps his head on straight while he's here.

Noah appraises Melody, clearly amused by what he sees. "I, on the other hand, am clearly as good a wingman as it gets. You two are free to have all the sleepovers you want under my watch."

Melody fumbles two attempts at tucking her hair behind her ear. When she glances at me from the corner of her eye, her cheeks flush as hard as mine.

Noah winks at me. "You're welcome, Coach."

~~~
~~~

"Every time I think you can't get any sweeter, you go proving me wrong. You and Noah are adorable together."

Melody caps the lip balm on the nightstand, flicks off the light, and crawls under the bed covers. I shift around to pull off my shirt and put out an arm, inviting her in.

"Noah's a good kid," I tell her as she curls into my side. "He deserves to have someone looking out for him."

"He's lucky to have you." She smooths a hand down my chest, grazing my stomach, leaving a light tingle over every inch of skin she touches.

Something's definitely different tonight. It wasn't just the jersey or the hug. She's left no air between our bodies, has melted into me so perfectly I feel her, soft and warm, in every rise and dip of my body.

For the first time in weeks, we don't feel like two people hovering in the awkward gray area between friendship and something more. For the first time in weeks, it feels like she's taken a step forward. Toward the finish line I've been standing at since I was fourteen, waiting—*hoping*—for the day she'll join me.

"Clover," I mumble as she runs her hand down my side. "What are you doing?"

"Feeling around for crazy scars. A third nipple."

I burst into a shocked laugh. "Why the hell are you inspecting me for a third nipple?"

"Because you only ever take off your shirt in the dark. Have you noticed that?"

Fuck. I've been waiting for her to call me out on that. "I guess I'm a little shy."

"You, shy? I don't think so." Her fingers curl and she grazes her nails over my chest, smirking at the groan it earns her. "It's okay if you have a third nipple. I promise to love it, same as the others."

I breathe out a laugh. "I don't have a third nipple, Clover."

She hums skeptically, and her hand rests over my pounding

heart. "You're so full of secrets, Zachary. The shirt. The lip balms." The moonlight streaming into the room illuminates her eyes. "You bought all my new clothes."

My stomach drops. *Fuck.*

That's two strikes against me in one night. Earlier, realizing how stupid I'd been not to break in the lip balms I've been leaving around for her. Now this.

I consider denying it, but she didn't ask a question. She's got me cornered, and I never meant for her to know this. Did everything I could to make sure she'd never know this. I got Brooks to initiate the shopping trip with Summer, called Callie with my credit card number and asked her to say that whatever Mel wanted would be on her.

There was no joy to be had in sneaking around Mel like that.

But the last thing I wanted was to make her feel like she owed me something for it, to wonder why I did it, what I wanted back. She lived through six years feeling like she owed that piece of shit for every way he spoiled her. As though the privilege of spoiling Melody Woods wasn't reward enough.

"Who was the leak?"

Her brows rise, like my copping to it caught her by surprise. "Drunk Callie let it slip at the game. Why'd you do it?"

Damn it, Callie.

"Because you deserved it. Because I knew you needed it, and I wanted to make you happy." When her brows crinkle, I add, "Are you angry? I wasn't sure . . . He paid for all your old stuff."

"He *chose* all my old stuff. Dressed me the way he wanted and then held it over my head that he paid for it. Every single thing in that closet had strings attached to it, and I didn't get a say in any of it. The stuff I got at Callie's—the stuff you paid for? I know it sounds stupid, but it meant a lot to me to have been able to pick it out myself."

"It's not stupid at all. And I don't want you to pile on the gratitude," I say quietly, hoping she believes me. "Like it wasn't the best money I've ever spent to see you feeling good about yourself again. Like you didn't deserve the gesture."

She reaches up, runs her fingers through my hair. "Zac, thank you. For the clothes. The lip balms, having me over every night, and cooking me breakfast every morning. For making me write that playbook, and making me feel like I could take back control of my life."

"I don't need you to thank—"

"No," she cuts in. Her soft skin rubs mine as she shakes her head. "Here's the thing. If I have to learn how to let you do nice things for me without looking for a motive, then you have to learn how to accept a *thank you*. Deal?"

There's enough moonlight filtering into the room to light up her smile, and thank God for that. "You've got yourself a deal, Clover."

She nuzzles into me. "I don't understand how you're single."

"I've never been single. I've been yours."

The words slip out without a thought, and I think I messed up. Showed my hand before I was ready to, and there's no way she won't put it together now that my heart has beat at a rhythm that called to hers since I was fourteen. That when she left Oakwood Bay, it was with a piece of me that I don't even want back, anyway. It belongs to her, just like the rest of me.

I haven't been single since the day I met her.

Mel shakes her head, though. Either she doesn't get it—still doesn't get it—or she refuses to accept it altogether. She heaves a sigh. "You're a real catch, Zachary Porter."

Her eyes shine as she looks up at me, and I sweep her cheek with my thumb. "So, catch me."

It comes out like a challenge. Daring her to take a chance on me. Because if it's not her catching me, it won't ever be anyone.

Chapter 23

Zac

It's the first Tuesday in October which, for me, normally means I get the night off at home to allow my coaches the utter indignity of pitting their partners against each other in a game of flag football.

I've never attended one of these, in all my years coaching the Huskies. Why would I? With Mel out there in the city with some dirtbag boyfriend who wasn't me, I never had a wife or girlfriend to show for.

And then Mel admitted she was invited to play. She said it in that nonchalant, scowly way of hers, but I've had this woman memorized for fourteen years. The way her nose wrinkled told me exactly how much she was into the idea of running around the Huskies field. So here I am, sitting in the stands. Still with no wife or girlfriend to show for, considering Mel's only here on Brooks's behalf, the lucky son of a bitch. But you couldn't have paid me to stay away.

The seats around me are buzzing with kids who've come to watch their parents amuse themselves for a night. Melody's already out on the field with the rest of today's players and their designated coaches, standing side-by-side with Brooks, her anointed fake boyfriend.

I'd be more annoyed about it if I wasn't getting such a kick out of watching her chat with the other women. Tentative at first, unsure of whether to play the part of the beaming ball of sunshine or just let herself be, snarky quips and all. As the minutes pass, though, her body visibly relaxes. She says something to the group that has them laughing, and I might end up decreeing that this annual game goes weekly, just to see that sweetly satisfied look on her face again.

"How'd you manage to get up here without anyone wondering why you came?" Brooks sits next to me, hiking up his feet on a seat in the row in front of us. I was too fixated on Melody to notice him break away from the crowd.

"I didn't. Had to tell them I got my days mixed up and came out for practice," I tell him. "Why aren't you down there with the rest of them?"

Brooks gives me a look. "Because your girl noticed you sitting up here with sad puppy eyes and she asked me to check on you."

I find her on the field just as she turns to glance over her shoulder in our direction. That's one way to get rid of the sad eyes. Melody, this attuned to me from yards and yards away? Instant mood shift.

Down below, a whistle goes off. Melody says something to one of the girlfriends—Emily, the one newly dating my offensive coordinator—and with a laugh, they both head for the middle of the field as the coaches make their way to the sideline.

"She looks like she's ready to crush skulls out there," Brooks says.

She does. Mel's got her hair gathered up on top of her head, the ends of her ponytail brushing her back as she tightens up her sneakers and adjusts the belt around her waist where the two flags are Velcro-ed to her.

She's wearing a yellow T-shirt with the Huskies logo on the front, and tiny shorts that have me glaring at my staff every so often, just to make sure I don't have to go down there and poke any of their eyes out.

"I haven't seen her play since gym class," I tell Brooks. "But if she's anything like she was then, this is going to be a hell of a show."

The Melody of back then was stubborn as anything. Never gave up on a play and refused to be told she couldn't keep up. Despite her size, she spent enough time with me and Parker to know exactly how to hold her own on a football field. And given that the stubborn thing still stands . . . I can't fucking wait for this game to start.

Looks like they've tapped Mel as a wide receiver, a smart move considering all those times in her parents' backyard catching for me whenever I wanted to get in a few extra practice throws.

Another whistle and they all move into position. But not before Mel swoops down, picks up some mud off the field left by yesterday's rain, and smudges a dark line under each eye.

Brooks releases a shocked laugh. "Did she just . . ."

I rub my mouth, trying to keep the pride off my face. After all, she isn't supposed to be here with me. But I'm gonna marry that girl one day. There's no other way about it.

"Ten bucks says they make it fifteen yards on the first down," one of my coaches calls on the sideline.

There's another whistle, Gina Matthews snaps the ball, and then it's spiraling through the air in a half-decent throw. Mel takes off, juking defenders pretty impressively for someone who probably hasn't played in years. She actually makes the catch, too—

"Oh, fuck," I mutter. "Look to your right, look to your right—"

Emily Davies—Emily damn Davies—comes out of nowhere and rips a flag off Mel's belt, ending the play.

My heart sinks. Brooks winces. A couple of kids sitting around us groan.

Money is exchanged on the sideline, but nobody looks more upset than Mel herself, who forfeits the football with a dejected shake of her head. I wish I could trade places with any one of them down there. Tuck her into a hug. Give her perfect ass a smack and tell her to get it right back on the horse.

"Not pretty," Brooks sinks in his seat. "Looked a lot like that play in the first quarter last game."

"Don't remind me," I say darkly. "It's been a recurring nightmare since Friday."

Melody stares at the opposing players all *whooping* their victory, and maybe this was a bad idea. It's been slow, but weeks into her return home, Mel's been gradually building back some of the confidence stripped away from her over the years. She's dead tired most days, but I know she enjoys being at the diner. I can see how much more comfortable she is in her own skin now that she's dressing for herself again, and I'll never forget that smile on her face when she discovered Baby Clark Kent.

But for a terrifying moment, I think this game might set her back.

"Okay, okay," one of the coaches shouts from the sideline. "Shake it off, people, it was only the first play."

Gina Matthews gives Mel an encouraging pat on the back, and I need to remember to give her husband a raise one of these days.

"Twenty bucks says they don't make it another yard." Never mind.

Mel heard him, and my heart cracks wide open when I see her cheeks redden from here. I'm supposed to be in charge around here, should probably stay above this. But I'm on the verge of taking his bet anyway, or at least telling them they're all fired, when Melody tightens her ponytail. She puts the same look on her face she had when we were camping, whenever I tried to get a rise out of her. The scowl I've become irrationally addicted to.

"I'll take that bet," Mel calls to the coaches.

Hell yeah.

Brooks snorts and laces his fingers behind his head, now entertained as hell. My tenacious, scowling girl shrugs when the coaches fall quiet. Flicks her eyebrows when she catches me staring and gets back into position at the line of scrimmage.

Is it too much to watch the game unfold from behind my fingers? Because that's the urge I get at the whistle, as the ball flies through the air again. The players converge. I lose sight of Mel completely, watch in horror as the ball bounces out of her teammate's awaiting hands and . . .

"Damn. There she goes—" Brooks recoils in his seat, hands halfway up to his face like he's getting behind the *peeking through your fingers* idea.

Mel fakes a defender, gets open. I swear to God I've never seen anything sexier than the way she hustles down the field, blowing past everyone as that ball tumbles toward the ground.

And she's fucking fast.

She's a few feet away, and then only another few, but there's still no way she'll make it there before that football hits the ground—that is, if she were anyone but the Melody Woods who tore down our high school football field in gym class.

That Melody Woods doesn't bother running the last few feet. She doesn't care that this is a for-fun recreational game with only kids as spectators. She's got a point to prove now. She wants that ball, and she's going to fucking get it by diving straight into the grass, shoulder first, catching it before it hits the ground.

There's a collective gasp. My heart is in my fucking ears as she lies there in a crumpled heap for what has to be the longest second of my life. I've got the seat in front of me in a death grip.

And then she stirs. Sits up, shakes out her limbs. Stands with a wince, covered in dirt. Her elbow looks scraped up as she calmly marches for the sideline, tosses the ball at one of the coaches and holds out an expectant hand.

"Pay up, Nathan."

The coaches burst into laughter. Mel clamps her teeth into her lip, trying to stifle a grin, and I settle back into my seat, tugging the sleeves of my sweater in place to distract myself from the raging urge to rush down there and carry her off the field, heading straight for the nearest bed.

Mel catches my eye, backing toward the yellow-clad players high-fiving behind her. I bask in the smile she gives me.

"Reel it in, man." Brooks nudges me with a laugh. "You look like you're about to bust a nut."

I might. I really fucking might.

~

"We adore your girl, Brooks."

Emily throws an arm around Mel, who half-smiles, half-winces at the contact. Not surprising, considering the state she was in coming off the field at the end of the game, all scraped up with bruises already blooming on her knees. Tufts of grass are caught in her hair.

She's hot as all hell with a bounce in her step, and it makes me doubly irritated that Brooks gets to be the one to claim her in front of everyone as we head out to the parking lot. She's walking in step with Emily, me and Brooks trailing them like a couple of bodyguards.

"Bet I adore her more, Em," Brooks says with a charismatic smile he knows will get her swooning over him the second he's out of earshot. He picks up the pace to squeeze Melody by the shoulders. "We'd better head home, huh, babe? Get you showered? Maybe an ice bath after that effort."

Surely—*surely*—he did not just call her *babe*. Does he have a death wish?

We come to a stop outside the stadium. The parking lot is near-empty. We were the last ones to head out, given the snail's pace Mel's moving at with her self-imposed bruises.

"Good idea . . . honey," she tells Brooks before turning to Emily. "Hey—thanks for including me today. I can't remember the last time I had this much fun."

Emily waves away her gratitude. "We expect to see you at happy hour next month. No excuses!" She turns to Brooks as she backs toward her car, where her boyfriend is already waiting at the wheel. "No excuses, Brooks. I'm holding you personally in charge of getting her there, you hear me?"

"You got it, Em," he says with a salute.

Emily turns to me. "Thanks for coming out, Coach. Glad to see your face outside a game for a change."

I lift a hand in farewell and we stand there, the three of us, waiting for their car to leave the otherwise deserted lot. The second they're out of sight, Brooks shakes out his shoulders.

"And *scene*. Great show, everyone. Excellent work."

Melody huffs a laugh. "You think they really bought that? You and me together?"

I despise the sound of the words *you and me* coming out of her mouth without referring to *me* and her, but seeing as I'm the one who got us into this fake-dating mess in the first place, I'm not really in a position to complain.

Brooks seems to know exactly what I'm thinking. He starts backing away from us. "Better not push our luck. You two have a good night."

He leaves us alone at the curb. Melody glances at me just as I glance at her, and I'm not sure why, but my heart picks up its pace. It's out of place, feeling this suddenly nervous, when I've been sharing a bed with this woman for weeks. But there's something different buzzing in the air around us tonight. I can feel it.

It's the same feeling I had in the moments after Friday's game, when I held her in my kitchen before Noah showed up. He's been staying over since, having dinner with us, watching a movie or whichever NFL game is on TV. Breakfast with us in the morning. I love having that kid around, and I can tell Mel gets a kick out of him, too, but it's made it impossible to ask any of the questions rolling around my brain since Friday night.

Would you have let me kiss you if he hadn't interrupted?

Are you changing your mind about me? Could you see us together?

This is the first time we've been properly alone since. Minutes pass in silence as we stare out at the empty parking lot.

At last, Melody clears her throat. "Tonight was great."

"I can't tell you how incredible you looked on that field. You kicked ass until the final whistle."

"I felt like me again out there. The me from before, you know? Who could just *do*. Didn't overthink every single step, expecting a trap door under my feet." Melody allows herself a half-smile. "I'm so glad you made me come here. It's nice being out of your house together—well, kind of together—without worrying about Parker. Hate to say it, but the fake-boyfriend idea was a stroke of genius."

Something's definitely happening here.

Deciding I may as well go for broke, I hold out my hand. Mel rolls her eyes the way she always does when I dial up the affection, but she takes it anyway. We walk to our cars in silence, where we parked them next to each other as we waited for Brooks to show up this afternoon to start the charade.

It's gray but still light out, somewhere around dinnertime by now. The air is sticky and humid the way it gets before a storm. It fits with the moment, though. We're sandwiched in the space between our cars, an unnecessary shelter in this empty lot, but it feels like we're in our own little world, just me and my Clover.

"Are you following me to my place?" I ask her.

"No. I was thinking I'd shower at Parker's before coming over." She doesn't make a move for her door handle, though. A half-hearted attempt at erecting a barrier, if I've ever seen one.

I pull a tuft of grass from her ponytail. "One of these days you're going to give in, Clover. And it's going to feel so damn sweet."

Her nose wrinkles. "Give in to what?"

"To me. One day, you're going to stop fighting it. You'll admit I'm exactly what you need in your life, and I can't fucking wait."

She rolls her eyes, but then gives me that smile. That perfect, flawless smile made even more special by knowing how rarely she offers it. The inside of my chest feels thicker than the pre-storm air, goes even warmer when she lets me pull her close, bury my face in the top of her head. She smells like a football field. Like grass and personal triumphs.

"You have no idea how bad I want to kiss you, Clover."

"You've already kissed me. In the woods."

My fingers run a line down her spine. "That kiss was . . . needy. Angry. And fuck, Clover, it was so good. But it's not how I ever wanted our first kiss to go."

"How would you have wanted it to go?"

I pull back to look at her. She's not smiling anymore. The curve of her eyebrows, the soft eyes, they scream of want. It was ten years ago, the last time she gave me a look like that.

"You and me kissing, after all this time?" I release a long breath. "It should have been at sunset, with rain pouring down on us. It should have been at the top of the Eiffel Tower, with Paris at our feet."

Mel bites her lip, body melting into mine. "You're a romantic."

"You bring it out of me."

"I hate it." Her eyes fall shut, but her cheeks go pink.

"No, you don't."

Her mouth pinches in a smile. "No. I don't."

I place a kiss on her cheek. The tip of her nose. Her forehead, the other cheek. Soft, fleeting kisses. Her skin feeling so damn smooth against my lips.

"Clover." I brush a lock of hair off her forehead. She opens her eyes. "Give in to me."

She sucks her lower lip into her mouth, eyes on mine. "But we're not in Paris."

"I can live without Paris." I press my forehead to hers. "Give in."

"There's no Eiffel Tower."

I grin. "I'm terrified of heights, anyway."

"It's not even raining."

Once in a while, these moments happen. I'll be thinking about something I've long lost, and it turns up a minute later. Lose my sense of direction on my way somewhere, only to end up exactly where I was headed. Those are the moments I feel Grams the most, know she's still looking after me from wherever she is.

Tonight, I feel her in that first drop of rain landing on Melody's cheek.

Her eyes widen in surprise. She inches away, staring at me and then the sky like she believes I had something to do with this, figured out how to command the weather just to steal a kiss from her.

But then the shock fades off her face, and her fingers dig into the hair at the back of my head and all I see are perfect, bright blue eyes blazing with want.

Fuck.

Our mouths press together. I'm pretty sure I'm the one who moans first, but there are so many sounds, so many incredible, sweet sounds coming from both of us now, lulling me into my favorite childhood fantasy. The one where Melody Woods kisses me, then runs her fingers through my hair and tugs gently to bring me in closer. The one where she lets me slide my tongue against hers, kiss her deep and needy.

Except this isn't a fantasy. It's real. It's real, right?

Mel's kissing me, and it feels nothing like the hate-laced kiss from the camping trip. It's slow. A fucking luxurious kiss as the rain falls around us, like we've got all the time in the world. The kind of kiss where you breathe into each other, break apart in simultaneous blissful smiles before coming back in for more.

Subconsciously, I know this could be nothing more than the product of overwhelming adrenaline. From winning her game, from feeling like herself again after working so hard at it. But I don't care. She can give me whatever she wants, take from me whatever she wants. I don't care what it means right now.

I back her into the side of her car, and we're getting soaked fast, the rain really falling now. Her hands leave my hair, clutching my hips instead, pulling me closer, only to find her way up my shirt to graze her nails along my back. My fingers curl in the hair at the back of her head and she moans her approval against my mouth. This kiss is fucking *everything*. Better than it ever would have been ten years ago, if I hadn't lost my head and left her behind.

Maybe we weren't meant to be back then. Maybe we were supposed to wait for these very raindrops in this very parking lot, to finally come together. Maybe she was supposed to be aching from a hard-fought game and I was supposed to have shattered my own heart just to appreciate how good it feels when it comes whole again.

A flash of lightning illuminates the world around us, followed by a clap of thunder. We gasp apart, my fingers in her hair, hers under my soaked shirt.

"We should get out of this rain." Melody's fingers fall to my waistband. "Let me show you around my back seat. It's surprisingly roomy. I promise, you'll love it in there."

I huff a laugh—a fucking painful laugh—and catch her hand as it drifts lower, over the front of my jeans where my dick begs for her touch. "God fucking knows I want to. But we can't."

"But you can kiss me all you want now."

I slick back her soaked hair. "Melody, I can't fuck you only to send you off to pretend-date my friend. It's not gonna happen."

Her eyes squeeze shut and she rests her head back on her car looking like she's in agony. She fumbles for her car door, but I usher her into mine instead.

"I need to get to Parker's. I need a shower," Mel says. I lean over to buckle her into my passenger seat anyway. Plant another kiss on her as the rain pummels the parts of me hanging out of the door.

"Shower at my place."

She threads her fingers through my hair. "I can't shower there. I don't have my stuff," she argues between kisses. "And you've got man towels."

"Man towels?"

"Too scratchy and manly for my delicate skin. Like your sheets." She moans against my mouth when I get my fingers in her hair. They dig in, because the alternative would be slipping them under her soaked clothes right here in this parking lot.

"My sheets?"

"The whole house has *man lives here* written all over it. It's only furniture—like you live there but don't actually *live* there."

"What else would you want there? Other than softer towels and sheets."

"I don't know . . . Curtains in your bedroom, maybe? Fluffier pillows. Artwork."

I nip her lip. "Hold that thought."

Melody gives an adorable grumble when I pull away, out of reach of her mouth. I round the car and hop into the driver's seat, soaked but not at all uncomfortable as I pull the car out onto the street.

"Where are we going?"

"We're getting curtains. And towels, and artwork. Fluffier pillows. Whatever means you'll like it there." Mel's eyebrows inch up her forehead. She's shocked, even though it's as natural as it gets for me. I've been dying for her to make her mark on the place. "We'll paint yellow polka dots all over the walls, if that's what you want."

Chapter 24

Melody

"If you had to choose between doing away with natural light at home or living with a possible mouse infestation, which would you pick?"

Zac pauses in the act of flipping through the playbook on the patio table in front of him. "Come again?"

Sticking the rest of a half-eaten waffle in my mouth, I nudge his laptop around and adjust the tilt of the screen so that he can get a look at it despite the beating morning sun.

"I'm looking at apartments in the city," I explain, scrolling through a few photos for the listing on screen. "These two are most promising so far."

Zac shuffles his chair closer, and though he leans forward to get a better look, there's an unmistakable stiffness to his shoulders as he does. Maybe it wasn't the best move, bringing up my moving away only a couple days after we veered into *sleeping buddies who make out whenever our live-in college kid isn't in the room* territory. But it's a product of the new wardrobe and the second job. The flag football and making new friends. Zac's unwavering encouragement. It's all got me feeling so good about myself lately, I figure I should keep up my momentum.

"Clover, why are your options a dilapidated basement or a mouse-infested apartment?"

I try to take a sip from my empty coffee mug, and Zac swaps it with his fresh one. He's drinking out of my old polka-dotted mug this morning. "Thank you. They're my options because I'm still waiting for inspiration to strike on the new career front. I was really hoping to afford something better, but I can't keep leeching off Parker forever."

Zac pushes away his laptop like he's seen enough. "Live here, then."

"I'm being serious," I say, tapping at his laptop. "Look at the photos. This place isn't half bad, if you ignore not being able to tell the difference between morning or night."

"I'm also being serious," he counters with a casual sip of the coffee we're now sharing. "I love having you around. And you've been spending more time here, so I have to assume you like being here, too. Hell, we spent the past couple days painting the main floor . . . What color is that, again?"

"Half seafoam."

"Half seafoam," Zac echoes. "So, why don't you stay here, enjoy your half-foam walls?"

It's funny. My ex moved me into an incredible downtown condo without so much as consulting me. Meanwhile, here's Zac—a man who owes me absolutely nothing—letting me decorate his home, helping me paint the place with a color of my choosing without a second thought. After our kiss in the rain, he drove us to the next town and let me fill a shopping cart with whatever I wanted. Soft yellow sheets, tasseled throw pillows, scented candles that make the house smell like a bakery. He's making room for me, opening his life to me, and it feels amazing.

But what feels even better is that I allowed myself to trust that his intentions were pure, that he wouldn't come collect his dues the way Connor always had. And Zac hasn't let me down yet. Neither have my instincts.

I have no idea what we are or where we're going. But there are moments, these days, when I dread the idea of leaving town. When I start to imagine what it would look like to make a long-term life in Oakwood, with Zac. In this beautiful house on the bay.

But all that reconnecting with my instincts, feeling like myself again, has me stopping those thoughts every time they come. I know I'd be staying here for him, not me. I've never seen myself living back here—at least not at this point in my life—and I let myself get lost in a man once, forfeited everything to keep him happy. I won't do that to myself again.

"Half-foam or not," I say slowly, "my plan is still to move back to the city. It's where I've always seen myself, and it's a point of pride at this point. I did everything on Connor's terms, and never got to experience it the way I wanted to. I want a do-over on my own terms."

"So you wouldn't stay?"

My chest throbs at the question, at the tentative way he asks it. "No," I tell him delicately. "I can't stay."

Zac fiddles with the edge of his playbook, smoothing out a crinkled corner. "And what does that look like? Doing it on your own terms?"

"Having a say in the apartment itself would be a nice start."

"All right, let's get another look at this." With a sigh, he pulls the laptop closer and scrolls quietly for a while. "Mel, I'm a supportive . . . sleeping buddy, right?"

"Yes, you are a supportive sleeping buddy."

"And you know I'm all for you fulfilling your playbook, living out your dreams on your own terms, the whole thing. Right?"

I frown. "Right."

"And that I respect you as a smart, capable woman?"

"Yes . . ."

"Great." Zac snaps shut his laptop with an audible clap. "So, at the risk of sounding like a misogynistic alpha-male prick, let me be very clear that there is no fucking scenario that could ever come about where I'd let you move into a rat-infested apartment. Ever."

A laugh bursts out of me. "They're *mice*. It could be cute, no? I'd be like Cinderella, cooking and cleaning with a bevy of capricious rodents."

Zac rubs his face with both his hands. "Melody, it's not happening. If you insist on moving away now, would you let me help you get something better? At least until you get a new job."

"I couldn't accept that kind of help. You'd be paying rent on an apartment that wouldn't be yours." I take in the shore at the foot of Zac's property, the water crashing over the few feet of sand. "Did you ever consider leaving?"

He follows my gaze to the bay. "What do you mean?"

"After your grams passed away. Did you ever think about leaving here? Trying out a new city?"

Zac peruses the open playbook in front of him. "Never. Staying always felt . . . I don't know. Important."

"But you live in this massive house. It seems like a lot just for you."

It occurs to me that it sounds like I'm trying to talk him into it—the idea of leaving Oakwood Bay. Insane, considering we're undefined. Sneaking around. That I'm fake-dating his friend.

"Well, when I built it, I had this idea that it wouldn't always be just me," he says with a smile. "And I think our kids will love having all this space to run around, don't you?"

I scoff. "We're having kids now, huh?"

"I was thinking two. Twins, if we're lucky, so they'd be as close as you and Parker." Zac tips his head thoughtfully. "That's all up for discussion, of course."

Whatever his feelings are toward Parker, it melts me that he thinks so highly of my relationship with my brother. Images of a life here with him and our own twins start fading in and out of my head.

The lazy sex we'd have before a chaotic morning of dressing and feeding the kids, the coffees we'd have in this very spot while they run around the lush lawn.

Except I can't stay. I owe it to myself to make another go of it in the city, minus the bad relationship. Zac's life is here. His job, his friends.

I nibble at my lip, reluctantly mopping the fantasy from my head. It leaves behind murky streaks. Images I can't let go of.

"But I'm moving away, and you'll be here in your house that's too big for one person." *And we're being reckless, getting attached while not knowing where to go from here.*

"Clover," Zac says after a lengthy pause in which I endeavor to look anywhere but at him. When I still don't muster eye contact, Zac drags my chair away from the patio table and tugs me into his lap. I curl into his chest instinctively—the safe space I carved for myself on the night in that tent, waiting for an animal attack.

"Listen, Mel . . ."

The glass door behind us slides open, and Noah sticks his head out from the kitchen.

"Hello, lovebirds," Noah calls. "How are we on this fine morning?"

Noah has stuck around Zac's house since last week's home opener. It was a little awkward at first, but I love how Zac and I have slipped into an organic domesticity together, with Noah as a nice bonus.

"Your timing is impeccable, kid," Zac says dryly. His thumb draws lines up and down my thigh.

Noah comes to hover behind us, holding the back of our chair. "Parenting one-oh-one: don't have kids and expect to maintain your personal space."

"You're twenty," Zac points out. "What do you know about parenting one-oh-one?"

"Absolutely nothing," he says cheerfully. He untucks his phone from his pocket, waving it at us. "My grade came in for that kinesiology assignment."

"And?" Zac shifts us to get a better look at him. I watched them both huddle in the kitchen over this assignment a few days ago, with Zac assuming the role of patient tutor. It had been his major in college, same as Parker and Summer.

"Got an A."

Beside me, Zac *whoops* with so much enthusiasm you'd think it was his own grade.

I shouldn't be surprised at this point. But seeing him interact with Noah has been an eye-opening experience. They're brotherly, sure. But Zac's also a proud, attentive, surrogate dad to Noah.

It's so unbelievably panty-melting.

"I'm heading to class early today," Noah says, fist-bumping Zac. "You two lovebirds enjoy the morning, Noah-free."

"Noah," I call before he disappears into the house. He pauses and I Frisbee a blueberry waffle that he manages to catch in his mouth like a happy puppy. "Don't make a habit of skipping breakfast, all right? You're the best part of my morning."

I'm not the best when it comes to sappy, touchy-feely stuff. But Noah's eyes round a touch over the waffle in his mouth, catching the sincerity in my words—that maybe he's not always wanted at home, but we sure as hell want him here. The corners of his mouth lift before he retreats inside.

"Best part of your morning, huh?" Zac tucks my hair behind my ears.

I blink innocently. "You're a close third, don't worry. After Noah and the waffles."

"Brat," he says, eyes crinkled in a smile. "But seriously, thank you for embracing the Noah thing. I get nervous every time he heads home these days. If I had it my way, he'd just stay."

"It's hard to imagine anyone mistreating a kid like that. He's so . . . full of life, despite what he's been through. Resilient."

"He is. Kind of reminds me of someone."

Zac kisses the tip of my nose. I grumble like I hate it and it only makes him smile wider. This might be my favorite thing, ever. The nose kisses, the seeing right through me.

"Does it sound like it's getting worse with his dad?" I ask.

"He doesn't say much about it, but this is the longest stretch he's been here. Usually, it's just a night or two before he's allowed back home." Zac pulls his massive playbook closer. "If only I could figure out how to win a game. Help Noah impress those scouts."

I peer at the binder. "Who are you playing this week?"

"The Knights," he tells me with a wry smile. "Fair warning that I'll consider anything you say next as potential sabotage in favor of your old college."

"Normally I'd say that's a fair assumption. But I'm pretty fond of Noah. His coach is all right too, I guess." I pull the playbook toward me, flipping through the illustrated pages. It would be a whole lot of gibberish if I hadn't grown up looking through Parker's playbooks in high school. I reach a tabbed section at the very back of the book, and this is more like it. Pages and pages of spreadsheets listing numbers, opposing team statistics. A language I speak.

"I assume you'll run a lot of play action passes on early downs?" I ask him, scanning the stats.

"That's the plan."

"It makes sense." I take a sip of the coffee we're sharing. "According to this, their defensive backs tend to cheat up toward the line of scrimmage on first and second down."

His eyes practically roll to the back of his head. "Fuck, you're so hot. I love it when you talk football to me."

I pinch his chin. "I've been talking football with you guys since we were kids. But look, this is a bit funny." I put down our mug, pointing at a column of data. "Maybe they play close to the line of scrimmage, but this shows the defense plays man-to-man coverage at a high rate on early downs. They probably won't bite on the play fake as much as you'd think. So, really—"

Zac pulls his playbook right off the table, holding it so close to his face it's like he expects the numbers to look different at that proximity. He turns, fixing an awed gaze on me. "Jesus Christ, Clover. Are you kidding me? You found this two seconds into looking at the book."

"I'm good with numbers." I shrug, helping myself to another waffle. "She's not as dumb as she looks, folks."

"Melody," he says, and he grips my chin until I meet his eyes again. "We pay a guy a six-figure salary to look for the kind of thing you just found me for free."

I *boop* the tip of his nose. "Don't say I never gave you anything."

"*Melody*," he insists. "Do you— Does this interest you?"

I frown. "What, numbers? Of course they do. It's what I do for a living, when I'm not shilling omelets."

"Numbers and sports," he clarifies.

"Oh. Yeah, numbers and sports are a much more appealing combination than numbers and making rich white men richer."

"Appealing enough not to get the Sunday scaries?" he asks, referencing my playbook.

I rub my lips together while Zac eyes me so quietly he might be holding his breath, waiting for my verdict. "You really think I could do something like that?"

"Hell yeah. You just did, Clover."

Zac flips open his laptop, grimacing when photos of the mouse-infested apartment pop up on the screen. He clicks away and pulls up a job search site. And despite the déjà vu of talking careers with a man in my life . . . this feels nothing like before. There's no telling, no shoving me at a job I never wanted. I'm almost shocked at the level of excitement now crackling in my chest. Why the hell didn't I think of this?

In true Zac fashion, he's radiating optimism as he scrolls through the search results. So much optimism that I feel it start to feed me, too.

Chapter 25

Melody

I've been around sports long enough to know that the best cure for a bad-game hangover is the next game itself.

But tonight also happens to be an away game, and that means it's my first night without Zac since we started our sleeping arrangement. I'm bummed out by the prospect of lack of sleep, sure.

What hurts the most is that I'll really miss it. The spooning. The sleepy kisses we have to keep quiet, with Noah staying over. The breakfasts before I head back to Parker's for my daily interrogation whenever I make the supposed walk of shame from Brooks's place.

I swear Zac held me extra tight in bed last night, like he was trying to get his fill before tonight.

"Hey, Coach," Noah calls without looking up from his textbook when I enter Zac's kitchen in the early afternoon. "Mom's home!"

I smack the back of his head on my way to the fridge. "I'm only eight years older than you."

Noah turns a pair of wide brown eyes on me. The expression makes him look even younger than his twenty years. "So, you're saying I have a chance with you?"

"I'm eight years older than you."

"That doesn't work both ways."

"It works however I want it to." I bend into the fridge, hoping for something easy to help myself to. I hadn't had time to grab lunch before heading here to catch Zac before he leaves. "How're you feeling about tonight?"

"Best I've felt about a game in years, actually. Are you coming to watch?"

"We don't tend to go to away games."

"Who's *we*?"

"My brother and our friend Summer."

Noah waves a hand dismissively. "So? I know it's a three-hour drive, but you should be there when we win. You're his girlfriend."

I examine a couple of blueberry waffles leftover from this morning's breakfast. "Am I? That's news to me."

A flash of color in a bottom drawer catches my eye, and I pull it open to find it stocked with green apples.

"Mel, we're friends now, right?"

I straighten, apple in hand. "Are we?"

"The three of us watched *Drive* together last night. Do you know how sacred that is? Besides, you guys told me about the fake-boyfriend thing. If being in on a scheme together doesn't solidify a friendship, I don't know what does."

"Then I guess that settles it." I bite into the apple.

"Excellent," Noah says briskly, snapping shut his textbook. "So, if I tell you something, you'll keep it between us?"

"That depends."

I study Noah. He doesn't look worse for wear today, but I know that he meant to go over to his parents' house after breakfast this morning, hoping his father had cooled down enough to let him return home. The fact that he's already back isn't a good sign. For the most part, it sounds like the rage-filled tirades are the worst he's endured at the hands of his father, which is bad enough. If he's about to tell me it's escalated into something more, the chances are slim I'd be able to keep that to myself. There's no way I'd leave him in that kind of environment.

To my relief, after a fleeting glance over his shoulder, Noah's mouth stretches into a smile. He presses his elbows on the island between us. "I've known Zac just over two years now. Since I was a freshman, right?"

"Okay . . ."

"And I've been staying over here at least a few nights a month since then."

"If you plan on making a point before your bus leaves today, you're going to have to pick up the pace."

Noah sits back on his stool. "The point is that suddenly there are nice sheets on my bed. Paint on the walls. I'm getting waffles for breakfast. There's all this weird artwork everywhere—"

"What's weird about the artwork? It's nice. Gives the place character."

Noah jabs a finger in my direction. "That there. That's my point. This place went from four walls and a couch to *character* overnight. I mean, look at this!" He gestures at the massive glass vase sitting in the middle of the island, filled with fresh daisies Zac picked from his garden. "Here you are trying to tell me you aren't his girlfriend. But I've never heard of a guy letting a *friend* decorate his place."

I stare at Noah, thinking back to the nonchalant way Zac let me load up the cart the night we went shopping for the house—*his* house.

My gaze drops to the green apple in my hand. "We haven't talked about that kind of thing."

"So talk about it. Sounds like a pretty cut-and-dry conversation to me."

Truth be told, I've been actively dodging that conversation. I swore to myself that, after the debacle that was my last relationship,

I'd focus on myself, a new career, somewhere to live, before jumping into anything serious with a man. And the playbook Zac had me write—my life plan—remains woefully underachieved.

What I need is more time. But I can see the question in Zac's face whenever I kiss him goodnight. When he first noticed me pulling a toothbrush from the bathroom drawer that sat empty for me since I started staying over. That'll be right around the time when I start kissing him some more, let my hands roam over him hoping to distract him. Or at least talk him into touching me back.

"What's a cut-and-dry conversation?"

The man in question emerges into the kitchen with an overnight bag slung over his shoulder, and my heart is instantly thrumming in my throat. Zac flashes me a grin before his gaze settles expectantly on Noah, who plasters an innocent look on his face.

"Butt out. You're eavesdropping on a conversation with the girl I'm trying to score with."

"If you plan to have a long and fruitful career in the NFL," Zac says, dropping his bag to the floor, "you'll want to remember I have sole control over the time you spend on the field showing off to scouts. Shouldn't you be upstairs getting ready?"

Noah laughs in reply and I lean against the counter, chomping my apple. Zac looks so damn good today. Even wearing a hooded sweatshirt, he looks solid and perfect, and I can't believe I've made it this long without seeing him shirtless. It's been weeks since he last touched me. My internet history is nothing but searches on the possible health risks of overusing a vibrator.

Without missing a beat in his back-and-forth with Noah, Zac's gaze drifts in my direction. It starts at my feet, at the ankle boots I have on. Trails up my bare legs, along the length of my sweater dress. By the time he reaches my breasts, he has a deep tilt to his head, dragging his teeth over his lower lip.

I can't help it. I shiver. The second I do, he meets my eye.

Shoots me a smirk that does something really wicked between my thighs.

Noah groans, grimacing at Zac. "I think I just saw your fuck-me face, Coach. Does that look seriously work for you?"

Zac's eyes don't leave mine. "I don't know. Does it?"

I bite my lip. Cross my legs. "You said you *aren't* coming home tonight?"

"This is disturbing," Noah whines.

"Then get lost, will you? We've got to be on this bus in half an hour. Go get your stuff."

He doesn't have to be told twice. Noah bounces off his stool, collects his textbooks off the counter, and leaves us in the kitchen without a parting look.

Zac stalks toward me, doesn't stop until our toes touch. I freeze with the apple to my mouth, in the act of taking another bite.

It's a really, *really* good fuck-me face.

Zac bends and takes a bite out of my apple. It pushes into my lips so that we're standing there with nothing but an apple's worth of space between our mouths.

He pulls away as he chews, smirking at what must be something of a feral look on my face, given the way my insides are buzzing.

"Don't know how you can stand Granny Smith apples. They're terrible." So, he *did* stock them for me, then. He flicks a strand of hair off my face when I still haven't recovered from his proximity. "You gonna miss me tonight, Clover?"

Blindly, I discard the apple on the counter. "I'll miss getting a good night's sleep, that's all."

"Little liar."

In a second he's gripping me, lifting me, dropping me onto the counter. The sound that comes out of me is so desperate it would be embarrassing, if I had it in me to care. But he takes another step so that he's standing between my open legs. The skirt of my dress rides up as he runs his hands up my thighs, coming to a stop just past their mid-point. His palms grip me as though he's fighting the urge to keep moving, and it sends something searing hot straight to my pussy.

"*God*, Zac."

He kisses my neck, and I thread my fingers in his hair to keep him close. "Tell me again how you're not gonna miss digging that perfect little ass of yours into my lap tonight."

"Oh, *come on*. Why did I need to hear that?" Noah stands in the doorway to the kitchen, looking utterly distraught.

Zac's jaw tenses, but he doesn't take his eyes off me. "Get lost, Irving. We're busy."

"Trust me, there's nothing I want more than to never make eye contact with you again. But any more of this and we'll miss our bus."

"Fuck everything," Zac mutters under his breath. With a deep, centering breath, he steps out from between my thighs with an impressive bulge snaking down his pant leg. "Go wait in the car, Noah."

With Noah safely out of the kitchen, Zac adjusts himself and helps me down. Leaning onto the counter to steady my shaking legs, I reach into the pocket of my dress.

Zac grins at the four-leaf clover I twirl between my fingers. "Are you sleeping here tonight?"

I shake my head. "Brooks is going with you, so the alibi's shot. We're all going to watch your game at Oakley's, and then I'll stay at Parker's. Take a break from rolling around in Brooks's sheets."

"Have I mentioned how much I hate your fake boyfriend?"

"He's your friend. And his sheets are imaginary." I pause, pretending to consider. "I bet they're really soft, though."

His eyes narrow. "Mention his imaginary sheets one more time and I can't be held responsible for my actions."

Zac Porter, jealous of my fake boyfriend. Tell me about this ten years ago and I'd never have believed it. I tickle the tip of his nose with the clover. "For the record, I like your sheets better."

"Because you picked them out?"

"Because I wake up and I'm here with you."

Wide-eyed, he accepts the clover in the palm of his hand, and I lift on the tips of my toes to give him a kiss. "Knock 'em dead, Coach."

He's halfway out of the kitchen before I call out to him. "Oh, and Zac? Thank you for the apples."

He flashes me that crinkle-eyed grin. "You're welcome, Clover."

~

I want to scream.

I want to do an outrageous celebratory dance around my bedroom, pop a bottle of champagne, cry tears of joy-slash-relief.

Most of all, I want to get into my car, drive the three hours to the city, and give that man the kiss of his life.

The game ended hours ago. I sent him a text the second the final whistle sounded, but I haven't heard anything back. Not that I expected it. He probably went out for a seriously deserved celebration with his staff after the press conference.

Out on the street, I hear a chorus of Huskies Howls from bargoers celebrating the team's twenty to thirteen win over the Knights. My insides twist with intense regret. Noah was right—I should have gone to the game. Pretended I was there for Brooks and celebrated with them all.

Screw it.

It's well past one in the morning, I have no plan to speak of, but I don't care. I need to see him, three-hour drive be damned.

I grab my purse from where it's hanging off the back of my desk chair. Bolt out of my bedroom, only vaguely aware that I haven't packed an overnight bag of any kind, and that I'm currently not wearing pants.

At Parker's front door, a notification flashes on my phone, and my heart almost busts out of my chest.

ZAC: Clover.

MELODY: I'm coming. I'm sorry I missed it, but I'm heading there now, okay? Where are you?

Three gray dots appear at the bottom of our text thread, flickering as he types.

ZAC: Open your front door.

Chapter 26

Zac

I stare down at my phone, heart hammering in my chest so hard and fast I don't know how I'm standing still right now.

I was terrified she wouldn't answer my text. That she managed to fall asleep on the first night we've spent apart in almost a month, concluding once and for all that we're cured of our insomnia. That she doesn't need me anymore, that I've lost my excuse to hold her to me every night.

But that's not why I came here. Not why I raced home the second the press conference ended, leaving Brooks in charge of getting the team back on the bus in the morning.

Parker's front door wrenches open and then Melody's there, long hair free flowing around her, wearing my high school jersey over bare legs and I swear, my vision actually flickers.

She blinks, eyes acclimating to the sight of me on Parker's doorstep, still in my game day outfit.

And then she breaks into a wide beam, and holy fuck, she throws herself at me so hard the momentum drives us back into the hallway. She slams us into the opposite wall as I catch her and let her wrap her legs around my waist.

"How are you here?" She's wound herself so tightly around me her voice is muffled in my shoulder, and I squeeze her like I'm sick of existing as two separate people. I want to consume her, soak her into me through osmosis.

"I begged an assistant coach's wife for her car keys. I was dying to see you." She laughs her approval against my skin before pulling back to look at me, eyes shining. I push the hair off her face, run my thumb over her cheek. "You tearing up?"

"You coached your first winning game tonight," she explains. "And I should have been there."

"Yeah," I agree. "I know you'd have had to play along with Brooks, but I didn't realize how bad I wanted you there until you weren't."

Her forehead falls against mine. "How do I make it up to you?"

"Show up for me next time. Front and center, for every game nearby."

"Deal." Mel scrapes her fingers through my hair. "What else?"

I hold her closer. "Kiss me. Hard."

She doesn't. She does me one better. Mel gives me *that* kiss. The Clover kiss. The slow, indulgent one that feels like taking a decadent bite of chocolate and patiently letting it melt on your tongue, just savoring the way it tastes.

Tonight of all nights, that fucking kiss just sets me off.

Mel tries to pull away, but I sink my fingers into her hair. Pull her back in with a fistful and she gasps.

"Did I tell you to stop?"

Her eyes go wide. Hopeful. Greedy.

I plant my mouth on hers and there's nothing slow about it this time. The deserted apartment hallway comes alive with us, our moans, the sounds of our hands roaming clumsily, feeling each other through our clothes. Her nails graze the back of my neck, and it takes her rolling her hips to realize that I'm painfully hard.

Fuck.

She grinds into my cock and it unleashes a hungry groan from deep in my soul. I drop my hands from her waist and fist her ass, the soft skin there barely covered by a flimsy pair of panties under my jersey.

"Please. Take me inside."

It's all Mel gets out before her mouth is on me again, and I cross the hall blindly, eyes closed, nibbling her lip as she moans for me. Feeling around, I find the open doorway and stumble us into Parker's apartment.

The door snaps shut behind us, and I stagger into the dark apartment so badly I end up slamming Mel into the wall. I only have a split second to panic that I've hurt her before she lets out a hungry moan into my mouth. And if this is a sign that she's into that kind of thing, getting rough, thrown around during a fuck, then goddamn, I don't know how I'm supposed to go another minute without—

"Mel?" Oh, fuck.

Parker's voice is a punch to the gut, the last thing I want to hear right now. We spring apart, Mel's eyes frantic and wide as I clamp my mouth shut to tamp down on the panting.

"Mels? Are you out there?"

His voice comes from the hall to the bedrooms. Mel swallows hard, sinking her nails into my shoulders. Maybe she does it to ground herself, calm herself down, but all it does is make my dick twitch against her.

"Y-yeah, I'm getting a glass of water! Go back to bed," she calls back, gulping down a breath as she stares at me frantically. Her hair is disheveled, lips pink and plump from playing with mine, and even if I could hide my hard-on, explain away my arrival, there's no mistaking what was happening here.

"Why did it sound like you were punching through a wall?" We hear a door creak open and the sound of a single footstep in the hall.

"Don't come out here!" Mel cries frantically. "Parker, I'm—I'm naked! I didn't get dressed— "

"Why are you walking around my apartment naked?"

"Because I thought you were asleep. S-so go back to bed unless you want an eyeful—"

"What the hell, Mel," he mutters irritably before treating us to the heavenly sound of his bedroom door closing.

"Jesus fucking Christ," I breathe, dropping my forehead to her shoulder.

Mel lets out a quivering breath into my hair, nails still digging into my back. "Go to my room," she pants. "Try to sound . . ." She drifts off and I find her bleary-eyed, like she lost her train of thought.

"Try to sound what?"

She blinks rapidly, gaze settling on my mouth. "Dainty. Not like a million pounds of muscle carrying his sister's incapacitated body."

I try my best. But at this point, I *am* a million pounds of muscle carrying his sister's incapacitated body, which happens to inadvertently rub against my cock as I move. There's only so much I can do.

The second we make it to her room I drop us on the bed and smooth a hand down her side, over my jersey, to the bit of her panties that peeks out from where the shirt's ridden up. It's been weeks and weeks of torture, sleeping next to her without touching her. Long, repeated showers, jerking off just to make it through the night. And again in the morning, to ease the torment of having spent the night tangled up with her.

I haven't changed my mind; I need us to be more than a maybe before I fuck her. But I'm on top of the world right now, and I'm aching to bring her there with me. I can't keep my hands to myself tonight.

But with Parker next door . . .

Mel reaches for the hem of my shirt. I almost let her do it, lift it off me. But I've got a few things I need to hold on to, at least for a while longer. Instead, I roll her onto her back and bury my face in her neck.

"You only take your shirt off in the dark."

"I know," I whisper back.

She shifts, wincing when her hair snags and I gather it out from underneath her, twisting it out of the way.

Her mouth pinches in a smile. "I love it when you do that."

I love everything about you. Every single thing.

I let my hand drift down her body, inching up my jersey and running a line along the strip of skin over her panties as she shivers.

"Zac," she whimpers. Her hips shift, searching for more of my hand, and I'd bet anything that if I moved any lower, I'd find her wet and ready for me. "Zac, I need you. Please tell me we can."

My fingers slide over her panties, just grazing the front of the fabric. "Can you stay quiet if I kiss you down here?"

Melody squirms under my touch. "I don't think so." Her fingers close around my belt buckle. My cock pulses at her proximity. "Can you stay quiet if I kiss you down there?"

"There's no fucking way."

Her eyes are pleading, like she wants my cock in her mouth that bad.

"I guess that only leaves one option." I roll onto my back, taking her with me, and coax her around so that she straddles my head, facing my body.

"What are you doing?" She clamps her mouth shut when I lift to kiss her pussy through her panties.

"Keeping my mouth busy."

That growing smirk of hers tells me she's perfectly on board with the idea.

Or maybe not. She arches her back, lifting her body out of reach from my mouth, and stretches out over me. Trails kisses down my chest, over my shirt, feeling me through the fabric like she's been craving to touch me. She lifts my shirt just enough to dot wet kisses over my stomach, hollowing it out.

My belt, pants, are quick to go. Mel shoves everything down before settling on her elbows over my cock, and I'm fucking captivated. Heart pounding, breathing hard. Craning my neck just to get a good look at what she's about to do.

"You're so fucking big," she whispers, wetting her lips. Staring down at my cock like she's taking stock. Like it's her Everest, and she's hellbent on conquering it.

And then I catch sight of what's above me. Melody's ass is in the air, still out of reach of my mouth, but the jersey she's wearing has ridden up so that there's nothing but a scrap of silky blue fabric covering her pussy. I reach for her ass and she hums her approval, kissing along my hip bone. A groan wrenches from deep in my chest. My grip on her ass turns so rough there's a chance she'll wake up with bruises in the morning.

She shushes me. "Stay quiet. You don't want this to stop, do you?"

"So sit down. Give my mouth something to do."

She doesn't. Mel, my perfect, stunning, bratty girl, fists the base of my cock, then hesitates a moment, letting her hot breath cover me before curving her tongue over the tip.

"*Ah.* Jesus fuck, Mel."

It turns out, when I'm not taking control, when I let her go at me just to see what she does and how she takes me, Melody likes to be a tease. She drags her tongue from base to tip, kisses me as though she's about to swallow me down before pulling away to watch me buck my hips, thrusting into nothing.

Mel drags wet kisses down my shaft, sucking as she moves along, licks at my balls like she means to do something with them, only to pull away with a devastatingly sexy laugh when I grunt with impatience. She shushes me again.

My cock goes a bit wet at the tip. She licks the pre-cum with an appreciative hum and I might really be dreaming. She's toying with me. *Torturing* me, making me sweat while I wait for her mouth and try to keep my sounds in check.

She pulls away again, and I finally snap. Gather her hair in a firm fist.

"Melody. Stop fucking with me or I'll show you exactly how brats like you deserve to take a cock like mine."

But I've been so shortsighted. This is Melody, my perfect Clover, so with a soft laugh she says, "Took you long enough."

That's the only cue I need. My grip on her hair tightens and I push her face down onto my cock, feeling her mouth stretch around me, drag down, surrounding me in maddening wet heat. I mean to pause partway down, because, without trying to sound like a conceited ass, I know I can be a lot to take. But Melody takes over. Swallows more of me, and then even more, and fucking hell, this girl is a miracle because she doesn't stop until she's got me in her throat.

I buck involuntarily, making her choke. But Mel draws back before sucking me back down to her fist, and again, and again with the kind of enthusiasm I'd have never believed if I wasn't seeing it for myself. Everything is so good, so wet, so fucking hot my eyes start to roll back into my head.

But she's stretched out over me, that tight body of hers barely covered by my jersey as it rides up with every deep bob of her head over my cock. I reach for her, running my thumb over her pussy just once before she jerks out of my reach.

"You don't want me to?"

She doesn't let up against my cock, but she makes a sound of denial. Then she squirms her hips over my head, and I swear to God I've never had to try this hard to resist pussy in my life.

"You're lying to me, Clover." I run the back of a finger over her panties. "You're soaked and needy, aren't you?"

She licks and sucks at my cock, this time her sounds acquiescing. I palm her ass, squeezing, so fucking ready to taste her, but the second I reach to push her panties aside, she jerks away again. And to add insult to injury, she drags her mouth right off my cock with the most breathtaking wet sound.

"It's your big night. I want you to take it and see what a good girl I can be for my game-winning coach."

I let out a mirthless laugh. "Good girls let me have their pussies whenever I want."

"Oh," she says with feigned innocence. "Then I guess I'm just as bratty as you say I am."

I grit my teeth when she takes me in her mouth again. And I damn near buck us off the bed when I watch her hand travel down her body, squeeze her tits through my jersey, crawl down her stomach, reach into her flimsy panties. She whimpers around my cock and I watch her fingers rub circles on her pussy, hanging over my head.

"Let me see," I demand. I'm doing my damnedest to stay quiet, but this is killing me. "Clover, let me see you."

She nods before bobbing down again and I yank her panties down to watch the way her fingers slide over her clit, rubbing fast, hard circles. She's making me crazy. Ruining me with her mouth and making me lose my fucking mind playing with herself for me to watch. I'm aching for her to cave in and drop onto my mouth, or else let me reach for a tiny taste.

"Melody. Do yourself a favor and sit that pretty pussy on my face." She whimpers at the words, and her hips drop a couple of inches.

Then another few.

I jerk up, pull her ass down, close my mouth around her clit and she stifles her moans around my cock.

Fuck yeah.

She squirms against my mouth, soaking the hell out of my face immediately. I suck on her, flick her with my tongue, groan against her. Damn near sob when she pushes back against my hands, lifting off me.

"Tastes so good, Clo," I mumble. "Let me give you more."

She laughs, messing with me like the brat she is, and I've had enough.

I toss her off me, crawl off the bed. Barely have a second to take in the disoriented look on her face before I grab her ankles, drag her to the edge of the mattress, and drop to my knees. At the first lick, she claps a hand over her own mouth.

Fuck, that's hot.

I reach for my cock, stroking hard and fast as I drag my tongue through her pussy. Dipping inside her, luxuriating in the way she tastes before moving back to give her clit my attention and sinking my fingers inside her. She's so wet and hot and making these beautiful sounds as she tries to stifle her moans. This is everything I'll ever need out of life from here on out. Right here—it can't be topped. My Clover on her back, legs spread wide for me, letting me devour her.

I drive my fingers in deep and Mel bucks her hips, taking them in all the way. My knuckles hit lower, grazing her ass and she jerks violently, letting out a single cry into the room.

"Zac. Holy fuck," she gasps.

I lift my head, searching her face. "Good or bad?"

"Good. So good—do it again—"

Oh, fuck me. This woman is going to ruin me.

I get to my feet and grab her ankle, and she gasps when I spin her around so that she lies with her head hanging just off the edge of the bed.

I hold out my dick, line it up for her. "Suck. Let me take care of all your pretty parts."

"I've never done that," she pants, eyes wide but undeniably excited.

"Not with fingers, either?" She shakes her head, and I nudge her lips with the tip of my cock. "We'll go easy, then."

She accepts my cock into her mouth, letting me drag it along her tongue, easing in, pulling back, easing in until she takes me as far as she can. At this inverted angle, she chokes easily, and I run my thumb along her jaw.

"Okay?" I ask. She nods, chest heaving in anticipation. "That's my girl."

I lean over her, spread her open, and my mouth finds her clit again. My fingers sink inside her pussy, while the others brush gently over her ass, barely touching her until I feel her start to relax into it and then rubbing over the sensitive skin in time with the pace of my tongue. She's squirming, damn near thrashing, whimpering as I pump my cock in and out of her mouth.

"Fuck, Mel. You're going to make me come so hard."

It's all so fucking flawless—her muffled sounds, the fucking feel of her—that I moan my relief when her pussy flutters around my fingers. I add pressure everywhere until she goes dead quiet, fists the sheets on either side of her. Reaches for me instead, feeling my body under my shirt. I'm relentless on her. Tongue, fingers, feeding her my cock—

It's stifled, but it's undeniable, and it'll probably be our undoing when the sun comes up and Parker decides to make us pay for this.

She makes the most mind-numbing, blissful sound as she comes. A thick, muted moan around my cock as she shudders into my mouth. When she goes limp, I reach for my cock, knowing it won't take more than a couple of good strokes. But Mel knocks my hand out of the way and, motherfucker, she guides me back toward her mouth.

I lift off my elbows, wanting to watch. She's a wreck, hair dangling off the bed, the skin around her mouth wet and sticky, lips open and inviting me back in. Staring back with a challenge in her eyes.

Oh my fucking—

My hips pull back, drive in, pick up their pace. Giving her what she wants, what I need, and I watch my cock disappear into her mouth, over and over. Both fighting and chasing my orgasm, because I don't want this to end. I don't—

Melody's hand closes around my cock, stroking me when my pumps start to get erratic, helping me finish in her mouth. The force of holding back my groan might leave my jaw sore for days.

Fucking. Bliss.

When I manage to make sense of the world around me again, I sink to the floor and pull her with me so that she's cradled in my lap. Melody wipes at her mouth, her chin, and when I move to wipe off a smudge of my cum on her lip, she guides my finger into her mouth to finish it off.

Jesus fucking Christ. If this is what it's like, if I can barely stay composed over a hot sixty-nine, there's no damn way I'll ever manage to survive fucking her. No way.

"Kiss me," I mumble when I regain my words. Her eyelids are heavy, but Mel sinks her fingers into my hair anyway. "And make it a good one. Your brother will murder me in the morning."

Chapter 27

Melody

Something vibrates near my hip, lifting me out of a deep sleep.

The sheets I'm lying on feel familiar, but the bed is different. The way the sun streams in through the curtains feels different, and it takes lifting my head off the pillow to remember we slept at Parker's last night.

I'm plastered against Zac, my forehead moving with the depth of his breaths. Without shifting too abruptly, I pat behind me for my vibrating phone. And my entire body goes cold the moment I catch sight of the screen.

CONNOR

Apparently, in the debate between fight and flight, I freeze. Connor's calling me. Why is he calling me?

I stare at my phone, shocked into stillness. My hand shakes like he can see me through the screen. Like he knows I'm here in bed with another man.

My thumb hovers over the screen. What would I say to him if I picked up the call?

Part of me wants to tell him I finally figured out his game—how he'd been manipulating me over the years—so he'd know he could never do it again. I crave that kind of closure.

But I move my thumb. Silence the call, and the screen goes dark.

Zac mumbles sleepily beside me, arches his back, and I watch, momentarily distracted, as he wakes up. It's the first time since the camping trip that I haven't woken up to him already out of bed and showered. His hair is disheveled over his pillow, eyes bleary as they take in my bedroom, and when he finds me, he gives me a lazy, sleepy smile.

"Hey, Clo," he mumbles, pushing the hair off my face. With a blink, his face goes serious. "What's wrong?"

The phone vibrates in my hand. "Connor . . . he just called me. He left a voicemail."

Another buzz, this time a text. I don't know whether I have the stomach to hear Connor's voice. But curiosity gets the better of me and I swipe at the screen, pulling up the message.

CONNOR: Melly, I know you'll have heard this on the voicemail, but I wanted to say it here too: I've been thinking a lot about us, and I miss you. Let's work this out. Give me a call when you see this.

What the *fuck*?

I hold out my phone to Zac, who props himself up on an elbow to have a proper look. "Are you all right?"

"I don't know. I guess I was expecting to hear from him at some point, in the back of my mind." I flop onto my back, grimacing at the ceiling. "He spent six years fucking with my head. It felt too good to be true that he'd break it off and leave it to that. Like I got away too easily, you know?"

Zac lies down, turning onto his side to get a good look at me. "Do you want to talk to him?"

"I don't want to hear a single word from him," I say definitively. "I should have picked up the call, right? I should be able to tell him off. For everything he'd been doing, for how he broke up with me and for trying to pull this *I miss you* crap now."

"Why didn't you?"

"Because he's so good at it. Slipping into the soft teddy bear of a guy he could be. Singing my praises. Making me feel like I'm the most important person in the world, and then turning on me on a dime." My eyes prickle with frustrated tears. "A couple months out of this relationship, and I still lose my cool at the sight of his name on my phone. How pathetic am I?"

Tears spill over the sides of my cheeks, hitting the mattress. Beside me, Zac shuffles closer. He gathers my hair from around me, under me, and moves it safely out of the way before laying his head so close to mine. We'd be nose-to-nose if I turned my face.

I really thought I'd been getting better. Getting my confidence back. I've been looking at jobs online, got rid of everything that reminded me of Connor. I feel a lot lighter than I have in a long time, and I feel so good about the direction I'm moving with Zac. So why the hell is my heart still pumping so furiously?

Zac watches me wipe my tears with the back of my hand. "Mel, I . . . I've never been in a relationship. So I can't pretend to know what this feels like—"

The guilt hits me square in the chest. "I'm sorry. You must be so sick of hearing his name."

"I could go an entire lifetime without hearing that fucker's name, and it still wouldn't be enough," he admits. "But what I was going to say is that I think it's normal to have good days and bad ones. Hell, I know how hard it is getting over someone you love, and I didn't even have a six-year relationship behind it. Never mind the kind of stuff you dealt with."

I turn my head, and I was right. The tips of our noses touch. "You loved someone?"

Zac rakes his teeth over his lower lip and nods.

Oh, that fucking hurts. I've worked hard at ignoring the thought of Zac in the ten years since we'd seen each other, and the women who must have had him. It's irrational, considering where we are, the things we did last night. It's silly, considering how much I know he cares for me. But I feel so viscerally jealous of her, whoever she is.

"What happened?" I ask him.

The corner of his mouth ticks up, just for a split second. "I screwed it up."

Apparently, I haven't adequately tortured myself this morning, because my next question is, "What was she like?"

Zac's eyes leave mine, sweeping the space above my head like he's casting around for the right words. "She's funny. The kind of sense of humor that has you hanging on every word, just to see what she'll come up with next. She's sharp and tough and has this way of making me feel like I can do anything. I'll be in the dumps and she'll be . . . she's that first ray of sunlight after a bad storm. Peeking through the clouds."

He says the words with such longing, reverence, that the envy in my chest thickens, feels almost unbearable. I hate her. Despise her.

Could Zac talk about me that way one day? I doubt Connor ever did.

"I wish I'd picked up his call," I say after a while. "I wish I'd told him off. But I knew I couldn't handle it."

"I think that shows you're doing a lot better than you think you are."

"Yeah? How's that?"

"Think about it. You said you'd always give in to him. Put him and his issues first. But you just put yourself first there by not picking up. Maybe one day you're ready to tell him to go to hell. You knew today wasn't that day, and you called it. That's tough as hell, considering how you've described the last six years."

His lower lashes brush below his eyes as his gaze travels over my face, and it looks so fluttery and delicate I shiver like they're sweeping my own skin.

"You really think so?"

"Not that you require my validation whatsoever, but yeah, I really think so." My chest swells. It actually *swells*.

With a single finger, Zac hooks a loose strand of hair lying across my cheek and tucks it behind my ear. His fingertip grazes my skin along the way, just a tiny whisper of a touch, but I feel myself sink deeper into this bed, drowning in caramel-colored eyes.

There's a voicemail waiting on my phone from the person who spent years decimating me. But right now, I feel safe.

Not because I know Zac would protect me if ever we faced a threat together. But safe in the way that I could go out into the world on my own, make all the stupid mistakes I want. Fail spectacularly, fall flat on my face, and I'd still have somewhere warm to come home to. I'd have someone who'd help dust me off, and set me on my feet to try again tomorrow.

It takes Zac breaking into a blinding grin to realize I'm smiling. So big I actually have to lift a hand to confirm the aggressive rise of my own cheek.

This man, and his impossible ability to fill me up when I go empty. I don't know what I did to deserve him. I push him onto his back and move on top of him, biting my lip at the small groan he gives when I straddle him.

"Thank you." I kiss along his neck, stretching the neck line of the T-shirt he never took off last night to keep the trail going over his shoulder.

I squirm my approval when he reaches for my ass. Last night was the kind of mind blowing that did nothing to satiate me. I'm starving for him. My hands fall between us, crawling under his shirt, feeling his stomach.

"Stay quiet or you're going on a kissing time-out," I murmur when he grunts at my touch. "You don't want Parker knowing what we're doing in here, do you?"

Right on cue, Parker's door creaks open, followed by footsteps across the hall before he knocks at my bedroom door.

"Mel?"

I take my time answering, licking up Zac's neck, feeling his cock throb against my thigh. "Yeah, Park?"

"I'm going out to grab a coffee. You guys want one?"

I jerk back so fast there's an audible sound to my mouth leaving his neck. I gape at Zac, horrified.

"You guys?" I mouth, like I need him to confirm I heard it right.

"Shit," Zac whispers.

Despite good intentions, I knew we hadn't exactly been subtle last night. I was kind of hoping the whole thing was awkward enough to go ignored.

But this is Parker, and I should have known better.

"I'm gonna take that panicked silence as a no," my dear brother calls through the door, unmistakably amused at having caught me. "I'll take my time coming back. Give your little friend enough time to sneak out with his dignity intact. Best brother ever, right?"

With a chuckle to himself, we listen, frozen, to the sounds of him making his way down the hall, keys jingling by the front door as he lets himself out.

"Oh my God," I whisper, even though he's gone. I scramble off Zac, tugging his jersey down my body. "Do you think he knows it was you?"

"Doubtful," he mutters darkly, sitting up and adjusting himself. "He probably thinks I'm Brooks fucking Attwood, here because he couldn't keep his damn hands to himself for one single fucking night."

"At the risk of missing out on jealous Zac, I'll remind you that you're the one who ditched your team because you couldn't stay away for one night." I hop off the bed to go sort through my closet. "I feel like we just got off easy. I wouldn't have put it past Parker to camp out in the kitchen, waiting for us to come out."

I dig my diner uniform from the bottom of a basket of clean laundry, tossing the skirt, polo, and apron onto the bed. I'm dying for the day off, especially after our strenuous late-night activities, but—

"Looks like you spoke too soon."

Zac hands me my phone to see our group chat lighting up.

PARKER: I know a couple of you just had a wild night . . .

PARKER: But let's all celebrate our game-winning Huskies at Oakley's tonight, huh??

BROOKS: HELL YES.

SUMMER: I'm in!

"Oh God." I stare at my screen in horror. "You're going to have to give Brooks the heads-up—*what the hell was that, Zac?*"

He surfaces from behind his own screen, wide-eyed. "What?"

I wave my phone in his face. "You texted *yay*? *Yay*, with a period, really? What is it with you and single-syllabled texts with periods? That's not suspicious at all."

He drops his phone to bury his face in his hands. "I panicked, okay? Knowing he heard us last night makes me want to crawl out of my fucking skin."

I toss my phone down, turning back to my closet. "Lucky for you, he *didn't* hear us last night. What he heard was a wild night between me and Brooks—"

I squeak when Zac yanks me onto the bed, planting his mouth on mine before I can get out another word.

Chapter 28

Zac

"Let's make this a winning streak, you hear? Do us proud, Porter."

Oakley's is loud. The bar has dimmed the lights so that it's just a soft orange glow lighting up the place. And true to its role as the only watering hole in town, it's packed to the brim: every mahogany table occupied, crowds surrounding the bar, and a live folk band taking requests up on a small stage toward the back, where tables were cleared for a makeshift dance floor.

I smile tightly at Jim, owner of Oakley's and frequent bartender whenever the place gets rowdy like it is tonight. It's funny how quickly things shift around here. Just last week, I got pelted with sour looks whenever I showed my face on the main strip. One win in, and it's like they've loved me all along—I haven't been able to walk around this bar without a round of celebratory howls going off.

On top of that, I'm the designated cocktail mule tonight.

I should have seen it coming. I don't know how I thought I was going to get away with buying all of Brooks's drinks as a thank you for fake-dating the love of my life—on top of buying drinks for myself and the aforementioned love of my life—without offering to get them for Parker and Summer, too. Tomorrow's hangovers are all apparently sponsored by my credit card.

Back at the table, Brooks throws me a shit-eating grin over the rim of his fresh beer. Beside him, Melody sneaks me a smile as she helps herself to hers.

Tonight's been . . . absolute torture.

I hate this. Pretending we're barely acquaintances. Sitting with a whole table between us, after last night. Acting like I'm not desperate to touch her, kiss her, play fucking footsie under the table with her. But if Parker knew the truth—that it was me and her making a racket across the hall last night—all hell would break loose.

It did once before.

Parker reaches for his drink, nodding his thanks before turning back to Summer. "Maybe it's the app you're using, Sum. I've never heard of someone with such a rich history of bad first dates."

"Or maybe it's me," Summer says, taking a sip of her cocktail. "Actually, no. It's definitely not me. Remember spaghetti guy? Someone failed him way earlier in life than I did."

"Who's spaghetti guy?" Melody asks.

She leans forward in her chair, shifting around like she's adjusting her outfit. But her knee brushes mine under the table and apparently the room's been upside down this whole time because it rights on its axis the second we touch.

"Oh my God." Parker sits back in his chair, closing his eyes as Brooks lapses into laughter. "Spaghetti guy. How could I have ever let myself stop thinking about spaghetti guy?"

"Oh, you'll die, Mels. This was, what? Two months ago? Three?"

"Last year," I correct.

"Really? That long ago?" Summer turns to me, her face screwed up in thought. "Well, spaghetti guy didn't know how to eat spaghetti. And he decided his first date with me was the right time to learn."

Melody frowns. "What do you mean, he didn't know how to eat spaghetti?"

"He ordered it all confident. Spaghetti bolognese, totally normal stuff. And then he picked up his fork and tried to sort of . . . stab at the noodles to pick them up. He didn't know to twirl his fork. So of course, that didn't work."

"Picture it, Mels," Brooks says, nudging her. "Our Summer, here, dressed to the nines for her date—"

Summer grins. "Trying not to choke from the force of holding back laughter as—I kid you not—I watch this guy then eat his spaghetti by hand. A couple of strands at a time because otherwise it would all slither from his fingers." She pauses thoughtfully. "Honestly, maybe I was too hard on the guy. In hindsight, his confidence might've been a little charming."

"I think you can hold out for someone who knows how to handle his spaghetti, Sum," Parker tells her, patting her arm.

Melody's shoulders shake with a laugh. The bar is so loud I can't make out the sound of it, and I actually have to stop myself from turning to the people standing by our table to bark at them to pipe down.

Don't they realize what's happening? Melody Woods is gracing the place with the rare, precious sound of her laugh, and they're all letting it pass them by without a care in the world.

It's more egregious than hearing there's a once-in-a-century comet lighting up the sky, only to close your curtains.

Someone kicks me under the table. This time, I look up to find Brooks staring at me, eyes wide as though to say, *reel it in, man*.

I realize I'm sitting frozen with my glass held up at my mouth, smiling stupidly at Melody. Thankfully, everyone else is still focused on Summer. I wipe the grin off my face. Replace it with a scowl.

Brooks blinks. "So much worse," he mouths. Giving up, I down half my beer in one go.

"You know the worst part of all this?" Summer says, gesturing at Melody with her glass. "I've been scouring a hundred-mile radius around this town for a decent man for years, and this one moves back and instantly shacks up with one of our most eligible bachelors."

My shoulders square with pride.

And they promptly deflate when I remember Summer doesn't mean me. She means Brooks.

One day I'll get to do it, right? Scream about her from the rooftops. Hold her hand everywhere we go, claim her in front of everyone. There'll be no doubt in anyone's mind that I'm the guy who gets to fall asleep with her every night. The one on her team, helping her get everything she wants out of life and then some.

One day she'll claim me back, and it'll make the torture of seeing her and Brooks sitting together worth it. I'll be able to look back on the last ten years of regret and think it wasn't so bad. We just needed time to become the right versions of ourselves. For life to shape us into puzzle pieces that fit perfectly together.

At least, that's what I have to keep telling myself. The alternative is agony.

"Aw, Sum," Brooks says, settling an arm over the back of Mel's chair. "You should have said something. I had no idea you wanted a piece of this."

In my peripheral vision, I notice Melody's fingers tapping the table. She has her chin in her palm, facing Summer, but she looks at me from the corner of her eye. The second my gaze connects, the side of her mouth flicks up.

It's like she sensed that I needed it. Like I'm the only person in this crowded bar who matters.

Like we're puzzle pieces.

"Have you heard at all from Connor since you've been home, Mels? Is he back from that trip?" Summer asks, drawing away Melody's attention.

She takes a few seconds to slowly digest the question, but Mel sits up straight and clears her throat. "Just this morning. He called me. Left a voicemail, sent a text."

"What does he want?" Parker asks tightly.

"To talk. He says he misses me."

Fucker.

Summer makes a face. "The balls on this guy. What we need is a good old-fashioned revenge scheme. Show him you've moved on with a better, hotter guy—assuming Connor's less attractive than Brooks, of course."

Mel's foot brushes mine under the table. "Can confirm. The new guy is definitely hotter."

Jesus Christ, I just giggled.

Giggled like a kid whose crush just made passing eye contact from across the schoolyard.

Parker gives me an odd look from across the table and I settle my face. Melody runs her fingers through her hair, apparently fixated on whatever Summer is saying. But she nudges my foot again. I nudge her back.

She pulls away. A second later, her foot returns minus the shoe, and she slips under the hem of my jeans to tickle my ankle with her sock-covered toes.

And just like that, this hellish night is worth it. Playing footsie with my Clover is the stuff of my fourteen-year-old daydreams.

"Oh, I have the best idea," Summer says suddenly. I force myself to look at her, pressing my lips together as Mel runs her foot higher up my leg, dragging my pant leg with her. "Let me take a picture of you and Brooks looking all cozy. You should totally send it to Connor."

Mel licks the corner of her mouth. She's trying to tickle the back of my knee without moving in her chair, and I'm pretty impressed at the athleticism required to do it. "I don't know, Sum. My plan is to ignore the hell out of him for the rest of my life."

"But that's no fun," Summer chirps, getting to her feet. "This'll really show him for thinking he can just breeze in and out of your life. Let him see what a hot couple you make. Even if you don't send them, you'll have some cute pictures with your man."

It seems she's actually fucking serious about this, because Summer rounds the table to stand right behind my chair. She holds her phone out over my head. Presumably because, as the one sitting right across the table from Mel and Brooks, I've got the best view of the *hot couple.*

"Come on," Summer says brightly. Above my head, she flicks her hand toward Brooks. "Get in his lap, Mels."

Slowly, I look over my shoulder at this childhood friend of mine who's suddenly decided to drive a knife into my back, aiming for the heart. Summer gives my deadpan stare a wide, oblivious smile.

She's totally fucking serious.

Mel's foot drops away from my knee and she squirms around, presumably trying to get her shoe back on. "What do you mean, get into his lap?"

Yeah, Summer. What the fuck do you mean, get into his lap?

"I mean, get in your boyfriend's lap and give him a kiss for the camera."

Without thinking, a laugh blows past my lips. It fizzles the second Parker throws me another weird look.

You have to be fucking kidding me.

Brooks shoots me an uncomfortable glance. "I don't think we're quite there yet with lap sitting, Sum—"

Parker lifts his eyebrows. "Did I mention I heard some very disturbing noises in my apartment last night?"

Fuck.

Melody and Brooks exchange a quick look. My jaw is killing me from the force of grinding my teeth together, and I try my best to stop, but I don't quite manage to.

At last, Mel gives a strained laugh. "Don't be shy, Brooks. Parker won't bite your head off if I sit in your lap for a second. Isn't that right, Park?"

"It's not Parker I'm worried about," Brooks mutters under his breath.

"What was that?" Parker asks Brooks.

"Nothing," he sighs. He pushes back his chair, making room for Mel. "Okay, babe. Hop on."

There's a devil on my shoulder. He wants me to reach across the table and spill a beer on my friend's lap.

It's the one time I've ever resented Grams for raising me right. Because all I do is sit there, watching Melody get to her feet. And it goes from bad to worse. She was already sitting at the table when I got here earlier, so this is the first time I'm seeing her properly.

She's wearing the dress. The green one from the dressing room picture she sent me all those weeks ago. The one that slices across the perfect swell of her tits, a green shiny fabric that might as well have been painted over her curves, cutting off above the mid-point of her thighs. She's wearing it with a pair of sneakers, a Melody look through and through, and she's utterly exquisite.

I've never wanted to kiss or fuck or fall to my knees and beg someone to love me back so much in my life.

Most of all, I want this to stop.

Melody perches herself on Brooks's lap. Face flushing, dress riding up, a furtive glance in my direction. She's sitting so stiff, like she's trying to make as little contact as possible. And to his credit, Brooks looks just as uncomfortable—

Mel starts to slip off his knees, and Brooks quickly reaches out. Then puts his arm around her waist, tucks her against him, and something green and ugly rears its head inside me.

Are we really letting this happen, man? it asks me, incensed.

I catch the look on Parker's face, who is apparently none too pleased with the sight of his sister on his friend's lap, and I work to smooth my expression.

Yeah. Looks like we're letting this happen.

"So sweet," Summer purrs behind me, and *no the fuck it is not*, Summer. She lines up her phone above my head, capturing this hellish moment for posterity.

Melody shifts in Brooks's lap. I zero in on the way her hair has snagged between them, itching to reach over the table and twist the strands out of harm's way.

Then Brooks gathers her hair, twists it, places it over her shoulder and that's it. My fucking breaking point.

Brooks Attwood is a good guy. Decent-looking. Responsible. A great friend.

He'll be survived by his parents, his sister Josie, and his three-year-old German shepherd named Peter.

Because that's our thing. *My* thing, the thing I do every night before we fall asleep, and it shreds my insides worse than Summer's next words.

"Kiss for the camera!"

I can't do this. I can't watch another second of this. I push back my chair as much as I can without smashing into Summer.

"I'm gonna get us another round," I announce. The last thing I see is Melody's anxious look pointed at me before I disappear into the crowd.

I don't go to the bar. I push through the mob until I break into the deserted hallway leading to the washrooms and lean against the wall, trying to get my head right.

It isn't real. It's not real, it's an act for Parker and Summer. She cares about me. That was me she was with last night. She has feelings for me.

Does she, though? She never said so.

"Zac." I turn to find Melody hurrying down the hall.

She stops just short of me, tipping back her head to get a good look at me. Her hair slides off her shoulder, dangles down her back, ends swishing by her waist.

"How did you get away?" I ask. She gestures down her front where I find a dark patch over the lower part of her dress. "You spilled a drink on yourself?"

"It's the first thing I could think of," she says with a chuckle.

But my brain is still wrapped in a thick, jealous fog and I don't manage to match her enthusiasm.

"Did you kiss him?"

Her eyebrows shoot all the way up. "Zac, it isn't real. You know that."

"Yeah, well." I plant my hands on her hips and walk her back until she hits the swinging door to the women's washroom. I push again, and we're inside. "I'm not feeling very rational right now."

Chapter 29

Melody

He's snapped.

Completely lost it. All semblance of control, restraint—gone. "Zac, what are you—"

The washroom is big, dimly lit, and smells like lavender and a touch of eucalyptus. I gasp when Zac turns me around to face the mirror, cornering me into the counter, a smooth, sparkling white surface away from the sinks. I plant my hands on it to steady myself, bending at the waist in the process. My dress is so skin tight it rides up right away.

"Don't move." In the mirror, I see Zac's eyes linger on my body, the way I'm bent over. I feel enough cool air to know my dress is barely covering my ass.

Zac walks the length of the room, checking to make sure the stalls are empty before locking the washroom door. By the time he makes it back to me, my chest is heaving. I'm breathing so hard my vision goes a little fuzzy.

He looks even more fired up than he did last night, and I really, *really* hope it means what I think it does.

"Are you—are we—" I swallow hard. "Tell me you have whatever you've been waiting for. I need you."

His eyes rake down my body with the same pent-up frustration that had us rolling around in the mud just over a month ago. "I'm not fucking you for the first time in a public bathroom."

"Then what ”

"Seeing him touch you, hearing you talked about like you're a fucking *couple*, like he's the one who has you in bed every night," he grits out, jaw pulsing hard, and I've never known Zac to be a possessive man. Then again, I've never witnessed him show other women affection, not even the girls hanging off him in school. "*I'm* yours. *I'm* the one who has you, and I'm getting some goddamn answers tonight, however I need to get them."

If I wasn't aching for him before, his words shove me over the edge.

Zac runs his hands down my sides, feeling my body hungrily. He grabs my ass and I'm so wound up, have been aching for more of this man since last night, that I moan from that alone.

"I could live off that sound." He drops his mouth to my shoulder. "Did you wear this dress for me?"

Of course I did. We both know it. But he's playing with me, making me confess it, and I've never been able to resist fucking with him given the chance. Last night, teasing him to his breaking point had been half the fun.

"I wore it for myself—"

"Liar."

He reaches under my dress, fingers curling in the waistband of my panties and dragging them down my legs.

In the mirror, I see him tuck the fabric into his back pocket. "Am I getting those back?"

"Nope."

God, I hate how hot that single word makes me.

Zac wrenches my dress over my hips. Kicks my legs apart. Lets out a soft groan at the sight of me bare, bent over, and spread out in front of him. My nails dig into the counter.

"So fucking pretty, Melody. I could stare at you like this all day."

I sway my hips, and he tips his head, enjoying the view.

"I'd rather you do something with it."

Agonizingly slow, especially for someone apparently trying for a revenge quickie in a bar bathroom, Zac smooths his hands up and down my thighs. It feels like a flamethrower running along my skin, lighting me up as it goes. His first touch is soft, just a gentle stroke with the back of his finger up and down my pussy until my thighs relax, knees spread a little wider. He finds my clit and my entire body melts. His finger strokes so gently it's a caress, but every brush sends something raging hot ripping through my body.

Zac meets my eye in the mirror. "No bra tonight?"

I look down at myself, the way my nipples strain against my dress. "What is it with men losing their minds at the sight of a nipple?"

"What is it with your nipples getting hard while you're locked in an empty bathroom with me, with that tight little ass of yours bent over the counter?"

"The dress is too fitted for a bra. And my tits are almost nonexistent, so it doesn't really matter."

That pisses him off. Zac rips the straps of my dress down my shoulders and shoves the top until my breasts pop out of confinement. I'm in feral disarray in this mirror, cheeks pink, hair spilling all over the place, panting absurdly hard. Now wearing this dress like a belt around my waist.

"Your tits are fucking perfect and I won't hear another word against them." He palms them. "Who'd you wear this dress for, Clover?"

"Mysel—" I cry out at the feel of him reaching to stroke my clit between two fingers. "*F-fuck.*"

Just as fast, his fingers disappear.

"You," I gasp. "I wore it for you."

"That wasn't so hard, was it?" He smirks, drops a kiss on my shoulder. "Here's how this is going to work, Clo. I touch, you talk. If you hold back—if you lie to me? I send you back out there soaking wet and needy. You got me?"

Zac's fingers find their way back, and there's a kind of dark gleam in his eyes that tells me just how much he means it. Zac is a great sport. He lets me endlessly tease him, push his buttons to my heart's content.

Apparently, he's taking over that game tonight.

He taps my clit, and it's like a lightning bolt through my entire body. "You got me, Clo?"

"I got you," I whisper.

"That's my girl. Now, tell me the truth: Did you kiss Brooks?"

"You should have stayed to see for your—"

Zac doubles his pressure on my clit, switches from strokes to tight, incredibly irritatingly perfect circles, and I can't help myself. My head falls forward and my moan echoes around us. And then he pulls away.

"I didn't," I practically sob. "I wouldn't. I have no interest in kissing Brooks."

"Good. Because as far as I'm concerned, you gave away your last first kiss the other day in that parking lot."

"That wasn't our first."

Zac's fingers gather moisture pooling out of me and smooths it over my clit. "It's the first time you kissed me without hating me."

"Don't I get a say in whether you're my last?"

He smirks, rubbing my clit over and over. "Fair enough. Do you want to kiss other people?" He really is serious about getting some answers.

"No," I admit, and the word is half-whimper. "I don't know about forever, but kissing other people is the last thing I want to do right now."

"I'm glad to hear that. Just in case it isn't already perfectly clear, there's no one else I plan on kissing. And I do know about forever." Zac takes a handful of my hair, turns my chin over my shoulder to kiss me as he strokes me. When he releases me, he catches my eye in the mirror again. "Let's drop the act with Brooks. Let's tell everyone it's you and me, for good."

"I can't—" I dart down to keep his fingers in place when they threaten to leave my throbbing clit. "Please don't stop. I'm not being difficult, I swear."

Whatever this is between us has grown so organically, it's hard to imagine ever giving it up.

But . . .

"For good is . . ." I gulp, eyes flutter when his fingers slip along my pussy, sink inside. All the while, he gazes at me in the mirror with rapt attention, hanging on every word. "*Fuck*, Zac. It's a lot to commit to right now. I'm—I'm looking for a job and some—somewhere to live and—it's a lot to figure out before I start thinking about forever."

This is . . . the juxtaposition is knee-buckling. I'm bent over a counter with barely a stitch of clothing, coming close to spilling my heart out to this man while his fingers fuck me slowly.

"But you feel something for me?" he asks, tone completely at odds with the sinful glide of his fingers in and out of my pussy. "Something real."

I think back to the way I could barely stand to watch him squirm at the table earlier. Every smile and embarrassing giggle he gets out of me without even trying these days. I think about seeing him at Parker's door last night, and feeling suffocatingly full.

"It—it hurts when you're upset. And when you smile, it's everything. It's real, Zac."

Zac nods, and he's so transfixed his fingers fall away. "What's it going to take? I want to be with you, Mel."

"I need time. And there's no sense rocking the boat with Parker until we're committed. Long-term."

"And you need your life to line up before you commit? The job and somewhere to live?"

"Do you think you can wait for me?"

His forehead hits my shoulder, and he shakes his head with a bit of a quiet laugh to himself. "Yeah, Clover. If there's one thing I can do, it's wait for you."

My confused reflection stares in the mirror at the way he lifts his head with twisted amusement in his eyes. Before I can ask what the hell just got into him, his mouth curls into a smirk.

"Glad we settled all that. Now, be my good girl and drop onto your elbows for me." Oh, fuck.

Every speck of air in this bathroom, which had sweetened a second ago, turns steaming hot.

Teeth digging into my lip, I do what he says. Zac crouches behind me, disappearing from view in the mirror. And even though it's perfectly clear what he's up to, what he's about to do, the second his mouth hits my pussy my shocked cry echoes around the deserted bathroom.

"Fuck, I missed you," he murmurs against my clit.

"Are you talking to me or my pussy?"

"Both of you."

He kisses me gently, tongue coming out to lash me, again when I moan, and then harder when I whimper. A light layer of sweat blooms at my hairline, and my baby hairs start to stick to it. You'd think last night would have desensitized me, at least a little. But I'm already a writhing, moaning mess bent over this counter.

"You taste so sweet—"

"Less talking, more licking, Porter."

I squirm, demanding his tongue, and he's the one who moans this time. A sound of pure gratitude. Like doing this, lapping my clit, clamping his lips to suck on me gently, is everything he's ever wanted.

If I thought he'd been enthusiastic last night, I was wrong.

The washroom is alive with moans that border on cries, his own enthusiastic groans, the wet sounds of his hot tongue running over my pussy. I'm grateful for the drunk shouting and pounding music on the other side of the door.

I know I should be clawing for my orgasm with everything I have. That's the point of a public quickie, anyway. But I've dreamed of having this man's face buried between my thighs for years, and the thought of squandering even one moment of Zac on something so fleeting feels unbearable.

Don't come yet, I beg myself. *Make it worth it. Don't come yet—*

Like he can hear my thoughts, Zac teases my pussy with the tips of his fingers. A threat and a promise.

Don't come yet—

It's a lost cause. He sinks his fingers inside me and everything tightens, gets scorching hot, goes utterly still. I reach back to grab his hair and shove his face in deeper, and he takes it as a sign to drive his fingers all the way inside my pussy, fucking me hard and fast.

"Oh, Zac—oh, *fu*—"

Outside the bathroom, the live band picks up a new song, and the bar goes wild. The sounds drown out my increasingly loud *fucks* and *Zacs* as the orgasm finds me, tears through my skin, my bones, sinks its claws into me and draws a violent shudder from my body.

Zac laps at me all the way through, until I'm boneless against the counter. I can feel his reluctance to leave the home his tongue has made of me. Panting, I yank him off with my fistful of his hair.

Zac grunts and staggers back on his heels, and I take that as my cue to turn around.

Oh my God.

Zac blinks up at me in a stupor. He looks barely conscious, like he's just been taking his drug of choice and loving every minute. He's a disheveled mess. Panting. Cock straining against his jeans. Hair wild from my fingers. Mouth, chin, everything glistens from me, from the force of his enthusiasm as he licked me.

"I wasn't done," he growls. It's as outraged as I've ever seen him.

"I just came—"

I must black out. Because I don't know how or when it happens, but next thing I know I'm sitting on the edge of the counter. Zac yanks me forward, kneels, and throws my legs around his shoulders.

"I wasn't done." He hits me with a look that dares me to tell him otherwise. "And neither were you."

And then his tongue hits my pussy again and my cry echoes around us. He slips a finger back inside me and I'm so soaked it finds no resistance. Nor does the second finger he adds, pushing all the way inside me, moving with the rapid pace of his tongue, making it all but impossible to suck in a breath until finally they pull back. They find the right spot and rub inside me. My fingers dig into the edge of the counter.

"Why are you so good at this?" I say through gritted teeth, almost an accusation.

He doesn't bother answering. He teases my other entrance, and I can't believe it's taken me this long in life to realize I like my ass played with. Then again, Zac seems to understand me better than I do myself. It shouldn't shock me at all.

The edge of my orgasm comes for me again. My pussy pulses around his fingers. I'm so close.

Then I catch Zac's eye. His laugh lines crinkle the second I do, and though he continues to attack my clit with the same eagerness, every filthy lash of his tongue feels almost sweet now. Adoring.

He loves this—actually *loves* doing this, doesn't he? He's getting as much out of licking my pussy as I am. I can see it in the way he looks at me. My grip in his hair turns soft. I comb the strands off his face and his laugh lines deepen. Zac closes his eyes, settles comfortably between my legs, fingers toying with me.

"Zac," I mumble.

Zac builds pressure on my ass, making me feel mindless and worshipped. He opens his eyes the moment he slips the tip of his finger inside, and it's over. He watches me cry out, chant a desperate *Zac, Zac, Zac*, and I'm all but screaming in this bathroom as I shudder, so fucking grateful for the loud music on the other side of that door as I fall back against the mirror.

"*Fuck*. Fuck," Zac mutters after I go still. "Nothing will ever top that. Ever."

Zac takes away his fingers and moves his mouth lower, kissing me everywhere, sucking at my skin, picking up the wetness he brought on and leaving none of it behind.

I sit up, completely shaky, as he gets to his feet to assess the mess he's made of me. Then he yanks open his jeans, pulls out his cock, and strokes it with the wetness leftover on his fingers.

Holy shit. He is so sexy.

"Let me," I urge him. "Let me do it for you."

Zac moves between my thighs, but I push him back, enough to slip off the counter and drop to my knees. His shoulders sag in defeat and I have no idea what he's defeated about, considering the sound that comes out of him the second he's in my mouth. He gives me these unbelievably deep moans, and nothing is more of a turn on than a man getting vocal when you're touching him.

"Oh, fuck yeah." He drops his head forward to watch, combing my hair back into a gentle fist. I don't take my eyes off him, either. "I'll never get enough of you, you know that?"

It doesn't take him long. Another stroke of my hand, lick of my tongue, and I'm pulling away to let him finish on me. He comes with a hard grunt, painting my chest and stomach, barely missing my bunched-up dress. He takes it all in with hungry eyes, the way he said he would back in the woods, before scooping me off the ground and back onto the counter.

"The day I fuck you, it's over. I'm done for. No way I come out of it alive."

"Pretty sure we'll be going out together." I shut my eyes, resting against the mirror behind me.

He kisses down my neck as he dresses himself. "Don't move, Clo."

Zac pulls a handful of paper towels from a dispenser nearby, wets them, cleans me off before helping me off the counter. I stand there weakly as he tugs my dress back into place, tidies me up.

"I don't think I can go back to that table," I whisper.

"Then get out of here." Zac kisses the tip of my nose. "Change out of that dress. I'll stay here a while as a cover, but I'll see you at home, okay?"

He dabs at the sheen of sweat along my hairline, runs his fingers through my hair so that it lies flat. Adjusts my dress some more. It's still soaked from the drink I spilled on myself.

"You're seriously capable of sitting with Parker, pretending none of this happened?"

He scatters kisses all over my face before turning me around and pointing me at the door. "Pray for me."

Chapter 30

Melody

"You're very popular this morning."

My highlighter pauses midair, poised over the Huskies playbook in front of me. Across the table, my phone goes off multiple times in rapid succession. An interesting phenomenon, considering there's only one person who messages me with that kind of enthusiasm, and Parker doesn't tend to surface from bed this early on a Sunday.

It's become my favorite day of the week. Since the away game a couple of weeks ago, I wake up, talk Zac back into bed so he'll fondle me a little, and sulk when he still refuses to fully sleep with me. We have breakfast on the back porch overlooking the water—sometimes with Noah, sometimes not. When he isn't recovering from a party somewhere, Noah will get in a couple hours of studying while Zac and I pore over the playbook for the coming Huskies game, trying to poke holes in the pages of player stats toward the back of the binder.

Ping, ping, ping.

There's a fresh stream of notifications lighting up my phone as Zac passes it to me, and the second I catch sight of them I emit a squeak rivaling the pitch of my incessant ringtone.

"That's a new one," Zac says. "What do I have to do to get you to make that sound tonight, huh?"

I tap at my phone, loading up a browser window. "That would require you to let me make *any* sound when you do things to me."

With Noah still living across the hall, I've been suffering through silent orgasms since that night in Oakley's bathroom. Obviously, there's nothing hot about getting fingered by the most gorgeous man I've ever seen as he clamps a hand over my mouth to make me take it in silence.

Nothing hot at all.

"Oh my God." My screen fills with a job posting for the Knights, my college team, one of the two schools out in the city. For weeks, I've been scouring a three-hour radius around Oakwood Bay for teams hiring sports data analysts. Naturally, I had to go and fall in love with the idea of a career so uncommon, nothing's turned up so far.

Until this.

"It's a predictive analytics job with the Knights," I tell Zac, scrolling through the posting. "I'd be working with their football team on game strategy."

Zac tugs my chair closer to have a look. "Is it what you want?"

"There's no way I'm getting this job," I mutter. "They're the top team in their division. I've got precisely zero experience in the field—"

"You've worked in data analysis for years, Mel."

I wrinkle my nose. "At a bank. It says they're open to applicants without experience in sports, but it still feels like a long shot."

"You're selling yourself short. You've basically been doing this job with me for weeks," he counters, nudging the Huskies playbook I've been working through this morning.

Right. He's right.

I've always hated my job, but the faith Zac has put in me since I helped get him his first win makes it even harder to sit through my nine-to-five. The Huskies have won another two games in a row now. It's the most useful I've felt in months, the most enthralled I've been with a career in stats since I graduated college.

Maybe the Huskies aren't strictly *my* team, but me and Zac? We feel like a team lately. As hard as I've worked to get my confidence up, I still find myself slipping from time to time, though I do have more good days than bad ones. Zac never lets me spiral, though. He really was made to coach.

"You do realize my sole purpose would be to help your rival team win games, right? Tell them exactly how your players fall short?"

It's the mark of the kind of man he is that Zac actually grins at the thought. "Never said I'd make it easy on you. Besides, you know what else felt like a long shot, just a little while ago?"

"What?"

He flicks a strand of hair off my face. "You and me. I started off sleeping with one eye open, thinking you might strangle me before sunrise. And look how well it's going."

I stare down at my phone, unable to help smiling.

I spent six years with Connor thinking I was the luckiest girl in the world, being spoiled rotten and loved so loudly. But all I'd been was a princess in a paper crown, forever trying to attain an inscrutable standard he'd set. Always trying to be *more*. Less. Whatever he decided he wanted from me that day. He'd chosen my first career path, and then spent years belittling me into believing it was where I was supposed to be whenever I showed a hint of dissatisfaction.

It's so night and day to Zac's calm, patient, and steady support—the way he smiles at me now, gently nudging me to take a risk, to try for what I want even when the outcome might not suit him. I feel spoiled by this man in life-altering ways. With power, courage, and choices, and belief that even my wildest dreams are possible.

"Okay, I'll apply. There's no harm in it, right?"

I've seen this man smile countless times since I was fourteen. It's as devastating today as it was then. I press a kiss to his cheek. "Here." I mark off the last player stat I was eyeing in his playbook and slide it over to him. "Have at it."

Zac scans the columns of data, the stats I've highlighted among the opposing team statistics. "You're a fucking genius, you know that? Forget the Knights. I'm about to fire my stats guy and roll you out a red carpet to a new office at UOB."

A giggle escapes me, and I might call off whatever this relationship is just for the sake of never hearing that undignified sound come out of my mouth again. "No way. The next job I get, it'll be on my own merit. Anyway, I'm sure not a single soul would think it's suspicious you hired the woman you're semi-sleeping with."

He clicks his pen and starts scribbling furiously over a legal pad of paper, referring to my notes. "They can all semi-kiss my ass. Besides, they think you're sleeping with Brooks fucking Attwood."

The door behind us slides open with gusto, and a worse-for-wear Noah shuffles onto the porch, shielding his eyes from the mid-morning light. "Damn, who turned up the sun today?"

"That would be the makers of Coors Light, or whatever other trash beer you drink." Zac glances at Noah. "Is this the state in which you plan on showing up to your meeting with those scouts tonight?"

"The beauty of youth is that I bounce back quick. Give me a waffle and a hot shower, maybe some hair of the dog, and I'm good to go." Noah drops into the chair facing mine, grunting as he goes down. His sandy hair is sticking up at all angles.

"Which scouts are you meeting with?" I ask, piling waffles on a plate for him.

"Ones for the Hornets in Florida. And the Rebels will be at our game on Friday." He dips a finger in a waffle square and licks off the syrup. "I don't know what good these meetings are, anyway, considering I'm not in a position to leave my mom—"

"Don't," Zac cuts in. He sets down his pen with careful precision. "Over my dead body will you squander your talent because of your father. It's not fucking happening."

It's not the first time Noah has brought this up, but it breaks my heart the same as it did then. The guilt and responsibility he feels for his mom, and protecting her from his father, are why he chose to go to UOB when he could have had a full ride anywhere else. He's told us his older sister has been trying for years to convince him to move in with her and her family a few states over, but he's never felt right about it unless their mom went with him.

Even when he stays here with us, he goes home to check on her every day.

"He's right, you know," I say as gently as I can. "Have you discussed it with your mom? I bet she'd say the same thing."

"She does," he admits. "She keeps saying she'll divorce him, kick him out of the house, but that's been her story for years. I wouldn't feel right leaving her."

Zac sits back in his chair. "You've been talking about playing for the Hornets since I've known you, and you have a real shot at it."

"We could check on your mom, if it gives you the peace of mind to leave," I chime in. And then pause awkwardly when I realize what I've just offered. Hard to do that when I don't plan to be here much longer.

Zac averts his eyes. "I'd do that. I'd check on her."

Noah runs a hand along his forehead, staring at Zac's open playbook across the table. He looks far too tormented for a talented twenty-year-old just trying to figure out his life.

"Would you consider coming with me tonight?" he asks after a beat. "To meet the scouts."

Zac's brows shoot up. "Me?"

"You," Noah confirms. "I could have my agent there, obviously, but it would be nice to have someone who doesn't look at me and see dollar signs. I know sometimes they like to meet the family, but that's . . . you know. Out of the question for me."

Beside me, Zac looks stunned by the suggestion. These are the moments when I can't fathom leaving Oakwood Bay. Leaving Zac and the utterly wholesome way he still doesn't see how much he means to people like Noah, or to Brooks, who found work with Zac's encouragement.

Or to me, who—despite having barely ticked off anything from the playbook Zac had me write—hasn't felt this content . . .

Probably since high school. When I could fool myself into believing those looks Zac gave me meant he felt what I'd felt for him, and I hadn't yet gone out into the world and disappointed myself by living under someone's thumb.

That's supremely sad, right? But it's better late than never.

Zac clears his throat, but his voice comes out all gruff, anyway. "Of course, I'll come with you."

"You really want to?"

"If you want me to meet scouts with you, then I can't think of somewhere I'd rather be tonight."

Zac's eyes go a little pink around the rims. Across the table, Noah's gaze floats to a point far above our heads. He blinks rapidly.

"Thanks, Zac. That means a lot, you know."

Oh my God, this has to be the most wholesome thing I've ever witnessed. Zac clears his throat again, and they're both avoiding each other's eye, trying desperately not to tear up.

Don't do it, I tell myself. *Don't ruin this moment—*

A clicking sound breaks the delicate silence, and they both whip around to find me with my phone held up to capture them both in the frame.

"I'm sorry. Please carry on." I stare proudly at the photo of them having a moment. "In a second this'll pass, and you'll both start bickering again. I really couldn't help myself."

You know what's funny?

Almost two months ago, I stared at my senior year vision board, thinking I had achieved nothing I'd dreamed of at eighteen. The job, the apartment in the city.

The little family of my own.

Maybe it's unconventional and kind of ambiguous. But staring at this photo, with the sounds of Zac and Noah's renewed bickering in the background, I don't feel so far off from that last one anymore.

Chapter 31

Zac

"Cut down the middle—*cut down the middle*, for fuck's sake!"

In true Brooks fashion, the words are muttered under his breath as we watch practice unfold from the sideline the following week. He'll stand here with me, rambling about which player should be doing what and who deserves to be benched until he gets the play right. His assessment is almost always spot-on. But as much as I appreciate his desire to be everyone's best friend, that leaves me to deliver the hard feedback to the team while he assumes the role of perpetual cheerleader.

I wouldn't say Brooks was made to coach. He belongs out on an NFL field, with other players of his caliber. But every time I've broached the subject of a comeback, it's clear his fear of mounting a failed return hangs over him like a dark cloud.

He turns to me, crossing his arms over his chest. "You gotta tell them to—"

"Cut down the middle. I got it." I shove my fingers through my hair. "You know, this good cop, bad cop act is starting to get old, man."

"Who . . . Isn't that Mike Irving?"

I look up to see Brooks squinting at something over my shoulder.

Behind me, the first thing I catch sight of is Harry—my boss, the bane of my existence— staring out at the field, apparently having been taking in the practice for who knows how long. He hasn't called me in for his usual decimating chats in weeks. Like the rest of town, his tune shifted with our first win of the season. Doesn't mean I trust him worth shit, though.

I could do without working for him and I'd jump ship without another glance, after the way he's publicly humiliated me on more than one occasion.

When he sees me looking, Harry touches the brim of his cap and turns to stride through the tunnel under the stands leading to the offices. Dick.

"Mike Irving," Brooks repeats beside me. "Noah's dad? Why does he look like he's about to light the place on fire?"

I see him now. A burly, red-faced Mike Irving marching past Harry in the direction of the field. If Brooks hadn't named him off the bat, it would have taken me a second to place him. The Irvings have lived in this town for years, and growing up, Mike had been a common fixture along the main strip.

Back then he'd been a charming, almost jovial man, the kind that you'd figure would raise a good kid like Noah. And then he got caught up in an accident on a fishing charter that left him with a permanent limp. He's never been the same. Stopped showing his face around town. Started hitting the liquor. Tormenting his wife and kids.

And by the looks of it, perfecting that nasty grimace, as he moves toward the field at an impressive clip despite the limp. Brooks is right. Maybe he's not looking to light the place on fire, but the fists at his sides, one holding badly crumpled papers, tell me this isn't a casual visit checking out his son's practice.

And then Mike pauses. His gaze sweeps the field before him and zones in on what he's looking for. "*Get your dumb ass over here, you little shit!*"

Oh, fuck.

The sounds from the field die off. I turn to watch Noah slowly remove his helmet, staring in the direction of his father like he's seeing a ghost.

"What the fuck is going on?" Brooks mutters.

"Get Noah," I say quietly, heart hammering in my chest.

He looks around incredulously. "You want me to bring Noah over to this guy?"

I stand perfectly still, frozen in dread as I watch Mike Irving only a few feet away. He's fisting the papers in his hand, glaring in positive fury at the field.

"No. Get to Noah and keep him away. I don't care how. Do whatever you have to do to get him out."

"Are you deaf or stupid, boy?" Mike Irving roars now. "I said, *get your ass over here*!"

"Should we call security?"

"*Go*," I tell Brooks. "Get to Noah."

The moment the words leave my mouth also appears to be the moment Mike decides he's had enough of waiting. He starts charging onto the field. Brooks takes off toward Noah as I throw myself into his father's path so abruptly that he slams into me, driving me back a few steps before coming to a halt.

"Mr. Irving, why don't we go talk in my office?"

Mike fixes his mutinous gaze on me. "And why the fuck would I want to talk to you? Get the fuck out of my way—"

"It's a closed practice. I can't let you onto the field, but if you want to wait inside while we—"

The next sound out of me is a hard grunt as Mike's hands collide with my chest to send me staggering back. And I'm suddenly glaringly aware of my mistake. Any thought of talking the man down was clearly a stupid one. He's here for blood, and considering I've never fought a day in my life—

Mike Irving closes the gap he created between us and shoves me again. "Look, this doesn't have to get physical," I say. "We can talk it out—"

"Talk it out? *Talk it out*? Tell that to my bitch wife who served me divorce papers this morning, spinning some bullshit about my being a shitty father."

Noah appears at my side, flanked by Brooks, who grips his jersey in an attempt to move him. "Dad—"

I grab Noah's shoulders, walking him back and away from his father with Brooks's help. "Get out of here, Noah."

"Is that what I am, you ungrateful shit? A shitty father?" Mike claws at the back of my shirt before taking a fistful and tugging so violently I hear it start to rip. "*Get the fuck out of my way.*"

"Dad, stop—"

"*Noah,* get the hell out of here—"

It happens fast. A couple of players closest to us rush over, taking Noah by the arms to drag him away. The momentum of having him ripped from my grip unsteadies me, giving Mike the upper hand. He gives my shirt another wicked tug, turns me around.

"You're the coach, aren't you? The one keeping him away from home," he spits at me, fisting the front of my shirt. "Keeping him away from his mother, making her cry—"

"We should go speak in my office—"

He jerks me closer. "I'm not interested in talking."

"I'm not fighting you—"

I only manage a glimpse of his fist before it collides with my face.

I stagger back, dimly aware of the sudden uproar around me. The blurred shapes of players converge on us as my ears ring. But Mike isn't done with me. He manages to catch my shirt again. To deliver another punch to the side of my face a moment before he's tackled to the ground, leaving me bent over and spitting blood.

~

It's the first time I've dreaded the sounds of Melody coming home.

In hindsight, I should have called her. Should have let Brooks call her when he asked if I wouldn't rather have her with me while I got checked by the team's doctors. As unsure as I was about whether our relationship is the kind where she'd want to show up for me and my bashed-in face, and as badly as I didn't want her to see me like that . . . it might have been better to give her a heads-up on what she's about to walk into.

"Zac, are you there?" she calls from the front door. I hear her bag drop onto the staircase before she moves down the hall.

"In the kitchen," I call back. I stand with my back to the doorway, holding an ice pack to the right side of my face. Just the act of raising my voice sends a sharp, searing pain through my brain.

"You're home early," she says, finding me. I hear her set something down on the counter behind me, and the smell of fried food fills the kitchen. "I was expecting to have time to snoop around before dinner. I brought takeout from Sheffield's."

"I thought you'd have finished all your snooping by now."

"It's a big house. Lots of nooks and crannies to inspect." I can feel her eyes on my back. "Zac? What's going on?"

I sigh, bracing a hand on the counter. "Don't freak out, okay?"

"Yeah . . . you can go ahead and assume that I'll start freaking out the second you ever say something like that. What's wrong?"

"Nothing. It's nothing bad. I just got a little banged up at work today."

"Zac." My name comes out a little shaky as she rounds the counter. Mel stares at the ice pack covering half my face. "What happened?"

She tugs at my arm until I let it fall away.

"*Zac*. What the fuck happened?" Her voice is several notches higher than usual as she stares at my face, horrified.

"There was a thing at practice today—"

"*A thing at practice*? Look at you—are you okay? Did you get this looked at? What *happened*—"

"I'm—hey, I'm fine. No, fuck, please don't—" Her eyes fill with tears and I pull her in just as she lets out a sob. She buries her face in my chest, letting me rub my hand up and down her back. "It's just a little bruising, okay? The swelling will go down quick—"

"You have a cut over your eyebrow!"

"Honestly, it doesn't even hurt."

She pushes off my chest to get a look at me, cheeks stained with tears. "What happened?"

"It was a—"

She wrenches out of my grip, eyes bloodshot but narrowed now. "Don't you dare downplay this. Who did this to you?"

"No one."

"Who did this to you?"

Shit. "Noah's dad showed up at practice."

I watch her digest the words. Watch the crinkle of confusion in her forehead smooth out, her mouth open over a syllable, but it takes her a couple of tries to get it out.

"Noah?"

"He's fine."

She nods. Over and over again, like she's letting it all sink in. And then she turns on her heel and charges out of the kitchen.

"Hey—where are you going?" I hurry after her, catching her around the waist.

"I'm going to give Mike Irving what he has coming to him." I tuck her back into me and she starts to fight it, struggling to wrestle out of my hold. "Let go of me!"

I double my grip. "He's not in a state to get a piece of your mind—"

"A piece of my mind?" she shouts, thrashing wildly in my arms, her hair flying everywhere. "I'm giving him a piece of my fist—*let me go*!"

I can't help it. The whole scene is so debilitatingly sweet that I laugh. And then immediately recognize my mistake when she starts to struggle even harder.

"How are you laughing right now? Get off me—let me do this!"

I pull her back into the kitchen as she drags her feet and then hoist her to sit on the counter. When she tries to duck around me, I plant my hands on her hips, holding her in place.

"Why are you so calm?" she demands, face contorted in fury. "Have you seen yourself?"

"I think you've got the anger quota filled." I cup her cheek, running my thumb over her eyebrow to smooth it.

"People don't get to go around hurting you with impunity—I swear to God, I will *kill* him—tear him apart, limb by limb until there's nothing left—"

"That's a lot of rage contained in someone so small."

She hits me with a withering look. "He's been terrorizing Noah for God knows how long. He *attacked* you. Let me go knock some sense into him."

I lift her arm so that her tiny fist sits between us. "With this thing?"

"What's wrong with my fist?"

I shake her arm and her fist rattles loosely between us. "Clo, you lost a standoff against a chipmunk. You think I'd let you face off against a drunk, angry bull?"

"We're not supposed to mention the chipmunk incident!" She scowls, taking back her arm. "At least tell me he got arrested."

"Noah didn't want that."

"And what stops him from crashing another practice?"

"Security's involved now. They'll be at all our practices going forward. And we fly out for a game tomorrow, so hopefully he cools off by the time we're back."

I smooth her hair where it got tousled in our scuffle, and after a while she starts to thaw. Mel eyes the side of my face, reaching to gently stroke above my eyebrow.

"Does it hurt?"

"The humiliation of going down on a couple of sucker punches hurts more than anything. Other than that, I've got a bit of a headache."

She sighs, settling her hand on the nape of my neck. "You've never been a fighter."

"No, I'm not."

"And you won't let me do it for you?"

"Definitely not."

I smile, but she doesn't return it. "Why didn't you call me?"

"I wanted to," I admit. "But I wasn't sure that was something we did. I don't know where we stand on the whole *calling your sleeping buddy when shit hits the fan* thing."

"I would have wanted you to call me. I'd have wanted to be there for you." She stares grimly at the side of my face. "Maybe we're due for an upgrade from *sleeping buddies*."

A bomb, warm and fucking *elated*, goes off in the pit of my stomach. Seeing me like this seems to have triggered something in her, and hell if it doesn't make every throb of my aching head worth it.

"I'm interrupting again, aren't I?"

We turn to find Noah hovering awkwardly in the kitchen doorway. My heart cracks wide open for him. He was distraught once his dad got escorted out, stayed with me while the team doctors had a look at the damage to my face. Now, he looks at me carefully, like he expects me to have turned on him sometime in the last few hours.

"Noah," Melody says, voice thick with relief as she scans him head to toe. She hops off the counter and crosses the kitchen to wrap him up in a hug. "You're not interrupting. You're *never* interrupting. This is your home."

She's tiny in his arms, doesn't even hit his shoulders, but after a second in which he doesn't seem to know what to do next, Noah sags into her. His chin hits the top of her head, and tears pool in the corners of his eyes.

He needed that damn hug. He looks about a hundred pounds lighter when they draw apart. He wipes dry his cheeks, and my fucking heart hasn't felt so full in years.

"Are you all right?" she asks, clutching Noah's shoulders.

"I'm fine. Zac got in the way before my dad even got close."

"Do you want to talk about it?" When he shakes his head, Mel turns to the brown paper takeout bags on the counter, blinking fast to hold back tears. "Well, then you're just in time. I brought home dinner—and before you ask, *yes,* I got your diablo spiced wings, though I still don't understand how you can stomach those. And I know you guys owe me a rom-com after the back-to-back doom and gloom movies you've been picking out, but I'm willing to give up my turn."

Noah starts fiddling with the takeout bags. They move in sync like they've been doing it for years, and there's nothing more thrilling than seeing them—two of the most important people to me—exuding domesticity, right here in my kitchen. It's exactly the kind of scene I dreamed up when I built the place. Me and my Melody, our kids. Quiet movie nights until we can escape upstairs for even quieter bedtime activities.

"Is it a forks-and-knives kind of night?" Noah asks her. "Or a sauce-all-over-your-face night?"

She waves away the cutlery. "Sauce everywhere. Drowning in sauce. Sticky fingers and stains on the couch we'll need to clean up in the morning."

With an approving nod, Noah piles the takeout containers in his arms—minus forks and knives—and crosses into the living room.

"What's that look for?" With her eyes on me, Melody closes the gap between us.

I sweep her hair aside. "Which look?"

"This look. That smile." Her fingers stroke the outer corner of my eye. My laugh lines? "What are you thinking about?"

"I'm thinking about never realizing just how lonely I've been until the very moment I felt full." When her brows pull together, I add, "Now. Here, with you. You make me feel so full, I can't even breathe, sometimes. Like my lungs are screaming at me that I don't need anything but you to survive. I am so far gone for you, Melody."

She stares down at her feet, bashful as always whenever I say too much. "Too sappy?" I nudge up her chin. "Am I scaring you off?"

Mel clutches the hem of my shirt. "I was ready to kick a grown man's ass for you—still am, if you'd let me. Sweet words like that don't scare me when they come from you. Not anymore."

"Hey, guys?" Noah calls from the other room. "What do we think about a comfort movie tonight? *The Silence of the Lambs*?"

"He considers *The Silence of the Lambs* a comfort watch?" I mutter as she huffs a laugh.

Melody leads me into the living room where Noah is already chomping down fries. "Come on, Porter. I'll hold your hand at the scary parts."

Chapter 32

Melody

I find Zac down by the water at the foot of his property, showered and dressed the way he is every morning before I'm awake. It's his attempt to keep resisting me, and the man has nerves of steel because I can barely glance at him anymore without having a visceral need to feel him everywhere.

He's sitting on the grass at the edge of the patch of daisies with a bunch of freshly clipped flowers at his side, probably destined for the vase he let me put in his kitchen after our shopping trip, what feels like years ago. He's taken it upon himself to put in a fresh bunch every week since.

I can barely believe we've only known each other again for a couple of months. It feels like I've been falling asleep with him for an eternity. I've got the fluttery feelings I'd felt for him as a kid only amplified.

I was right to have called it puppy love the night I first showed up here. It feels so different this time around.

Zac's voice carries over the lawn as I make my way over. He spots me when I'm a few feet away, and gestures at his phone with the hand not holding it.

The bruises along the side of his face have darkened overnight and sheer rage bubbles inside me again. The thought of someone putting their hands on him—hurting him—makes me want to draw blood. Fret over him. Kiss him until the bruises disappear.

"Mom, I better go get breakfast started," he says, looking into his phone. I realize he's on a video call.

"And by that you mean, *Mom, I need you to stop talking my ear off*," a voice answers with a laugh. "Unless you've really started cooking breakfast for Noah, which would be very sweet indeed."

I've never met Zac's mom. Growing up, his parents had always been somewhere on the other side of the world, wherever his dad was stationed.

I smooth my hair, flushing at the delighted way Zac's brows inch up his forehead when I sit beside him in the grass and lean into the frame of his phone.

I've seen photos of her over the years, scattered around Grams's old house. At first glance, the woman on the screen doesn't look much like Zac. She's got deep red hair and gorgeous freckles dotting her face. But even through the phone, her brown eyes are as striking as Zac's. They crinkle the same way his do when he smiles.

"I can vouch for the breakfast alibi," I tell his mom with a small wave. "I'm a very needy house guest. My name is—"

"Melody," she finishes for me. Through the phone, it's hard to tell which one of us she's looking at given how close together Zac and I are sitting. But she appraises us with obvious interest. "I'd know you anywhere."

In the tiny square in the corner of the screen where we're reflected, I can see Zac is wincing.

I suppress a laugh. "You know, I've long suspected you kept photos of me plastered to the walls of your teenaged bedroom, somewhere between the Nirvana and Power Rangers posters. This settles it."

Zac bumps me with his shoulder. "You saw my teenaged bedroom, you brat."

"What I saw were suspiciously empty walls. Who knows what you did away with before I came over," I say with a shrug. I turn back to his mom. "It's nice to meet you, Mrs. Porter. I heard so much about you growing up."

"Call me Andrea, please," she tells me. "Between the things I'd hear from my mother and Zachary, it feels like we met ages ago. It was always Melody and Parker this, Melody and Parker that. Sprinkle in some extra Melody all over the place."

Oh, this is so fun.

Zac's head falls forward in such defeat, I can't help but laugh.

"I'm gonna go ahead and take this from you," I tell him, prying the phone from his hand before he does anything rash, like hang up on his mom to save himself further humiliation. "I've only been awake five minutes, and this is already the best day of my life."

"You know, you're exactly how I pictured you," Andrea tells me.

Zac lets out a mournful groan. "Here we go."

I nudge him quiet. "Really? How did he describe me?"

"'She looks like the sun, Mom,'" Andrea says, voice dropping in apparent imitation. Zac stiffens at my side. "'Mixed with a little bit of rain.' I'll never forget it. The sweetest words coming from a fourteen-year-old boy."

Here's something I never expected: meeting Zac's mom and having her steal my breath away within the first minute and a half. My body—every organ contained within it—goes still.

She's that first ray of sunlight after a bad storm. Peeking through the clouds.

They're the words Zac used to describe the girl he'd once loved. The one he screwed up with.

"I can see what he means now," Andrea says, clearly oblivious to the thick silence on the other end of the line. "The blond hair, beautiful face. But your eyes are all trouble, aren't they? I've seen you two together all of two minutes, but it makes perfect sense now."

Zac looks off to the side, staring at the tree-lined edge of the property.

"What makes sense?" I ask quietly, terrified to hear what she'll say next, yet completely riveted.

"Why he refused to leave Oakwood Bay after my mother passed," Zac's mom says. "Why he built himself a beautiful home and left it almost completely blank on the inside, like it wasn't his to finish."

"Mom," Zac says softly. It sounds like he wants to warn her to stop speaking, but doesn't have the heart to do it.

I stare up at the house. It's the first time I'm really looking at it from a distance. The stone façade, the wraparound porch. The porch swing facing the bay. The patch of daisies we're sitting by.

He has a yellow front door.

It looked so familiar my first morning here, but I hadn't been able to figure out why.

Now, I place it clearly. It's the house I'd pinned to my vision board before moving away for college. The one Zac had stared at the last night I saw him. The picture that went missing sometime over the years.

But that's crazy. Right?

Because like it or not, he *did* leave me that night. He didn't speak to me for a decade after. Men don't go and build the dream home of a childhood friend they no longer speak to. They don't wait for her to move back and fill it the way she wants, paint the walls to her heart's content. They don't. Nobody does that.

Except . . . "I'm going to go ahead and take this from you." Zac steals his phone back. "All right, Mom. You've done enough for one day. I'll talk to you later."

I can't see the screen anymore, but I don't miss Andrea's satisfied laugh. "Take care of those bruises, honey. I love you."

I'm on my feet and picking up the daisies Zac had clipped by the time he hangs up the phone.

"So—"

Zac lifts me before I get the words out, squeezing me to him. "Thanks for meeting my mom." He breaks the awkward tension so easily. I adore that about him.

"She's very interesting," I tell him when I'm back on my feet. I tickle his nose with one of the daisies I'm holding.

"What makes you say that?"

"Oh, I don't know. Maybe because she made you seem obsessed with me."

"I am obsessed with you. I'm not sure how to make that any more obvious."

I bite down on a smile. As I stare up at him, I realize something: I have no real idea how he felt about me then. But I'm dying to hear that he loves me now.

What a liberating thought.

After months of agonizing over my breakup and the disastrous six years that preceded it, feeling down to my bones that I'd be ready to hear those words from Zac is shedding a hundred and something pounds of brown-haired, blue-eyed toxicity.

I don't say a word. Don't do anything other than stare up at Zac, willing him to say it.

"I fly out with the team in two hours," he says, without taking his eyes off me. He looks at me like he knows exactly what I'm thinking. "Wait until I come back. Don't make me say it just to leave you."

I have grass under my toes, but in my head I'm levitating.

~~~

MELODY: Safe flight, Z. Bring me home another win, okay?

ZAC: Anything for you, Clo. Miss you already.

I'm a pessimist. Most of the time, anyway, and usually only when it comes to myself. But I have no trouble visualizing tonight. That
~~~

fourth win for Zac, Noah, and Brooks, and then the fifth, and every win after that. They deserve it, and I feel it down to my bones that they'll get it.

I'm a pessimist, and the Connor revelations of the past couple months should be enough to keep me that way, at least when it comes to love. But standing by this empty table at Sheffield's, I've never felt more hopeful.

All I can think about is how badly I already miss him, too. How seeing him that way yesterday, all battered and bruised . . . The utter fury I felt knowing someone had hurt him, had even looked at him the wrong way, it broke me open. That's my guy, my person.

There are a thousand open questions. I'm set on moving away, and his life is here. We'd need to confess to a relationship that I'm not sure my brother would support. And after my breakup, I really wanted to get my life in order before committing to another man.

I pull a crumpled piece of yellow paper from my apron, with *Clover's Playbook* written across the top.

1. Find a job that pays better (and doesn't give me the Sunday scaries)
2. Purge my life of everything that isn't mine
3. Cut all ties to my ex
4. Do something I've been dying to do, but never have
5. Never hold back how I feel (dirty thoughts excluded)

I thought this playbook was going to be my secret sauce to life. I thought that if I focused on this list, and only this list, that I could get myself to a happier place. And it's gone largely unachieved. I don't have my dream career. I still live with my brother. I chickened out at the sight of Connor's name on my phone not long ago.

In a lot of ways, it seems like I'm still back where I started when I moved home a couple months ago. And yet, I'm not. I'm working hard at two jobs, found a career path that could really make me happy. I've been making new friends—the WAGs; Brooks and Noah, who I've come to adore—and reconnecting with old ones. I've . . . God. I've fallen in love with a good man, who encourages me at every turn. Motivates me and supports me in being my own person, finding my joy.

And the kicker, the most exhilarating part of it is . . . I think I could go off to the city on my own and make it this time. I really think I could. I don't *need* Zac or anyone else to get it right.

But I don't *want* to go a day without Zac.

What if my life doesn't have to be perfectly squared away with frilly pink bows and sprinkles on top before thinking about forever? Maybe a little mess is okay, as long as I can trust myself to have my own back if my world goes to crap again. As long as I can trust Zac to be my second line of defense, in the event I stumble too hard.

My body is buzzing, a steady vibration through each of my extremities, and it takes me a second to realize what it is. I'm excited about the future. I'm *happy*.

To hell with waiting for things to fall into place.

The diner around me is almost dead quiet, on the tail end of another slow lunch shift as I get a head start wiping down my section before heading out for the day. Wynn is off by the register, counting out today's earnings before the dinner crowd comes in. I turn back to my phone.

MELODY: Zac?

He'll be on his flight already. My thumbs hover over the phone, trying to figure out how to convey the way he makes me feel through text so that the second he lands and turns on his phone, he'll feel some of it, too.

I jump at the sound of two quick raps at the window beside me. Only catch a glimpse of a vaguely familiar knit sweater before the diner door chimes open. And Connor strolls in.

"Melly, thank God. I've been so worried about you."

I freeze. Just stand there like an inanimate concrete block as Connor's face stretches into a painfully familiar smile. In my head, his face has taken on a sinister look, cast in shadows with arrogant, malevolent smiles.

But here he is, at Sheffield's, looking like he always has. Connor with the dark hair neatly pushed back, blue eyes bright and earnest. The deep dimples denting his cheeks as he takes stock of me.

I don't realize I'm holding my breath until he reaches for my hand. My lungs expel everything they have as I jerk away, bumping into the table behind me in the process.

I'm not seeing things. He's really here. "Melly?"

I've got my phone in a death grip. With a concerned crinkle in his brows, Connor pries it from my fingers and pockets my phone before reaching for me again. It's such a sinister move, confiscating my only method of communication with the world outside this diner, and it leaves me in such dead shock that I keep my hand in his.

"It's okay. I'm nervous too," he says gently. "These past few months have been torture without you, Melly. Please say something."

Say something, I echo. *Tell him to leave. Tell him this good guy act doesn't work anymore.*

"What are you doing here?" I say instead. My voice is shaking.

His thumb runs lines up and down my hand. "You scared the living daylights out of me. Your phone goes straight to voicemail. I knew there must be something seriously wrong. You'd never leave me hanging like that."

My heartbeat is in my ears. "How did you find me?"

He tips his head to the side, seemingly dumbfounded by the question. "We've been together six years, Melly. I know where you grew up."

"We're broken up," I say, gaining a bit of awareness. I take my hand away, blinking around me. Somehow, we're still at Sheffield's. "Connor, we're broken up. You shouldn't be here. We're over."

"That's why I've been trying to reach you." He takes a long breath. "I'm here to get you back. To bring you home and get things back to normal. It's not been the same without you. You should see the state of our plants; they might miss you even more than I do."

He flashes me that smile I used to love. Bright, wide, so beautiful it made me feel special to receive it. Now, all I want to do is sob. I want to feel enraged at seeing him. I want to claw that manipulative smile off his face, shove him out of this diner. But I never expected this kind of ambush.

When I don't say anything, he fingers the end of my ponytail. Invading my space. "You look so different. Your makeup—"

"I know. You like it natural. Look, Connor, you shouldn't be here."

"I never said that."

I frown. "Never said what?"

"I never said I like it natural."

"Yes, you did," I say. I don't even know why I'm entertaining this. It doesn't matter what he thinks about my makeup. "You said it looks like a mask otherwise, that I don't need to try so hard—"

"Melly, I would never say that. Why would I care what makeup you wear? You know I think you're beautiful, regardless."

"You did, though. You threw out all my lipstick and eyeliner and said it looked like—"

"That's crazy. There's no way I'd do something like that." He shakes his head with such conviction I'm scrambling to think back to the moment I remember—I *think* I remember. "God, you're breaking my heart, Mel. I'm so sorry you thought I did that."

"You—you did, though. I swear, you threw it all out—"

I jump at the sound of another knock on the window acting as the backdrop to this nightmare. Parker peers into the diner, and a wave of relief crashes straight into my chest.

"You all right over there, Mel?"

At the counter, Wynn is fixed on me, frozen in the act of refilling straw dispensers. His gaze flicks to Connor, and it's barely perceptible, but his brows pinch in distrust.

"I'm—I'm fine, Wynn."

"Do you *work* here, Melly?" Connor seems to be taking in my attire for the first time. His eyes linger on my apron, and there's nothing subtle about the appalled downturn to his mouth. "You should have called me if you needed help this badly. The second you come home, you're getting your own card to my account. You can buy yourself anything you want, okay? My treat."

I see four curious eyeballs staring at our scene over the tall back of a nearby bench seat. "Connor, maybe we should step outside—"

Parker blows into the diner with his glare glued to Connor, apparently not remotely concerned about causing a scene.

"What the fuck are you doing here?" he barks.

Connor's grin doesn't falter. "Hey, Parker. I understand why you're upset. I came here to make things right with your sister, but I know I owe you an apology, too. She's had to crash with you, disrupt your routine, and if you give us a few minutes to sort this out, I'd be happy to come speak with you. Apologize for these past couple of months. Make up for you having to look after her—"

"I don't need a thank you for looking out for my own sister, asshole. Least of all from you, after the shit you pulled on her." Parker turns his unimpressed gaze on me. "Did you tell him he could show up here?" Brutally aware of Connor's eyes on me, I shake my head. "You wanna be listening to his bullshit?"

I shake my head again and Parker charges for the diner door. He throws it open. "Get out," he tells Connor.

"Whoa—what's with the aggression? I'm only here to talk."

"She doesn't want to talk to you. Get out of the diner, jackass."

"Why don't you let your sister speak for herself, Parker," Connor says derisively. "She's a grown woman capable of her own choices—"

Oh, hell fucking no.

It's a whole new low. Letting those words out of his mouth without even a hint of irony, after years of manipulating me out of choices.

"Get out of here, Connor."

"Melly—"

"Fine, then I'll go."

I march around him for the open door, but Connor reaches for me, fingers grazing my wrist as though to grab it. He doesn't manage to get a grip on me. In a second, Parker fists his shirt and wrenches him out of the diner. He follows behind, shoving Connor down the sidewalk and away from the door.

"Parker!"

I rush outside. Connor's hair has escaped confinement from the way he styles it, and he takes a moment to brush it back despite the way Parker seethes in his face. "That was completely uncalled for. There's no reason to get scary aggressive—"

"You think I'm scary?" Parker says, taking a step toward Connor. I grip his arm to stop him. "Consider yourself lucky it was me finding you. Other people wouldn't be so forgiving. You'd be a pile of limbs on this sidewalk."

Connor narrows his eyes. "Who—"

"Leave, Connor." The last thing I need is to see him put on a sad puppy show when he hears about my fake boyfriend. "I don't want to talk to you. This is over. Let it go."

Connor's eyes are still narrowed at my brother like he never even registered my words. Like they're irrelevant. Parker glares right back, and it's a look so foreign to my sunny twin's face that it sends a chill through me.

"She asked you to leave, asshole."

After another long moment, Connor rips his gaze off Parker. Somehow, he manages a smarmy smile in my direction. "I know you're in shock, Melly. It must be hard to see me, and you need time to digest this. Think it through. I'm willing to be patient for you. Take all the time you need and we'll talk again, all right?"

"My phone," I call to him when he's already several steps away. "You still have my phone. Give it back."

I think he almost looks disappointed I remembered he'd taken it from me.

~

"You sure you're okay, Mels?"

Parker pokes his head into my bedroom for what's got to be the fiftieth time since I made up a hasty excuse to leave my shift at the diner in favor of burying myself in bed. I'm shaken up and embarrassed I let Connor get in my head, rattle me over a memory I *know* was real, and the only person I'm aching to talk to is miles away. About to coach a game he's nervous enough about, without having this added to his plate.

"Yeah." I clear my throat when it comes out scratchy. "I'm fine. Just in shock, I think. I never thought he'd show up here."

"You want me to call someone?"

"I'm okay, I promise. I just need a few more minutes."

Parker nods, shutting the door behind him, and a moment later I hear his own bedroom door close. I ignore my phone when it chimes on the night stand, turning to stare up at the ceiling instead.

Fuck. I am such a weak, stupid—

My phone chimes again. And again, and again, texts coming in quick succession. Finally, I reach for it.

PARKER: Connor just showed up at the diner. There was a scene.

SUMMER: WHAT?

SUMMER: What did he want?

BROOKS: Today of all days.

BROOKS: Mels, are you okay?

I appreciate that he might have wanted me to have the support, but why would Parker feel the need to broadcast it in the group chat like this?

And then my heart bounces into my throat when my phone goes off and **ZAC** flashes across the screen.

"Zac—"

"I swear to God, I will murder him. I will tear him to fucking *shreds*." Zac's voice is shaking, livid. He must be out on the field already because I can hear vague sounds around him, and the wind rushing into the phone. "Melody, are you okay?"

Even in his anger, his voice is enough to soothe me. I melt back onto the bed. "I am. I'm okay. Thank you for calling. I really needed to hear your voice."

"Calling? I'm already halfway out of this godforsaken stadium. I'm coming home, Clo."

I jerk upright. "No—don't do that. I swear I'm fine. I don't need you to come home."

He sighs into the phone. "Then I'm coming home for my sake. There's no way I can sit here like this—"

"You have to, okay? It's a whole plane ride, and you just landed, and I really want you to coach this game."

"Did he put his hands on you?"

Shit. "He—he tried to, but Parker got in his face—"

I wince at the barrage of angry curses now streaming out of Zac. His voice sounds far away, like he's moved the phone from his mouth, but I can still feel his fury.

"Did he hurt you?" he says into the phone.

"No, he didn't. I swear," I whisper. "Zac, your team needs you. Please stay there."

"I can't. Ask me for anything else, because that's the one thing I can't do. I'm losing my mind," he pleads. "It was bad enough coming here missing you. But this is unbearable."

My eyes prickle at the thick emotion in his voice. "I miss you, too. I was thinking about you when he showed up. How happy you make me." I listen to the sounds of his breathing slow down, even out. "You've really got some kind of nerve making me care about you like this."

Making me love you like this. Those were the words you were supposed to say.

Zac breathes out a laugh, and I'm relieved to hear the return of some of its usual warmth. "Hold on a second, okay? Stay on the phone."

The sounds on his end cut off abruptly, and I sit there a few minutes until he comes back.

"The next flight coming here leaves in an hour and a half," he tells me. "You think you can swing that?"

My heart leaps in my chest. "I think so."

"Good, the ticket's in your inbox. If you won't let me come to you, then come to me."

Chapter 33

Zac

The game was unbearable.

The post-game debrief was downright torture. The fucking bus ride back to our hotel was agony.

I'm the first one off the bus the second we pull up to the hotel doors, but things aren't working in my favor today because my bag is nowhere to be seen in the undercarriage. It takes a dozen of the coaches and players filing past me to clear enough bags to spot mine toward the back of the pile, and I dive for it like a man out at sea reaching for a lifesaving buoy. I motor around the guys filing into the hotel, loud and still riding a high from our narrow win.

She should have landed half an hour ago. May be just getting here, too . . .

I spot Melody up ahead by the elevators. Golden hair tied up on top of her head, the ends tickling the letters of my last name on the back of my high school jersey, and I've never known relief like this.

"Zac!" My heart.

My heart, my lungs, my entire fucking body melts at the sound of those three letters put together, voiced by the only person who matters. Before I can make up my mind about whether to charge her right here in front of my team, Mel takes off across the lobby and throws herself at me, letting me catch her mid-jump and winding herself around me so tightly it's like she's afraid I've somehow lost my mind enough to insist she gets off.

"Clo—"

It's all I manage to get out before she crushes her mouth on mine, kissing me unabashedly wild and desperate, giggling against my lips when the guys around us erupt in a smattering of suggestive whistles.

In the past twenty-four hours, these people have seen me pummeled by a parent, and are now watching me devour a woman on a road trip, kiss her like it's a matter of life or death. Never mind that she's supposedly dating Brooks. But I don't care what this looks like. I don't care about the example I'm supposed to be setting. I walk us across the lobby, smashing at the elevator button until it arrives. The second the doors close, I turn Mel into the wall, setting her ass down on the railing lining the elevator as she drags her mouth along my neck.

"Twenty-fourth floor. Room twenty-four-fifteen," she mumbles against my skin, and I split away only long enough to hit the button before I'm on her again.

"You're really okay?" I say, already breathing hard as she nibbles at my lip. My hands are everywhere. Through her hair, along her jaw, her shoulder, palming her tits through my motherfucking jersey.

"I'm really okay," she says, licking a path up my neck, then scraping the skin with her teeth. "So much better now."

I grip the hem of her jersey and it seems we're on the same page because her arms go up, letting me whip it off her body, leaving her in an insane green lacy bra that wrenches a hungry groan from my chest.

"Do you think there are cameras in here?" she pants, hands crawling under my shirt, feeling her way up my stomach as I drop my face to her body, kissing, biting the perfect swell of her tits, desperate to leave my mark on them.

"Probably. You wanna stop?"

"God, no," she breathes. "We're almost on our floor."

She pushes her tits together, letting me bury my face in them before she slides the straps off her shoulders and tugs down her bra, freeing her nipples for me.

"Clover," I groan. "God, you're fucking killing me."

Mel breathes out a laugh. "Why? They're yours to play with, aren't they?" Her words send something base and feral clawing through me.

"That's fucking right. They're mine." I palm her tits, squeeze, bend to capture a nipple between my lips, reveling in the way she squirms against the elevator railing. "You're mine." My hands roam, grip her ass, lift her off the railing and grind her into my dick. "This is all fucking mine. And, Clover? I don't do takebacks."

The elevator doors ping open and I sweep her stuff off the ground before powering us down the hall to our room, smashing the door open once it's unlocked, throwing her onto the bed, and ripping the bag off my body.

Mel loses her bra and lifts her hips to strip off her leggings as I rip open my pants. It's a wild flurry of clothes raining down around us. Harsh, hungry breaths. Wild eyes devouring each other as we strip down. Her lips part when she watches me throw off my shirt, and I catch the way the spark of anticipation in her eyes fades to confusion, and then to lust.

I've been careful to keep a shirt on since I've seen her again until I get the chance to explain. But right now, I plan on keeping her good and busy, too distracted to get a good look at anything.

I crawl onto the bed, coaxing her onto her back. "I want you," I tell her, running a hand down her body. "Everything. Right now."

Fuck it. Fuck everything. To hell with waiting for her love, her commitment. I fucking *need* her.

"Really?" Her nails scrape down my back when I bite down on her nipple. "This is the magical moment you've been waiting for? Who knew all it would take is a run-in with my crazy ex."

"I wasn't waiting for some magic moment. I wanted to win you over."

She threads her fingers through my hair. "Oh? And you don't want to win me over anymore?"

"I already did."

She throws her head back in a laugh and I lift my head from between her tits just to soak it in. "You're awfully confident tonight. Is it because I let you fly me out here at the drop of a hat, or the fact that I'm naked underneath you?"

"Neither. It's the way you're looking at me tonight."

"I'm looking at you differently?"

"You are. It's the first time since you've been back where I haven't seen it once. That look you give like you're not sure about me." I pause, assessing her. The way not one single part of her stunning face feels closed off. "Are you sure about me, Clover?"

She rolls her eyes, but they twinkle when they find me again.

"You don't even need to say it. I know you. I know what it looks like when you hate me. What it looks like when you're trying to figure me out. You're giving me none of that tonight."

"You're not about to tell me you've already named our kids, are you?"

Our kids.

The last time I brought up the idea of a family together, she looked at me like I was insane.

I shake my head. "You're in with me, and that's all I care about. The rest of it . . . I'll throw in a counteroffer here and there, because that's what I'm supposed to do. But just so you know? You'll get your way every time."

"You're in a sappy mood tonight, Porter." She runs a hand down my bare chest, pushes me until I'm sitting, and crawls over to straddle me. "I'm not sappy. It's just not me."

"I'm well aware," I say, pulling her closer.

She toys with the waistband of my boxer briefs, fingers grazing the tip of my cock. "And you still want to be with me?"

"Need, Clover. I'm so past *want* it's unhealthy."

She kisses my neck. "But I wouldn't write you sonnets. And I'd probably never remember to light candles when I make you a nice dinner. In fact, I'm an awful cook. So you'd have to do all of that, too."

"We can make that happen."

She nips my lip. "You'd never get me to serenade you."

"I can live with that."

She takes my face between her palms, stroking her thumb over the bruised side of it. "I won't ever be sappy. But I'll always be willing to throw punches for you, in all my tiny-fisted glory. I'll nurse you back to health every time you get sucker punched, take in as many college kids as you can care for, find you as many wide receivers as you need to win all the championships you deserve."

It's a whole surge of adrenaline, being so close to having everything you've always wanted. In football, it's where you really show your worth. That Super Bowl game where you either show up and perform, or fold under the pressure and lose it all.

In the moments when I dared to let myself dream of a time that I'd be right where I am now, I swore I'd never botch it. I'd make the most of the opportunity, leave it all on the field.

I need to tell her, in case it isn't already painfully obvious. How desperately in love with her I am. How having her in my life again took the love I already had for her, turned it on its head. Propagated it, deepened it, making a damn mockery of the way I felt before.

You thought that was love? Let me show you what the real thing looks like.

Melody places a soft kiss to my lips, then leaves a trail of them along the bruised side of my face, down my neck, over my bare shoulder. My heart is beating a mile a minute. The words are ready to tumble out of my mouth. *I love you, I've always loved you, I'll never stop.*

She rests her forehead on my shoulder and I run my fingers through her hair, feeling my heartbeat everywhere.

"Melody—"

"What is that?"

I frown, trying to figure out what she means, what she's looking at. And that's when I remember I took my shirt off.

I stiffen, jerk back, but the second her eyes find mine, I know it's too late. "Zac, what is that? Show it to me."

Heart sinking into the depths of my stomach, I move my arm out away from my body, watching her duck to have a look at the side of my ribcage. With a finger, she traces the skin there, over the cluster of black four-leaf clovers tattooed along my side, down to my hip.

I can't get a read on her face. Can't figure out what that wrinkle between her eyebrows means. "When did you do this?"

I think maybe she's hoping I'll confess I popped out to get it done an hour ago, though there's no way she'd actually believe the lie. I go with the truth.

"I started ten years ago. I have one for every year I lost you."

She eyes my side, and I can tell she's counting. Double checking. Her gaze flicks to mine. "Why?"

"Melody." Her name is a plea out of my mouth. "You know why."

I know she does. It was in the way she looked at me, just this morning. The way she was adding up my mom's words, the way she stared at the house.

It's in the way she stares at me now, rubbing her lips together. I think she's trying hard not to cry. "You—you left. You didn't want me."

"I've loved you since we were kids. I've wanted you since I figured out what it meant to want someone. I loved you so fucking bad, and then you said what you said that night and I . . . You were my best friend's twin sister."

Her brows pull together. "What does Parker have to do with it?"

I feel the sting of it all over again. The fucking torture it inflicted on my immature teenaged brain. "He had this stupid rule—the one fucking rule he made sure to drill into every guy who ever came within spitting distance of you. He'd bring it up all the time, out of nowhere, like . . . like he had some kind of internal clock telling him, *oh, it's that time of day again. Better drill it into this sad fucker's head that he can't have the one girl he's ever wanted—*"

Mel disentangles herself from my lap, shuffles back onto the bed, and my entire body aches from the void she leaves behind. She finds the jersey she threw off only a handful of minutes ago and pulls it on.

"That's why you left—the Hands-Off Melody Woods Rule? You actually listened to that?"

"I left to tell Parker how I felt about you, and that I was going to do something about it. It was so fucking senseless that I left without explaining that, Mel. But I had it stuck in my head that I was going to do it the right way. I was going to clear the air with my best friend, my brother. I wasn't going to turn you into this dirty little secret. He blew up on me. It was—it was bad."

"This—" She rubs her face in both hands. "You let me sit there, waiting for you all night. Ignored me when I reached out the next day. I cried myself to sleep for months. You left me hanging for years, all because you couldn't get my brother's blessing?"

"You know how he can be. You haven't wanted to tell him about us."

"But I never let it stop me. I've come to you every single day for months. I've been pretending to date your friend to get more time with you. Maybe I've been slow and closed off, and a bit confused about my feelings for you. Maybe I didn't want to rock the boat with my brother, but I never stayed away. I've been choosing you. Over and over again."

She's so fucking right, it kills me.

"I told you I had no good excuse. I chose my friendship with Parker over my love for you, and it was the biggest mistake I've ever made. He and I have never been the same since, anyway, and . . . I lost you both that night."

There's no humor in her chuckle. It's pure incredulity. "Leaving me like that wasn't love. If you loved me—"

"I do—"

"You didn't—"

"*Do*, Melody. Are you hearing me?" I get to my feet, agitated, and shove the hair off my face. "Don't do that. You don't get to tell me I didn't love you then and haven't loved you since. You don't get to tell me that I haven't been *aching* for you—*down to my fucking bones*—since the minute you left town."

She clamps her jaw shut and I pull on a shirt, unable to believe how fucking sideways this night has gone.

"I endured ten years without you, Mel. And while you were out there getting over me, building a life with someone else, I was here. Waiting. Hoping. Praying to gods I don't believe in for another shot with you."

I think she's getting it. Finally getting it, because the fight in her body seems to go out then, replaced by something that seems almost stunned—overwhelmed. But I'm not stopping now. I've held all this in for as long as I'm capable. I crouch at her feet, take her hands from where she's tucked them underneath her on the bed.

"I am in love with you, Melody. I have *been* in love with you. And frankly, given the way the past fourteen years of my life have gone, I don't see a way out of it. This is it for me. You, with all your—your inability to start a conversation with a simple *hello*. The way you don't give me an inch, make me work my ass off for the ghost of a smile. I will never stop working for it, working to earn you, because that's what you deserve. And I'm so utterly and completely gone for you, anyway, that I wouldn't know what to do with myself if I weren't."

Her face crumbles at my words, eyes fill with tears. "Then why didn't you reach out? Why didn't you try? Getting over you was . . . It was the hardest thing I've ever done. I can't tell you how much I missed you. How long it hurt me to leave things the way we did, even to this day. I was upset, but I'd have heard you out, eventually."

"I tried, a few years in. I got Summer to get your address out of Parker and I came to find you in the city. You were already with Connor. Melody, I am so sorry. I'm sorry for letting you believe for a second that I didn't love you. I'm sorry that I hurt you badly enough that you pulled away from your life here, and that I wasn't there for you for ten years, in whichever capacity you needed me to be."

Mel rubs her lips together, now looking anywhere but at me. I get to my feet. She loves me back—I know her, I *know* she does—and she won't even look at me.

It's utter bullshit. "Let me off the hook."

Two swipes of her arm, and she looks at me with hastily dried cheeks. "What?"

"You heard me." I fiddle with the red shoelace around my wrist, tugging at it compulsively. "I made a mistake, but it was years ago. I'm different now—you know I'd never choose anyone over you. You *know* that, Mel. Let me off the hook. Get out of your head and let us finally have this."

"Are you asking me to get over something I just learned about, after a decade of believing something else entirely—"

"Yes. That's what I'm asking."

"And if I need to process it?"

"Then process it with me. We haven't come this far just to throw it away over a ten-year-old fuckup. You're stuck with me, and we're not doing anything else until we get past this. Staying up all night if we have to."

I flick on the bedside light just to drive the point home. Stride across the room and turn on the floor lamp, too. She stares down at her hands. I pick at the flimsy shoelace.

At the sound of my sharp breath, Mel twists around to look at me.

My red shoelace sits on the ground, snapped in half, frayed ends curling up. I stare at it, this thing I held on to, pretending it meant that the woman now standing feet away from me was mine. Even from miles away, without a word spoken between us in years.

The sight of it broken on the floor kills my frustrated momentum. Is this some kind of sign, then? That I'll never really have her?

I pick up the string, but I know it's beyond help. It had already been hanging on by a thread. I sink down at the foot of the bed.

Melody moves for the hotel room door. I think she's really about to fucking do it and walk out on me. With my jersey on, just to twist the knife. But she crouches to fiddle with her backpack instead.

Her keys clang together in her hand as she makes her way back and stops just short of where I'm sitting.

"There's no hook, Zac. Okay? There's no hook to be let off. But it's been fourteen years of thinking things were a certain way, only to find . . ." She looks at my side, the part of me I branded with her, over and over. Her eyes soften, and the second they do, so do my shoulders. "Only to hear I had it all wrong. I'm processing. That's all."

I nod, take in a breath. "I love you. I always have," I say again. Just so I know she heard it.

She's still a bit guarded when she looks at me, but her mouth pinches into a relenting smile. Her cheeks flush in that way I love. Mel pries the broken shoelace from my fingers, tosses it onto the bed. My gaze drops when she starts fiddling with the keys she pulled out of her backpack.

She picks at a knot on her keyring until the matching red shoelace comes free.

I can't take my eyes off it. I haven't seen the thing in years, not since I tied it around her wrist. I'd assumed she tossed it the second she realized I wasn't coming back for her. Never for a second thought she might have kept it. That she'd dig it up again one day.

"Where'd you find it?" I ask, voice thick.

Melody takes my arm. "Find it? What do you think was important enough to go back for in that storm?"

"This is what got us stranded together in the woods?" I am flying. I am weightless, made of air and hope. "You always had it with you?"

"I always had it with me."

She loops the rope around my arm. Double knotting it. Triple knotting it. Every sure flick of her wrist whispers *mine, mine, mine* in my ear, and it really feels like she's staking her claim on me with this shoelace.

Finally.

Melody lifts my hand and kisses the inside of my palm. "Take good care of it for me, okay?"

Chapter 34

Melody

Coffee stains down my front. Milk froth in my hair.

That's the distracted state in which I'm finishing my shift at Sheffield's this afternoon. I regret every bit of the offer I made Wynn to pick up the shift, to make up for quitting early after Connor showed up yesterday.

You don't get to tell me I didn't love you then and haven't loved you since.

I tied that shoelace around Zac's wrist last night, and we both clung to it like a desperate white flag. We crawled into bed and kissed goodnight, both suddenly drained yet aware we'd have more to talk about the next day.

Zac's confession doesn't matter—not really. We've spent months organically growing this relationship. I've spent months fighting him at every turn, only to fall flat-on-my-face-in-love with him anyway. Last night doesn't change any of that. He did a stupid thing years ago, took accountability, and has shown me the kind of man he's grown to be. He's quietly proven his love for me every day since he crawled out of that tent in the woods.

Still, though. I've spent all day obsessing over fourteen years' worth of ill-founded memories and hurt. I assumed I'd been the one to ruin our relationship by asking for a kiss he never wanted. I spent ten years so upset by his supposed rejection that I avoided my hometown so that I'd never run into him. Fell into a relationship with an abusive man because of my own inexperience, coupled with the insecurity born the last night Zac and I saw each other.

It was the most restless sleep I've ever had in Zac's arms and a quiet flight back this morning, during which he let me pretend to read whichever book I haphazardly clicked on my Kindle. It's a miracle I've been able to make it through my shift at all.

Fourteen years. We wasted *fourteen years*. I can't decide who I want to shake more. Myself. Zac.

"Hey, Mels." Or my brother.

I look up to find Parker eyeing me cautiously. Possibly, he's been watching me mindlessly wipe down this pristine table for the past ten minutes. He's wearing shorts and a damp T-shirt. A sheen of sweat glistens at his temples.

"I came in for a post-run coffee," he explains, jerking his chin at the register. "You okay?"

I don't know how I expected to feel seeing my brother today. Maybe some resentment. Anger.

But more than anything is deep curiosity. He admitted to the Hands-Off Melody Woods Rule when I first moved back to town. It hadn't entered my mind that Zac had been one of the people warned off me.

"Not really." Blowing out a breath, I drop into the booth I've been cleaning. "Parker, I need to ask you about something."

With a look around the emptying diner, he slides into the seat opposite me. "Okay. Hit me."

I push aside my spray bottle, fiddle with my rag. "What happened between you and Zac? How come you're not as close as you were when we were younger?"

Parker doesn't seem all that surprised by the question. "Why do you ask?"

"Just something I noticed since moving back. You're both out there acting like everything's fine, but I know it isn't. You're so awkward around each other."

He pushes the sweat-wet hair off his face, sinking lower in the bench seat. Parker looks me in the eye, but the guilt there is palpable. "You're going to want to murder me. You remember the night before you left for college? When he drove you home during the party at his grams's house?"

I nod, working to keep my face blank.

"Well, he came back all . . . I don't think I ever saw him like that, Mel. It was like he was on another planet. On top of the fucking world."

I grind my teeth together, forcing myself to stop picturing a younger Zac coming to my brother, in love with me, asking for his blessing. On the heels of asking him to kiss me.

Of tying matching red shoelaces around our wrists. With my four-leaf clover in his pocket, before he'd go on to tattoo them for years.

"What happened?" I ask when Parker doesn't go on.

"Honestly? It took me a while to figure out what he was getting at. He was talking a mile a minute. About how much our friendship meant to him, how grateful he was that our parents basically took him in like he was one of us . . . I was drunk and confused as hell, Mel. There was a whole party going on around us." Parker rubs his jaw, staring off at the wall like he's back there again, listening to Zac. "And then I realized he was asking—*telling* me he . . . well, he told me he had a thing for you and that he wanted to act on it."

Listening to the pained way Zac told his side of the story, it would have been impossible to believe he was making it up. Still, there's a relief in Parker recounting an identical version.

"I was drunk," he says again. "I mean, it felt bad enough, back then, that my best friend was telling me he wanted to screw around with my sister. But add the alcohol, and it was . . . irrational and ugly. There was a lot of yelling. Shoving around. We made a scene in front of everyone at the party. In front of his grams. I . . ." He clears his throat, stares down at the table; I've never seen him this ashamed in my life. "I threw a punch. My aim was shit and I barely made contact, but some of the guys had to break us up. And then he just . . . shut down. I didn't see him again until school started a couple weeks later, but it was never the same. Every time I tried to talk to him about it, to apologize for what I did, he'd find a reason to cut the conversation short and acted like everything was okay."

I want to ask him whether he'd still hate seeing us together now. But it doesn't feel right letting on about my relationship with Zac without having him in the room with us.

Instead, I stare out the windows, looking out onto the colorful street. The bright storefronts and the yellowing leaves falling off trees.

We wasted so much damn time.

Ten years of longing, on both our parts. I can admit that now.

My matching shoelace got us stranded at that campsite, like it knew how badly we needed it. How much I still missed him. I never had the heart to get rid of that bracelet, to leave that piece of him behind. Not ten years ago, when I took it off the morning after he left, nor on that stormy night.

That should have been my sign that this is meant to be for us. And here I am wasting precious minutes obsessing over a *ten-year-old fuckup*, as he put it.

"You don't look murderous," Parker ventures after a while.

"No, I'm not murderous. What's the point? Things are totally different now."

My brother gives me a long look. "Things are going well with Brooks, then?"

With a noncommittal shrug, I get to my feet. Parker follows me to the counter.

Get out of your head and let us finally have this.

On a whim, without a single thought, I fire up the espresso machine. Pour milk into a canister and froth the hell out of it. When I slide the steaming latte across the counter, topped with a modest but un-exploded heap of foamy milk, Parker catches it in both hands. He lifts his brows, impressed.

"Are you coming around on the idea of us together?" I ask him.

And would you still be coming around if you knew it was Zac that I love?

With a carbon copy of the loaded shrug I just gave him, Parker takes a long sip of his drink.

Chapter 35

Zac

Even with her car in the driveway, it takes seeing Mel sitting at the kitchen island with my own two eyes to really believe she's back home, where she belongs.

I took me and my shitty mood over to Brooks's until she finished her shift at the diner, unable to stomach a waking moment in this house without her. Now, Melody sits hunched over a to-go coffee cup, fingering the strands of hair framing her beautiful face, and I stand at the entryway to the kitchen, just basking in her presence. The way the place feels brighter, the house feels warmer.

"How much longer do you think you'd stand there staring if I keep pretending I don't know you're here?"

I've never been so relieved to be greeted by her signature snark. The day she greets me with a *hello* will be the day I know I fucked up good.

"Long enough that you'd have to excavate my rigor-mortised body. You're my favorite thing to look at, Mel." I move into the kitchen as she turns on her stool. "How was your shift?"

"Enlightening." She lets a breath balloon her cheeks and blows it all out. "Parker came in. I asked him about that night."

"And?"

"And it would mean a lot to me if you both made up. He's my brother and you're my . . . my Zac. And I hate that your friendship changed over me."

"Then we'll work it out."

She runs a finger around the rim of an unlit candle on the island. "It's occurred to me that there are a bunch of things I have all wrong from back in school. I was hoping to ask you about them."

My stomach squeezes nervously, but I pull up the stool next to hers. "You can ask me anything."

She clears her throat. "True or false: Your prom date never fell through. You canceled on her to go with me as friends, because you knew I was upset no one asked me."

She's really not fucking around.

I shove the hair off my forehead. "False. I pretended to have a date because I didn't want to ask anyone but you."

Mel looks touched, rubbing her lips together. "I swear, I didn't know you felt that way. All the girls you'd have around you . . ."

"There was no one until college, when I figured I should attempt to move on. I gave up on that pretty quickly. Then I saw you with Connor a few years later and tried dating again for a while, but . . . they weren't you."

It feels so good to finally let all this out. Euphoric.

Melody hasn't taken her eyes off me. "True or false: you never left Oakwood Bay because you . . ."

"Because I hoped you'd come back one day. Because I wanted to be here if you ever did."

"And this house? The reason it looks almost identical to the one on the vision board I made for school?"

"You wanted it. I wanted to give it to you."

"Just like that, huh? I want something, you give it to me?"

I lift and drop my shoulders. "I like it when you're happy."

Her gaze travels around the kitchen, taking it in. Maybe finally getting that it's hers. Not an inch of this place was built without her in mind, and it never felt right painting it, filling it, without her say.

"Thank you," she whispers. "For the house, and for caring that much. I really do love it here."

I cup her cheek and she leans into my hand. "True or false: you kept my jersey because you missed me."

"A lot," she says.

I lift my wrist. "You kept this shoelace because you still thought about me."

"All the time." She hesitates. "You really did start getting those tattoos because you were in love with me back then."

"That's true, Clover." I tuck a strand of hair behind her ear. "I want to show you something."

I hold out my hand to help her down from her stool, and she follows me to the wall of bookshelves lining the back of the living room off the kitchen. Most of these are books of Grams's that I haven't had the heart to give away. But I slide four of them from the very top shelf and hand them to her.

The tattoos are proof that I've longed for her for the past ten years. But there were four years before that, too.

Melody balances the books in an arm. They're our high school yearbooks, and with a glance at me, she opens the topmost one. Flips through it to find dried-out four-leaf clovers preserved between the pages.

Mel stares down at a page, at the clover pressed into it. She nods, slowly, over and over, curling her lips into her mouth, and a single tear hits the yearbook, right next to the clover.

"All of them?"

"One for every game I played, all four years." We stare at each other. "Why are you crying?"

She dabs the corners of her eyes. "I think I'm mourning what we could have been this whole time. Knowing I could have had you . . . It's such a waste of a decade."

I reach for her and sweep the back of a finger along her cheek, collecting tears. "It wasn't time yet. I had a lot of growing up to do for you."

Melody balances the yearbooks on the back of the couch. She moves to me, fiddles with the hem of my shirt. Runs a hand up my side, where her four-leaf clovers dot my body.

"You were right, that night after the WAGs game," she tells me. When I only frown, she adds, "You told me that, one day, I'd realize you're exactly what I need in my life. And you were right."

My heart seems to know something I don't. It picks up speed, banging inside my chest so hard I'm sure she must hear it. Something flutters around my diaphragm, light and heavy at the same time, rising up my throat.

Melody sucks in a long breath. "I feel happier than I have in years, and I have you to thank for that, Zac. You're still everything I loved about you back then—kind and thoughtful and caring. You see the potential in other people, and you don't let them think any less of themselves. You're exactly what I need, and what I want to keep, for good. I don't want to hide this anymore. I want to tell Parker. To end this thing with Brooks and tell everyone about us."

Mel wraps her arms around me, and the fluttering feeling surges upward. "I loved you so much back then," she says. "I know I took a break in the middle, but maybe that's what I needed to really appreciate the way I love you now. The way you love me now."

Nothing.

Nothing will top this. Ever.

With her hands anchoring my face, Mel presses her mouth to mine. The force of the kiss sends me stumbling back into the bookcase. And then she flattens her body to mine, searching, demanding, lifting onto her toes to kiss me harder, and I scoop her up so that she can wrap her legs around my waist.

She scrapes the nape of my neck with her nails. I groan, everything going tight with need. "Noah isn't home," she mumbles between kisses.

I fist her hair. "Thank G—"

Right on cue, the front door blows open. *You have to be fucking kidding—*

"Hey, Zac?" Noah calls from the front hall. I can hear him kicking off his shoes and moving toward the staircase.

I swallow hard, forcing a breath into my lungs as Melody laughs silently at my winded state. "Yeah?"

"I'm getting changed quick and then heading out for a date. I don't think I'll be home tonight. You guys need anything before I go?"

Thank fuck.

Melody dots kisses along my jaw. "We're all good. Thanks for the heads-up."

We listen to his footsteps move up the stairs. When he's safely on the landing, Melody breaks into the kind of teasing grin that makes me fucking weak in the knees.

"What should we do while he's away?"

Chapter 36

Melody

"What's taking him so long?"

I dig my nails into the back of the couch behind me. Zac stands a few feet away, staring at me from the bookcase. His arms are crossed tightly against his chest like it's the only way he can manage to keep himself from lunging at me as we stand here waiting out the agonizing minutes before Noah leaves for the night.

I squirm, every inch of my body uncomfortably hot and sensitive. My nipples rub against my bra. My clit throbs against my leggings.

"One more minute. Just another minute, I can hear him getting ready," Zac murmurs, chest rising and falling fast, rivaling the pace of my own.

I'm hurting. Everything actually *hurts* right now. Without thinking, I let my fist drift to the inside of my thigh. And then an inch higher and another, and then—

I whimper at the feel of the heel of my hand grinding over my pussy. It's not enough. It's not nearly enough. I've been dreaming of fucking the man in front of me for years, and then spent the past couple months in a tantalizing sleeping arrangement that's made everything so much worse. Nothing but the feel of him inside me will be enough tonight.

"Melody, stop that," Zac says sharply. He sways forward and back, as though thinking better of coming anywhere near me right now. Eyeing me as I rub my fingers over the damp seam of my leggings. "Take your hand off your pussy. Now."

"Zac, I can't. I'm dying."

"And what do you think this is doing to me? Don't you dare come without me. Not tonight."

His cock is fighting the front of his jeans. Jaw is pulsing in frustration. Biceps are flexing from the force of keeping his arms crossed, exercising every bit of the restraint he has left. The sight only makes me hotter, makes me rub harder.

He's grinding his teeth, and this is fun now.

Smirking, I dip my hand into my pants, finding enough room to slip under my panties. "*Melody*," he says through clenched teeth when I release a quiet moan. "I swear to God—oh, *fuck me*."

"That's the idea." Zac's eyes go wide when I withdraw my hand to suck myself off my fingers. "What's wrong, Zac?"

"What's wrong is that the longer you keep this up, the worse it'll be for you the second we're alone."

"Worse how?" I find my way into my panties again, rubbing circles over my clit, releasing every little whimper and moan just to tease him.

"You ever been spanked, Clover?"

"Can't say I have."

"It's what brats like you deserve. Your ass is mine the second that front door closes."

"Keep on threatening me with a good time, Porter. It's making this so much better."

I eye the doorway leading out of the living room. We're at the very back of the house, as far away from the staircase as we can get. I bend at the waist. Peel off my leggings, take off my shirt. I toss them at him, leaving only my bra and panties on.

"That's better."

"*Fuck*, Mel."

I close my eyes, push my panties to the side, and dip my fingers into my pussy. God, I'm already so wet it's tempting to beg him to skip the foreplay. To bend me over right here and fuck me so hard and messy I see stars.

Zac doesn't say another word. For a while it's nothing but my whimpers, his harsh breaths, and the wet sounds of my fingers moving inside me. When I open my eyes, blinking away the sex haze, I see his hand moving over the front of his pants. His gaze is stuck to me as he touches himself.

God, he's so fucking hot. I can barely believe he's mine.

Because he is. He's mine. He always was, always should have been.

Finally—*finally*—we hear Noah up on the landing. My heart is in my ears as my fingers freeze inside me.

I'm ready to dive behind the couch for cover if for some reason he decides to come all the way back here. But the second he's down the steps I hear him fumbling with his shoes, listen to the sound of his keys glancing off the table by the door.

The front door opens.

It closes.

And the lock clicks.

"Give it a second," Zac tells me as I move my hand out of my panties. "Just in case."

We stand perfectly still, listening, panting, eyes glued to each other. A car door slams shut. There's the roar of an engine coming to life.

Thank God. *Thank God*—

Zac takes a step toward me.

But I'm not ready to stop toying with him. I want to drive him to the edge of his sanity. See what it looks like when he takes what he wants from me—what he's apparently always wanted from me—without apology.

I move around him, toward the hall, smirking at the look of surprise when I dodge his hands as he reaches for me.

"Melody."

I dash down the hall with his footsteps behind me. I'm at the foot of the stairs by the time he catches up, and when I turn to face him, it's clear he's not impressed with my antics. I back up and climb one step up the staircase.

"What's your game, Clover?" Zac's voice has dropped deeper than I've ever heard it.

"I figure if you're going to teach me a lesson, I may as well earn it."

I reach behind me to unclasp my bra, but Zac takes a step toward me, slow and careful, like he's trying not to spook an animal out in the wild. "Don't. Don't take that off. Let me."

Oh, Zac.

I let my bra drop to the ground. He releases an angry breath. He takes another step forward and I hook my thumbs into the waistband of my panties.

"Don't you fucking dare," he growls.

My panties hit the floor; the second they do, he snaps.

Zac rushes me. I turn, barely make it up another two steps before he hooks an arm around my waist, drags me back down the stairs so that I fall on the lower steps on hands and knees with a desperate, hungry cry.

He drapes himself over me, fisting my hair to uncover my ear and nipping my earlobe. "Just so you know, I had every intention of making our first time romantic as fuck."

"What, like candlelight and rose petals shaped like hearts?"

"Something like that. Should've known better. I forgot who I was dealing with." He palms my ass hard. A shiver runs down my spine at the threat behind the move. "Melody, yes or no?"

No hesitation. "Yes. I want it—"

The next sound out of me is a loud cry as his hand comes down to smack my ass. The sharp sting spreads under my skin until he rubs it away with the heel of his palm. "*Fuck*, Zac."

He licks a path up the side of my neck. "Good or bad?"

I whimper. "Do it again."

He smacks me again, just harder than the first. Letting it sting a little longer before soothing it this time. *Fuck*. How is it I've gone so long without having this?

How is it he knew I'd like it?

I'm soaking wet. I can feel myself start to drip between my thighs. Zac punches his hips forward, dragging his denim-clad cock up and down the back of my thigh, and groans into my ear.

"Again," I pant, curling my fingers, digging my nails into the wooden staircase. He smacks my ass so perfectly that my moan sounds like a plea.

"Ready to behave?" Zac trails wet kisses up my neck. I nod frantically. "That's my girl."

He backs off, and I wince as my ass hits the step underneath me. With a smirk, Zac wrenches open his pants, drops his zipper. My chest heaves when he pulls out his cock, holding himself out for me.

"Open up. Let me fuck that bratty mouth."

Oh my God, I love seeing him like this. Sweet Zac, all riled up over me.

Pressing my lips together, I plant my hands on the step behind me, dragging myself up. His mouth flattens into a hard line.

"Where do you think you're going?"

I pull myself up another step. And another. Zac lunges for me, and with a yelp I dodge his hands. I scramble all the way up the stairs and take off toward the bedroom. My foot snags on the rug lining the hallway. I fall, catching myself on all fours.

My breaths are so fast and shallow, the edges of my vision start to fade. I turn over to see Zac stalking toward me. With his eyes on me, he rips off his shirt, and the dim lights cast shadows over his mouthwatering body. He's all bunched-up muscles and ridges and the obscene bulge where he tucked his cock back into his pants. He looks big and threatening and so damn sexy I almost give up my game. I can't wait to fuck him—

Apparently, I'm living out all kinds of fantasies I never knew I had tonight.

My stomach drops when Zac reaches out, grabs my ankles, and drags me to his feet with so much force the rug comes with me. I end up flat on my back. I think he's about to pull me up, claim my mouth the way I love, the way he wanted downstairs. But Zac drops to his knees. Throws my legs wide open. And buries his mouth in my pussy.

"*Zac.*"

He groans, running laps over me with his tongue, kissing every part of me.

"I thought I was being punished," I pant. "This feels a lot more like a reward."

"Uh-uh." He pauses to lash my clit relentlessly with his tongue. "It's *my* reward. I think I fucking earned it after your performance."

This is it, right here.

All my good karma coming around in the form of a man who eats my pussy like it's his favorite thing to do. I sink my fingers into his hair, encouraging his pace. I'm immersed in the full sensory experience of it: the slow drags of Zac's tongue, his greedy sounds, the way he meets my eye, looking cocky as hell at whatever he sees in my face.

I'm so worked up, it doesn't take me long. His fingers sink inside me, curl the right way, hit the right spot, and I burst, back arching off the ground, clawing at his hair so hard I must be hurting him. Zac licks at me, letting me ride out my orgasm until I fall back limply on the floor.

He crawls up my body to hover over me on hands and knees. "I swear I'm not just saying this, Clo. But you're the best I've ever tasted, hands down."

I reach up to smooth out the mess I've made of his hair. "You're very welcome."

With a laugh, he heaves my limp body over his shoulder and stands, then shoves open his bedroom door and tosses me onto the bed. He freezes in the act of unzipping his pants, gazing down at me where I lie in the middle of his mattress. His face softens in a way that pumps my chest full of warmth. Makes me feel like I'm an unexpected piece of glitter falling from the sky.

Fluttering down toward him as he watches in wonder.

"Don't," I whisper, nose prickling. "Don't look at me like that. You're going to make me cry."

This is why I love us. He was spanking me a handful of minutes ago. Just as quickly, the pendulum swings, and candlelight and rose petals wouldn't feel so out of place.

Zac drops his pants. He stretches out, covering my body with his, hard pressing onto soft. Brown eyes gaze over my face like he wants to soak this in.

"How am I looking at you?"

"Like you've waited years for this."

A corner of his mouth tugs up. "You know that feeling of wanting something for so long, so bad, it starts to feel unattainable? I'm scared I'll wake up in the morning and realize I dreamed all this."

It's really something special. Realizing you've been loved this hard, for this long, without even knowing it.

"I'm here." I stroke the hair off his face. I trail my hand down his neck and chest until it sits over his pounding heart. "Right here. I love you, and this is as real as it gets."

Zac lays the sweetest kiss on me, slow and full, filling me with something so light I think I could float off this bed. Somehow, I manage to pull him in closer. I lick at his tongue and his hips jerk, grinding his cock into my thigh. Just like that, the kiss turns frantic. His grip on my face turns greedy. He shifts around, and the next stroke of his cock hits my clit.

"Zac," I moan. "Condom. Now."

Nipping my shoulder, he goes to sort through the nightstand and tears open a sealed box of condoms. His body really is something else. The muscular shoulders, the way his thighs flex as he moves. The crinkled eyes. Whoever made him really took their time. Got every detail right.

"How have you pictured it?" I ask him.

Zac looks up from the box in his hands. "Pictured . . . this? You and me?"

I sit up, reach for him. He sucks in a breath through his teeth when I gently stroke his cock. "Tell me and there's a good chance I'll do it for you."

"I've pictured us fucking so many times over the years, there's no one way to tell."

"But our first time?"

He licks his lips. "You riding my cock. Me enjoying the view of a lifetime."

I get to my feet and lift onto my toes to kiss him, maneuvering him onto the bed so that he lies on his back. He rolls on the condom, looking so big spread out on the mattress, and I crawl over him. I run my tongue over the smooth skin of his stomach, pausing to admire the ten four-leaf clovers before kissing them all, one after the other. He groans when I climb on top of him, dragging my pussy along his cock. Simultaneously, we look down to watch the way the condom glistens with what I leave behind.

"Fuck. Look how wet you are," Zac murmurs.

I shift my hips, stroking him with my pussy again, again, kissing him hard. On the next stroke I reach down, and he lifts his hips—

"Zac," I gasp.

I'm so wet, so ready for him, that I think he could easily sink in with just one stroke. But we seem to be on the same page because neither of us rushes it. My nails dig into his shoulders, feeling him stretch me inch by inch. It's so good that my eyelids go heavy. Through a fog, I watch his lips part, brows twist, and I know he's right there with me.

"That feels so good," I mumble, bending to kiss him once he's inside, hitting me deep. My muscles ease, like they'd been tense and waiting for him as long as he's been waiting for me. "God, that feels so good, Zac. We're made for each other."

He chuckles, stroking the hair off my face. I'm on another planet. "Clo, I'm not even . . ."

"Mm?" I say lazily, kissing his jaw.

Zac takes my hips. Pushes down, gently, but my eyes snap open anyway. His cock surges deeper and I release a shocked cry as he keeps stretching me.

"Oh God," I gasp, lifting my head to get a look, and *holy fuck,* he's not even halfway inside. He's going to ruin me.

Zac scrapes his teeth over his lip, and I can see him struggling to ease me into this. See exactly how badly he wants to pound into me. "I need you to take more. Can you do that for me?" His fingers tangle in my hair, keeping me close as I nod in frantic response. "That's my girl."

He moves slowly, thrusting off the mattress, feeding his cock into me slowly as I writhe on top of him.

"Zac," I moan, and it comes out like an accusation. "It's so much."

He runs soothing fingers along my back, dots kisses over my face. "You quitting on me, Clo?" I mumble words that make no sense. Shake my head. "So, fucking take it."

With a whimper, I sit up, balance myself with hands on his stomach, and swivel and grind my hips, working to stretch around him, take in the last of him. Twisting around, I feel my body relax and adjust for him. Zac reaches for my clit and rubs soft circles. Any tension left fades to nothing.

"I'm so fucking proud of you." His eyes roaming my body. "Look at you. My girl knows how to take a fucking cock, doesn't she?"

I nod frantically, glowing under the heat of his praise, feeling stretched so fucking thin in every kind of way. Everything feels so good. I tip my head back. My hair sticks to the sweat rolling down my spine.

"There you go," he murmurs, staring at where we connect, watching his thumb work my pussy, softening me. "Are you going to fuck me now, Clover?"

I dig my teeth into my lip as his finger picks up the pace. "I'll have you know my first instinct was to say no, just to mess with you."

Zac smirks. "But?"

"It just so happens I really want to fuck you now."

I lift, just a little. A couple of inches just to test the waters and feel this out. I drop, fit myself on him again. And then I'm rocking over him, taking him in and out of me and my eyes shut because it's good, so good, so full.

"Jesus fucking *fuck*, Clo." His voice is thick, strained, a little slurred. "So fucking tight. You're so fucking hot. So . . ."

He seems to forget he was speaking. Zac reaches for me, eyes hungry as he watches me ride him. He palms my breasts, squeezing, tugging my nipples. Runs his hands down my waist, settles them on my hips. He looks captivated by the way my body rocks back and forth. Like he's drunk or drugged, on some kind of wild trip with edgeless shapes and lightning bolts flashing around us.

My skin prickles, pussy warms. I've never been so damn turned on by a man's eyes on me in my life. I brace myself back on his thighs, drawing my body all the way up his cock so that he nearly slips out. Then I roll my hips and he's back inside. My abs work hard to take him, because it really is work, taking a cock like his.

"Fuck me back," I pant. "Please, Zac. Fuck me back—"

Zac meets my movements with thrusts of his own, up when I come down, sending sharp flashes of heat down my legs with every one. But it seems he's set on giving me most of the control, letting me set the pace, the angle. He's enjoying the view like he said he'd do and looking like he's floating in another galaxy as he does.

"See how sweet I can be for you?" I move my weight forward and dig my nails into his chest. "Making all your dreams come true."

He smooths his hands up and down my thighs, so firmly my skin ripples under his palms. "I've got dreams of fucking you dating back fourteen years. You could spend the rest of your life on your back with your pretty thighs spread wide, and it wouldn't scratch the surface."

He darts up, wraps an arm around my waist, and draws me closer, then crushes our lips together. It's rough and fast and it seems Zac's done playing second fiddle because he meets my pushes with hard drives of his hips, hitting me so deep, over and over.

My body overheats, goes weightless. "Zac," I gasp. "Zac, Zac, Zac—"

"Come for me, Clo," he says against my lips. "Let me feel it."

I whimper into his mouth, sinking my nails so deeply into his shoulders I'm surprised I don't break skin. I'm frantic against him, working with him on our rhythm, but the second he slips a hand between us and presses my clit, it's over. I still and he takes over, fucking into me like he's trying to shove the orgasm out of my body.

"Oh my G—"

My cry borders on a scream and I claw at him, reach for his hair, desperate for something to clutch. Our sweat-soaked skin slips together as I thrash violently on top of him and I swear he's just tapped me like a fucking tree. Fucked the soul right out of me.

"How—why—so good." I give a pitiful moan into his neck, and

Zac stills his hips, tucks his chin to press his lips to my forehead. God, he's so sweet. So gentle—

"Buck up, Clover."

My eyes fly open. Oh, fuck. "You didn't come."

Zac gives a soft laugh into my hair. "Playtime's over."

He rolls us so that I'm flat on my back, then lurches off the bed and disappears into his closet.

"How are you even functional right now?" I'm lifeless on his bed, the soft comforter we bought together lulling me into a sex-induced coma, but just as my body starts to melt, he reappears.

He tosses some fabric onto my body.

"Put it on, turn around, and stick that tight little ass in the air for me."

Oh, *fuck*.

I lift my head, fumble with the fabric. It's a Huskies jersey, same as the one framed behind his desk at work, with his name across the back.

"Stereotypical jock," I say, sitting up. "How many women have you fucked with your name on their back?"

With a cocky-as-hell smirk, Zac plucks his jersey from my fingers. "Get your fucking arms up, Melody."

He slips his jersey over my body. Stands me up and turns me so that my back hits his chest, holding me tight like he knows full well my legs wouldn't carry my weight. He bites my neck, kisses my temple.

"I've been saving this move just for you, baby. Watching you ride my cock was a pretty sight. But my name on your back and streaming out of your smart mouth while I fuck you senseless? That's what real dreams are made of."

He shoves me back toward the bed and I fall onto my elbows, scrambling to kneel at the edge of the mattress. I lift the hem of his jersey over my hips, wriggling my ass in the air like an eager offering.

"Fucking fuck," Zac mutters under his breath.

"Even better view?"

"You have no idea."

He runs his hands over my ass, down to stroke my pussy. I'm so sensitive I cry out just from that, then even louder when I feel the tip of his cock brush over my clit.

"You know what this means, Clo? You wearing my name like this?"

I whimper, dropping my forehead onto the mattress, clutching my own hair. I squirm again, seeking him out, trying to get him back inside me. But Zac only teases me with his cock.

"The second I'm inside you like this, it's over. This is the last cock you'll ever get. This pussy is mine in this lifetime, the next, and the one after that. You get me?"

"I get it," I pant. "I get you. Put it back in."

He drags his cock up my pussy, then notches himself just inside, but not nearly deep enough. "Whose pussy is this, Melody?"

"*Ah*. God, Zac. Yours. It's yours. I'm fucking yours."

"Fuck yeah, you are."

He drives inside me, so smooth and hard that flashes of light erupt over my vision. He's relentless—draws back, punches in, and the air's out of my lungs. I moan when his thighs hit mine.

"You're taking it so good, baby." His thumbs stroke the space between where he holds each side of my waist. "I'm gonna get a little rough, okay? Tell me if it's too much."

I nod eagerly, desperate for him to use me, to fill me up the way he wants.

I thought he was deep before. But at this angle, on elbows and knees with my ass in the air, he slams so far inside me that I'm thrust forward on every pump. He reaches for my shoulder, holding me in place and making me take even more.

The sounds in this room are obscene. Desperate whimpers and

hard grunts, skin slapping furiously together, wet sounds as he just fucking possesses me. It's raw, hard, and relentless. It's years' worth of need, coming to a point. He claimed it wouldn't be as romantic as he'd have wanted tonight, but I can't see it getting any sweeter than this.

"Touch your pussy," Zac grinds out. "You're gonna come for me again. Do it now."

I'm damn near sobbing at his words, tortured and grateful at the same time. I reach between my legs. Peer around for as much of a look at him as I can get. I watch his abs contract with effort as he fucks me, the sweat dripping down his temples. The deep furrow in his brow as he fixates on the sight in front of him, his cock disappearing inside me.

I feel it building again, the hot current burning up my spine, down my legs. Suddenly I'm face down on the mattress, crying out, biting his sheets. Zac's thrusts get sloppy. With a breathtaking groan, his body jerks one last time. He tenses and collapses forward so that his forehead hits my shoulder. I mumble senselessly into the mattress, feeling him throb inside me.

"Fucking . . . Jesus . . . Clover," he pants into my skin.

With a pained groan, he pulls out of me and turns me over. He's gentle with me again, gaze traveling over my face, my limp body. He pushes back the hair stuck to the sweat on my forehead, and I make a weak sound of protest.

I'm lifeless. He's ruined me. I can't even see straight. "Baby, I'm gonna need signs of life. Give me words."

"Sex coma. Go away."

Apparently, all attempts at sweetness faded with the third orgasm.

Zac barks out a laugh. He draws back the covers at the head of the bed and drops me carefully onto the soft sheets, tucking me in. When he returns from the bathroom, he crouches at my side.

"You wanna wash up?"

"I can't get up," I sigh, feeling pathetically weak. "But I need to get my makeup off."

Zac disappears into the bathroom, returning with one of the makeup wipes he must have pulled out of my drawer in the vanity. With the same keen focus he had when cleaning me free of mud back in the woods, he gently wipes it along my cheeks and forehead. He flips the wipe around and coaxes my eyes shut so that he can carefully work on ridding me of my eyeliner.

"Keep them closed," he murmurs when I open my eyes, thinking he's done. He lifts a wet cloth from his lap. "The package says you have to rinse your face after."

Oh my God, he's so sweet I can't stand it. "You read the directions for makeup wipes?"

"You're too beautiful to mess around with." He runs the cloth over my face, as gentle as anything, and kisses the tip of my nose when he finishes.

I never thought I'd feel this way again. That I'd willingly let—*want*—a man to care for me, dote on me, the way Zac does. It makes every bit of me tingle in the most heavenly way.

"Anything else?" he asks.

"I'm overheating."

Zac peels his jersey off me and tucks me back in. "What else?"

"Stop being so attentive and spoon me already."

"There's my girl." With a laugh, he climbs into bed and pulls me to him. Twists my hair up and out of the way. "At the risk of nauseating you—"

"That was the best sex of my life," I mumble into our pillow. Zac kisses the back of my neck.

"You're very welcome."

Chapter 37

Zac

I wake up to a slow, steady heartbeat against my cheek.

The bed is a fucking furnace. I have a light layer of sweat on the back of my neck, even though we only have a thin sheet covering us and we're wearing absolutely nothing. My face is smothered against Mel's smooth, warm skin, rising and falling with her breaths. I've ended up asleep with my head on her chest, holding her tightly like I was afraid she'd evaporate in the middle of the night. Like I made it all up. Last night, and the months before.

I knew it would be that way for us. The way we were last night, teetering back and forth between sweet and teasing, the way we do with our clothes on. It was pinnacle Melody. Pushing me to my breaking point one second, and the next asking me to describe the way I imagined our first time and giving it to me. Blowing my imagination right out of the water, because no amount of fantasizing could have ever measured up to the real thing.

She loves me. We're the *us* I've always wanted, and I don't know how I got this lucky.

Just as I consider waking her up for the sake of feeling her eyes on me, Mel shifts, breathing deep.

"How do you wake up already looking this pretty?" I ask her without moving an inch. I'm not ready to give up the sound of her heart.

"You haven't even looked at me." Her hand comes to rest on my head, fingers sinking into my hair.

"Doesn't matter. I know what I know."

"My hair is sticking to my sweat."

"That's just sexy."

"I have total morning breath."

"Yum."

I pounce, crawling up her body. Find her chin and lift her face as she squeaks and tries to squirm away. I love how especially grumpy she is in the mornings before her first cup of coffee. Nothing thrills me more than seeing that perfect scowl.

"Your ability to go from zero to a hundred like this should be studied by the world's most advanced scientists," she grumbles.

I grin. "Kiss me good morning."

"I can't."

"Why not?"

"Morning breath, remember?"

"Doesn't matter. Kiss me."

"It'll matter when you get so turned off you never want to see me again."

"Impossible." I kiss her cheek, the tip of her nose. "Here's the thing about me, Clo: I learn from my mistakes. I was an idiot once and I don't plan on letting you go again. You and me? This is it. Lock the cuffs and throw away the key."

She tries to hold the displeased downturn to her mouth, but I kiss the tip of her nose again and her body sinks deeper into the mattress, relenting. She lifts her head to kiss me, and my satisfied moan echoes around us.

I pull back before I get carried away, crawl off the bed, and pull on a pair of sweats. Mel lifts her head. "Where are you going? I'm barely awake."

"I'll be right back. Stay here."

I collect the trail of clothes down the hallway, by the front door, in the living room. Flip on the coffee machine and fire up the waffle-maker as I pull out my phone.

ZAC: Are you good?

NOAH: Sure am. Date went well.

NOAH: I assume your first night without me in weeks did too? Am I allowed home today?

ZAC: You know she'd kick my ass if I said no. Just give us the morning and get your ass home.

NOAH: Yes sir.

At some point, I become aware that I'm staring out the window with a dopey grin and I laugh at myself.

I take the stairs slowly, balancing two coffees and a plate of blueberry waffles, our clothes hanging over my shoulder. It really doesn't get any better than seeing Melody turn over in bed, covered in nothing but a thin yellow sheet.

She tosses her phone on the nightstand. Stretches out like a cat, my grumpy cat, and sits up without bothering to tuck the sheet around her. It drops onto her lap, leaving her bare from the waist up.

This woman is actually mine. It's crazy, right? Total freak accident.

"You are such a cliché," she says with an amused look at the breakfast I place on the nightstand. "You get a little tail and suddenly it's breakfast in bed. Don't tell me you're about to pull out a diamond, too."

"I wasn't going to do it today, but there you go tempting me." Her eyebrows shoot up, and with a smirk, I take a waffle and stick it in her gaping mouth. "Eat your breakfast, Clover."

I lift the sheet covering her body and crawl underneath it, settling between her legs. "What are you doing?" she says, chewing a bite of waffle.

"Eating breakfast."

She squeaks when I yank her down to give me better access. Her legs fall open for me, and I kiss along her thighs. She gives a full body shiver, whimpers when I press a kiss to her clit.

Nothing will ever, *ever* top this.

I'm addicted to her pussy. The sounds she makes for me, the way her hips squirm, draw me in. It's probably unhealthy, will somehow come back to bite me one day.

"*God*, Zac."

Hard to care about unhealthy addictions when she moans like that. I lick at her, slow and soothing this morning. Trail a hand up her thigh, teasing her ass with my thumb, and she slumps onto the bed with a drawn-out moan. I inch my fingers into her pussy, and—

She whimpers. One tiny note, and I know it's not right. Not the same as the others, the good sounds. I surface from under the covers to see her biting her lip.

"Sore?"

She nods. I trail kisses up her body, all the way up to her mouth, and then roll off the bed. In the adjoining bathroom, I wash out the clawfoot tub I don't think I've used in all my time living here and fill it up with water, squirting in a bit of Mel's vanilla-scented body wash.

Not sure it's the best substitute for the proper bubble stuff, but it'll have to do until I can get her some.

Besides, it fills the room with her scent, and I'm thrilled to find that it follows me out into the bedroom, too. She scowls, pretending to be annoyed when I pick her up off the bed and carry her into the bathroom.

"Warm enough?" I ask her as she sinks into the water.

"It's perfect." She slicks back her hair with water and her scowl melts away. "You better be coming in with me."

I strip off my sweats. "Where else would I be, Clo?"

The bathroom is bright, the morning sun pouring in through the massive window beside the tub, giving us a perfect view of the water out back. But neither of us take it in.

Why bother, when the best view is right in front of me, in the form of the woman sinking cozily into the warm water. She stares back at me without even bothering to hide her smile or the sweet twinkle in her eye. She sends ripples through the water as she slides toward me and straddles me. I let out a helpless groan at the feel of her body pressing into mine, all wet and hot, smelling like vanilla.

"How long until you go to work today?" she asks, cupping water in her hands and soaking my hair.

"Forget work. I'm taking my first day off in years. We're winning again, and I've run enough overtime practices this season for them to owe me the time. How about you?"

"Forget work. My days there are numbered, anyway." She plays with my hair, molding it with her fingers. "I got an email from the Knights while you were down making breakfast. About my application."

My heart lurches. "And?"

She beams. "I have an interview next week." It's a simultaneous pang of euphoria and dread.

Her days are numbered here, too, a nasty voice says in my head. *The second she gets that job, she's leaving town.*

"You're going to ace it," I tell her, shoving my own shit aside. "There's no way you're not getting this job."

She shrugs noncommittally, but she hasn't stopped smiling. "Want to play hooky from work again and drive me to the interview? Spend the day in the city with me?"

Do I want to go out there with her, basically enabling her ticket out of Oakwood and away from me?

"I'm there." I must really be some kind of masochist.

"Great. So, assuming I do get this job, and setting aside the persistent ex-boyfriend issue, that only leaves play number four in my playbook."

"'Do something you've always wanted to do, but never have,'" I recite. "What do you have in mind?"

Mel hums, moving my arm out from my side and tracing the topmost tattoo. "Did this hurt?"

"Getting a tattoo? It's not so bad."

"I'm thinking of getting one. I've always thought about it, but never had the guts to." She grips my shoulders. "I'm thinking a skull tattoo on my butt cheek—"

I cough. "*What*—"

"As a symbol of the new me," she finishes proudly. "I'm tough. Strong. Not to be messed with."

Melody curls a tiny bicep to drive the point home. Fucking hell, I must have broken her last night. Fucked any good sense right out of her. That's what this is, right?

"Please tell me you're kidding." I sit up straight, taking her with me as water sloshes around us. She sours at my alarm. "Tell me you're not going to ruin your perfect ass with a fucking *skull tattoo*. Seriously, my heart couldn't take it."

"Don't panic. I'll make sure it looks great." With a laugh that does nothing—absolutely nothing—to ease my panic, Melody trails light kisses up my neck, along my jaw. "What do you want to do with your day off, Coach?"

She knows exactly what she's doing when she holds my face and kisses me hard like this, flattening herself against me. Pushing out the water floating between us, along with every panicked thought from a minute ago.

"This," I get out in between kisses. "Definitely want to do this."

"This," she agrees. "And we can strategize how to tell Parker about us."

My stomach squeezes. "You want to do it tonight?" When she nods, I lurch us out of the bath, dripping water everywhere.

"Where are we going?"

"Back to bed. If I'm going down tonight, it'll be in a thick, post-sex haze."

Chapter 38

Melody

"Do we even know if he's home yet?"

Zac is nervous. I can feel the anxious energy radiating off his body as we reach the nondescript blue door near the opening of Oakley's that leads up to Parker's apartment.

"I was too scared to text him," I admit, slipping my key into the lock.

"*Scared*? You're supposed to be the calm one here. He's not allowed to kill you. Me, though? I'm a walking dead man." He shoves his hands into his pockets with unnecessary force.

"For someone who's sworn up and down he no longer cares about what my brother thinks of us, you're looking a little green."

"Yeah, well, I'm full of it," Zac says grimly. "You're mine, and he's your brother. Of course I care what he thinks."

How does this man make me swoon, even when he talks about Parker? And how—seriously, *how*—do I get to be the lucky one who has him?

I rub his forearm, hoping the contact helps calm him. "I realize I should have said this before, but here goes: as much as I'd love to have Parker's blessing, not having it won't change a thing between us. I'll still love you." I quirk a smile when his shoulders visibly relax. "Even after my little brother kicks your ass."

Zac snorts. "You came so close to sticking the landing."

I shrug. "You know full well whose wagon you hitched yours to—"

"Whose wagon is hitched to whose now?"

It's a bucket of ice water dumped over my head.

I freeze, still in the act of rubbing Zac's arm, and his gaze drops to watch the way my hand now tightens in a steel grip. Nails dig into his skin.

It can't be. *It can't be.*

I look around slowly, even though I already know what I'm about to see. Connor is standing behind us on the sidewalk. He moves around Zac to appraise me, then bounces an intrigued gaze to Zac, trying to place him. He shoots Zac a pleasant smile when he sees him looking right back.

Zac doesn't recognize him. It's only when he looks at me again, presumably noticing the way I'm now standing rod straight, nails damn near piercing his skin, that his face dawns in understanding.

"Hey, Melly," Connor says, turning that sunny grin on me. I grit my teeth. When I don't manage a word, he holds out a hand for Zac. "I'm Connor. Melly's boyfr—"

"Finish that sentence." Something strange seems to be happening to Zac's face. It contorts in a way I've never seen. His mouth is in a near snarl, a dark cloud eclipsing the light in his eyes. His jaw pulses angrily. He doesn't take his eyes off Connor. The hands in his pockets have turned to fists. "Finish it. I fucking dare you."

"Pardon me?" Connor asks, giving Zac an odd look.

"Connor, what are you doing back here?" I cut in quickly.

He shrugs. "I never left. You're going through something, clearly, and I couldn't bear being back home without you. Without being around the corner, in case you needed me."

"I had to leave that home when you broke up with me," I point out. "You have to go. I told you I was done with this—"

"You didn't mean that." The condescending prick flashes an apologetic smile at Zac, as though asking him forgiveness for my lapse in judgment. "Besides, don't you think you owe me at least a conversation after six years?"

That does it for me. The tension in my body snaps. This absolute. Fucking. Dick.

"I don't owe you a thing, Connor. Get out of here."

I catch a barely perceptible flicker in his bright expression. His mask slipping as he realizes he's not getting his way? I've never seen it before.

"I just want to talk to you. It's the right thing to do, Melly."

"No. I don't want to talk to you."

"All I need is five minutes—"

"*She said no, motherfucker.*" Zac's voice echoes angrily around us, and a few people across the street pause to stare at us. "You got a problem getting a two-letter word through your head? Because I've got a way to make it sink in."

Connor's attention fixes on the fists in Zac's pockets. "Who the fuck asked you to get involved?"

Zac's eyes meet mine, imploring. *Ask me to get involved.*

It's so contrary to the Zac I know. The calm, controlled one who dishes out easy smiles. Incapable of aggression, not even with Noah's angry, drunk dad charging at him.

Now, I can tell he's working hard to keep his cool. The last thing I want is for him to lose it in the middle of the street, because of Connor of all people. Already, people are staring. I see Jim, the owner of Oakley's, peering through the bar's window. It makes me stand a little taller. I'm not about to let this asshole get the best of me, and especially not of Zac.

I shake my head at Zac, and his teeth grind so hard I'm sure I'd be able to hear it if my heartbeat wasn't in my ears.

"That's what I thought," Connor says with a derisive chuckle. "Come on, Mel. Let's leave your little guard dog here and have a chat inside, huh?"

"I'm not going inside with you," I tell him coldly. I nod at the alleyway beside Oakley's, away from prying eyes. "You can say whatever you have to say over there."

When I start to move around Zac, he gives me a last pleading look, asking me to stay, not to go with Connor. But I've been chasing this feeling for weeks, the ice-cold strength to stand up to him, and I refuse to derail my own momentum.

"I'll be right back. Stay here."

He stares at me for another long moment. With a bitter sigh, he moves out of my way. Connor laughs. "Good little guard dog. *Woof, woof.*"

"Did you just—" I whip around, fucking *praying* I heard him wrong.

But Connor's still smirking at Zac, who only calmly crosses his arms over his chest with a look that plainly says *I fucking hate you.* Which is noble and all. But I go from cold, simmering fury to white-hot rage in the span of a second.

It's the same kind of rage that had me trying to hunt down Noah's dad the moment I saw Zac's banged-up face. Because Connor just fucking—

"Did you just bark at him?" I snap at Connor. "Tell me you didn't *bark* at him, you sick, narcissistic piece of—"

"Mel, it's fine," Zac says evenly. He doesn't take his eyes off Connor, though. "Don't let him get to you."

It's far too fucking late for that.

Connor appraises me. Maybe I'm misinterpreting it, but he seems fascinated by my reaction. I turn on my heel and march into the alley, Connor's footsteps behind me.

"Who the fuck is he, Melly?"

The alley is dim, walls cutting off the setting sun, and it casts ominous shadows over the sharp angles of Connor's face. He glances at the mouth of the alley, like he expects Zac to have followed us in.

"None of your business. *He* is none of your business. And let me tell you something, Connor: if you ever bark at him again—even *look* at him the wrong way again, I swear to God—"

"Oh, I get it now. This is what you've been up to, then? Why you broke up with me?"

My jaw drops. "*What*? You broke up with *me*."

"I'm holed up in a tiny inn down the street, worrying about you. Meanwhile, you're out there fucking some other guy—"

"I—*me*? Are you kidding me, Connor?" I hiss. "You dumped me to be single on a boys' trip!"

"And I want to undo it. I want you back, and you're the one refusing."

I let out a bitter laugh. "You really are deranged. You're not even denying that's why you did it. How many people did *you* fuck days after dumping me?"

I don't know what catches him more off guard—the bite in my tone or that I'm not backing down. Connor tips his head to the side, eyes calculating.

"Everyone makes mistakes, Mel. I can forgive your cheating if you drop this bullshit attitude and come home with me now."

He's serious. Staring down at me completely steady, as though he didn't just spew a whole load of garbage at my feet.

"Fuck you, Connor."

His brows shoot up his forehead. "Excuse me?"

I take a step toward him. "I regret every second of our relationship—*every second*. Do you hear me? I wasted so many good years trying to keep you happy, while you did *nothing* but drain the life out of me for your own sick satisfaction." I fist my hands at my sides. "So yeah, you heard me. Fuck you and fuck your twisted mind games. Get out of this town, and out of my life."

I brush past him, but his hand closes around my arm, tugging me back.

"How are you going to be like this after everything I've ever done for you? The apartment, the job, anything you could ever need—"

"I never asked you for any of that," I spit at him. "I never asked for it, and still, you've had no problem hanging it over my head. *Threatening* me with it, even now. Breaking up with me was the best thing you ever did for me."

I tug my arm back, but he tightens his grip. I'm not sure I've ever been afraid of Connor. He was a manipulative ass—emotionally dangerous—but never once did he come close to getting physical with me. Then again, he always got his way.

But now, with his fingers digging painfully into my arm, I feel a terrifying prickle of awareness raising the hairs on the back of my neck. The steady whirring of alarm bells in my head tells me this isn't right; to get out.

Have I sensed this before? Is it why I always kept my mouth shut—as a way to protect myself from this side of him?

"Let go of me, Connor."

"We're not done talking."

"Yes, we are, and you're hurting me." I try to wrench out of his grip. "*Let go*, Connor—"

"Stop struggling and talk to—"

The words are cut off by his own hard grunt as his back hits the alley wall, head bouncing against the bricks. The momentum releases his hold on me and I stagger back to see Zac looming over Connor, forearm pressed against his throat to keep him in place against the wall.

"Clover." He's right up in Connor's face, jaw pulsing in fury. "Tell me you're okay."

Connor blinks rapidly, dazed from the impact of his head smashing into the brick wall behind him. "*Clover?*" he says derisively. "She let her fuck buddy give her *nicknames*—"

"Boyfriend," I snap. "He's my boyfriend. Get it right."

Connor finds me over Zac's shoulder, but Zac releases him a fraction off the wall just to slam him back into it, drawing back Connor's focus. "Don't look at her. Look at me. Give me one good reason why I shouldn't snap your fucking arm for touching her."

I fist the back of his shirt. "Zac, don't do something you'll regret tomorrow."

"Yeah, Zac," sneers Connor. "Don't do something—"

Zac doubles his pressure on Connor's throat, cutting him off. "Not another word from you."

"He's not worth it," I say quickly, tugging at his arm. "Zac, he's not worth it."

He huffs a breath. And then another.

"If I were you, I'd get down on my knees and kiss her feet in gratitude. Because as far as I'm concerned, she just saved you a trip to the hospital." Zac grinds his forearm threateningly into Connor's throat, but it's the soft, eerily calm tone of his voice that really makes him frightening. "But seeing as you're never getting within spitting distance of her again, here's what's gonna happen. You're going to walk out of here, straight into your car, and you're going to drive out of this town. Look at her again, I will rip your eyes out. Contact her again, I will snap your fingers. Touch her again, and I will end you. Do we understand each other?" When Connor doesn't move, doesn't do anything but stare at him mutinously, he adds, "This is the part where you nod, motherfucker."

For a second, I wonder if Connor has a death wish. He glares at Zac like he's working up the courage to call his bluff, see how far he can push him. But that's the thing about manipulators, right? They only go after the weak links.

Connor nods at last, sags down the wall when Zac releases him. He's agitated, shoulders bunched under his shirt, but when I drop my hand into the one he offers me, his touch is so gentle we might have just woken up from a blissful nap together.

I push the hair off his face and Zac manages a smile. "Let's get you upstairs, girlfriend."

We make it a single step away before Connor's voice floats from his spot behind us. "Lucky you. She's an ungrateful bitch, but at least she was good for a decent fuck."

Oh, shit.

Before I can process the right words to stop him, Zac whips around, grips the front of Connor's shirt, and jerks him upright like a puppet on strings. His fist collides with Connor with enough force to put him on the ground.

"What the hell?"

We spin to find Parker, flanked by Brooks and Summer, frozen on the sidewalk at the mouth of the alley, staring wide-eyed at the scene before them.

God, how can this go from bad to worse?

"Holy shit." Brooks rounds Parker to stand at Zac's side, watching Connor wipe the fresh cut on his lip. "Did you just throw down?"

"Get him out of here before I do it again," Zac answers. Connor gives Zac a mutinous look but doesn't spare me a glance.

"Who is he?" Brooks asks.

Parker appears at my side, his face completely unreadable as he moves his gaze from Zac to Connor. "Mel's ex."

Brooks grimaces as Connor rises, steadying himself on the wall he'd just been pinned against. "You'll be hearing from my lawyer—"

I snort. "No, we won't. That would require you to admit you let some guy knock the snot out of you."

"Get him out of here," Zac says again, eyes still glued to Connor.

Brooks takes Connor by the upper arm, and the entire thing must have really done a number on him because Connor doesn't even protest. "Come on, big guy. What do you say we help get you on your way, huh?" He digs into Connor's jacket pocket. "Found his keys. Sum, you'll follow us in my car? I'll ride with him a while, make sure he ends up in the right place."

"I've always wanted to be a getaway driver," Summer says, catching Brooks's own keys. God, I love my friends.

As they escort him away, Parker pats Connor on the back far harder than necessary. "I told you I wasn't the scary one, asshole."

The second they all disappear from the alley, Parker turns, looking back and forth between me and Zac.

"So. Shall we head inside?"

Chapter 39

Melody

Zac and I eye each other in the living room, listening to the sounds of Parker rummaging in his bedroom. He headed straight there once we got upstairs. I don't know about Zac, but I'm feeling a lot like a kid who's just been ushered into the principal's office, waiting for the hammer to drop.

I take Zac's punching hand, running a thumb over his knuckles. The skin isn't broken, but it's red and angry-looking and he'll wake up with bruises tomorrow.

"You didn't have to do that, you know."

Zac takes my chin between his fingers. "Yeah, I did. No one talks about you like that. Ever."

"You don't fight."

"I'd burn everything to the ground for you and walk away without another look." He thumbs my chin when I chuckle. "What's funny?"

"You know, I love it when you smile at me. I love it when you leave lip balm everywhere you think I'll need it. But I *really* love it when you lose your mind over me. You're just so good at it."

"That's because I've been doing it all my life, Clo. You really held your own out there. I was so proud of you."

I huff out a laugh. "Your *I'm proud of you* face looks a lot like your *I'm about to dismember someone* face."

"Since when do you have an *I'm about to dismember someone* face?"

Parker leans his hip against the kitchen island, dressed down out of his work clothes. I don't know whether it's a force of habit, but we simultaneously move away from each other on the couch.

Parker blinks. "I'm sorry—are we still doing that thing where we pretend you two aren't sneaking around?"

My stomach drops. Parker snorts at whatever he sees in my face. You have got to be kidding me.

"How long have you known?"

"Known what?" he says innocently.

"*Parker.*"

He looks from me to Zac. "*Oh.* We're *not* pretending you haven't been hooking up?"

Zac clears his throat. "Listen, Parker. Before we get into all that—as far as I'm concerned, this is only one of two conversations that need to be had. I know things have been a little off between us."

"Are you ready to stop hating me?"

I shift uncomfortably. "Would it help if I left the room?"

"No, stay. I'm never hiding anything from you again." Zac presses his forearms onto his knees. "I don't hate you, Parker. It was misdirected self-loathing, and I've always known that. Still didn't make it any easier to look at you the same, though."

"Self-loathing because I didn't want you to sleep with my sister?"

"It was never about sleeping with her, man," he says, frustrated. "Why is that what you reduced it to?"

"Because I was in those locker rooms with you. With the team. I saw the way they'd look at Mel and Summer, like they were candy. You did too, when it came to Mel. I know it was overprotective, overbearing brotherly shit, but hearing the things some of the other guys would say made me sick. There was no way I could turn a blind eye to it. I don't think anyone could blame me for wanting to protect my sister from that."

"But you *knew* me, Park. You were the closest thing to a sibling I ever had. And still, I got lumped in with a bunch of horny jackasses." He stands abruptly, pointing at me. "You had to have known it was bigger than that. I was crazy about her."

Parker fingers the roll of athletic tape sitting on the counter beside him. "I swear to God, I didn't. I had my head so far up my own ass with football, and whatever other bullshit I had going on back then. I didn't realize it went that deep for you. It doesn't excuse the way I reacted, but it's the truth of how I felt at the time."

"Yet you don't seem surprised to hear me say it now."

"I thought we had one bad, drunken fight, but that we'd hash it out in the morning. It's not like things hadn't gotten heated between us before—we disagreed over football all the time, and we always got over it. I put two and two together by the next time I saw you, but you'd already written me off. You never wanted to talk about it whenever I tried."

"I was angry with myself," Zac admits. "I could have been clearer with you about what I wanted with her. I could have told you to shove it and gone for it, anyway."

Parker stares at him a moment. "I'm sorry for the way I acted that night. I'm sorry that it cost you this." He gestures at us, then fixes on me. "You're clearly . . . You're happy right?"

I try to fight the flush in my cheeks, but it's a lost cause. "I really am, Park. Please be okay with this."

He turns to Zac again and says: "Do I get my best friend back?"

"As far as I'm concerned, this thing between us is squashed. It should have never been a problem to begin with. I'm sorry I let it become one."

Parker smooths down the front of his jeans. "Well look at us, dishing out apologies like grown adults. Who knew it would be this easy?"

"Hang on." I look back and forth between them. "That's it?"

Parker blinks. "What do you mean?"

I get to my feet. "I mean, after ten years of holding a senseless grudge, acting like you barely know each other . . . that's it? You apologize and things go back to normal?"

Zac gives me a funny look. "Would you rather we duel at dawn?"

"No, but . . . but what about tears? Don't you want to take your time reconnecting? Falling in love all over again? What about grand gestures, and angst, and tension, and outside forces working against you?"

"*Falling in love*? She's lost it," Parker deadpans, turning to Zac. "Lucky for me, you just claimed responsibility for her. This is all you, man."

Zac reaches for me and hesitates, like he's afraid touching me will pass on some kind of disease. He rests the back of his palm against my forehead. "She doesn't feel feverish," he tells Parker. I swat away his hand.

Parker takes a step back, anyway. Good to know these two can hit their stride again so soon after making up.

"So . . . you're okay with all this?" I say to Parker. "Me and Zac together?"

"Mels, I thought you knew me better than that. Why the hell would I send you off on a camping trip where you'd have to share a tent if I weren't okay with the possibility of it?"

My jaw drops. "You said you stayed behind because you had a girl over!"

"Nah, just trying to help you two make up for lost time. Though I *was* fascinated by the lengths you were going to to hide this."

Parker's front door blows open and Brooks and Summer appear. They take in our scene: the way Parker leans against the island of the open kitchen, me and Zac standing in the middle of the living room. The mutinous look I'm giving my brother.

"I take it the jig is up?" Brooks says.

"Wait, it's over?" Summer looks around in disbelief.

"Yup," Parker says proudly, popping the *P* for emphasis.

"*Damn it*," she bursts. She reaches into her purse and produces a fifty-dollar bill, then thrusts it in Parker's direction. "I thought for sure they'd manage to stay oblivious at least another month."

"Oblivious to what?" Zac frowns.

"To the fact that you really aren't as clever as you think you are. Did you seriously think we didn't figure out you were hooking up the whole time?"

"The whole—" I look from her to Parker. "How long have you known, exactly?"

"I've known since the camping trip." Parker pockets his money. "But neither of you seemed willing to talk about it, so we played along. I figured you could use some time to be blissfully in love before Summer kicked off her Spanish Inquisition."

My brother gives me an affectionate smile, and despite the shock, I'm gripped by the urge to cross this room and throw my arms around him.

Brooks's shoulders slump in relief. "Thank *God* it's over. Do you know how terrified I've been that I'd let something slip?"

"Slip about what?" Zac grimaces. "He just said they knew from the start."

"Not slip about you two. You couldn't have been more obvious." Brooks gives him a look. "You two made me swear not to tell Summer and Parker you were seeing each other, *they* made me swear not to tell you they already knew . . . I haven't had a good night's sleep in months."

"But Brooks and I—"

"Mels, even *I* have more chemistry with Brooks," Parker says. "If we didn't already know, that joke of a *relationship* would have been the ultimate sign."

Zac presses his palms into his eyes. "And you let us keep pretending because . . ."

Summer plops down on the sofa, spreading out comfortably. "It was fun to mess with you. You did this thing when we were all out together where actual smoke would come out of your ears whenever Brooks breathed near Mel. Cracked me right up."

"Entertaining as hell," agrees Parker.

"But now that it's over, please allow me to begin," Summer starts, lacing her fingers and cracking her knuckles. "Question number one: Is this for real or are you just hooking up?"

Zac turns to me, eyes crinkled in a grin that makes my chest crackle. I suck in my cheeks before I embarrass myself with the loopy, lovesick smile begging for release.

"It's for real."

Zac's smile grows impossibly big, taking over his face, and I feel myself start to blush furiously. I shake my hair onto my face for some coverage.

"Okay, cute as hell," Summer says, tone a lot softer than it was a minute ago. "Question number two, Zac: Is this the part where you ask her to stay? Forget the city, move back here for good?"

Trust Summer to stumble onto the one sore subject—even worse now that we're in as good a place as we are.

"No." Zac gazes at a spot on the coffee table as he answers. "No, I'd never ask her to stay—her dream was always to live out there. In fact, she just heard back from a job she applied for in the city. She's interviewing with the Knights next week."

I can tell the words burn coming out of him. I know he'd love nothing more than to have me stay, in the house he built for me—for us. With our patch of daisies and half-foam-colored walls. But when he meets my eye, there's not a shred of resentment there. He's putting me, my needs, first, like he always does.

I love him so damn much.

"We'll figure it out," I say, mostly to him.

"Okay, I think we got too deep, too quick with the questions there, Sum," Parker says, but I catch them exchanging a look. He shoots an exaggerated smile my way. "Next question, Mels: When you snuck Zac in here for the night a few weeks ago, did you or did you not forget that the walls are paper thin?"

Chapter 40

Zac

"*Fuck*, Mel. What a way to wake up."

It takes me a second to grasp why my body is on fire even before my eyes open for the day. What that hot, wet feeling is dotting down my chest.

And then comes the telltale sight of a Melody-shaped hump under the covers, covering my stomach in delirium-inducing kisses. I roll onto my back and she settles between my legs. Neither of us bothered with clothes last night, and she's rewarding me for it.

Neither of us have bothered with clothes for days, since we finally confessed to Parker. Wouldn't have it any other way.

"You were stabbing me with this thing in my sleep. It's only fair that I get to wake you up, too," she murmurs, and her hot hand closes around my cock.

I groan at the soft way she strokes me, and rake my fingers through my own hair. "Why do you think I was always rushing out of bed before you woke up? I can't believe this is the first time you've felt—oh, *fuck*."

Mel licks my cock, pausing at the tip to shush me. "Noah's downstairs. He hasn't left for class yet."

I clamp my jaw when she kisses along my length, pausing to dip the tip into her mouth.

Jesus fucking . . .

My hand falls over her head. I'm not even trying to rush her or control this. I just want to confirm she's there. It's been weeks of feeling her like this, but still, it's too good to be true.

All of it has felt too good to be true. Walking down the street holding hands. Finding her stretched over the fence between the stands and field at the end of our games, wearing my jersey, waiting to give me congratulatory kisses in front of everyone. I'm still not convinced I haven't been in a deep sleep since the day she showed up in town.

Sure, it was pretty awkward explaining to people that I hadn't, in fact, stolen Brooks Attwood's girlfriend. Nor was this some kind of *why choose* situation. But the people of Oakwood are resilient. They move on quick from fake-dating scandals.

I grunt when my cock hits the back of her throat. "Mel, get up here before you make me come."

Mel pushes back against the weight of my hand, drawing her mouth off me. She crawls up my body and surfaces from under the covers with her hair a mess. She's everything I've ever wanted to wake up to.

"I need you," she whispers. She drops her hips, grinding down on me. She's not lying. She's already soaked, dragging her pussy over me, needy and impatient.

I don't need to be told twice. I flip us over so that she's on her back, but she takes fistfuls of my hair to stop me when I start to kiss down her body to make my way between her thighs.

"Please." I kiss her stomach. "Don't you want it?"

"I do. You know I do. But I really need you inside—"

"Please, Clover? I need my fix. Need it bad."

Her laugh bounces her stomach against my face. "It's for you, is it?"

"It's for me." I lick a path to where her thigh meets her body, admiring the way she squirms for me. "And it's for you."

"Then you can have thirty seconds."

"One hour."

"One *minute*," she says, squirming again. "Hurry up."

The fingers in my hair turn gentle, stroking over my scalp as I run my tongue over her pussy. She's doing her best to stay quiet, and I think that's why she's squirming so hard. She thrashes underneath me, moving her fingers in my hair, trying to release the pent-up feeling any way but by screaming into the room.

"So good," she whispers.

I drag down my tongue to catch what's started to drip out of her. "One hour?"

"One hour. One day. Take a whole fucking year down there—"

I take her clit between my lips and her entire body starts to shudder, thighs lift off the bed. And that's when I pull away. When she realizes I'm not coming back for more, she allows herself a long, mournful sound. I surface from under the covers to find her sulking, skin so dewy, eyes dazed.

"We agreed on one minute." I kiss her pout. "Next time, let me have my way."

"Next time, don't look so smug that I cancel the sex." Mel starts to sit up, but I hold her still, pulling her hands over her head.

"You're gonna want the sex," I say, kissing her neck. "It's good luck. For your interview later."

"Good luck sex?"

"Yeah. My version of your four-leaf clovers. It'll work, you'll see."

She lets out a weak moan when I rub my cock over her clit, and her legs fall open, then wrap around my hips, drawing me closer. The second I slide inside her, she throws back her head, crying out.

"Shh," I say, covering her mouth with mine, swallowing her sounds as I start to fuck her, slow so that the bed doesn't squeak. I take my time with her and I feel everything, every part of her. This is almost too much.

"Melody," I mumble against her lips. "Fuck, I think I'm gonna come fast. I . . ."

It's the groggy morning sex. How her nails scrape gently up and down my back. It's her smooth skin slipping along mine, the heat of her pussy sending a sharp rush down my spine.

It's—

My eyelids wrench open.

"Melody." I slick back the hair sticking to her forehead, trying to get her attention, and she whimpers. "Mel, I . . . I didn't—"

Her dreamy gaze travels over my face. "What?"

"I didn't put on a condom. I'm clear, but . . ."

"Oh." She's barely alert, but there's a tiny spark of recognition deep in her eyes. She lifts her hips when mine slow down, drawing my cock in and out of her, doing the work for me.

I stroke her cheek. "You're gonna have to give me more than an *oh*, Clo. Are you on something?"

She blinks fast, clawing at consciousness. "Yeah. Yes," she says, looking me in the eye now. "I have an IUD. And I got checked after my breakup—" She gasps when I take over fucking her again.

"You're an angel." My forehead presses against hers. Skin-to-skin like this with nothing between us, I can barely suck in a breath. "I need you to stay nice and quiet while I fuck you. Can you do that?"

She nods frantically, but when I drop to suck her nipple into my mouth, she cries out my name.

"That's not gonna work for me." I lick a path back up her body, and I'm momentarily distracted by the sight of her blissed-out face rocking up and down on her pillow every time my hips meet hers. "Those are my pretty sounds. No one else gets to hear them anymore."

I flip her onto her stomach and settle my pillow under her hips.

God, this view. I palm her ass, squeezing hard. "You've got the perfect ass, you know that?"

"Then do something with it."

She squirms, offering herself up, but there's no way I can spank or finger her without making it crystal clear to the kid downstairs what's going on in this room.

"You can get some of that later." She turns her chin, looking for my lips. I let her have them just long enough to line up my cock. "Bite down on your pillow, Clo."

Her moan is muffled this time, and I almost regret telling her to curb her sounds, missing them instantly.

But it lets me fuck her rougher, and the absolute fucking ecstasy weaving its way through my body almost makes up for it. With her hips at this angle, I can tell I'm hitting her good, in the right place. She's squeezing around me so fucking hard I'm about a second away from exploding. After a while I need to focus elsewhere, because the sight of her ass in the air, my cock disappearing inside her, it's just too fucking much.

"I'm almost there." It's taking everything I have not to go off. "Come with me."

"I'm close," she says into the pillow. "Just wait."

Mel's muffled sounds become labored, relentless, when I wrap an arm around her to play with her clit. Some garbled syllables, some that sound like my name. Some that sound praising and others more like threats.

"*Now*, Melody. Come with me. Come with me, or the second I fill this tight pussy with my cum, I'm bending you over the edge of this fucking bed"—she looks over her shoulder, eyes wide, eager at the words—"spanking that ass so hard you'll never forget that when I ask you to come"—she gasps, nods frantically—"I fucking mean it, Mel. Now, come for me. Come on my cock, scream my fucking name."

"Fuck. Z—"

Yes.

I push her face into the pillow to drown out her cries, and she clenches everywhere, spasms violently. I shove my hips forward, sinking myself inside her as far as her pussy allows. Go off like a motherfucking bomb, biting her shoulder to hold back my own sounds.

"If that sex was good luck," she pants, surfacing from her pillow a few blissful minutes later. "Then I've got this interview in the bag."

~

"You're going to ace this," I tell her between kisses. "You're smart and competent. You know football better than half my coaching staff. You're funny, and you're really, really pretty—"

Melody draws back, huffing out a laugh. "I hope those last ones don't factor into a job interview."

"Oh. I forgot I wasn't just listing things I love about you."

She beams at me, and I don't know what I expected from her this afternoon, but she's already made me so damn proud.

I took another day off work to make a day of it in the city with her. She was nervous on our three-hour drive in, sure. But she got through my prep questions with quiet confidence.

Now, her shoulders are squared and self-assured, and it's such a far cry from the woman I met again a couple of months ago, I want to lift her up and squeeze her to me. Twirl her around in this busy parking lot outside the Knights' football stadium. But she's about to land a job here—I'm refusing to think about the alternative—and I don't want to embarrass her in front of her future colleagues.

"All right, Clover. Go kick ass." With a last kiss, she turns, and I can't resist giving her a little tap on the ass as she walks away, basking in her parting scowl.

I make sure she gets all the way across the parking lot and into the building before letting the smile slip off my face.

Because she's about to get this job, and then she'll find an apartment. And soon she'll be living hours away from me. Creating for herself the life she's always wanted, out from under the thumb of the guy who ruined her first venture into the city.

I'm excited for her. I'm desperate for her to have everything she wants. I'm fucking devastated for myself.

Three hours away is nothing, I tell myself for the thousandth time since she landed this interview. *There are weekends, and video calls, and you can drive back and forth on weeknights as much as she wants you to.*

But I can't, can I? Not with the way the team practices every night of the week. And with our games fluctuating between Fridays and Saturdays, that leaves . . . Sundays. One day a week.

It's soul crushing.

I'm blowing out a long breath, about to get back into my truck, when I hear a voice call my name. I almost ignore it. It's not like *Zac* is unique as far as names go. But then I spot a man squinting in my direction, clad in a windbreaker emblazoned with the Knights logo.

He takes a few tentative steps forward before I realize I'm looking at Luke Bailey, the Knights' head coach. He's bearded, salt-and-pepper-haired, probably a good thirty years older than me. He's everything I would have wanted to have as a coach while I was playing, and everything I hope to be as one now myself. Good-natured but tough. Commands the respect of his team, and everyone else in the league.

"Luke, hey," I say awkwardly, suddenly aware of how questionable my presence is. "I swear I'm not here as a spy."

"That's exactly what a spy would say." He chuckles, reaching me at last. He strips the hat off his head as he offers me a hand to shake. "What brings you here?"

"Ah . . ."

Fuck. Mel and I had discussed that it was probably the right thing to disclose her connection to me as a possible conflict of interest. But I really wasn't prepared to speak about this myself today.

I stick my hands in my pockets. "My girlfriend's in there interviewing for a job. I swear she's not a spy, either."

Luke raises his brows. "What job is that?"

"The predictive analyst one," I say, and he nods in recognition. "She's very good at getting things out of me, so if anyone should be concerned about her having this job, it's my boss. She'd be the best spy you'd have. I hope this isn't a mark against her."

He barks out a laugh. "Are you kidding? You just scored her some major points. She's got guts, going after a job with your rival team. I like her moxie."

"Trust me, if it's moxie you want, she's the one."

Luke eyes me a moment. "If I told you something, could I trust you to keep it to yourself?"

"Sure."

He turns to stare out at the stadium at the end of the parking lot. "This is my last season."

I frown. "With the Knights?"

"With anyone. I've decided it's time for me to retire. Well, my wife's decided it, and I wouldn't dare cross her," he says, eyeing me again. "It's not being announced for another month. But my bosses are aware, and they're already working through a list of potential replacements."

"Ah," I say with a nod. "Well, as great as that is for you and your family, I'm sorry to hear that. It'll be weird playing an entire season without seeing you on the sideline."

Luke waves away my words. "I appreciate the ass-kissing, but that wasn't my point. You're on the list, Porter. A recent addition, if I'm frank, because those were some rough opening games. But the way the Huskies have played the past few weeks hasn't gone unnoticed."

"They're looking at me?"

"Don't sound so surprised. I think if you keep turning your team around the way it looks like you are, you'll probably have a damn good shot at the job. It would be smart of them to bring in someone young. A whole lot fresher than I am, after thirty years in the league."

I stare at him, shocked, but overtaken by flashes of what it could mean if I had this job. It would mean only a handful of months of long-distance with Melody. I could finish up the season with the Huskies early in the new year, assuming we make it to playoffs. And then I could move here, too. We could be here together.

"I'm happy to let them know you're interested, if you want me to," Luke says.

"I . . ."

Fuck, I want that. I want it so damn bad. Luke raises gray eyebrows in the wake of my silence.

"I need to think about it," I say at last, and it feels like ripping away a piece of my own soul. I nod at the stadium. "Need to talk to her about it. She's got first dibs on a job here, and I won't crowd her space without her blessing."

"Assuming she gets the job." Luke pauses. "Coach to coach, is she any good?"

"Coach to coach, she's the smartest person I know. And she's been unofficially doing the job for us on the side."

Luke nods, smiling from behind his beard. "You're a good guy, Zac. Good coach, too. You'll let me know what you decide about that recommendation, yeah?"

Chapter 41

Zac

Brooks and Parker stare out onto the field as Noah launches ball after ball at his teammates.

Parker spots me first as I near them on the sideline. He's dressed in workout gear, meaning he probably hit the Huskies' training facility after wrapping up work at the athletic rehab center. It's been slow and a little awkward, but after he and I met for a drink the other week, it feels like we've got a good shot at getting our friendship back to where it used to be.

"I've watched this kid play for two full seasons and I still can't get over how good he is," he muses, following the arc of Noah's throw.

Watching Noah play with that kind of ease really never does get old. And it's all the more amusing knowing that he's also the guy who walks around the house in unironic Iron Man pajama pants. He's also been the one with a front-row seat to my relationship with Mel—an actual, real as hell relationship—in the weeks that have passed since our talk with Parker.

In the moments when I'm driving home alone from work, or falling asleep after Mel, there's been nothing more soul crushing than realizing that, eventually, that house is going from a pseudo-family of three to just me.

Mel's on the verge of hearing back from the Knights. Scouts from all over the NFL have been chatting up Noah what feels like every couple of days.

And I'm on the verge of going from having everything to having nothing.

"How was your meeting with the big boss?" Parker asks when I don't say anything.

"Oh, you know," I say, glancing at Brooks as I shove my hands into my jacket pockets. "He pretended he hasn't spent the past few months threatening my job. Called me *son* a bunch of times, like he hadn't embarrassed me in front of the media more than once. He wants to talk about renewing my contract."

"Can't stand that guy," Brooks mutters.

"But that's good, right? Why don't you seem into it?" Parker asks.

"Because I don't care to coach for him." I exhale a stream of condensation into the crisp November air. "And because it would keep me here."

Parker stares off at the field, nodding like he knows exactly what I mean. That Melody would be hours away, working days while I work into the evenings and coach games on the weekends. It means going half the year with barely a scrap of her.

Brooks runs a hand over his jaw. "What's the alternative?"

"I found out the Knights are looking for a new coach and that I'm on the shortlist." I mold the brim of my hat as their heads whip around to look at me. "Their head coach keeps texting me, asking if I'm interested. It really sounds like they want me."

"They should—the Huskies are a completely different team this season," Parker says. "Have you told Mel?"

"I'm working up to it. Considering she'd have to work for me if she gets that job . . . I can't decide if the news would go down well."

Brooks tugs at the sleeve of his sweater. "Well, if you need any more motivation to leave the Huskies, Noah's definitely getting drafted this year. He won't be back for another season."

"I know."

"And . . . I was planning on doing this more formally. But if it gives you the kick in the ass you need, here goes." Brooks straightens. "I plan on resigning from the team, Coach. I'm out at the end of the season."

I glance at Parker, who doesn't seem surprised by the news. "I hope it's for the reason I think it is."

It hasn't been great watching Brooks coast through life in the year and a half since his injury. He's a top-tier football player, an even better friend, and if he's about to tell me he's going to give playing football another shot, I'll be the first one to celebrate his departure from the team, even if I'll miss having him around.

Brooks exchanges a quick look with Parker, who almost guiltily hikes his gym bag over his shoulder.

"You know, I got the idea from Mel," Brooks says. "She mentioned once that you got her to write a playbook of things to make her happy again after her breakup. I was thinking about what mine would look like, and it always came back to the way I left the NFL. It never felt like a real end, you know? I was forced out by an injury, and then kept out by my own insecurity about never being able to play the way I did before I got hurt. It's probably a long shot, but Parker agreed to help get me back into playing shape. I'm going to attempt a comeback."

My employee just resigned, and one of my best friends just told me he's working up to leaving Oakwood Bay. In the reality where Noah and Mel are about to do the same, losing Brooks will sting.

But I'm really fucking happy for him.

"You couldn't have given me better news, man," I say, clapping him on the shoulder.

"Not even when I add that it'll mean me parting ways with Mel? You know, we never formally broke up."

The pride on my face turns sour.

Parker snorts, shaking his head. "You're both idiots. A fake boyfriend . . . Doesn't get any dumber than that."

I shrug. "The things you do for love."

"I remember those days," Brooks says, almost wistfully. "Naomi had me in a chokehold from the day I met her."

His gaze drops to the grass under our feet, and I swear, there's nothing like the PTSD I get from listening to Brooks talk about his breakup with Naomi, and the way she shacked up with an ex-teammate of his while he recovered from his concussion. It had been a killer cherry on top of the darkest time of his life.

"You ready to date yet?" I ask, knowing full well the answer to that question has been a resounding *no* in the time since it happened.

Predictably, Brooks flinches at my words. "The comeback comes first. Then the rest of my life can happen."

"Famous last words." Parker raises an eyebrow, fixing me with a piercing look he and Melody must have rehearsed in the womb. "Talk to Mel. You're kidding yourself if you don't think she'd jump at the idea of having you out there with her."

Chapter 42

Melody

"You don't think it's too sappy?"

I smooth down my shirt in the passenger seat of Summer's car as we pull up to Zac's house. We were only out on our top-secret excursion for a few hours, but I've missed the hell out of him.

Which is why this has to work. It *has* to.

I can barely make it an afternoon without missing him. Putting a permanent three hours between us would break me.

"Oh, it's sappy as hell. There's no getting away from that." Summer hops out of the car and follows me to the yellow front door. "Trust me, he's going to lose it when he sees it."

"In a good way or bad way?"

"Good way, I think. I mean, the whole thing is adorable. Hearing how gone you've both been on each other since high school has me swiping right all over my dating app. Crappy first dates be damned." She pauses at the threshold, scanning the hallway into the house. "Is it safe to come in? Will he maul you the second he finds out you're back?"

I don't blame the apprehension. Zac and I have made it a habit of leaving nights out with our friends within just a couple of hours of arriving. In my defense, it's not easy to sit so close to him when I'd much rather be sitting on him. I don't know how my body is functional at this point. We've had fourteen years' worth of tension to blow off.

During our fourth round yesterday, Zac spent God knows how long between my legs, doggedly determined to make me come with his mouth no matter how long it took. It could have been an hour by the time I did—I wouldn't know. He ripped the alarm clock off his nightstand and threw it across the room when I tried to take pity on him after the first twenty minutes.

I swear, he looked more pleased with himself after giving me that orgasm than he did when the Huskies hit a four-game winning streak.

"You look like you're spiraling deep into another sex fantasy," Summer says.

"No, I wasn't." I snap out of it. She gives me a look. "Okay, I totally was. I'm sorry, he's a bit of an animal. I think he keeps trying to distract me with sex so that we don't talk about the other stuff."

"The moving away stuff?"

I nod. Zac refuses to let on about it, but I know him. I have every line and tilt of his smile memorized, and I know when it's only halfway there. He's been nothing but encouraging on the surface, but I know he's been stressed since my first interview. And now that . . .

"This is going to work, right?" I ask Summer for the thousandth time. "He's going to say yes?"

"The man's been obsessed with you for half his life," she says soothingly. "He'll say yes, Mels."

Inside, we listen to the sounds coming from upstairs. There's a lot of shuffling around from somewhere near the bedrooms, and the kind of bickering only Zac and Noah could get into.

I drop my keys on the table by the door, and the noises stop abruptly. "Clover?" Zac calls into the house.

"Clover, baby, love of my life," Noah sing-songs. "Are you home?"

There's a loud grunt, and I picture Zac digging his elbow into Noah's side.

"We're down here," I call back, and two sets of footsteps make their way over to the stairs.

At my side, Summer pouts the moment Zac appears at the top of the stairs, beaming wide as he takes the steps two at a time with Noah tailing him.

"He's definitely saying yes," she mutters as he hits the landing. She pats Zac on the shoulder, turning to Noah. "Take cover, kid. It's about to get real mushy around here. I'm leaving before I get too nauseous to drive."

"You have no idea." Noah reaches for his own car keys. "Every time I think they can't get any worse, they prove me wrong. I'm right behind you."

With a parting eyebrow wiggle, Noah follows her out and shuts the door behind him, leaving me, Zac, and our bewildered expressions behind.

"What's Summer talking about?" Zac asks, reaching for me and picking me up so that I'm plastered against him.

We'd been sneaking around for months, have been official for a few weeks, and still, it feels so surreal having him to myself like this. It's funny how it changes things, admitting you love someone. Confessing to your family and friends that it's been you and him all along.

Since you were kids. Until you're old and gray, with kids of your own.

"What's Noah talking about?" I counter, but Zac only buries his face in my neck. It wrenches a stupid, embarrassing giggle out of me. He surfaces from the crook of my neck, looking pleased as punch.

"Wipe that smug look off your face or you don't get to hear my news," I tell him.

He quickly rearranges his expression into an emotionless mask. "Go on."

"I got a new job today."

Zac jolts. "With the Knights?" When I nod, he looks even happier than I was hearing the news. "I knew. I fucking *knew* it. They'd have been idiots not to hire you. You're going to kill it."

I hold his face between my palms, trying to absorb his elation into my skin. That's one out of two discussion points out of the way, and I'm nervous as hell. I need every bit of strength I can muster here.

"That's only part of the, uh . . ." I squirm in his arms until he sets me down. "Okay, you know I'm terrible at this. The sappy, cheesy stuff is definitely more in your wheelhouse, but I want to ask you something important."

He tips his head. "Hit me."

"Well, I was thinking that . . . Look, I know you like it here, that you've always lived here, did the whole waiting around for years until I came back thing. Which is incredibly romantic, and kind of what I'm banking on when I ask you this."

Zac's gaze drifts off to the side. I've confused him.

"I have no idea how it would work, because there are only two college football head coach positions in the city and they're currently occupied. So there's a chance you'd be without a job for a while as we figure it out. But I think that we could. Figure it out, I mean. Together. If you lived there. With me."

Zac's brows inch up his forehead. "You're asking me to move with you?"

"It's crazy, I know. I was thinking it through, how to ask you, and then I realized . . . In movies and books there's always this big, grand gesture, and some sort of panty-melting speech asking their lover to take a leap of faith. But seeing as I'm terrible with love speeches—clearly—I came up with something . . . different."

The flush in my cheeks feels like I've dipped my head straight into an open flame. But I guess there's no turning back now—*definitely* no turning back now—and so I lift my shirt, carefully peel away the bandage at my side, and twist around to show him.

"Melody." Zac traces around the small four-leaf clover tattoo over my ribcage, freshly done this morning after I put in my notice at both my current jobs. "That's . . . that's very permanent."

"So are we, as far as I'm concerned."

I watch a smile take over his face. "You matched my tattoos."

"Yes, well." I release a breath. "You've been full of grand gestures this whole time. So, I . . . you know. Thought I'd throw you a bone."

Zac bursts into laughter. "It's a good bone. I love it."

"What about the other stuff? I know it's unconventional, that I'm supposed to be the one moving for my man because *patriarchy*, blah, blah. And it would probably require you to be unemployed for a bit, but . . . please move with me."

Instead of answering, Zac holds out his hand and leads me up the stairs to the bedroom. The curtains are open, letting the moonlight spill through the window. Pillar candles line the entire perimeter of the room, and on the bed is a confetti of yellow rose petals.

He stops us at the foot of the bed, letting me take it in. "What's all this?"

"My grand gesture," he says, looking around. "It's not as good as yours. But it does involve several orgasms with the intent of making you see what you'd be missing if you said no."

"Said no to what?"

"I was going to beg you to let me move with you."

Hope bursts in my chest. "Really? You'd quit your job?"

"Sort of." Zac takes in a breath. "I ran into the head coach for the Knights' football team while you were interviewing with them. He told me he's retiring at the end of this season, that the team's interested in me as a replacement. That he'd put in a good word for me if I want it. It really sounds like my chances are good."

I stare at him. Zac looks so edgy, telling me all this, that I'm convinced I must be missing something. "Are you not interested in working there?"

"I'm very interested. It's a great opportunity, if it happens."

"Then I'm confused. How are you not bouncing off the ceiling right now? I mean, it's the *Knights*, Zac. The top team in your division. Don't you want to coach for them?"

"Well, yeah. But—"

"And, more importantly, why are you not thrilled by the prospect of eventually moving there? With me, your girlfriend. Who's usually the dour one between us, but who'd probably burst into fucking song and dance over this, if you weren't looking like such a sourpuss. Talk to me. Tell me what's wrong."

"If I did get the job . . . You'd work for me, Mel."

"We'd be a team," I say, throwing out my arms, barely able to contain my excitement. "We do it every Sunday anyway, don't we? I help you with your playbook. You tell me how clever I am—honestly, it's about time you paid me for it. Besides, I got this job on my own merit. Zac, this is perfect."

"You're really happy about this?"

I grip the front of his shirt. "No. I'm freaking *thrilled*. Excited. Exhilarated. Me, of all people. We'd live together there, and split our summers between the city and Oakwood so we could keep seeing our friends. Noah will be off being some hotshot NFL star, but we'd still see him when he visits his mom, and . . . Please tell me you want this, Zac. Please? Because I kind of described my dream life just now, and you're looking at me like I've lost my marbles."

"That's your dream life? You and me working together, the city apartment and this house here?"

I hold his face and watch my fingers thaw whatever doubt was there. "What else could I want?"

That does it. Zac grips my thighs, picks me up, and flops us down on the petal-covered bed. He lets me have his full weight only for a second before pulling back to peel off my shirt, just to get another look at my tattoo.

Zac dots a kiss on the tip of my nose. “So, does this mean you’ll get a new tattoo every year, same as I did?”

His smile is blinding, brighter than the moon shining through the window. I trace his laugh lines and I’m glad there isn’t a mirror around, because I’d bet my smile is just as absurd.

“In your dreams, Zac Porter.”

Epilogue

Two and a half months later

It's a weird feeling.

There was a heavy, sinking thing in the pit of my stomach as thick disappointment swirled around the Huskies locker room. Players and coaches only half-listened to my championship game post-mortem because, at the end of the day, a loss is a loss. Nothing I say will put time back on the clock, give us the opportunity for one last run that could put us on the winning side of this.

What makes it a weird feeling is the simultaneous absolute fucking thrill of watching a stunning, five-foot-five blond woman get pelted with streams of champagne out in the middle of the football field. She's as elated as I've ever seen her, my scowling girl, with purple and silver strips of confetti stuck in her hair as the team celebrates their narrow win to get that trophy.

I fish out the four-leaf clover Mel handed me before tonight's game, twirl it between my fingers. I shouldn't even be out here.

When you're on the losing side, you tend to high-tail it out of the stadium at your first opportunity. Instead, I'm standing inside the opening leading to the locker rooms, watching Mel and my future team celebrate their win. Both wishing I was in her shoes, and so fucking glad it turned out this way.

Because she deserves it.

Because she's had a hell of a few months piecing her life together, a hell of a past six years, and she deserves to have everything good this world has to offer her.

"Hey, Coach. I'm heading back to Oakwood with the team." Over my shoulder, Noah pauses, presumably catching sight of Melody celebrating her win out there. He's in his post-game tracksuit, and there's a small tug at his mouth that wasn't there in the locker room. "Well, that kind of makes all this feel a bit better, doesn't it?"

I pocket the clover. "You have no idea."

It's been a listless couple of months of long-distance after Mel moved out to the city for her new job. Pair that with my boss's renewed wrath at learning I'm leaving to coach the Knights at the end of the season, plus that he's losing Brooks to an NFL comeback attempt, and Noah once the draft comes around in a few months . . . This game couldn't have come any sooner.

I have the whole house to myself again, now that Noah and his mom have moved into a rental in the next town over. It's been painfully quiet. Brooks, Summer, and Parker must be sick of my constant company.

Even over the screams from the stands, still full of Knights fans watching their team celebrate, I can make out the distinct yelp of Mel struggling under the weight of the championship trophy someone hands her. They pluck it out of her arms before she drops it and she's really on top of the world tonight because she actually laughs at herself. Big and unabashed.

I don't know what makes her turn around. There's no way she could have heard Noah and me laughing at the sight of her getting crushed by the shiny trophy. But she does, and the moment she finds us hiding out, she splits from her coworkers and beelines for us.

Her face goes all funny as she makes her way over. Her cheeks struggle as she wrestles away the joy, trying to tone it down for me and Noah. But the second I crack a smile, probably wider than hers had been out there on the field, she gives up on fighting it. She takes the last few yards at a run, jumps, and winds her legs around me when I catch her.

"I'm sorry—" she starts.

"Don't be. You did good, kid," Noah interrupts, squeezing her shoulder. "I assume you'll both be sticking around your apartment to celebrate in peace. I'll see you back in Oakwood."

The second he's out of earshot, I turn Mel into the wall and plant my mouth on her before she can try for another pointless apology. Like having her be this light and content isn't worth every minute of that Huskies loss.

She goes for it, anyway. "It could have been either one of us out there." She runs her fingers through my hair. "I can't believe how close it was. I'm sorry you lost."

"Are you happy?" I ask her with a kiss to the tip of her nose.

"So happy." Mel nods, rosy-cheeked, rubbing her lips together. "And it's not just because of that. *You* make me happy. I can't wait for you to move out here. To kick some ass together next season."

Every time I think a moment between us can't be topped, it happens. This night should be a low for me, but I'm so fucking proud of her, so glad I get to be the one to do life with this woman.

This, here. This is the moment that can't be topped. "Then I didn't lose. Not at all."

In the pocket of my jacket, I pull out a slightly crumpled piece of yellow legal paper. Unfold it to show her the words *Zac's Playbook* written at the very top, and the six words I scribbled down that morning on the porch, when we both wrote down the ways we'd work at getting our lives on track.

I was supposed to write down the ways I'd get the team here

tonight, playing in the championship game after two abysmal seasons.

But then she challenged me to think through how I'd work to get myself happy. So, I did.

Get her happy. Keep her happy.

Melody takes my playbook from me, staring down at the words. "This is all you wrote?"

"It's all that matters, Clover."

She takes my face between her hands. "God, I love you." I can tell she's working hard not to tear up. "Thank you for loving me that much."

I feel so full right now, I could explode. It's the same feeling I get every single time we manage to have a rare day together. Mel looks at me like she's feeling it, too. She nibbles at her lip, holding my face between her hands, and for a while all we do is listen to the cheers out on the field. Someone on the mic announces the game's MVP; the Knights coach makes a speech I don't catch a word of.

It kind of feels like I'm in the middle of a surreal dream with my perfect woman—the woman I've always wanted—and I could wake up and lose all this any minute.

I don't know what the hell I'm waiting for anymore.

I could wait until we're home, back in Oakwood. I could take out the little velvet box rolled up in a pair of socks where it's been hiding for the past couple of months, just waiting for the right moment. I could wait for things to fall into place like I did ten years ago, the night she asked me to kiss her. Or—

"Marry me."

Melody's lips part. It takes her a second to catch up. "Really?"

"Yes, really. Mel, I swear I'll do it right the minute we get home. I'll get down on a knee, give you a ring, light candles, plan a party with our families, the whole thing. But I love you so fucking much and I'm done letting perfectly good moments pass us by." I push the hair off her shoulder, loving the way her eyes go round at the words. "Clover, ten years ago, we tied shoelaces around our wrists, and I pretended it meant you were mine and I was yours. I wanted it to be that way so bad."

"It was," she tells me. "It was that way. We just didn't know it."

I nod. It still doesn't feel real. "Now that I know it, there's not a single thing I want more than to keep it that way. For good. To keep making you happy, for good. Marry me, Clover."

Mel squeezes her eyes shut, little wet beads forming in the corners. I don't think I've ever seen this particular shade of pink on her cheeks, but it's my new mission in life to get it to reappear daily.

"I can't stand how sappy you are," she mumbles. "You're too sweet for your own good."

"You love it." I grin, fishing a long strand of silver confetti from her hair. "Is that a yes?"

"Of course, it's a yes, Zac. You've always been a yes."

I loop the silver strand around her finger, fitting it into a ring, and I was wrong. So wrong.

This is the moment that can't be topped.

Or maybe it can be. Maybe that's the point. Because as long as I have her, my four-leaf clover, we'll have a lifetime of topping the last moment.

Acknowledgments

This story wouldn't exist without the love and support of my readers. Thank you for reading, sharing, and reviewing my debut series (the Sunset Landing series) and making me believe that my stories are worthy of existing outside of my own computer hard drive. Your excitement is truly what keeps me going!

Thank you to my husband, who carried such a load while I wrote *Only in Your Dreams*, allowing me to focus on drafting, carrying our first child, and working a full-time job somewhere in there, too. No way any of that would have been possible without you.

To Shruthi and Chris, whose brilliant insights made *OIYD* the book it is today. This story is light-years ahead of where it was before your feedback, and I cannot thank you enough! And to Jenn, who kept my writing in check and story straight. Your feedback and words of encouragement were just the kick in the butt I needed to get it over the finish line!

There's something so special about writing a story about attaining your dreams . . . only for it to go making my own dreams come true. When I first wrote and released *OIYD*, never in my wildest imagination did I think that little indie baby would find a home within the traditional publishing world.

Thank you to Lauren, Hannah, and the team at Folio, for championing my stories and believing that I wasn't completely off my rocker for attempting to give this book a second life.

To Melanie, Elizabeth, and the teams at Atria. Thank you for believing in *OIYD* and the Oakwood Bay series. I am so excited to be working together to bring these stories to readers!

And finally, thank you to Jillian for being so gracious about a total stranger's thousand questions and for giving me the courage I needed to put myself out there. I fear you may never get rid of me now. This is why you don't feed the pigeons!

About the Author

Ellie K. Wilde is a Canadian writer of contemporary romances and romantic comedies that make you laugh, swoon . . . and maybe require a cold shower or two to recover. She enjoys writing stories with dirty-mouthed, cinnamon-roll heroes and the fiery women who bring them to their knees.

When she's not daydreaming about her next book, you'll find her devouring other romance novels, bingeing reality TV, and snuggling with fur babies. You can keep up with Ellie through her website at www.elliekwilde.com and on Instagram and TikTok @EllieKWildeAuthor.